I0564515

Miss Goodone

Anne O. S.

Published by Anne O. S., 2025.

MISS GOODONE

First edition. September 15, 2025.

ISBN: 979-8900462493

Written by Anne O. S..

Miss Goodone

The Truth Behind the Door

Anne. O. S.

ISBN: 979-8-90046-249-3

COVER DESIGN BY: ART PAINTER

LIBRARY OF CONGRESS CONTROL NUMBER: 2018675309

PRINTED IN THE UNITED KINGDOM

Chapter One
The Rainbow

———◦✦◦———

NINA SANK INTO HER favourite armchair. It was a bit shabby, sure, but that didn't matter. It had that perfect way of wrapping around her. Tucked away in the back of her old library, it was her little sanctuary, far from people and noise. As if there were many people or much noise to begin with. But that spot? No doubt it was perfect for reading a good book. Even at thirty-one, she had the heart of an old soul. So peace, quiet, and comfort? That was her thing.

But before she could even dive into the story, the flames in the fireplace went mad, shooting out and turning the whole place into a blasted sauna. With a sigh, Nina had to get up. As she pushed it back, her leg flared with the usual annoying pain. After giving it a quick rub and muttering a few choice words, she managed to limp over and put out that devil of a fire. It was about time, as her pale skin had already turned completely red.

Looking around at the emptiness, she nearly forgot the days when the library buzzed with life. The ache in her heart grew when her eyes landed on her assistant, sitting up front at the reception desk, playing with her short, wavy blonde hair. Tessa had been with her for seven years, not just as an employee but as a true friend. Nina liked her—one of the few she did—not because of Tessa's personality (that wouldn't have been possible), but because of her rare yellow soul.

Her gaze moved to the small table stacked with envelopes, unpaid bills staring back at her like a silent accusation. How on earth was she supposed to pay Tessa's salary now? Of course, she didn't have to worry about rent since the library was hers. But those utilities still had to be paid, and, let's be honest, the expenses weren't exactly pocket change.

Beep-beep! A message popped up on her phone, the one she'd been anxiously waiting for. A few days ago, someone had called, expressing interest in buying her library. Yes, her library. Her baby.

Now, they had finally sent the time and place for their meeting. Nina stared at the screen, thinking hard... and harder. Should she go through with it? Or not? Sleepless nights had already been spent worrying over the choice. Thinking about it. Overthinking about it. Thinking about overthinking about it. It was exhausting. And yet, she was still unable to decide. Not for her own sake, but for Tessa's. Although she was bloody curious. Who, in the name of tea and biscuits, would actually want the library? And why? The whole thing felt strange, even a bit dodgy.

Sighing, she pulled on her 100-year-old jumper, gave Tessa a quick wave, and called out, 'I'll be back soon! Just need some cigarettes, you know,' in that practised Yorkshire accent of hers.

Tessa raised an eyebrow. 'What? But you've got a whole pack under the desk,' she said with that deep accent, also Yorkshire, but pure Bradford, genuine.

'Err... the lighter, I meant,' Nina shot back, and with that, she hurried off, vanishing before she could be asked any more questions.

Tessa had a feeling. At forty-one, she'd seen enough to pick up on things, and when it came to Nina, she probably knew her better than Nina knew herself. Still, instead of asking, she just shook her head with a quiet laugh.

Meanwhile, Nina wobbled down the street towards the Chinese restaurant. It wasn't far, thank goodness for that, just around the corner. Any farther, and she wouldn't have managed it, poor thing, not with the constant ache from her illness.

Finally standing in front of the glass door, she took a deep breath to steady herself. 'You've got this, Nina,' she muttered. 'Just a few people and some guy. No big deal.'

Squeak... she pushed the thing, trying not to breathe through her nose to avoid catching the souls. Her eyes swept the place, grateful it wasn't packed. Still morning, after all. But there was no one waiting for her. Just a couple who looked like they'd been through the wars and a young man in a hat sitting in the corner, staring out the window.

'Nina, well, I wouldn't have expected to see you here!' shouted Lisa, the restaurant owner. Nina knew her well; after all, they were neighbours.

'Oh, hi there. Err, I've got a meeting with someone from my school, you know...' Nina replied, coming up with a quick excuse.

'Aww, of course, that's lovely! Go on, sit down, and I'll bring you something,' Lisa said, already rushing off behind the counter.

Nina sat down with a smile, though it wavered a bit as she checked the clock and then her phone, wondering whether to call or just wait. She decided to give it a bit longer but couldn't help herself; she took a fine sniff of the air, trying not to make it obvious.

And there it was, that heavy, disgusting smell, like something straight out of a septic tank. Frowning, she quickly held her nose to block the awful stench. Yet another bad soul.

Nina, in fact, had a gift, or perhaps a curse, for sensing people's souls. And not just sensing them, but seeing them too. Inhaling near someone, a green smoke would show, smelling rotten and foul; that was a bad soul. Yellow smoke, though, scented like roses, meant a good one. She had been born with this ability, or at least, she had believed so. Long ago, she'd given up questioning why or where it came from, accepting it as part of who she was. Even if deep down, the feeling stayed, like she didn't quite belong in this world.

'Nina? Shall I sit down?' The young man in the hat startled her a bit. She'd been looking out the window and hadn't noticed him.

'Oh, it's you. I didn't realise... Sure, sure, please.' She gestured for him to take a seat. Nina sighed, a bit thrown off that it was this young man.

'Beautiful weather, isn't it?' he said. 'I'm Martin.'

'Lovely, yes. I know. I remember. It's a very nice name,' Nina replied, feeling a little nervous and fighting the urge to sniff him. Yellow souls were rare, like Tessa's, and she wasn't sure she was ready to find out more about this stranger.

'Would you like something?'

'Oh, no, no, thank you. Lisa is already making something for me.'

'Hmm, I see you know each other well.'

'Yes, I've been coming here for years. And you?'

'Me? No... I've just moved here, which is why I'm interested in your library.'

'Aww... I see. And where did you move from?'

'Not far,' Martin said, leaning in slightly. 'But I'm a librarian, and I noticed your library is, well, a bit outdated and perhaps not very busy,' he added.

Nina forced a smile, and Martin quickly pressed on. 'So I'm making you an offer,' he said, sliding a cheque across the table.

Nina looked at it and tried not to let her mouth drop. The cheque was three times what the library was worth.

'Well, that's quite a sum...'

'It's a sum that shouldn't be refused,' he said smoothly.

Nina swallowed hard. 'I... I need to think about it. Can you give me a few days?'

The young man nodded, offering a pleasant smile. Just then, Lisa came, and Nina felt relieved to have a break from the tension. Lisa set down two plates full of noodles and a Coke.

'Thanks, Lisa, but this...' Nina began, but Martin interrupted again.

'It's on me,' he insisted. Nina wasn't much of a cola fan; she preferred water but didn't want to be rude.

'Anyway, I need to get back to the library,' she said.

'But there's no one there,' Martin pointed out.

'My friend is there, and I left a pot on the cooker, so... you know.' Nina quickly made up an excuse.

'Of course, take your time... I'll wait,' Martin said, and Nina could only nod, feeling more anxious.

Then she just couldn't help it. As she turned to leave, she did it: sniff... sniff. And that's when she nearly had a heart attack.

For the first time in her life, she saw a rainbow—neither green nor yellow, but spinning, colourful smoke with no scent at all. Nina froze, staring, her brain struggling to make sense of what she was looking at.

Martin noticed.

'You all right, Nina?' he asked.

'Erm... yes, yes, just a bit of leg pain,' she replied, trying to sound calm.

'I'll walk you,' he offered, his voice gentle.

But Nina's eyes widened in alarm, and despite the throbbing pain in her leg, she did her best to make a quick exit. Her heart was beating. She walked back, slightly peeking over her shoulder. Her hands were trembling; that rainbow-coloured soul had shaken her to the core. There was just something about that young man that didn't sit right.

The fresh air helped, though, and she took a few deep breaths, tucking the cheque into her pocket. Too young, too handsome, and honestly, Nina had never seen that much money in her whole life. But his soul... no. Absolutely not. She wanted nothing to do with him. Pulling out her phone, she blocked his number without a second thought. Right now, coffee—please. Oh, and a cigarette. Anything to settle her nerves. She opened the creaking library door, and there was Tessa, holding her sweet, milky tea like it was a precious gem.

'All right, spill everything!' Tessa demanded, stomping her foot for added drama.

Nina took a breath; she really didn't want to say anything that might upset her friend.

'I was just eating at Lisa's,' Nina said.

'What? Without me? That's just too much!' Tessa said, slamming her tea onto the table and crossing her arms like a pouting teenager. 'I'm not talking to you now,' she added, nose in the air.

'You're funny! Calm down.' Nina replied. 'Lisa just needed help with her tax forms.'

'Oh, my God, you should have said that right away! Want some coffee?' Tessa's face lit up instantly. Anything involving paperwork was basically a swear word to her.

Chapter Two
The Hat

—⁓—

Two days ago...

ASIM SAT ON HIS BED, arms crossed, staring at the ceiling as his phone took its sweet time charging. It was a small flat above his father's butcher shop. The smell of meat drifted all the way up, but he was used to it by now. Meat-scented perfume, edition number five. Pure butcher shop essence. Even though they hadn't lived here long, since they'd only just moved in, Asim had basically grown up with meat. Literally. His dad was a proper butcher; cleaver in one hand, salami in the other, and most importantly, a never-ending supply of unwanted life advice.

School? Pfft, as if... He was only twenty-one, smart as hell, had potential, actually wanted to do more. But no. Daddy dearest had decided Asim was going to be a butcher, and that was the end of that. And when dad makes a decision, it's like a death sentence, except without the mercy of actually dying.

Now he was staring at his phone. And nothing. Big fat nothing. How the hell could he just leave his phone sitting there like that, totally exposed? It was like waiting for a text from your ex and getting an ad for hair loss treatment instead. Fantastic. Oh well. He sprayed on some aftershave, fixed his hair, because that mattered. Style was everything. And ugly? Not a chance. Tall, slim, tanned skin, dark hair... basically a walking heartbreaker. If he were a kebab, he'd be the extra expensive one with all the sauces.

Downstairs, he could hear his father, Samir, speaking to a customer. His deep, commanding voice carried through the thin walls, authoritative as always. Asim sighed and rubbed his temples, but something wasn't right. For weeks, he had the feeling his father was hiding something, slipping away at odd hours, talking in hushed tones on the phone. And tonight? Samir was acting strange, moving slowly toward his room, which was suspicious.

Asim's instinct told him to stay put and mind his own business. Sensible advice, really. Completely reasonable. Naturally, he ignored it. So he stepped into the hallway, moving carefully, his socks doing an admirable job of keeping him quiet. His father's door was slightly open. Carelessness? Odd. His heart pounded as he moved closer, careful not to make a noise, and discreetly peeked inside.

And what he saw nearly knocked him off his feet.

Samir stood in front of the mirror, his back to Asim, adjusting something on his head—a black hat. A hat Asim had never seen before. And then it happened. As soon as Samir set it right on his head, his body changed. His skin pulled taut, shifting like something alive. His face reshaped itself, smoothing out the years, and even his hair darkened and grew. Before Asim's eyes, his father was gone, replaced entirely by someone else. A younger man. Tall, slim, sharp-featured, with a birthmark just below his left eye.

And then Samir, or whoever he was now, picked up the phone.

'It will be done, my lord,' he said in a voice Asim barely recognised. 'The library will be ours.'

Asim's breath caught. The library? What the hell did a library have to do with anything? Who was his father speaking to? What had he just seen? His father, or again, whoever he was now, put the phone away, grabbed his coat, and left. Asim stepped back, slipped into his room, and closed the door quietly. His heart was pounding, but he needed answers. There was only one way to get them. To follow. So, he waited exactly ten seconds after hearing the front door slam before opening his own. Grabbing his hoodie, he pulled it over his head and walked quickly down the stairs.

Outside, it was cold and heavy with rain. He spotted his father, or the man pretending to be him, walking down the street, determined. Asim kept his distance. His father didn't look back once. He passed through the market, walked past the bakery, and entered a Chinese restaurant. Asim stopped on the other side of the street, hidden behind a parked car.

What was his father doing here? Through the window, he saw him sit in the farthest corner, head lowered, as if he were waiting. But for whom? Minutes passed.

And then, she walked in. A woman with long dark hair, slippers, an old worn-out jumper, and she looked tired too. She sat down at the table, and then Asim saw his father sit opposite her. They talked, and he saw him give her something like a cheque, and even her eyes widened. Asim couldn't hear what they were saying, but the woman seemed tense, nervous, like she didn't trust him. And then she left. Strange, really. On the street, she stopped, typed something into her phone, and walked on.

His father stayed seated. Asim waited a few minutes. Who was she? And more importantly, why had his father met her? Asim followed his father back home. This time, he didn't rush up the stairs; this time, he waited. His father entered the flat, took off his coat, and the moment he removed his hat, his body changed back to normal. The young man was gone. Samir was Samir again.

Asim watched from the hallway as his father pulled out his phone, typed a message, and left the flat again. But this time, Asim didn't follow. Instead, he slipped into his father's room. He only had a few minutes. So he searched, rummaging through his things carefully but quickly. He opened the wardrobe—nothing. Then, in the drawers under the bed, he found something.

A small wooden box.

He pulled it out and opened it. Inside was a book. On the cover, it said: The Guardian of Hell. Asim's stomach tightened. He flipped through the pages, but they were blank. *What the—?* Then he searched deeper. Under the book were loose papers and a photograph. It was the exact same woman from the restaurant. Asim stared at it, his thoughts racing. Why did his father have her photo? And why *The Guardian of Hell*?

Then came the footsteps. His father was coming back. Asim shoved everything back into the box, but a key fell out, a big, golden one. He had no time. He spotted a suitcase by the door and quickly tossed it in there, acting like nothing had happened. Samir walked in, glanced around, and held his breath.

'What are you doing here?' he said.

'I was just looking for... socks.'

'Socks?'

'Yeah, I didn't wash mine.'

'Oh, right. Shall we get something to eat?'

'Yeah, why not?'

Chapter Three
The Thunder

Back in the present - Tuesday.

JUST AS NINA WAS ABOUT to sit down, a flash of lightning lit up the sky, followed by a deafening clap of thunder. Moments later, the rain began hammering down like the heavens had a score to settle.

'Alfie will be here!' Tessa shouted from the kitchen. Nina glanced at the door, and sure enough, there he was, stepping inside, right on cue.

Alfie was the only regular who showed up every Tuesday at the exact same time, like clockwork. He never spoke. He just gave Nina a nod, followed by that delightfully charming smile of his, and she couldn't help but smile back. He removed his coat, causing droplets of water to splash onto the faded green wallpaper. He then wiped his shoes on the red carpet, as if testing how much more dirt it could take. Not that he seemed to care.

Nina widened her eyes at the mess but said nothing. She made her way back to her armchair, pretending not to watch him too obviously. Although she couldn't stop herself from peeking. Then he threw his brown briefcase onto the table, almost like he had something to say. Nina sighed and forced herself to stop staring.

Finally, she opened her book, desperate to lose herself in its pages. Reading was her only solace, the one thing that eased her racing mind. But Alfie, with his heavy, wary footsteps, wasn't making it easy. He picked up an old book and set it on the table with a thud that disturbed her delicate focus.

Nina noticed how he gave her a quick, slight peek, a little habit he never seemed to break. She offered him a smile, and, as usual, he quickly turned away, pretending he hadn't spotted her. A bit shy, a touch odd. But undeniably handsome, at least in Nina's brown eyes. His tanned skin, neatly styled dark hair, and tall, lean frame gave him a natural charm. According to the registry, he was thirty-four, yet he carried an air of mystery that made him seem ageless.

Tessa returned with that coffee Nina had been craving, and, genuinely, it might as well have been liquid gold.

'You're a legend,' Nina said, clutching the cup like it could save her life. She pulled out a cigarette, but because of those ancient British smoking laws, she had to trek outside, even though the hidden kitchen in the back had a window that practically screamed, "Come on, one cheeky smoke won't hurt." Even so, Nina wasn't the type to take risks or challenge old rules.

With a sigh, she threw on her raincoat, walked out, and finally lit up.

What a day, she thought, blowing out smoke like she was trying to exhale her stress. Martin was still bouncing around her mind, bothering her like a bad plot twist. And

Alfie? Well, he wasn't exactly a calming presence either. She'd known him for roughly two years, and while he'd never done anything sketchy, there was always something... weird about him. Weird enough that she never flirted with him, even if he did sometimes drift into her late-night thoughts.

Truthfully, a part of her was terrified of him, and not without reason; Alfie didn't have a soul. She'd sniffed him plenty of times before and never sensed or seen a thing. At first, it scared the hell out of her, because who doesn't have a soul? But in the long run, she got used to it. Alfie was the only person she'd ever met who was soulless. Still, he seemed harmless enough, just a bit strange.

The cigarette calmed her nerves, and the coffee was still enjoyable, even with a hint of rainwater mixed in. Whatever, she'd had worse. Back inside, she took off her raincoat, washed her hands, and sprayed on some perfume. The last thing she wanted was to smell like an ashtray. A bit of chewing gum usually did the trick too.

'Hey, sniff me,' Tessa tried to whisper, but it was obvious she failed.

'Shit, are you mad? Alfie is here,' Nina whispered back, quickly scanning Alfie's way. He wasn't looking, thank God, and she really hoped he hadn't heard anything.

'Oh, come on, he's not even paying attention, please.'

'For God's sake, I sniff you every day!'

'Well, you never know! I had a date, and you know how it is. What if I smell bad?'

'You're such a goose. All right, come closer,' Nina sighed, sniffing around Tessa's face like a dog hunting for a snack. A yellow mist appeared, sweet as roses.

'Don't worry, you're clean as always,' Nina reassured her. Tessa lit up with relief and rushed back to the desk. But an unmistakable trumpet-like sound escaped as she bent over to grab her phone.

'Oh, shit,' Tessa muttered, cheeks flaming as she tried to act casual, sneaking an embarrassed glance at Alfie. Thankfully, he hadn't moved an inch. Didn't see or hear a thing, she thought. But oh, he had seen and heard; he just ignored it.

Nina shook her head, thoroughly entertained. Some things never change.

Tessa ran for the bathroom, holding her backside and waving at Nina like she was trying to flag down a taxi. 'Nature calls,' she tried to mouth, but Nina wasn't exactly a lip-reading genius. Still, it wasn't hard to figure out, especially with Tessa clenching her bum like her life depended on it. Nina just slapped her forehead and went to sit behind the reception desk, fully aware that Tessa would be in there for ages.

Meanwhile, Alfie sat there, nose deep in a book, looking ridiculously put-together as usual. Nina caught a whiff of his perfume, some pricey stuff that smelled like it belonged in a high-end fashion ad. And really, so did he. Alfie always had that aura, like he should be walking down a runway instead of creeping around in her library.

Nina couldn't stop thinking, for the millionth time, who or what he really was. She'd tried talking to him plenty of times, desperate to find out why he didn't have a soul. But conversations with Alfie were as effective as yelling into a golf hole. He'd just gesture with his hands, shrug, and leave her questions hanging. In time, she'd given up, figuring some mysteries were destined to stay that way.

But today, she decided to give it another shot.

'Crazy weather, isn't it? It was so nice, and then boom, storms and rain,' she said, trying to sound relaxed with a smile.

Alfie looked up and nodded before falling straight back into his book. Well, that was a dead end. She felt a bit silly. 'Err,' she mumbled, glancing at her nails, which were a proper mess. She grimaced, remembering the days when she wasn't battling constant pain. Days when she could paint her nails without exhaustion sucking the life out of her. It wasn't laziness; it was something only someone who'd been there would get.

Then, to her surprise, Alfie stood up, placed his book neatly back on the table, and slipped on his cream-coloured coat. A loud crack of thunder exploded outside, making Nina jump. 'Oh my God, that scared the hell out of me,' she said.

'Sorry,' said Alfie in a deep voice before walking out.

Nina's jaw dropped, and her heart began to race.

'Tessaaaa! Alfie said "sorryyy"!' she shouted.

'Seeeee? I told ya! He's some kind of weirdo!' Tessa yelled back, finally emerging from the bathroom.

'Can you believe it? He talks! And his voice is so... beautiful,' Nina said, turning wide-eyed to Tessa.

'Okay, okay, calm down... Wait, why did he say "sorry"?'

Nina paused, thinking it over, and then it hit her. She'd mentioned being startled by the thunder, and he'd apologised for it.

Tessa's eyes went wide with excitement. She'd always had her suspicions about Alfie and his connection to the weather. Every time he showed up at the library, storms and lightning weren't far behind.

Tessa, who loved movies and bingeing TikTok conspiracies, was convinced he was some kind of supernatural being. Nina had always written off her theories as rubbish.

'Well, what about ya?' Tessa said, crossing her arms. 'You can feel and see souls, so you're not exactly normal either! Maybe Alfie's some kind of Thunder God.'

'Thanks, Tessa. I didn't know you were going to start calling me a freak too,' Nina said, feeling a bite of hurt.

'Oh, stop it! You know I'm jealous of your cool abilities,' Tessa said, plopping back into her chair and waving for Nina to do the same.

Nina thought back to how she'd always felt different, like the odd puzzle piece in a box of perfect matches. It had taken her years to piece things together, and even now, she still didn't know much about herself. Digging around in the dark, never getting any clear answers, it got old fast.

But there was one thing she did believe. Thanks to everything she'd been through, something beyond this world existed. She just didn't have a clue what it was. It was like she'd been waiting her whole life for something to show up, something that would finally make it all make sense.

Living with her so-called gift or curse hadn't exactly been a walk in the park. In the beginning, it felt more like torture than a blessing until she'd somehow learned to get control of it. She tried not to think about it too much because it made her chest feel heavy, like carrying a bag of stones. Her teacher always talked endlessly about letting go of negative thoughts and holding on to positive ones. *Yeah, cheers for that.*

But over time, she learned how to stop holding onto things that dragged her down. As a result, she was able to keep going, taking careful steps one at a time. For her, a chapter read was a minute well spent. Everything else? Massively overrated.

'Oh, for God's sake, look at the time. Shit, got a date.'

Tessa pulled out a mirror and lipstick, looking ready to save the day, and carefully applied it to her lips with the focus of a high-caffeine surgeon.

'Can't show up looking like I've been trapped in this bloody library all day,' she muttered, adding a hurried bit of blush and a touch of mascara, transforming from "haunted librarian" to "acceptably human" in record time.

Then she turned to Nina. 'How do I look? Lovely, innit?'

'You look beautiful!' Nina said, yet secretly she thought, way too much makeup, as usual. Friends were friends, though, and honesty only went so far, even if it did give her a sting of guilt.

'Anyway, does this dress look too tight? My washing machine's on the defect, you know.'

'No, it's lovely... Anyway, who's looking after your mum?' Nina asked, quickly changing the subject.

'My sister, of course... Oh yes, and don't forget your pills. I'm off.'

'Will do. Have fun.'

When Tessa left with a smile, the weight of the evening crashed down on Nina. She ran her eyes over the library and then smelled the air. Hmmm. Beautiful. No souls. Her body throbbed as if it had been holding out for Tessa to leave.

Spotting the small brown suitcase still sitting by the table, clearly Alfie's mistake, Nina shoved it under the desk, only to be hit with a bloody strong smell. Not just any scent, either. More like old leather mixed with something floral, unusually captivating, like it was basically whispering, "Go on, have a peek." She leaned in, trying to pinpoint it. Oh, the smell was intense, almost compelling, pulling at her interest in the most desirable way.

The urge to open it was real, even though it definitely wasn't hers. A risky move, for sure. But Nina wasn't one to go poking around in other people's things. Even if the temptation was maddening, she wasn't that rude. So she straightened up and shook off the feeling.

Chapter Four
Sunaruh

———⊱◦⊰———

NINA WAS IN THE SHOP, mid-morning, already down to her last cigarette from the pack she'd bought just the day before. Yes, it had been one of those nights, long and restless. Martin's messages haunted her, even though she'd blocked his number. He'd found new ones to text from, asking if she'd reconsider, offering even more money. She'd tossed and turned, finally giving up, and messaged back that she needed a few more days to think.

'Miss? Hello? It's £10.50, please,' the cashier snapped, clearly fed up with Nina zoning out.

'Oh, right, sorry,' said Nina, fumbling with her purse and handing over the money.

She noticed a boy next to her who couldn't have been more than twelve, holding a box of chicken nuggets and looking painfully lost. He kept counting his pennies, his brow furrowed, his eyes flowing longingly to the sweets by the till. He swallowed, his face falling as he looked down. A woman nearby decided to stick her nose in.

'Shouldn't you be in school?' she asked.

The boy just shot her a glare that yelled, *What's it to you, you nosy cow?* The woman sniffed and walked off, acting like she had somewhere important to be.

Nina's heart clenched. This wasn't about school; the kid was hungry, broke, and alone. God knows what else he might be dealing with. She took out some extra coins and bought his nuggets and the candies he wanted. The boy's eyes lit up as he mumbled a thank you, trying to hand her his change.

'Keep it,' Nina said and added a juice to the bundle.

'Why are you here on your own? Got any trouble at home?' she asked gently as they walked out together. He didn't speak, just shaking his head with a big "no," eyes still wary. As they reached the doors, she spotted a man standing there who looked like the boy's dad, or at least someone responsible for him. He was thin, messy, and chain-smoking like it was his full-time job.

Nina's stomach heaved. The guy looked rough, and she couldn't shake the worry he might hurt the boy. She took a quick sniff of the air, ready to brace herself, but instead, a sweet, yellow mist came by. *Well, that's a surprise,* she thought, a little relieved.

'Thanks, miss,' the man said, nodding before taking the boy's hand and leading him away. Nina stood there, feeling off-balance. *What if my gift was lying to me? Should I have called someone? But who would listen?*

She shook her head, trying to let it go, but it hung onto her. That ache of seeing kids suffer. It always got to her. She headed back to the library, hoping and praying, really, that the boy was alright and that it was just poverty, nothing more sinister. 'Please, let them just be poor,' she whispered to herself.

She was about to step into the library when she saw the scene: flashing ambulance lights, police cars parked all over the place, and enough yellow tape to make it look like a dodgy murder mystery. Brilliant. Just what her day needed. For a second, panic gripped her. *What if something had happened to Lisa?* After all, the whole mess was right in front of her shop.

She crept forward, trying to blend in with the crowd, which was hard to do when her anxiety was already at a solid eight out of ten. Nina wasn't keen on getting too close; crowds made her nervous, and for good reason. The last time she had tried sniffing the collective souls of too many people, she'd ended up flat on her back, and it had taken days to recover. She let out a breath of relief when she saw Lisa standing there, perfectly fine, just behind that yellow crime tape.

Lisa jumped as if electrocuted. 'For heaven's sake, Nina, you scared the shit out of me!' Then, in her usual "I'm too chill to care" way, she added, 'Some poor old lady got hit by a car. Really sad, yeah?'

Nina looked over at the scene: a body covered by a tarp with medics standing close.

'Dementia, apparently. Yeah, yeah,' Lisa continued, with all the emotion of someone reading the back of a medication box. 'You probably knew her.'

'Knew her?' Nina frowned. 'Who was she?'

'No idea. But she was in my shop asking about you.'

'About me?'

'Yeah, I thought she was your granny or something, so I sent her over to the library.'

Nina's stomach twisted. If the lady had come looking for her, she must've been in the library right before... well, the car incident.

'Right, it's freezing,' Nina muttered, more to herself than Lisa. She turned and made her way to the library. But she had to stop. This itch to find out more about this elderly woman wouldn't let her go.

Part of her felt a bit guilty, sure, but mostly she found the whole thing just plain weird. And well... curiosity killed the cat, right? But Nina figured satisfaction might just revive it.

So, she couldn't resist and sniffed. Big mistake. The unpleasant smell smacked her in the face like an old sweaty sock. A thick, greenish fog blew up, and she had to pinch her nose shut before she choked. Good thing nobody noticed her standing there, looking up at the sky and holding her nose like she'd just walked into the world's smelliest fart cloud.

In the end, the green mist faded away, taking the bad smell with it. A gentle breeze passed by, as if nature was saying sorry for the olfactory assault. Nina knew what came next: the soul would just... poof. Gone. But where the hell did they actually go? Heaven? Hell? Or maybe they got sucked into some cosmic black hole of nothingness? She'd been dying to know the answer for ages. It was one of those questions that stuck in her mind like a bad pop song: irritating, endless, and impossible to shake off. As much as she hated it, she couldn't help but wonder.

Tessa was sticking her head out the library door like a nosy meerkat.

'Oi, what's all the noise?' she yelled.

Nina motioned for her to get back inside, but Tessa was having none of it. Frustrated, Nina quickened her pace, ignoring the sharp pain in her leg. Ugh. It felt like her thigh was trying to detach itself.

'Just get inside, will you? You're letting in the bloody Arctic,' Nina called.

'Fine, fine,' Tessa said, stepping inside.

Nina sighed and told her what Lisa had said, hoping for some clue about the old lady.

Tessa sat down heavily, looking only a little shocked.

'Blimey,' she said. 'That old bat? Yeah, she was here, asking for you. I told her to come back later.'

'Who was she? Did she want a book or something?'

'Nah,' Tessa said, then winced. 'I know it's bad to talk badly about the dead, but honestly, she was really strange!'

'Oh, come on, out with it.'

'Alright, as you wish,' Tessa said, obviously feeling guilty. 'She had, you know, hair like she'd been fighting with some kind of bush—*and lost*.' Tessa showed two fingers. 'Twice.'

She carried on, 'And she talked like she wanted to do some dodgy business with me, you know... And she smelled like dog shit. No joke.'

Nina tried not to laugh, but it slipped out anyway.

Tessa carried on, 'Now, you should sit! Listen... She sniffed me, like you do, then stepped back like I was the one who stank. Can you believe it?'

'No way!'

'Yes way! I thought you knew her. Well, she was on about some promise you made her? You owe her something?' Tessa said. 'But then she just left, saying she will be back, like from some horror film, you know? A stinky witch, so I had to open every window!'

'I've never seen that woman in my life. And I definitely haven't promised anyone anything. What the hell is going on?'

Tessa gave a half-shrug. 'Weird, innit? Maybe she was just mental. You know, she was like a hundred years old anyway.'

'Yeah, probably. Lisa said she had dementia.'

'You see? Sorted. Poor woman, though. Anyway... a coffee?'

'Of course.'

'Lovely,' said Tessa.

Even though Nina was putting on her best everything's-peachy act and blaming it all on dementia, deep down, something was screaming at her that this wasn't just some harmless old granny, especially after Tessa went on about how the old woman had a good sniff at her and how Nina had evidently promised her something. Or better yet, owed her. Disturbing.

These past few days had felt like the universe was dropping hints left and right. All Nina wanted was for her illness to sod off so she could go hunting for answers. But no, of course, she was absolutely knackered. So, she popped some painkillers, dragged herself into the shower, and tried to wash away the dirt.

Meanwhile, Tessa was glued to TikTok, chewing away—biscuits this time. But enough was enough. She smacked her tea down on the table, grabbed the vacuum cleaner, and got to work on the never-ending grime. Then she headed straight upstairs to Nina's flat, where she could hear the shower running. 'Oh gosh,' Tessa groaned, pinching her nose and racing to the window, her eyes watering from the reek. It smelled like wet dog—no doubt about it. Overflowing ashtrays, abandoned coffee mugs everywhere, and even knickers thrown about.

But for Tessa? Just another day. She'd seen it all before, no big deal. Stretching her lips into a grin, she turned up the music and danced around the room like a footballer celebrating a win. Good thing it was only a one-bedroom flat.

Bloody hell, Tessa thought, tugging at a piece of fabric as if she were skinning a rabbit. 'What the hell is this?' she muttered, spotting a torn-out page from a book. Strange. Nina might be messy, but careless with books? Never. A torn page? Now that was a sin. Whatever. She scanned the first few words. Something about a Guardian. What a load of bollocks, she thought, chucking it in the bin. Done.

Before heading back downstairs, she yelled, 'And don't stay in there too long. Work's waiting!' But Nina acted like she hadn't heard, conveniently ignoring the dreaded word "work."

Down in the library, Tessa sipped her wine, feeling smugly accomplished, when something caught her eye. Alfie's small brown suitcase, still tucked under the desk from the other day. Her fingers trembled with nosiness; Nina wasn't there. Perfect. Heart beating, Tessa crouched behind the desk and carefully opened the suitcase flap just enough to peek inside. Her face fell. Boring. No gold, nothing worth the effort. A quiet huff escaped her lips, and she felt like she'd wasted her time.

Oh, if only Tessa knew what she was looking at. With a quiet snap, the suitcase flap closed, and she straightened up, brushing off her hands as if dusting away the evidence. Wine glass in hand, she took another sip, settling back into her chair and pretending nothing at all had happened. Lovely.

Nina was finally walking down to the library, still thinking about that woman who had died on the road. Being the absolute professional nitpicker she was, Nina had perfected the art of fantasy. She remembered an old story about a witch called Sunaruh. She had absolutely loved that story because this witch could sense souls. For a while, Nina even fancied herself as Sunaruh. Who wouldn't want to be a soul-sensing witch, right? But obviously, it was just a made-up fairytale. Still, that's why the story stuck in her head.

For some reason, the whole thing reminded her of that weird old woman. She started digging through the bookshelves. In the second section, she found it: a thin little paper book with pictures that looked like they were meant for kids. She opened it, and ta-da! There it was. The woman in the story had hair that looked like she'd had a brawl with a bush. Proper wild. But Nina still wasn't sure. She felt a bit mad even thinking about it. What if, though?

She rushed over to Tessa and asked again what the old woman looked like.

'Well, like I told you, she had hair that...' Tessa started.

'No, not that! I mean a proper description. What she actually looked like,' Nina said, clutching the book like it was made of gold. She didn't want to just hand it over yet. Instead, she took her time to be sure.

'Alright. She had proper dirty grey hair, ugly green eyes, and she was massive. Like, really massive. She was three times my size. And you know I'm big, hmm?' Tessa said.

Nina had a little laugh at that.

'Fine, you silly thing. Anyway, have a look at this,' she said, showing Tessa the picture from the book.

Tessa took one look and swallowed, her face going pale.

'Oh, bloody hell, you're joking. Let me see that,' Tessa said, pulling the book closer. She stared at it like she expected it to bite her. 'Nina, that's her. It's actually her!'

'Shut up! Don't mess with me, Tessa! I need you to be serious.'

'I swear, I'm telling you the truth. That's her! What on earth? Was she some sort of famous witch or something?'

'Gosh, no. It's just a short fantasy story. You know that witch I told you about? The one we joked about being me, remember?'

'Oh shit, yeah. I remember. My God, are you telling me she's real? I need to sit down before I have a bloody heart attack.'

Tessa dropped into a chair.

'I need tea. This is too much. She was here, Nina. I was lucky she didn't eat me!'

'Yeah, it's mad, isn't it?' Nina said, sitting next to her, feeling well and truly freaked out.

Tessa gave her a long, serious look. 'Listen... Do you think you're a witch?'

'Oh, don't be ridiculous. I'm not a witch... or am I?' Nina said, not so sure now. Just thinking about it made her shiver.

'Hang on. It kind of makes sense. You can sense souls. She could too. And why would she turn up here, in this library, just for you? Shit, what if that accident outside wasn't really an accident?' Tessa said, narrowing her eyes.

'Oh, come off it, Tessa. You can't seriously think that... or maybe you can? Flipping hell, I have no idea.'

'I'm not just going to sit here pretending nothing's wrong. I'm not letting my best mate turn into some smelly old witch,' Tessa said, standing up.

'I'm not turning into anything. Come on!'

'Well, not now. But anyway, look. What if she's your aunt? A gran? Or your mom? Or worse, what if this is serious? What if someone's out to kill you? Okay, I might not be into books, but films teach you more, you know. Trust me,' she said. With a dramatic wave, she added, 'So, I'm off!'

'Don't worry, I've got my own kind of magic.' She shut the door behind her.

Nina just sat there, staring into the emptiness. She even whispered a prayer to God, begging for some answers. She went off to make herself a coffee, and that cigarette was non-negotiable. She desperately needed to calm down. She was even starting to scare herself. I mean, she'd tried countless times to sense her own soul, but nothing. Zilch. Maybe she didn't know the right technique, or maybe she simply didn't have a soul at all. A lovely thought. Puffing away, she noticed the light drizzle of rain, but then she spotted Tessa in the distance and couldn't help but smile. Tessa always managed to lift her mood, even if she did look like a hyperactive meerkat.

There she was, bustling around by the doors, bombarding people with questions, and swinging her arms and legs like a string-puppet. Pure entertainment. Then she disappeared into a shop, leaving Nina chuckling as she headed back inside. It was bloody freezing. She shivered, switched on the strange fireplace, and before she knew it, Tessa was back.

'Flipping hell, that was quick! Right, spill the beans,' Nina said.

'Well, not much to tell. Sit down, have an egg one. On the house, by the way. Ali's a gem, you know, and can you believe he's just had his fifth kid?' Tessa said, handing Nina the sandwich.

'Oh, Tessa, you were supposed to get some juicy details about the witch.' She smacked the sandwich on the table.

'Oh yeah, alright. But this sandwich, Miss Skinny—you're going to eat it!' said Tessa.

'Anyway, apparently some young bloke took care of it. Turns out she was his nan. And really, Nina, she had dementia.'

'Hmm, a young bloke? What did he look like?'

'He had a mole, a hat, and was proper good-looking. Tall, young. Martin, what a beautiful name, innit?'

'Lovely, yes. So maybe we are just making things up,' Nina said, trying to keep her cool, but inside she was bricking it.

'Yeah, don't stress. You're not a witch. But still, that old woman, she's exactly who I've been going on about,' Tessa said, heading back to the reception desk.

Meanwhile, Nina swallowed, feeling even more spooked. She knew, deep down, that the old woman had to be a real witch. And Martin, the guy wanting to buy her library, must be connected. Maybe he was a wizard too, who the hell knew? Especially with that rainbow soul of his. Suspicious, much? That was probably why they wanted to get their mitts on the library. Nina was beyond confused. All she could do was mutter a silent prayer, hoping that some higher power she'd long since stopped believing in would finally give her a bloody clue.

Chapter Five
The Day

———⟨◈⟩———

TESSA WAS IN LINE FOR a sandwich, just wanting a quick bite, when some man started shouting behind her. She turned and saw him flat on his back, yelling, 'This is assault!' An elderly man stood over him, fists flying, and snarled, 'You little bastard, you're going to pay for that!' before ripping a half-crushed baguette from the guy's hand.

Then, as if one outraged elderly man wasn't enough, another joined in, and they started kicking the homeless man on the ground—it was brutal. Shouting filled the shop, and the woman behind Tessa pulled out her phone, all too eager to start filming, probably thinking she'd get a million views on TikTok. One of the workers from behind the till jumped over, and before you knew it, all three of them dragged the homeless guy outside like they were throwing out rubbish. Tessa just stood there, frozen, her chest tight.

'I'm just hungry, just hungry,' the homeless man kept shouting in a breaking voice.

Meanwhile, people were recording on their phones, and some were calling the police, but Tessa couldn't move. The whole thing caused a deep, uncomfortable feeling in her stomach. She grabbed a couple of sandwiches and some drinks, paid quickly, and stepped outside into the cold, where everyone was still standing around, making a scene. She walked over to the guy, now curled up on the pavement, and handed him the food bag.

He looked up at her, eyes full of tears, and choked out a quiet, 'Thank you.'

Tessa just gave a small nod, waved him off, and kept walking. No looking at anyone, no looking back. But this was something she couldn't overlook—the woman from the shop was holding the torn baguette in one hand while holding her phone in the other, staring off into the distance as if she were waiting for someone, probably the police. Yet Tessa knew all along that the baguette would end up straight in the trash; they'd rather throw it away and make a drama.

But this is the world we live in. Even though she knew all the usual talk, how people said homeless people were drunks, druggies, whatever; they'd screwed up their own lives, right? It still squeezed her. Tiny tears rolled down her face as she walked, the world feeling harsh, broken, unfair as hell. She didn't judge the homeless man, even if he stank of strong drink. He was starving; you could see that clear as day. By the time she got to the library, she felt weighed down. But it wasn't just the fight bothering her. Today was a heavy day, one she always felt in her bones. The 24th of October. A date she'd never forget. A date full of pain that never really went away.

She walked into the library. Nina was still upstairs. But today wasn't just about tossing her bag behind the reception, making some tea, and digging into lunch. Tessa collapsed into her chair, not feeling it at all. She started picking at her fake nails, which were clinging on for dear life. Today was supposed to be the day. The one where they went to that restaurant that had way too many feelings attached. When Nina finally came downstairs, she acted like it was any random Tuesday. She just crashed into her kingdom, book in hand, coffee on the side table, feet kicked up like she was queen of the universe.

Tessa's jaw nearly hit the floor. Seriously? How could she forget? Or worse... was she just done with it? Over their tradition? Tessa's mind flew. Nina then stood up and went back upstairs without even looking at Tessa, not even noticing her sad face. Tessa just looked down and decided to let it go. She couldn't exactly drag Nina out kicking and screaming. But now, she was left with the whole emotional load to handle solo, and it sucked. Big time.

Just then, someone came in. Tessa's eyebrows shot up, and she perked right up. It was a young lad asking about a job he'd heard was available. Tessa was a bit taken aback. She had no clue what he was on about. Still, she hollered up the stairs.

'Ninaaa, get down here and hurry up!'

Now came that awkward moment, silence, and those typical smiles. 'Have a seat, lovely weather, isn't it? Want a cuppa?' she asked him finally, doing her best to sound casual while they waited for Nina. But the young man shook his head, turning down both the tea and the seat. He seemed a bit fidgety, scratching his calf, neck and back to his calf. Tessa tried not to stare, smiling until Nina finally came.

'Oh, hello there. How can I help you?' Nina asked, eyeing his glossy black hair. And that fresh smell.

'Hello, err, I just came to ask about the job you're advertising,' he said with a hesitant voice, like he wasn't quite sure of himself.

Nina raised an eyebrow. 'A job? Sorry, but we're not hiring anyone.'

Tessa, meanwhile, kept smiling like a loon, sneaking looks at his legs, thin as matchsticks. The young man had this effortlessly posh look about him: tanned skin, dark eyes, and dressed so sharply you'd think he was on his way to a photoshoot.

'Hang on,' he said and dug through his pockets. Out came a set of keys, a phone, and finally, a scrunched-up piece of newspaper. When he unfolded it, his eyes widened in horror. 'Oh no, it's a flatmate ad, not a job one. I must've grabbed the wrong clipping. Sorry about that,' he stammered, turning beetroot red.

'No worries,' Nina replied, even though it did feel a bit awkward. 'But as you can see, we don't have much need for staff.'

The young man glanced around the empty library, the hope in his face slightly fell.

'It's lovely, though. Got that charming, old-fashioned vibe,' he said.

Tessa couldn't resist. 'Lovely, yes. What's your name, then?'

'Asim,' and offered this hopeful-like smile.

Nina sighed. 'I'm really sorry, Asim, but I'll be honest: we're just kind of surviving here,' she said, feeling a stab of guilt as his face fell even further.

'That's exactly why you need me!' Asim said, rapidly looking energised. 'Look, I don't mean to be rude, but this place could use a bit of modernising. You know, a fresh touch.'

Nina and Tessa exchanged he's-got-a-point look.

'Hmm, you're not wrong,' Nina admitted. 'But I haven't got a penny to spare, really.'

'See? Another reason you need me,' said Asim, with a sparkle in his eyes.

'I wish, but I can't afford to pay you, Asim,' said Nina.

'I'm not asking for a wage. I mean, not straight away,' he added with hands up. 'Let me work, and when this place starts pulling in, you can start paying me. Until then, I'm happy to help.'

Nina sighed, softened a bit. There was something about the fire in his eyes. It was genuine, and that kind of passion was hard to come by.

'I don't know. It just doesn't seem fair, you know,' she said.

'Please,' Asim begged, leaning forward. 'Give me a few days to try, and if I'm wrong, you won't owe me anything.'

Tessa kicked Nina's leg under the table, not so subtly.

'Ow! Alright, alright, I get it,' Nina moaned, rubbing her shin. 'That's Tessa, my assistant, anyway,' she added, throwing Tessa a playful look. 'Okie-dokie, Asim. You can stay and do your magic.'

Next day

Tessa planted Asim behind the desk, handed him a sandwich and tea, and then shone a lamp at him.

'Where are you from? How old are you? Do you have a girlfriend? Married? Kids?'

Nina slapped her forehead. 'Oh my God, Tessa, please, just show him around. He's just a boy!'

Huffing, she sank back into her chair as Tessa smirked and said to Asim, 'She's a bit moody, but otherwise, she's a really nice lady.'

Asim was relieved when Tessa finally dropped the detective act and started showing him around the library. He soaked up every corner, the massive wooden tables, the old-school charm, all of it. Then he pointed to a door.

'What's behind there?'

'Rubbish, it's a dirty old basement.'

Tessa rattled off the rules and everything about the library, but Asim just nodded along. 'Helloo? Are you even listening to me?' she asked.

Apologising, Asim said he'd get right to work. He pulled out his phone, took notes, and parked himself at the desk where the old computer rested. It was a piece of crap, sure, but he didn't care. He wasn't here for a job.

As Tessa drummed her fingers impatiently, Nina buried herself in her book, quietly praying that Asim might pull off a miracle and save the library from selling it off.

Tessa noticed the envelopes Nina had carelessly left on the table. Her heart tried to bust out of her chest like it fancied legging it down the street.

'Why didn't you tell me about this? Oh my God, Nina, I'm your friend; I could maybe help,' she said.

Nina put down her book and sighed. 'Sorry, it's my business, not yours.'

'Well, you could've at least told me you were thinking of selling it so I could find another job.'

Asim stretched his ears to listen, pretending to type on the keyboard. Nina quickly set Tessa straight; selling wasn't on the table, just something she'd been throwing around. Sure, she'd received an offer, but she'd trashed the lot. And, of course, she'd thought about Tessa; no way was she selling the place just to leave her high and dry.

Tessa fluttered her eyes. 'I just... even when I'm bored, I still love you and this library; it's my life, and you know that!'

Asim spoke up. 'You don't need to sell a thing, I promise. Just give me time.'

Nina felt a warm satisfaction and gave him a firm nod. Tessa tried to stay positive, and even she wanted to forget about this day. But there was no hiding it. No matter how much she tried to play it cool, deep down, it messed her up. She picked up a cloth, pretending to dust the already-clean books as she edged closer to Asim. She wiped the desk, giving him a sly look.

'How old are you? Just curious, you know?'

Asim lifted his fingers off the keyboard. 'Twenty-one, and no, no girlfriend. I live just around the corner.'

Tessa quickened her pace with the cloth. 'Hmm, that meat shop?'

'Yeah, it's my dad's. We live upstairs.'

'Oh yea, there used to be a phone shop. Why the move, and where's your mum?' Tessa wasn't letting up.

Asim looked down, twisting his lips to the side. 'You're nosy. I don't mean to be rude, but I've got work to do.'

Tessa didn't blink. 'Cup of tea?'

Asim started hammering the keyboard again.

'Who are you writing to?'

'My fiancée!'

Tessa had never been one to hold back, but today, her patience was even thinner than usual. The conversation with Asim had started simple enough—just small talk, nothing serious. But the moment she'd brought up his fiancée, something in the air shifted.

She hadn't meant to dig, hadn't even planned on asking, but curiosity got the better of her. He told her they were set to marry next year, that she'd be arriving soon. That should have been the end of it. But instead, she kept talking. A harmless comment, or so she had thought. Something about arranged marriages, about how she knew how it was with Asians.

As soon as the words left her mouth, she noticed the change. Asim had stopped typing, his shoulders rigid. When he turned to look at her, his face was unreadable. Then he asked if she was being racist.

Tessa barely held back a sigh. Racist? Her? She had lived in Bradford her whole life. She knew how things worked. But Asim didn't know that, didn't know her, and clearly, he wasn't letting it go.

She turned back to the bookshelves, smacking the cloth harder than necessary against the spines. She was done with this conversation, or at least she wanted to be. But something about his silence, about the weight of his stare, pushed her to say more.

Her words came out without much thought. A jab, sharp and direct. Something about him being a spoiled brat, about how he still needed his mum.

The reaction was instant.

Asim shot up from his seat, the chair scraping loudly against the floor. His entire body tensed, fists clenched at his sides and without another word, the door slammed behind him.

Tessa exhaled, rubbing her fingers over her forehead. And then, just as if on cue, Nina walked in.

She had obviously seen Asim leaving, his tense posture. She didn't even need to ask what had happened. The look she gave Tessa said enough. But Tessa wasn't in the mood for a lecture.

Nina folded her arms, staring her down.

'Excellent,' she said.

Then, in a calmer tone, she told her to act like an adult, not a child. She reminded her how much they needed Asim, how much he had already offered to help them, and now Tessa had practically chased him out.

Tessa scoffed, throwing her hands up dramatically. She wasn't going to apologise. She hadn't done anything wrong. That was the last thing Nina wanted to hear.

But before she could say anything, Tessa cut her off. If the library was really going to be sold, then fine. Nina could do whatever she wanted with it. At least then, she could finally pay her what she owed instead of sneaking around like a book dealer, pretending things were fine when they clearly weren't.

'What the hell is wrong with you today?' Nina asked.

Tessa let out a harsh laugh. Oh, she could list a few things.

For one, Nina had been hiding the fact that she was selling the library. And to make things worse, some kid had just accused her of being racist, like she was some ignorant idiot who didn't know better.

But Nina wasn't having it. She dismissed it all, saying Tessa was just being paranoid, that no one was accusing her of anything, and no one was doing dodgy deals behind her back.

That only made it worse.

Paranoid? Right. Of course she was. Tessa clenched her fists, her mind racing.

'You know what? Forget it,' Tessa said. 'And don't forget to send me a cheque when you sell the place. Cheers. Have a lovely life.'

And with that, she walked out, slamming the door behind her. Tessa felt broken, completely done in, and it showed in the way she drove. Her eyes were blurry with tears, her head lost in some hellish fog, curses running through her mind on a loop. Truly, it was a miracle she didn't crash or have someone slam into her. Somehow, she made it home in one piece.

But she didn't go inside, just sat there, staring at the house. 'Sorry, Farhan. Hope you didn't catch any of that,' she muttered. 'This day's been too much. I can't do it... not on my own.' She wiped her face, smearing the tears. Then she slipped in through the back door, careful not to be seen by her sister or the kids. Her mum was upstairs in bed, thank God.

But she needed something strong to take the edge off. The house was dry, and with her sister in the kitchen, sneaking anything was out of the question. So, she grabbed some cash and headed off to the corner shop.

Now standing outside, she took a breath, forced on her best "I'm fine" smile, and stepped in. Tessa knew the shopkeeper too well to let him see her falling apart, so she threw out a joke, hoping it would stick.

Bag in hand, a bottle of the hard stuff inside, she went back to the car, climbed in, shut the door, and opened the bottle. One sniff, and then a long, burning drink. It stung, but it took the pressure off, even if only for a bit. Still, the day wasn't over. The evening was crawling in, and Tessa didn't look anywhere close to ready to just slink into bed and let it all go.

Chapter Six
The Meat Shop

———❦———

NINA TOOK HER PHONE and stared at Martin's message. Maybe it really was a lost cause. Rainbow soul, whatever. But the price he was offering. She could clear Tessa's debt and even have enough to take a break from her soul-crushing job. Not that it made her feel any less like crap about it. 'Fine,' she muttered, typing back that she'd take his offer. Martin replied in a flash, like he'd been lurking by his phone, desperate. He'd be over tomorrow afternoon, apparently. Lovely. More awkwardness on the horizon.

And then it hit her: those memories of Tessa. She kept thinking about what day Tessa had been talking about and why she'd been so angry. Nina knew Tessa well. Sure, she could be fiery, explosive even. They'd had plenty of arguments before. But things always worked out in the end. One of them just had to make the first move, send that message or make the call. Usually, it was Tessa who did it. But not this time. No, this time, nothing. So, it was up to Nina.

She sent the message, swallowing her pride. Ego didn't matter now; she needed Tessa more than ever. In the message, she apologised and waited, hoping for a reply. But nothing came. It was marked as read, which was interesting, but still, no response. Alright, she's still mad, Nina told herself. She needs more time. She tried not to dwell on it. It'll be fine.

But Asim was still on her mind. Even though she hardly knew him, there was something about his yellow soul that Nina liked. She wanted to at least apologise to him on Tessa's behalf. The young man hadn't done anything wrong. She threw on her favourite cardigan, grabbed her keys, and then she saw it: Asim had left his phone on the table. Well, at least she had a good excuse to go see him, so she wouldn't show up empty-handed. Slipping the phone into her pocket, she was almost out the door when her leg flared up again painfully. She hobbled back, took her meds, and felt upset with herself.

The library was empty; it was still mid-morning. Breaking the rules for once, she pulled out a cigarette and lit it. But bloody hell, her conscience wouldn't let her rest. The smoke filled the library with a thick, nasty smell. No, she thought and put it out. Locking the door behind her, she headed out. Facing the faded sign for *Samir's Halal Meat*, Nina braced herself and pushed through the door. The heavy smell of raw meat nearly knocked her out.

'Hello, err, I'm just looking for Asim.'

'He's not here,' came the flat reply. A cleaver cracked down, splitting flesh with a sharp, frightening sound.

Samir, a mountain of muscle with a shiny head, kept his eyes on the meat. He sliced with precision, never bothering to look up. Nina swallowed hard, taking in the sheer size of him. The shop was cramped and felt alive with too many souls, but she didn't dare sniff this time.

'I know you,' Samir continued in a proper Lancashire accent. 'You're the librarian. What's with my son?'

Nina's pulse kicked up.

'I'm Samir,' he said, stepping forward. 'Come with me.'

He grabbed her shoulder, pulling her into a back room where the noise from the shop disappeared.

'How do you know my son?' Samir said in that dangerous tone of his. 'You realise he's just a kid?'

'Oh God, no, no, it's nothing like that,' she stammered. 'He just ran out of the library and left his phone behind. He was...'

'And why was he at the library, huh?'

Nina's throat tightened as his tone sharpened.

'He just needed some books for... school?' she managed to say.

Then he softened, sounding like a genuinely nice guy.

'Right. Well, he's off visiting his mum. At the graveyard.'

'Oh, the graveyard... that makes sense,' she blurted out, then winced at how stupid she sounded.

'What?'

Nina quickly apologised, ready to leave. But Samir surprised her by offering coffee. She hung back, considering her options. Something about him made her pause. Then she did it; sniff... sniff... oh gosh, his soul. And froze. Her heart raced as if it was the rainbow again, the same one she'd seen in Martin.

A rainbow soul? Around Samir? What the hell is going on?

'Black, no milk, no sugar,' she finally said, trying to hide her shock. There was no way she could leave now, not without figuring out what this meant.

Upstairs, Samir's flat was clean and reasonable. A neatly arranged bookshelf hooked her eye, and she made a comment about it. Samir's smile was faint, just about there.

'I don't read,' he said, 'but Asim does. Can't get enough. Just like his mum.'

Nina didn't know what to say. So, she made up an excuse about needing the toilet. After actually using it, Nina saw something through a half-open door: a shiny black hat. Her stomach dropped. It wasn't just familiar; it was the same hat Martin had worn, the man who wanted to buy her library. Same weird sparkle and the same unique style. Weird, she thought. Maybe they were relatives? It sort of made sense, the rainbow soul and now that hat. She wanted to find out more, staring at it, anxious, before shaking off the feeling and moving on.

Back in the living room, the atmosphere had changed. Samir's tone had turned cold.

'I don't want Asim in that library,' he said. 'He's got other responsibilities. No time for bookish nonsense. He belongs here, in the shop. Not messing about like an old woman.'

Nina clenched her jaw but kept quiet. Samir clearly wasn't being honest, and she could see right through him. His words were harsh, and the threat was clear. 'There will be no more chit-chat if I see him there.'

'Do you understand?' he added.

Nina set her coffee down, her hands trembling. What a bastard. She'd come here hoping to learn more, but instead, she was more pissed off than she'd been with Tessa.

'Nice talk,' she said and slammed the bloody door.

Well, this wasn't at all how Nina thought things would go. For one fleeting moment, she'd been sure she was onto something, some small, tidy answer wrapped up in a neat cosmic bow. But no, of course not. That would've been far too simple. Instead, she was left with nothing. Not just nothing, but less than nothing. The sort of nothing that practically laughed in your face while... let's just say, it's only the universe giving her the middle finger again.

Then she remembered that gem of wisdom from her old teacher: Don't think negative thoughts. Focus on something nice. *Oh, sure, because that's so easy when your brain's doing somersaults.* Still, she gave it a go, sitting there with her coffee, pretending it was all fine and dandy; it wasn't.

Her mind kept travelling back to Tessa. And Asim. Oh, poor Asim. The kid couldn't catch a break, could he? First, losing his mum, and now having to deal with Tessa and her drama. And then there was Samir. That man wasn't exactly the picture of fatherly compassion. Nina checked her phone for the millionth time, but surprise, surprise; nothing from Tessa. Maybe she needed more time. Whatever.

Nina sent her a quick message: "Went to see Asim. He wasn't home. Samir said he's at the graveyard visiting his mum. Thought you'd want to know." Done. Delivered without the slightest bit of satisfaction.

Chapter Seven
Graveyard

———⁓❧⁓———

TESSA WAS WIDE AWAKE, even though it was already past midnight. She wasn't exactly drunk, just a little lightheaded from the whiskey she had in the car earlier. It gave her a slight buzz, but that faded when she saw the messages from Nina. She ignored the first ones, still upset with Nina and, if she was honest, with herself.

But then came the others. The ones Nina sent after hearing about Asim's mum. Those struck a chord. Even though Tessa didn't reply, the words lingered, pressing heavily on her chest. She had said some harsh things to Asim about his mum. And now, she found out his mum was gone. He had gone to visit her grave.

That thought wouldn't leave her, circling in her mind like an irritating fly. She felt an overwhelming need to make things right, no matter what it took. Even if it meant facing the consequences. She understood that kind of pain. She hadn't lost her mum, but she had lost someone else. Someone who left a permanent, painful scar on her heart. That made this day, October 24th, especially difficult. She never really knew how to cope or how to just get through it.

Usually, Nina helped her. But not this time. And that stung. Tessa realised she had to face it alone. That was just life, right? Maybe it was better this way, learning to handle these heavy days on her own, building the strength to deal with them without anyone else. By now, she had calmed down and even managed to scrub off the whiskey smell in the shower. Without a second thought, she headed out to find Asim.

Finding him was easy enough. He was right there, near the front, sitting alone under the glow of a single streetlamp. She dropped down beside him. Asim just looked over, gave a small nod, and didn't say a word. There was no anger on his face, just a deep, aching sadness. Almost like he didn't want to be alone, even if he didn't say so.

Eyes on the graves, she asked, 'Can I have some?'

Asim made a face like he was jammed and said, 'Aren't you a bit too old for this?'

Still, he passed her the spliff like it was a secret document. They both took long, lazy drags, sinking into the chill of the moment. One joint wasn't nearly enough. They dropped back, high as a kite, staring at the stars and the graves, holding their stomachs like they had just heard the funniest joke ever.

Tessa stared at her feet.

'You know, I had a son once. He died when he was just a child. It was a long time ago... It's... well, his birthday, you know. And I was upset, angry, whatever, and I know that is not an acceptable apology. I'll be honest with you. It was childish and...'

'Oh, I didn't know that. I mean, I'm sorry, Tessa. I really don't know what to say. No need for an apology anyway. I wasn't thinking straight either...' Asim said and lowered his head, while Tessa still couldn't take her eyes off her feet.

'No, no, Asim, please... It was dumb, like really. We always used to go with Nina to his favourite restaurant and chill there, and it was always easier for me and...' Then she finally looked up, quickly wiped her tear so Asim wouldn't notice, and continued. 'I got mad because I didn't celebrate his birthday, you know, and what if he is watching? Anyway, how about your mum?'

She had never liked talking about it, and she certainly hadn't come here for therapy. But she knew the sting of loss better than most.

'I never knew my mum. I was just a baby when she passed,' Asim said, a bit sombre.

'Bet you were an ugly baby, though! Probably for the best, she missed that bit.'

Laughter exploded out, cutting through the tension like a chainsaw through butter, brilliant and exactly the relief they both desperately needed.

Tessa waved a hand with a half-smile. 'Sorry, that was awful.'

'No worries. I've been called worse.'

'Fun is something that keeps me up, you know. Keeps me... well, me.'

He gave her a look that said he understood. Maybe he actually did, more than most. Tessa told him she had gone through not one but two marriages, both wonderfully wrecked. The usual. She went on about life's special knack for scraping her down, like the earth had a hobby of making her its personal chew toy.

Asim pressed his lips together.

'Yeah, I guess that's life in this world,' he said. 'Do you believe in Hell and Heaven, Tessa?'

'Hmmm... that's a good question, and I don't know, Asim. Hard to tell. It's more like yes and no.'

'Interesting. Same here. I just keep wondering where those dead people really go, you know. I wish I knew the truth...'

'And I wish I knew the truth about you. A boy like you, in our library? You know, I'm not as dumb as I look.' She winked at him.

It was quite cosy. They were chatting away under the stars, dead folks all around, but it was a lovely spot.

Asim totally chilled out. He revealed his past in a stream of thoughts: a lifetime spent on the move with his father, never staying in one place long enough to call it home. It wasn't just travel. It was a way of life, an endless series of new beginnings and goodbyes. No siblings, no extended family, just him and his dad, like a duo moving through a messy world. Friends came and went.

As Asim's words painted a picture of isolation and thirst, Tessa, properly stoned, looked at him, trying her absolute hardest to understand what on earth the boy was on about. He described a deep-seated loneliness that coloured his childhood, a desire for a stable family dynamic, a brother, a sister, maybe an aunt. His father was a constant but distant human being, more consumed by work than present in his life. The jealousy he felt for people with strong relationships bothered him and made him feel even more disconnected.

'Can you imagine that my dad has secrets? I found out who he really is and what he's like. You won't even believe it. This is why I came to the library, Tessa!'

Her head was bobbing, dangerously close to a full-on snore. Then, as if the world couldn't bear to watch her embarrass herself, the phone rang, rescuing her from a nap she'd deny ever happened. It was Lisa, who spilled the beans about the police cars outside the library. And even though Tessa was knackered and just about holding it together, the fight with Nina vanished from her mind like a fart in the wind. Her heart started thumping like she had just chugged five cups of espresso, and without even a look at Asim, she ran straight to the car.

'Tessa, drop me home, please!' Asim shouted, pushing into the passenger seat.

Tessa just waved at him to hurry up. As she put the pedal to the metal, Asim started looking more anxious than a squirrel in traffic.

'You know, maybe you should pull over and get a taxi,' Asim suggested, clinging to the seat like a cat hanging from a curtain. His face was turning a shade of ghostly white. 'Driving in your state is, uh, a bit illegal, you know.'

'Oh, don't be such a softie, Asim!' Tessa shot back, speeding like she was auditioning for the next *Fast & Furious*. 'What's the point of life if you don't take a few risks? I'm a free woman! You believe in Heaven and Hell, innit? Well, we might get a straight look if we keep this up! Want the truth? We'll find out soon enough!'

Asim just held his breath, internally regretting every choice that had led him to this moment with this complete lunatic. Even through his terror, he couldn't help but wonder how the hell she could afford such a posh car on a librarian's salary.

'Look, seriously, slow down a bit, okay? What's got you in such a hurry?'

'Lisa said there were police at the library.'

'What? Seriously? What the hell happened?'

'That's what I need to find out, obviously. We've never had police at the library before.'

'Yeah, that's proper weird. I'll come with you,' Asim offered, trying to sound brave.

Tessa shook her head. 'No, it's late. Go home, get some rest. We'll talk tomorrow. I'll pop by for some meat,' she said, as they whipped around a corner so sharp Asim nearly saw his life flash before his eyes.

'Bloody hell, that was close!' Asim squealed, sounding like a choirboy hitting the high notes.

Tessa just laughed, enjoying the madness. Luckily, the streets were basically empty, and there were no police in sight. It could've ended up a right mess.

'By the way, how do you afford this expensive car?' Asim asked, still clutching his stomach.

'Inherited a ton of money, actually. My ex was loaded,' Tessa replied, like it was the most normal thing in the world.

'Lucky you. But why do you still work at the library if you don't need the money?'

'I love that place, alright? I love Nina too. Plus, the library was my lifeline after my son died. You know, Nina's always worrying about money. She even talked about my salary and the possibility of selling the library,' Tessa continued. 'See, Nina knew I'd inherited something, but we never dug into it. I didn't want her to think I didn't need the job. What if she'd sacked me, eh? But really, if she'd told me sooner how deep in the muck she was, I could've helped. And I still will. I'm not letting that library sink. Don't worry, your job's safe. I'll make sure of it.'

'Well, you're full of surprises,' he said.

Tessa slowed the car near Asim's door so suddenly he nearly head-butted the window.

'Thanks for the heart-stopping ride,' Asim muttered, desperately trying to keep his dinner down.

'See ya,' Tessa said, nearly parking on the curb near the library. But there were no police cars. Weird, she thought, as she banged on the library doors and waited. No one answered.

THE LIBRARY

A sudden bang on the door made Nina jump. Sweat beaded on her forehead as she covered her mouth, heart pounding. *Shit, what now?* she thought. Fear, her oldest enemy.

Then she heard a usual scream, 'It's me, Tessa. Let me in!' Nina's heart slowed, inching back to normal. *Oh gosh, calm down, Nina. Breathe.*

'Why are you here so late? What's happening?' she asked, trying to sound calm.

Tessa's eyes darted around the library like she was expecting a lost zombie to pop out from behind a bookshelf. 'Oh gosh, are you alright?' She flicked an eyelid, looking both concerned and a bit like she'd walked in on a murder mystery. 'Lisa called, said there was a police car outside. Talk.'

'What? Oh gosh, you know her—she's just crazy. She probably made that up because she was bored. Don't forget, she has a green, stinky soul,' Nina mumbled. 'Anyway, you're not upset?'

'What a witch, anyway, upset about what? Oh, you mean the fight? I totally forgot about it. Sorry for that...,' Tessa said.

'But why were you so upset?'

'Because it was our day. Well, my son's birthday and you forgot, you know? And then there's the whole thing with selling the library. But, you know, it was actually good that it happened. We can't keep doing this anymore. It's the past, and I shouldn't have acted that way.'

But Nina sat down and burst into full-on tears. She had forgotten, and it hurt more than anything else. She started apologising, but Tessa stopped her, saying it was nothing and to just let it go. Life moves on. Tessa also told her not to sell the library, adding that she had spoken to Asim and sorted everything out. Everything was fine now, and Tessa made it clear she didn't need her salary.

Tessa hugged her tightly, like she could squeeze the despair right out of her and maybe a bit of her own pain too.

Nina felt relief wave in, warm and grounding, like a long-awaited drink after a rotten day. Tessa offered to stay the night without waiting for permission.

'I'm fine, really,' Nina tried, but Tessa was already halfway up the stairs.

Nina let out a breath, watching her go, feeling that weird, unusual appreciation. For once, the loneliness and fear backed off, like they'd finally had enough of her for one night. But there was one thing she had to do right away. She wrote to Martin, the man with the hat, telling him she wasn't selling the library. Even though it was past midnight, the message was read almost immediately and that was all that important to Nina right now.

Tessa pulled out an inflatable mattress. She dragged it and threw it down beside Nina's bed.

'You take the bed. I'll sleep on the floor,' Nina said, but Tessa's response was immediate, her eyes narrowing. The kind of look that said, *Seriously?*

'I'm not that heavy, alright? Just... solidly built! Like a tank. But a cute one.'

'Stop it, Tessa, you are perfect.'

She threw herself onto the inflatable mattress with full confidence, and immediately, it let out a tragic hiss, deflating in defeat until she was basically lying on the floor.

'Oh my God, my back. Shit, my back!' Tessa sucked in a breath.

Nina jumped up, helping her onto the bed, the laughter they shared tinged with more than a little pain. It was funny, in that way life can be when you're both too tired to care.

'Shit, I'm getting old and fat,' Tessa said, rolling her eyes. But her words knocked hard.

Nina hated to see Tessa so down. Grabbing a damp cloth, she wrapped it around Tessa's sore back, handed her painkillers, and settled her under a duvet. Nina then dropped to the floor.

They lay there. Breathing. Waiting.

'Nina? How much do you weigh?'

'Why?'

'I've always dreamed of being slim. You know, at least slimmer.'

Nina kept it casual, assuring her that weight didn't matter—health did. Tessa just hummed, but there was a weight to it, like something unspoken hung in the air. Nina felt a stab of guilt for not noticing how much it bothered her before.

'Thanks for being here, Tessa.'

It felt good. Safe, even. Like coming home to a quiet place, where someone was waiting to make everything feel a little less heavy.

After a moment, Nina asked, 'You know, have you ever thought about God? Hell, do you actually believe in it?'

'Once, I did, Nina. But... since my son died, I don't believe in God anymore.'

'Sorry, Tessa. You're right. I don't believe it either. I've always respected you. You're so strong.'

'I'm not, Nina. I'm trying to be. But there are days when I think... enough. When does this end, you know?'

'What do you mean? You don't mean...'

'No. I tried, but I couldn't do it. You know that. Those days are gone, but still... happiness doesn't just come back. You can't force it.'

'Yes, I understand. Life's hard, isn't it?' Nina sniffed, then added, 'Hm. Anyway, do you smell weed?'

But Nina didn't realise she was talking to dead air; Tessa was already snoring like a bear. A noise came from downstairs. Footsteps, or maybe her mind playing tricks. She shot upright from the floor.

'Not this,' she said, shaking Tessa's shoulders. 'Get up! Someone's downstairs!'

Tessa was, well... dead to the world. The room wasn't so dark, thanks to Nina's half-arsed curtains. She picked up her phone and was about to dial 999, but paused. The phone landed on the bed with a loud thump. She sniffed the air, recognising the soul right away.

'Asim? Is that you?'

Sure enough, there he was. Nina threw on a robe and headed down.

'You scared the shit out of me! Thought you were a thief. What're you doing here at this hour?'

'Had a fight with my dad. Got nowhere else to go.' He paused. 'I know it's late, but can I...'

'Course you can stay. Sofa's yours.'

Chapter Eight
Secrets

OH, THE SMELL OF TOAST and margarine. Just what Asim needed.

'Come on! Get washed, breakfast's on the table. Don't make me say it twice,' Tessa barked. He smirked and raced off to the bathroom. Tessa called after him, 'And keep it down; Nina's still out.'

But Nina wasn't asleep. No, she lay there, every muscle rebelling, eyes swollen and dead tired. Her thoughts were a tangled mess until Tessa's voice stabbed through the fog, talking to Asim about her. He wanted to know why Nina was still in bed.

'Rare disease,' Tessa said, more to herself than anyone else. 'Painful as hell. Pills don't do much.' She sipped her tea. 'No cure, so, you know, life, innit.'

'Hmm.' Asim played the part of the curious guest. 'So, how'd Nina land the library?'

Tessa looked both ways, as if someone was watching. 'You won't believe it. Some stranger handed it to her, just like that.' Then she whispered, 'Even this flat, all in one day.'

Tessa wasn't one to settle. She leaned in, changing the subject. 'So, what happened? Why'd you end up here, huh?'

Asim looked down, hardly chewing. 'Just my dad, you know.' He paused, then poked at the toast. 'Me... working here. He isn't really happy.' Then he looked into her eyes. 'Things got a bit messy, you know?'

Tessa gave a knowing smile, recognising it was all part of the game at his age. She had been through it too. The same rows with her mum, no dad around to smooth things over, just the usual mess.

'I was even worse. You're a good lad. I brought a baby home to my mum.'

'Oh, and how old were you?'

'Sixteen,' said Tessa.

'What?'

'Problem? I was the best mum in the world, and...'

'No, I'm sorry, Tessa.'

Asim let out a half-smile, nodding toward a photo hanging by the tall lamp, something catching his eye.

Tessa looked at it, then said, 'Oh, I was a lot skinnier and then... Ermm. Tea?'

'No, not that one. I'm talking about the man in the other picture.'

'Oh, him? That's her ex, proper smelly one.'

'Smelly one?'

'Yes, like a wet dog. Smelly bastard. More toast?'

And he enjoyed that toast, along with the tea that Tessa kept refilling for him. He felt safe and welcomed with her, like he was at home, like being with an auntie, and Tessa liked that too. After all, her son would be his age now if only he had lived, she thought to herself. But maths wasn't really her cup of tea. *Nope, not today. Sad brain, you can take your emotional baggage and bugger off.*

Meanwhile, Nina, still listening in her room, caught every word and wasn't exactly chuffed about it, but she shoved her feelings aside and dragged herself to the shower. In and out, quick as a flash. After drying off, she opened the grey cupboard where her tablets were stashed. Painkillers first, like clockwork.

Nina gave her wardrobe a look, as if searching for gold in a skip. With a weary sigh, she grabbed the long grey dress, the fashion equivalent of a damp rag. Her smaller wardrobe was a stroll down memory lane. Her attention was drawn to two old pairs of heels. She used to walk around in these like they were a second skin. Then she looked down at her feet in the orthopaedic slippers. *Flipping hell.* A far cry from her former glamour.

When she finally dragged herself downstairs, it was coffee and cigarette time, appreciated like they were gold dust. The clock read nearly 11:30 AM, but that didn't bother her in the slightest.

Tessa was slouching with her tea, doing a half-hearted job of cleaning. Meanwhile, Asim was lost behind the desk, staring keenly at his computer.

Nina immediately went still. Her eyes did a double take. An older gentleman in a slightly scruffy suit was waddling through the library. Right behind him was a younger woman in a red dress. Was she with her fella or what?

'Oh, hello! How lovely!' she said, visibly excited.

Tessa stared at her, mouth hanging open. 'Who are you chatting to?'

Asim just kept watching.

'What's wrong? Oh, right, I'm meant to be quiet,' Nina said, her tone dropping as she realised her mistake. Tessa's face turned white, looking like she was about to bolt, clearly thinking Nina had lost her marbles.

Nina slowly made her way to Asim. 'Nice job! Didn't think it'd kick in so soon. I'll be in the back,' she said, flashing him a cheeky wink.

When Nina turned around, Asim said his work wasn't finished yet and he was still working on it.

'What are you on about? Who are these people then?' Nina asked, pulling her brows together.

Tessa stomped over and gave Nina a sharp pinch on the shoulder. 'What the hell's wrong with you? What people? There's no one here!'

And then, someone walked in. A young woman with no hair.

Nina pointed at the shaved woman, her brows scrunched up like she'd just bitten into a lemon. 'Oi, isn't she here too?'

Tessa just pointed to the back with a smirk, like sending her for coffee was just part of the job description. So, Nina did just that, flashing a grin at the folks she probably shouldn't have been smiling at. They smiled back. Even the old lady who waggled her finger, shushing Nina like she was a naughty kid disturbing story-time. The older gentleman at the table shot her a look, fed up with the library racket.

It wasn't anything new for Nina, and that's exactly why she took those pills—to avoid seeing those bloody ghosts. Sensing souls wasn't her only strange ability; she could see ghosts too. But seeing them was a whole different ballgame compared to feeling souls. It was far more serious, especially when she was a kid. Poor thing even had to spend months in a psych ward, but in the end, things worked out. Ever since then, Nina never dared to skip her medication. And she never forgot to take it.

Still, it bothered her. How was it possible? She wasn't afraid. Ghosts had never done her any harm. But it was weird as hell. As she thought about it more deeply, she realised something odd. It happened just when Asim was sleeping over. After all these years, had she forgotten to take her pills? But no, she was positive she had taken them. It didn't make any sense. Could Asim have swapped her pills? The thought spun around in her head.

Meanwhile, Tessa was off making fresh tea for Olivia, the newbie who had just signed up on Asim's computer. Olivia was lost in the fantasy section when she piped up, asking where the bathroom was. With a cup in hand, Tessa led Olivia to the restroom, balancing like a circus act. When Olivia came out, she awkwardly kicked a bottle. The pills scattered all over the floor.

'Sorry, didn't see them,' she said, rushing to lift them up.

'No worries, I'll give you a hand,' said Nina.

They both bent down to gather the pills. As she picked them up, something clicked. Those pills looked familiar.

What the hell? How did these end up here? Why? What's going on? I was right. It was Asim.

She rushed to the bathroom, a lightbulb going off in her head. Of course, she recognised them. Those were her pills, and the ones she had taken were totally different. She had been taking these since she was a kid. *Hell, now I look like a psycho... again.* Now it was clear to her. It had to be Asim who switched her pills. What she couldn't understand, though, was why and how it was possible when he had a yellow, pure soul. It didn't make sense. She even started to wonder if her ability was deceiving her.

But then she remembered her teacher, who had told her that her gift never lies, and she still trusted him completely. She wished more than anything to speak to him now, to at least hear his voice and learn more. But she had stopped searching for him. *Useless.* Yet, she wasn't about to let this go. She decided she would get the truth out of Asim, whatever it took, just to make those ghosts disappear, including that new girl, Olivia, with no hair. Then she would handle Asim her way.

She wasn't afraid. She trusted her ability and knew Asim was a good, pure-hearted boy. Maybe he had a reason for what he did. *What if he knew something about me? What if he just wanted to find out the truth?* And so, she walked out, pretending that nothing had happened.

Meanwhile, Asim rubbed his eyes while Tessa worried over Nina. But Nina had her head screwed on tight; she saw things others couldn't, meds or no meds. She was a proper pearl, if only she had a bit more self-confidence.

Asim dropped down next to Olivia. He asked where she was from. She went bright red.

'I'm from here. I mean, I live close. And you?'

Asim told her he had just moved in.

'Nice, do you like it here?' Olivia asked. Just then, his phone rang.

Well, it wasn't exactly a quiet library; it might have been better when it was half-empty.

'No, I'm not,' Asim said. He strode back to reception with the phone glued to his ear. 'Chal teek hai, ok, bye.' He slumped back in his chair, serious as a heart attack, not even looking at Olivia.

But she didn't bat an eyelid. She was too busy with her book, pretending Asim's call was just background noise.

Meanwhile, Tessa was at the back with Nina, near the wild fireplace.

'What's up with you today? I'm getting worried,' Tessa said softly, or at least she tried.

'I'm fine,' Nina said. 'Just took the wrong pills and felt a bit off.'

'Listen, how long have I known you now?'

'Seven years?' Nina said.

'Right, well, you've never taken the wrong pills, alright?'

'It just happened, ok? I felt dizzy and... don't worry about it.'

Tessa sighed, glancing around. And then, Asim's phone rang again.

'Yeah, that's sick. He smashed it, bro,' Asim said.

Nosy Tessa perked up, then got up, pretending to wipe the threshold.

'I don't give a shit, bro,' Asim grumbled. He spotted Tessa messing with his keyboard. 'Let me call you back, bro.' He hung up.

And suddenly, Tessa didn't see any threshold.

'Oh, look, everything's nice and tidy, bro,' she quipped. She couldn't hold back a laugh, but Asim chuckled too.

Olivia tried to keep quiet as she packed up. She didn't even look at Asim, just gave Nina and Tessa a quick wave goodbye.

Asim then stretched his long legs and walked back to Nina. He was checking if she was fine.

'I know it was you. Why did you do it, and how do you know?' Nina asked, locking eyes with him.

Asim was quiet, giving her an earnest look.

'Who are you, Asim? Why are you really here, hmm?'

Asim pulled up a chair and settled across from her by the fireplace. Meanwhile, Tessa sat at the table, a bit farther from them, pretending she was listening to songs on her headphones and eating sandwiches.

'I'm sorry, Nina, but trust me, I'm not a bad person. I don't want to hurt you or...' Asim trailed off.

'Listen, I know you're not bad, but be honest with me, ok? We can't work together like this,' Nina said firmly, eyes locked onto Asim.

'You are right. Sorry, Nina, and yes, I swapped your pills. I just needed to know if it's really you,' Asim admitted, lowering his gaze.

'What do you mean?' Nina asked, crossing her arms.

'You won't believe me, but what I know sounds mad, and I don't want you thinking I'm a nutter. I respect you and...' Asim hesitated, rubbing his hands together.

'For God's sake, Asim, just talk!' Nina snapped, losing patience.

So, Asim laid it out.

Nina was quiet and listened closely. Meanwhile, Tessa, pretending to listen to music on her headphones, was actually fully tuned in. Her eyes widened like a cartoon character who had just seen a ghost—full-on what the actual hell mode.

'I found his stash of weird stuff, you know...' Asim started.

'No, Asim, I don't know!' Nina shot back.

'Well, some kind of... It was a document about the library's ownership,' he explained. 'Even your full name, the real one, I mean—Beatrice Nina Wright.'

'What? Why would your dad have my documents?' Nina asked, her confusion growing.

Tessa, who had gone from *cartoon-character shock* to *detective-in-a-crime-show* mode, narrowed her eyes.

'That's the thing, Nina. That's not all...' Asim continued, he had found some old photos, pages from books and a gold key.

He then leaned in, his face serious. 'You don't believe me, do you? I knew it. That's why I didn't say anything, OK?' Asim said, leaning back, bracing for her reaction.

'Nope, no. Carry on, please,' Nina said, now more curious than anything.

Asim hesitated, like he was about to drop something heavy. 'One day, I saw my dad do the unbelievable,' he admitted.

Nina frowned. 'Unbelievable how?'

'Hidden away, I watched as my dad put on some weird, old hat. And just like that—bang! His face, his voice, everything changed. It was like watching a totally different man take over,' Asim explained, shaking his head as if still trying to process it.

'Wait, so you're telling me your dad can... what? Transform?' Nina asked, struggling to believe it.

Asim nodded. 'I didn't know what the hell to make of it, so I followed him. Then I saw him with you, sitting and chatting in that Chinese restaurant.'

Nina's mind raced. A hat that changes your identity? *Bollocks, surely.* But then, she remembered—when she had seen Samir, she had noticed a shiny black hat in his flat. And then there was Martin, the man who had tried to buy her library, he had the same hat. At the time, she hadn't thought much of it. Only now... Something about that hat felt off.

'Wait, wait, slow down. What did you just say? So your dad changed into Martin and then you followed me?' Nina asked.

'Martin?' Asim repeated, looking confused.

Nina walked around, pacing, unsure if she could believe it herself. 'Listen, that guy, whoever he is, is not your dad or whoever the hell he is. That's the man who wanted to buy this library, and now it all makes sense,' she said, running a hand through her hair.

Asim just sat there, deep in thought. 'See? At least you believe me now. I'm telling you, this is no joke anymore,' he said, exhaling sharply.

At that moment, Tessa walked in, dropping the act with her *headphones*. 'Alright, you two. While you're in here spinning fairy tales, I'm out there trying to listen to you two

birds, and my hearing isn't that good. So, what is going on?'
she demanded, plopping onto a chair, sandwich in hand.

Then, in true Tessa fashion, she immediately added, 'And
Asim, eat a sandwich to calm you down. You're too skinny
and stressed out. Come on, chop chop.'

Asim shook his head. No, no, this really wasn't the time
for food.

Then he spoke in a low voice. 'Anyway, the pages say
you're the bloody Guardian of Hell. You got it, Nina?'

'Guardian of Hell? Are you taking the piss?' Nina
blurted out, nearly choking on air.

'No joke. You've got some mad skills. That knack for
sniffing out souls? Huh?' Asim insisted.

He revealed the breathtaking truth—that her memories
and other powers had been wiped and stored away in those
old books. But Nina stayed quiet. It sounded like *bullshit* to
her. Well, half of it, anyway. He also mentioned a door in the
basement. He knew it existed, had heard about it, but didn't
know exactly where it was hidden or what was behind it. All
he knew was that it led somewhere else, a different magical
world.

Nina's heart was going crazy; she was *dying* to accept it.
'So, I'm some kind of magical freak? Or worse, some devil,
Satan? Right. And what door? What magical world?'

'Well, still better than an old smelly witch!' Tessa chimed
in.

'Yeah, still a weirdo, Tessa!' Nina shot back, rolling her
eyes.

'Not a weirdo. You're the proper real deal, Nina. You
can even bring back the dead,' Asim said, watching Nina

carefully as she wrestled with the shock. The pages made it crystal clear.

'I know. I only know what I saw in that book, okay? I don't have all the answers, but if we dig deep together, we can find out!' Asim urged.

'Anyway, what makes you think this is about me?' Nina asked, still sceptical.

Asim leaned back, dead serious. 'I know it is you. This is why you can see ghosts and smell souls.'

And there it was again, that bloody heavy quietness.

Chapter Nine
The Door

Part One

NINA HAD TO LIGHT UP. It was either that or risk collapsing from all the pent-up stress. She grabbed her lukewarm coffee and attacked jumper. It was cold, but well, smokers weren't exactly treated like royalty these days. More like the unwashed peasants of society. So, she took the long way around the library, hoping to puff in peace, far from judging eyes.

Her mind, in the meantime, was a disaster. Asim and Tessa had dumped a truckload of existential noise on her earlier, and she was still trying to sort out the wreckage. Guardian of Hell? What a joke. Or... no? It was like signing up for a marathon when walking to the post box already left you winded. She could nearly hear the earth having a good old laugh at her expense.

Just as she was getting sucked into her dramatic mental spiral, in waltzed Lisa. And by waltzed, I mean stomped in a coat red enough to blind you and slippers that screamed *I've given up*, complete with white socks. Lovely. Lisa was trouble. Not because she was a nosy gossip with more tea to spill than a Harrods' afternoon service. Though that too. But because her soul had the charm of week-old bin juice.

'Oh, hello there!' Lisa beamed as if they were long-lost friends. 'I'm so glad to see you! Had to sneak all the way over here, you know. Can't have anyone seeing me with a cig in hand.'

'Yep, same,' Nina replied, in a tone so dry it could have started a brush fire.

'So, what's new? How've you been?' Lisa asked, exhaling a fog bank of cigarette smoke.

'Ah, you know, all good. And you?'

'Fantastic! Rebecca's pregnant. Can you believe it?'

'Really? Wow! Who's Rebecca?' Nina was already regretting this detour into the Social Torture Pathway.

'Oh my God, you don't know? She's the baker's daughter! You know, next to that nasty meat shop. Samir's place!'

Ah, yes. Samir. Just hearing his name made Nina's stomach turn over like it was trying out for Cirque du Soleil. But she splashed on with a neutral expression. Lisa, of all people, couldn't know she even knew Samir. That would open a can of lice bigger than Godzilla.

'Oh, right. Of course. I just haven't... met her,' Nina said. 'But obviously, you know everything.'

'Oh, stop! I wish... I mean, I don't know everything!' Lisa said, as if modesty wasn't allergic to her. 'But she's, well, a big girl. Enjoys her pies. Speaking of, how did that date go?'

'What date?'

'With that young gentleman! The one I saw you with in my restaurant. You left him there, poor thing, looking like a lost puppy.'

'Oh, him? Just a friend. He was interested in the library,' Nina said, hoping this interrogation would end soon.

'Good, good! I was thinking, surely, you're not into cradle-robbing. How old was he, 18?' Lisa said, grinning like she'd cracked some grand conspiracy.

'I don't know, Lisa, and I don't care.'

'Of course, course. It's quite cold, isn't it?'

'Yes, but I'm sure your socks keep you warm.'

'Of course, they're lovely. Anyway, that poor old lady... did you ever sort that out?'

'What old lady? And what am I supposed to sort?'

'Oh, haven't you heard? Word on the street is she was your grandma, and you didn't even pay for her funeral.'

'I'd love to know who's spreading that garbage. Whoever it is deserves a good slap.'

'Oh, totally, Nina! Couldn't agree more,' Lisa chuckled, looking about as honest as a used car dealer. 'Anyway, got to run!'

'Yea, see ya,' Nina said, watching Lisa waddle away, slippers flapping. What a sight.

'Ugh, she really does deserve that green soul. What a witch,' Nina mumbled to herself. 'Just wait until I'm a Guardian of Hell. You'll be first in line to roast, you bitch!'

When she came back inside, she just wanted to wash her hands, but of course, Tessa and Asim were already waiting by the door. Not the main one, obviously, that would be too simple, but the one that led to the basement.

'Ready?' said Tessa, basically vibrating with impatience. Asim just stood there, tapping his foot. Nina sighed, knowing full well she was about to regret every life choice that led to this moment, and nodded. The door opened with a creak that yelled *horror movie cliché*, but the basement was... well, disappointingly normal.

Tessa took the lead, turned on the light, and they all clomped down the creaky stairs. Honestly, it was more junk storage than a proper den of supernatural intrigue. Just a cramped room, smelling like someone had bottled "Ye Olde Musty Shoppe" and left it to ferment.

'See, told you, no other doors here,' Nina said, gesturing at the mess of old books and done in boxes spread around.

'Hmm, strange,' said Asim, scratching his head. 'I was sure there was a door here?'

Tessa rolled her eyes like she was dealing with two clueless tourists. 'Come on, you two, help me move this wardrobe. The door's behind it.'

Of course, she was already trying to manhandle the wardrobe, and Nina couldn't help but wonder how Tessa even *knew* this.

'Wait, what?' Nina asked.

Tessa, in her oh-so-casual way, explained that the door had annoyed her while she was cleaning—so she just blocked it with a wardrobe. Because, you know, that's just what people do. Asim, who was suddenly all for the adventure, ran over to help. They moved the olden piece of furniture together, and Tessa wiped the sweat off her face.

'Blimey, my tits are sweating now,' she joked, and Asim turned redder than a traffic light in Piccadilly.

'Tessa, for God's sake, behave,' Nina said, giving her a look and flicking her eyes on Asim.

'Oh, come on, let the lad learn,' Tessa grinned.

'Anyway, here are those doors. Can we just open them now and forget about your sweaty tits?' said Asim.

Tessa pulled the handle, and the door opened... to reveal bricks. Just bricks. Total, boring bricks.

'What the heck? How's that possible?' Asim said, looking like he'd just been told there were no more sausage rolls left at Greggs.

'See? Nothing,' said Tessa, hands on her hips. There was an awkward, squeezing quietness.

'Well, you could've said so from the start,' Nina said.

'Where's the fun in that?' said Tessa.

'Seriously? Fun? Everything is a joke to you...' Nina started, and the two launched into their usual bickering.

Meanwhile, Asim's attention floated to the room itself. He started poking around.

'Oi, you two, stop the fighting and get over here,' Asim called.

He found an old photograph stuck behind a stack of dirty books. Something about it immediately felt... turned. When Nina hooked sight of it, her face drained of colour. And Tessa? Well, she looked like someone had just told her Yorkshire tea was permanently out of stock.

On the photo was a man, lounging on what could only be described as a *flaming throne*. A massive red gate stood behind him, while storm clouds filled the sky above, glowing with flames.

'Oh my God, is that... Alfie?' Tessa said, staring at the picture like it had personally offended her. Nina peeked at it, then leaned in closer. And closer. Until her nose was basically touching the thing. She didn't say a word, just shot a wide-eyed glance at Tessa and Asim, who were already brimming with their own opinions.

'That's Alfie?' Asim whispered, like saying it louder might summon him.

'Yeah, but why the *bloody hell* is he on a flaming throne?' Nina muttered with this wobbling voice. Her hand trembled as she flipped the photo over, and there it was: *Death – 1978*.

'Death? What the hell does that mean? Like he's dead?' said Nina.

Tessa took the photo out of her hands with zero regard for her personal space.

'He's not bloody *dead*, Nina. It says he *is* Death. As in, Mr Black Robes, Big Scythe, King of the Dead—Death himself.' She let the words hang in the air with a voice louder than it should have been, like she was trying to prove herself too. 'Bloody hell, I *knew* he wasn't normal,' Tessa added, but for once, her usual smug grin was nowhere to be seen. She looked pale, her bravado clearly on life support.

For a moment, the three of them just stared at the photo in a silence so thick you could have sliced it with Alfie's imaginary scythe.

'Lovely, well,' Tessa said finally, breaking the tension like a dropped plate. 'I'm going to make tea.'

Because when life slaps you with the fact your regular customer is Death, tea is what you bloody well do. She walked upstairs without waiting for an answer, leaving Nina and Asim still iced up.

Nina's brain was doing the intellectual equivalent of cartwheels. Alfie? Death? Not the slightly awkward guy who showed up every Tuesday to like a ghost read books and sip tea? But the actual picture of Death? The celebrity people joked about at Halloween parties? The Grim Reaper? She couldn't process it. And the more she tried, the worse it got.

Did that mean Alfie had come for *them*? Was this it? The end? It was one thing to joke about Death being an idea, but it was another thing entirely when he in fact lived down the street and had a taste for Earl Grey.

Asim looked like he'd just solved a riddle only to realise the answer was terrible. He muttered something about how Nina being the Guardian of Hell somehow made it all fit, but his expression said otherwise. The pieces of the puzzle might technically go together, but it didn't make the picture any less horrifying.

'So, Death and the Guardian of Hell,' Nina said, her voice teetering on the edge of hysteria. 'What are we? Some sort of afterlife power couple?'

'No idea,' Asim muttered. He'd sunk into a chair that looked like it would break any second, his face a mix of confusion and factual fear. 'But if Alfie's Death... does that mean we're done?'

Nina's panic climbed to new heights. Her thoughts spiralled from mild concern to full-blown *end-of-days-level dread*. Was Alfie here to drag her to Hell? To finish whatever punishment she was evidently meant to suffer? Or worse—was she about to be collected?

'Calm down,' Asim said, though his voice shook like a leaf in a storm. 'We'll figure it out. Somehow.'

Somehow. Brilliant. Nina's chest tightened. Sure, let's just "figure it out" when Death himself is involved. Fantastic plan.

Before they could work out any brilliant plan (which, let's face it, was probably not happening), the evident sound of footsteps came from the library. Nina took Asim's arm, taking him closer.

'Shhh,' she whispered, pulling him to the stairs. They crept up, hearts beating, and stayed hidden behind the door.

They could hear Olivia's voice travelling in from the library, all casual-like. And of course, Tessa was up there too, making tea as if she hadn't just been involved in some cosmic showdown. Nina rolled her eyes. Seriously, Olivia had to show up now? Timing really was a sadistic bastard sometimes. Nina muttered something about how the woman couldn't have picked a worse moment, and Asim, in usual Asim fashion, pointed out that she should have locked the door.

Oh, brilliant, Nina thought. Thanks for that insight, Sherlock. She bit back a response about how annoying he could be, but it was true—he was definitely capable of being smug at the worst possible moments.

Then, before they could properly argue or even think of a plan, Tessa's voice rang out from upstairs, loud. 'Oi, you two, come out! Olivia's here, and I'm making tea.'

Part Two

NINA QUIETLY SLIPPED into her armchair, trying to appear calm, while Asim went straight to the reception desk. He welcomed Olivia with exaggerated cheer, loud enough for anyone to hear, and she responded in kind, waffling on about how lovely the weather was. Asim couldn't help but glance outside, where the rain was beating against the windows like a drum solo gone wrong, and the sky was a sheet of grey misery. Very lovely indeed. Then came the lightning and thunder, loud enough to make you wonder if Thor himself had popped by for a visit.

It wasn't just Tessa shouting, 'Alfie's coming!' anymore. Even Nina had joined in, and this time, the dread was very real. Now that they knew Alfie was Death himself, not just some man with a weird sense, they had every right to panic.

Asim was trying his best not to sweat through his shirt, while Tessa came in with a tray of tea, her hands shaking so badly she was basically watering the carpet with spilled tea. Nina sat wide-eyed, her heart thudding like it was training for a marathon. And Olivia? Well, she was pretending to be buried in her book, but you could tell she was paying attention, subtle as ever.

Then the door creaked, and he walked in. Alfie. Wiped off his shoes, this time, unusually gently. His umbrella gripped in one hand like a soldier holding a rifle. He threw

Asim a grin, all wide and toothy, and Asim nodded straight, moving like a robot whose gears had stopped. Alfie turned to Tessa and gave her a faint smile. Tessa smirked back, trying to avoid his eyes, looking as if she was half-heartedly reading a newspaper she'd rather chuck in the bin. The room suffered heavy, like an awkward family reunion where everyone knows the big secret, but no one's brave enough to mention it.

And Alfie? He clocked Olivia, and his smile slipped, eyes narrowed, like he recognised her but really didn't want to confess it. Olivia pretended she hadn't noticed, her head still buried in her book. Alfie sat opposite her, and Tessa, trying to walk on tiptoe, carefully set the tea down on the table. She didn't even dare look at Alfie.

Her voice trembled as she asked, 'Tea?' It was a first in two years of serving him, and yes, of course, he noticed. But he just shook his head and smiled, acting like nothing was wrong. Tessa took a cloth and started wiping down books, pretending to be busy, as usual. But her heart was doing an Olympic run in her chest.

Asim saw Alfie give Olivia a sharp kick under the table. Olivia struck him a direct glance, then hid her nose even deeper in her book.

Nina whistled up with a bright 'Hello,' forcing a wide, daring smile. Alfie's mood lifted immediately, and it was like watching a storm cloud suddenly decide to bugger off.

What a day. The door opened again, and voilà, it was Martin. Dripping wet, hat on, long coat, the whole ominous stranger package. He shook his shiny shoes, directing water splashes everywhere, and scanned the room. Asim's face went tight, like he half-recognised him but couldn't quite place it.

'Ufff, isn't he handsome?' Tessa whispered to Nina, hand covering her mouth but not nearly quiet enough. Nina shot her a look, eyes wide, and then rushed off to the kitchen, not happy to see him.

Martin stepped forward. 'Good afternoon, mind if I have a quick look around? Nina's expecting me. Is she in?' he asked, flashing a smile so polite it reasonably belonged in a posh tea advert.

Asim exchanged a glance with Tessa and replied, 'No, I'll call her, hang on a sec.'

Martin was all charm and smelled like money. He barely paid any attention to Olivia or Alfie, his eyes fixed on the library. But when he wasn't looking, Alfie and Olivia swapped a sharp, knowing look. Great, thought Asim. They all knew each other.

Martin wandered around the room, running his fingers over the books, brushing the green curtains, and even pressing his hand to the carpet like he was a detective in a period drama. He paused by the door to the basement, hummed, then moved on, eyes flying over the shelves that Tessa was still pretending to clean.

Asim slipped into the kitchen, where Nina was hiding.

'Shit, that's my dad! I know that hat. He's turned into that lad, do you get it?!' he whispered, trying to keep his panic under control.

'I know, it's him. I know that hat too, and that's the Martin, I told you about, the one who wanted this library,' Nina whispered back and added, 'And you were right, Asim.

I don't know if I'm ready for this,' her voice trembling. 'Magic, all of it, Asim; you were right.'

'Are you joking? Of course, it is!' Asim whispered back, clearly irritated.

'Flipping hell, and even Alfie—I mean, Death—is here. Are we all going to die?' said Nina.

'No one's dying, and listen, Olivia and Alfie—they know each other. I saw it,' Asim whispered.

Then those bloody oiled doors creaked again. Samir walked in. Asim's dad.

Tessa's face flushed bright red as she called out, 'Come on in, sorry, I really need to oil these bloody doors again; sounds like a horror film!'

What a day for this supposedly quiet library. Asim and Nina peeked out from the kitchen, looking like a pair of nosy neighbours spying over the fence.

'What??' they both said at the same time, quickly ducking back.

'My dad? Then who the hell is that lad, Martin?' Asim whispered, baffled.

'Shit, we got it wrong. Maybe he's got a brother?' Nina whispered back, still hiding.

'My dad doesn't have a brother! I'm telling you, he changed once he put that hat on, ok?' Asim said, sounding desperate.

'I know, I believe you. But maybe you saw someone else?' Nina said.

'Yeah, probably just a different bloke,' said Asim. 'But I swear, they looked identical!'

Meanwhile, in the library, Samir was soaked, but he didn't give a toss. He walked straight to the reception and asked for Asim. Tessa told him to wait. As she headed toward the kitchen, Samir stepped back, squinting. He shot a strange look at Olivia, then locked eyes with Alfie. Alfie stared right back, and this time, even Olivia joined in. The tension was thick, or at least as thick as it could be when Martin, wearing a slightly ridiculous hat, was skulking between the shelves, eyeing books as if he expected them to suddenly do a tap dance or reveal some hidden secrets. He stopped Tessa on her way to find Asim.

'Do you have any more books here? I mean, some older ones, perhaps?' he asked, with a smile so painfully charming it could've sold ice to a penguin. Just not to her.

'If you don't know what you're looking for, I can't really help you,' she replied, her patience wearing thinner than cheap loo roll. His smile vanished.

'Hmm, is there another room, or maybe a basement where you keep more books?' he tried again, this time with a tone that implied he might know something she didn't. Which, let's be honest, was unlikely.

'Look, handsome, do you want tea? Because I'm heading to the kitchen now.'

'Yes, please, darling,' he said, giving a small, theatrical bow before sliding into a nearby chair. Just as she turned to go, he piped up again, 'Sorry to bother you again, but was an old lady with silver hair a customer here?'

Tessa was already at the kitchen door, hand on the handle. She stopped, mildly exasperated. This was weird even by her standards, and those were standards that had seen all sorts.

'Old lady? Of course, this is a library; we do have some old ladies coming here—old like me, old like my mum, and all sorts of old and old and old,' she said, with a look that screamed she was dangerously close to losing her patience. Honestly, she only said it in the hope he'd finally get off her back. He was persistent, the kind of annoying that made you want to swat him like a fly that just wouldn't sod off.

Finally, she entered the kitchen.

'Listen, you two hiding in the kitchen, something stinks, alright? So get your arses out there and sort it!' Tessa called, setting the old kettle down with the kind of care you'd reserve for a bomb. She tried to whisper, though whispering had never really been her forte.

'Shh, they can hear you!' hissed Nina, her eyes wide and flashing with a mix of shock and anger.

'Tell him I'm not here, that's my dad!' Asim whispered to Tessa, looking like a kid caught with his hand in the biscuit tin.

Tessa, not very much impressed, grabbed the kettle and poured the water into the cup with slightly more force than necessary, spilling a few drops in her rush.

'What? The bald one is Samir?' Tessa half-shouted, absolutely failing at being discreet.

Nina slapped a hand over her mouth. 'Shh, are you mad? Look, something's going on with that lad in the hat. Watch out, he's the one who wants to buy this library,' she whispered, eyes running to the door with the over-the-top concern of someone in a spy film.

Tessa then raised her voice a little louder than needed. 'What, that's him? What a bastard! No way, he isn't getting anything!' she said, with a tone practically daring the world to argue.

If the neighbours hadn't heard before, they absolutely had now.

Meanwhile, back in the library, Samir froze, eyes glued to the young man in the hat, Alfie, and Olivia. They weren't just staring; they were caught in one of those weird, strong face-offs that felt like a flashback to the days when Sylvester Stallone was king of the screen—back when men didn't draw back, and explosions were a sign of respect. The pressure in the room was thick enough to cut with a spoon, and just when you thought it couldn't get any more dramatic, the sky let out a thunderclap so loud it probably startled pigeons three towns over.

Samir started circling Alfie and Olivia, visibly in the mood to threaten, before finally pulling up a chair across from the man in the hat. He leaned in and gave him that look—you know, the one meant to say, *I see you, and I don't like it.*

'Nice hat, mate. But you don't look like you belong here,' Samir said.

Martin gave him a rusty, unimpressed look, as if to say, *Congratulations, Sherlock, you cracked the case.*

Then, without breaking eye contact, Martin reached into his coat and slowly pulled out... a pair of white, sparkly gloves. He did it like he was drawing a gun in the Wild West, except instead of a Colt .45, it was sequins. Alfie and Olivia exchanged looks, and a bead of sweat popped out on

Samir's forehead, like he'd just done a 5K. They all knew: these gloves weren't your usual winter wear.

Just when you thought things couldn't get any weirder, Tessa marched out of the kitchen, slamming a cup of tea down in front of the young man with all the subtlety of a sledgehammer.

'Listen, mate, don't go all Michael Jackson on us here. You're not reading? Then you're not drinking either! This isn't some charity. Anyway, this tea is probably too old for you,' she barked before turning around to Olivia. 'Cup of tea, love?'

Olivia's eyes virtually yelled, *back away, Tessa.*

As a miracle, Tessa took the hint, breathing hard and stepping back, slowly—like *really* slowly.

Martin slipped on the gloves with a tap, pointing his finger at Samir like it was a loaded weapon. Samir, as if trying out for a jungle cat documentary, leapt forward. In a flash, a blue, laser-like beam shot out of the glove, slicing a chair in half like it was butter.

Poor Olivia let out a scream and dove under the table faster than you could say, *"Not my problem."*

Alfie shot to his feet, whipping around just in time for it. Bam!

Then came another. Bam! A lightning bolt crashed down with the force of an explosion, shattering the entire shop window in an instant. The blast sent shards of glass flying like deadly shrapnel, slicing through the air with terrifying speed. It was as if a grenade had gone off, hurling razor-sharp fragments in every direction, each piece a miniature missile of destruction.

Martin, now looking like a pincushion for glass pieces, even his hat bleeding somehow, didn't waste a second. He ran.

Samir, only just noticing the spikes digging into his shoulder, shielded his head and shot after him, tearing through the door like a man who'd seen it all. And still had zero intention of backing down.

Alfie? He'd vanished into thin air, like he was part of the storm itself.

Tessa, ducked behind the bookshelves, watched the whole thing unfold. Tucked low on the floor but with a look that said, *oh, I'm missing nothing*.

Nina, for her part, ignored the pain and ran outside after Samir. Asim, shaking with fear, turned under the table after Olivia.

'You alright?' he blurted.

Tessa pushed her head out and shouted at Asim, 'Yes, I'm alright, thanks for asking!'

The danger had vanished, but the thirst lingered. Not for wine. Something stronger. Whiskey. She poured herself a shot.

Meanwhile, Nina was slowing down, struggling to breathe. She saw Samir grabbing Martin around the neck and pulling the hat off him. In an instant, Martin transformed into some elderly man, a proper grandad. *Who the hell is that?* Nina wondered, shocked, wiping her eyes, not sure if she'd seen the real deal. She pressed a hand to her thigh to steady herself, blinking into the weak light.

But it was too late. Samir saw her, let go of the poor grandad he had been gripping, and the man collapsed in a heap. In a flash, Samir sprinted back into his shop. Nina hobbled back to the library, her slipper betraying her. Flipping hell. She kicked off the sole and walked barefoot, boiling. It stung, yes, and she was proper pissed off, but more than that, bloody confused.

'Oh my God, my window! Shit!' Nina stood outside, staring at the smashed glass, scratching her head.

Inside, Tessa was downing the old whiskey. Raising her hand, she passed Nina a glass through the broken window.

'Have some. It'll calm you down.'

Nina exhaled, took the whiskey, and drank it. Meanwhile, Olivia slipped away without a word, avoiding eye contact.

'Well, we've lost the hook-up, I guess,' Asim said, finally getting up from under the table and staring at the broken window.

'Forget her, she's got no hair anyway,' Tessa replied, handing him a glass.

He took a sip and coughed. 'Ugghh.'

'It's nothing. Here's another. This'll help with your cough,' Tessa said. She swallowed her own, eyes locked on the broken glass.

'Well, here it is. I was right about Alfie, and so was Asim about the other things he said. I just saw it with my own eyes,' she added, drinking down another glass.

Nina stood there, eyes fixed on the smashed window. Asim shuffled, his gaze bouncing between Tessa and the broken glass.

'What the hell just happened?'

'Oof,' Tessa screwed up her face, having downed another shot that burned like chilli. She looked at them both and said, 'Alfie just disappeared. Puff. One minute he was standing there, and then he simply wasn't. Magic. Magic is real. It exists.'

Chapter Ten
Stepping Through

————◦❀◦————

SHARDS WERE EVERYWHERE. Some smeared with blood, a few lodged in books. The place was a wreck, but no one seemed to care. No one got hurt. Or did they?

'Omg, Tessa, don't move!' Nina's eyes went wide as she grabbed a cloth. 'You've got a shard under your chin!'

Nina started to panic. Asim slammed his glass on the table and reached out for Tessa. She didn't shy away. Either she was too drunk to feel it or just made of steel.

'Where? Shit, yeah.' She just glanced at Asim as she pulled the piece out herself, cool as you like. 'Sorted.' She wiped the blood away, took a dustpan, and carried on like nothing had happened.

Asim's and Nina's eyes nearly popped out. Tessa moved as if she had a tuatara in her backside.

Now that's what I call a woman, Asim thought, shaking his head.

The rain kept spilling down, and the humidity felt like hell. Asim stuck some boxes over the broken window, and the room swelled with quiet. They were tired but mostly confused. Sitting at the second table, their hearts running like a Bugatti. Each of them had that far-off look, like they were replaying their own private crime scenes in their heads, waiting to see who would speak first.

'Cuppa tea?' Of course, it was Tessa. The anxiety in the room pressed down. Asim and Nina just rolled their eyes at her, both thinking, *How the hell can she be thinking about tea right now?*

Asim moved, catching the slight wriggle of Nina's fingers on the table.

'So, shall we go over what you're saying?' Nina finally asked.

Asim and Tessa threw quick side-eyes, the kind that didn't need words. Then, like an unwelcome guest, the silence slipped right back in. Unbelievable.

'Well, there is magic, the door is full of bricks, Alfie is Death who just vanished, then some bloke, who, by the way, was or wasn't Samir, shot from gloves. Lovely day, isn't it?' Tessa said.

At least she smashed the dead air. Asim admitted he had no clue how to get into that other world and was starting to feel proper shaky. Nina was right there with him, feeling it too. Their chat was a bit of a non-starter, like something out of a dodgy film, except not as interesting.

Nina confessed she felt as if she belonged to another world. Asim kind of summed it all up. And Tessa made tea. Then she added that it all started when Asim arrived, but Nina disagreed with her. After all, Alfie had been going to the library for quite some time, and she had come into possession of the library under strange circumstances. Olivia was also quite strange.

Asim said he no longer knew who his father was and admitted fear was creeping in. Nina told them what she had seen outside, that Martin had changed into an elderly man, but it didn't lift their spirits much. Tessa reminded them of the theft and the picture.

'Weird, he didn't nick anything,' Tessa said, taking a sip of her tea, 'but what if he's the one who put the picture in there?'

'What?' Nina replied, doubtful. 'You're saying instead of stealing something, he brought rubbish?'

'Well, yeah,' Tessa insisted. 'It wasn't there before, I'm telling you.'

'Tessa's got a point, Nina,' Asim chimed in, leaning forward. 'Look, maybe it wasn't random. Maybe someone wanted us to find that picture, to figure out the truth about Alfie. There's got to be something deeper going on.'

Nina puffed out a breath slowly. 'Shit, you're probably right. It just feels like we're in even more darkness than we were before.'

They fell into break-time mode. Just sat there, thinking. A little scared, sure, but their interest wouldn't let it go. There was no way they could just move on and pretend nothing had happened. Not after today.

Nina was on a tear, questions battling through her mind faster than she could pin them down. Why the hell was she the Guardian of Hell? Where was this Hell anyway? What did it even mean to be its Guardian? Why all the secrecy? And what was the deal with her memories being hidden in books? And why the hell the library window? The more she thought about it, the more the questions piled up.

Meanwhile, Asim was left with absolutely nothing but a massive blank. Not a single answer. Just a void staring back at him, as if to say, *don't look at me, mate.* They sat in anxious hush, both knowing full well they were in deep trouble. Were they in danger? Oh, absolutely.

'If we just sit here and talk like old grandmas—oops, sorry, and grandpa—we're not going to figure out anything!' Tessa shouted, slamming her teacup onto the table.

'Listen, look at the pic. I just remembered something,' Nina said.

Asim and Tessa both turned to her, eyebrows raised, then shook their heads in unison like a pair of confused penguins.

'No, seriously, look again!' Nina huffed.

Still nothing. Just blank stares. Honestly, she could've told them the Mona Lisa was winking, and they'd have the same reaction.

'Fine!' Nina snapped. 'I'll just say it. The briefcase! It's on the floor, right next to his bloody throne. That briefcase is here! He left it. Here!'

And then—Bang! Bang!

Tessa ran to the door, shouting, 'I nearly shit myself! It's Lisa. Let me sort her out! That sneaky bitch!'

Meanwhile, Asim grabbed the suitcase and dropped it onto the table with a certain thud.

'It's time to open it,' he announced, his tone leaving no room for argument.

Nina sighed, wishing aloud that there might at least be some money inside. Something useful, for once.

By the time Tessa returned, tea in hand and Lisa thoroughly dealt with, Asim was already prying the suitcase open. She raised an eyebrow, not quite impressed.

'What's all the fuss about this thing? It's just a book. Fat and old, but not like me, of course.'

It wasn't surprising she'd already had a peek. Of course, she had. Nina and Asim didn't even bother pretending to be shocked at her nosiness. But as Asim finally opened the suitcase, all three of them froze. The book inside was a riddle. No letters. No markings. Just blank, empty pages staring back at them like some cruel joke. Asim threw it aside, muttering about how ridiculous it all was.

Nina couldn't help but joke, though with a hint of suspicion, 'Maybe it was our Alfie's old teaching notebook.'

Tessa breathed in so hard she nearly spilled her tea.

'What? That's the biggest load of bollocks I've ever heard. Alfie's not normal, Nina. He's Death himself. He vanished right in front of us, remember? Pfff, *our* Alfie, did you hear that? She said *our* Alfie!'

Asim just shrugged.

'Forget that, Tessa. Listen, my dad has the same suitcase. I remember—I dropped a key in there. Accidentally, I mean. But why is the suitcase here? And it's not Alfie's, it's my dad's,' said Asim.

'Omg, I'm more confused than ever. Can we forget all this? Just let it go,' Tessa said.

Nina knew Tessa was right, but something about the idea still didn't sit right.

Alfie had always seemed so... normal. A nice guy. A person you'd never guess had a cosmic blade hidden in a sweeping brush closet.

'You've lost it,' Tessa muttered, but Asim said nothing, lost in his own thoughts.

Nina couldn't look away from the book. Something about it drew her in. Her fingers brushed the aged cover, feeling its texture as if it might whisper answers.

'It's alive,' she said, startling both of them.

She inhaled sharply, catching the strange dual scent of white roses and sour milk. It didn't make sense, but neither did any of this. Suddenly, the book came to life. Light poured out from between its covers, brightening the room like a searchlight. The three of them jumped back.

'Shit, I need another drink,' Tessa muttered, though her voice betrayed her fascination.

Before anyone could react, letters began forming on the pages, glowing as they appeared, one by one. The book quickly turned its own pages, the letters pulsing as if they were alive. Then, as though called by an invisible power, three golden letters rose from the page: KEY.

Tessa screamed in joy, bouncing in place. 'Oh my God, it's like something out of a film!'

Asim, acting on impulse, reached out for the book but quickly pulled back when a spark flew out and slightly burned his finger. He looked at it, shocked, as Tessa cried out in fear. He waved her aside. It didn't hurt much, but they were completely focused on the key taking shape in front of them. The letters bent and flowed before coming together to form a big, golden key that gleamed like something from a fairy tale. For a moment, no one spoke. No one moved.

'Are we drunk, or did that actually happen?' Tessa finally asked, her voice a mix of awe and disbelief.

Nina and Asim exchanged glances, both unsure whether to laugh or scream. Asim broke the silence first, mumbling that it must be the key to the mysterious doors in the basement. Nina wasn't so sure. She reminded him, again, that the doors were already open with nothing but bricks behind them.

'Maybe it's still worth trying,' Tessa said. 'We just saw magic happen, Nina. You can't deny that.'

The three of them sat in tense hush, swapping looks of confusion, fear, and a spark of hope. Deep down, they all believed it. This wasn't just a coincidence. This was something bigger.

Tessa broke the quiet again, her voice lower this time. 'We're not safe here,' she said. 'This place feels like a bloody powder keg.'

Nina stepped closer, eyeing Tessa. 'Why are you so desperate to open that door? What do you think is waiting for us there?'

Asim jumped in. 'I lost my mother,' he said simply. 'If you become what you're meant to be, Nina, maybe you could bring her back.'

Nina frowned. She wasn't sure if Asim was making it up or holding onto something he desperately wanted to believe.

'I don't even know what I'm supposed to be,' she said.

Asim stepped closer. 'I want the truth, Nina. No more lies. And I'll help you, no matter what's waiting.'

Tessa nodded, her face serious now. 'Asim's right. This library, those doors, these weird people around, the bloody key. It's all connected. We've got to try.'

Nina was deep in thought, but the fire in Asim's eyes was impossible to ignore. She finally gave up.

'I'm in,' she said.

Tessa, of course, wasn't done. 'Hold on,' she said, standing up. 'I'm not going through some magic door empty-handed like some idiot in a horror film.' She started walking, muttering about snacks, tea, and a cricket bat.

Nina and Asim just stared after her, not quite sure whether to laugh or groan. Typical Tessa.

Bang! Bang!

Nina shot out of her chair. 'Run now!'

With their hearts pounding, they bolted for the basement, legs moving as fast as they could. They slammed the door behind them.

Asim: 'Who's hammering away like that, though?'

Nina: 'Just wait till the muppet banging realises it's only boxes up there.'

Tessa: 'Bloody hell. Why are we running? I'm going up to beat the shit out of him!'

Nina: 'Don't you dare move, Tessa. We don't know who it is! You forgot what just happened?'

Asim, already at the door: 'Will you two quit yapping and help me open this?'

In a split second, a gravelly voice roared from upstairs.

'Don't open the door! Asim, don't do it!'

It was Samir, yelling.

Nina pushed at the doors, but they weren't budging.

She shouted, giving Tessa a nudge, 'Shift your fat arse, Tessa!' but it was no good.

Asim grumbled, 'Give over, let me have a go. We haven't got all day; Dad's going to smash through any second.'

Finally, he unlocked the door with the golden key. All of a sudden, where there had been bricks, a brilliant light burst forth, so intense it burned their eyes. Tessa, shielding her face, muttered something about it being the gates of heaven. But there was no time to think, no time to argue or second-guess. Hearts racing, nerves frayed, they moved forward blindly, their fear pushing them faster than their sense of caution. Without a second look, they crossed the doorway, running straight into the... unknown.

No sooner had they stepped through than the door behind them slammed shut. Nina spun around, her hand slapping against cold red bricks. Tessa's heart nearly exploded, and Asim was dripping with sweat.

'Brilliant. Now we're stuck,' said Tessa.

Chapter Eleven
Alfie

---❧---

'THIS IS BAD...' ALFIE'S voice carried through the hall, smooth and measured. He didn't do anger. That was for people who hadn't yet figured out how to make disappointment more effective.

Still, the way he leaned against the golden railing, fingers dragging over the needlessly intricate patterns, suggested he was at least vaguely irritated. Not enough to raise his voice, but perhaps enough to reconsider his life choices. He had always tried. He had done everything to make sure Nina never learned the truth. Not because he wanted to hurt her. Quite the opposite. He was protecting her. But not just her. He was protecting the world. Protecting Hell from her.

Now he was home. There was no need to pretend to read in the library. He already knew. It was too late. Although home wasn't Hell. It wasn't Earth, either. He had his own place, his own world. Because Alfie? He wasn't just anyone, and he certainly wasn't just human. His dark eyes flicked toward Samir, radiating quiet menace and offering no customer service whatsoever. Samir shifted. Not nervous, no, definitely not, but also not exactly sprinting into action. He was just standing there, like a man who had clicked "Order Now" and immediately regretted it.

'This is all my fault,' he admitted.

Alfie sighed, rubbing a slow hand over his jaw.

'How did they cross the door?'

Samir looked away.

'I don't know, my lord.'

'Of course you don't,' Alfie said, pushing off the railing.

His footsteps made no sound on the marble, which was odd, since marble usually liked to make itself known. Golden veins crackled through it like lightning caught mid-strike. Hopefully, they were decorative and not ominous.

The palace wasn't lit by fire or lamps. It simply told darkness to sod off, and apparently, that was enough. The walls stretched so high it was either impressive or overcompensating. Above, the sky had lost the sun and moon and was stuck with some strange silver light that flickered like a dodgy bulb.

A warm breeze drifted through, carrying a smell that didn't belong. Rain on stone, perhaps, or that feeling when you walk into a room and forget why. Outside, the gardens sprawled in every direction, packed with wildflowers that had no business existing but did anyway, just to be smug about it.

Alfie finally turned back to Samir and said, 'I failed, Samir... I failed.'

Samir's jaw tightened.

'No, my lord. I failed. Someone else was trying harder. Someone wanted them to cross the door from Hell.'

Silence settled. Not uneasy, but full of empathy.

'It was Olivia, Samir. My own sister. Life.'

He exhaled sharply.

'Anyway, forget that now. It happened. You're the only one who can bring them back,' Alfie's voice was quiet but firm.

'I can't interfere. If I step in, thunder will strike, and innocents will pay the price.'

'I know, my lord,' said Samir.

'They need to understand what that means before it's too late.'

'Yes, my lord.'

'Go. Find them.'

'I will. They won't get far.'

Samir sighed, rubbing his temple. He turned to leave, but Alfie's voice stopped him.

'Samir.'

He stilled.

Alfie studied him. 'Crossing from Hell to the real world isn't just reckless. It is forbidden. The consequences...' He ran a hand through his dark hair. 'It could undo everything.'

Samir nodded once. He knew exactly what Alfie wasn't saying. If the wrong beings caught wind of this, they would not be saved.

'And Tessa?' Alfie asked, quieter now.

Samir swallowed. That was the worst part. Tessa. She wasn't supposed to exist in the real world. Not like this. The world knew. Hell knew. Alfie didn't press further. He let the silence stretch, heavy and unspoken.

Finally, Samir spoke.

'I'll bring them back before it's too late. I promise.'

'It is already late, Samir,' Alfie said.

He tilted his head slightly.

'And when it's too late?'

A pause.

'Then I'll do what needs to be done, my lord.'

Alfie studied him. Whatever he found on Samir's face, he accepted with a slight nod.

'Good,' Alfie said softly. 'Don't forget. Once Nina gets her powers back, she will no longer be Nina.'

'I'm aware. And I'm not going to let that happen,' said Samir.

'I will send our people after them if you fail.'

'I won't, my lord!'

'And Samir... your son. Don't bring him back. His time has come. He belongs there, in the real world. He is old enough, and there is no place in Hell for him.'

'But my lord...'

'Go, Samir,' said Alfie.

Samir straightened his shoulders. He stepped toward the edge of the palace, where the air shimmered like water on glass. Without another word, he vanished into the real world.

Alfie stayed where he was, staring after him. Then, without looking away, he muttered, 'This is all my fault.'

1993. The good old days. Well, not really.

Thirty-one years ago, the morning was nice. Warm, but not let's-sweat-our-souls-out hot.

Alfie sat in his massive palace. He didn't sit on the throne, because that was too predictable. Nor did he sit in the great hall, which was far too echoey. Instead, he chose his study, where he could have a bit of peace. A moment to think. Classic moody immortal move. He stared at the fireplace, watching the flames do their little dance. Meanwhile, his heart was doing a different kind of burning. The kind that came with unwanted emotions.

It was ironic, considering Alfie was literally Death itself. But even the Grim Reaper could have a soft spot. He was debating. A big decision. Should he do it or not? It wasn't just about Nina. It was about everything. Humans. Souls. Hell itself. The whole mess. He sighed, pulled out a cigar, and lit it without a lighter. A reminder of his power, though even he had limits. The most powerful, yet bound by rules. He couldn't simply interfere with human lives. Free will existed for a reason.

And now, he had to decide whether he was willing to break that rule. But this was far beyond whoopsie-daisy territory. This was oh crap, we need to fix this before it turns into full apocalypse territory. And some poor souls were going to pay the price, but that was the nature of sacrifice. Decision made. He called his servant.

Knock, knock.

'Yes, my lord? You called for me?'

Alfie nodded. Goodbye, cigar. Hello, expensive grey coat. Time to be dramatic.

'Take over the realm until I return.'

'Yes, my lord.'

Alfie nodded again. Lightning flashed. Boom. He was gone.

Straight to London. Specifically, a lovely dark alley filled with human screams. Ah, the ambience. The smell? Less great. Blood. Bodies. Lots of bodies. A butcher's shop, but straight out of a horror film. Alfie's heart clenched. Not from fear, just sheer disgust. And there she was. Nina. Long black hair, dripping in blood, holding some poor man who wasn't moving any more. When she spotted Alfie, she casually threw the body aside and stood.

'You shouldn't be here, Alfie,' she said coldly.

'I could say the same for you, Nina. What exactly do you think you're doing?'

'I am doing what I must. This is what I am. I am stronger than ever, and soon, Hell will belong to me.'

'No, Nina. You are the Guardian of Hell. The souls are not yours to take. They belong to no one.'

She scoffed. 'You're wrong, Alfie. You always have been. This world belongs to me now. I will take what I please, and when I have consumed them all, I will restore Hell to its true form. They will kneel before me. The Hell you created is nothing more than a joke. A cage. And I will not be caged any longer. I will rule. I will be queen. You cannot stop me.'

'Your power was never meant for this, Nina. You were meant to protect, not destroy. Did you really believe you could do this without consequence? That you could claim a throne that does not belong to you?'

'Oh, Alfie, you are so sentimental. Always have been. Look at what you've done. All of this? It is your fault. You pitied them. You gave them another chance. But that is not how it is meant to be. The dead belong in Hell. The real Hell.'

Alfie's voice hardened. 'No, Nina. You belong in Hell.'

And then it happened.

Power move.

Alfie raised his hands, and suddenly, a book appeared. Not just any book. The kind that makes powerful demons very, very nervous.

'We'll meet again, Nina,' he said, locking eyes with her.

Then it happened.

She shook. Screamed. Dark yellow and green smoke burst out of her, sucked straight into the book. She dropped to her knees, wheezing like someone who had just run a marathon in stilettos.

'What... have you done?' she gasped.

'I have sealed your power, Nina. And that is just the beginning. Watch carefully.'

One book turned into two. Then three. Then more. Black smoke swirled, shooting back into her. She collapsed completely. Her power was gone, and as a bonus, so were her memories.

Alfie crouched beside her and ran a glowing finger over her cheek.

'Now you will know what it means to be human.'

Snap. Nina was gone.

Alfie sighed. He snapped his fingers again. The books vanished. And then came the dramatics. Lightning struck. The sky blackened. Clouds gathered like they had nothing better to do. And then came the thunder. Boom. Boom. Boom. Lightning rained down like an overenthusiastic fireworks show. Buildings were smashed. Roads split open. People... some of them didn't make it. And Alfie knew. He bloody well knew. And he still did it.

Why? Because Nina had been killing for weeks. She wasn't stopping. Someone had to end it, and that someone was him. The problem? Lightning and Alfie weren't exactly mates. In fact, they were enemies. And once he interfered, lightning struck, wrecking everything in its path. That was how the world worked. It was on him. The people who died because of it? Also on him.

So, what did he do? He took their souls with him. Gave them a place in his kingdom. Somewhere safe. Somewhere to live, work, and exist. One of them was Samir. Alfie liked the man. He gave him angel powers. Now he was his right-hand man. Because the gates of Hell were shut. Souls were lost. But Alfie knew that sooner or later, a new Guardian of Hell would be born. The gates would open. The souls could move on. And at least it was better than letting Nina become a full demon queen. Hell wasn't flames and brimstone. Hell was a copy of the real world. And Alfie? He was just trying to keep it from turning into something even worse.

Chapter Twelve
Behind the Door

———⊗———

TESSA LOOKED AROUND. Everything seemed a little too perfect, almost like it was not real. The lights and buildings sparkled strangely, as if something was hiding beneath the surface. The air was light, carrying the smell of petrol and car fumes, or at least that was what Tessa thought.

Asim stood beside her, staring at the traffic lights with wide eyes, as if he were waiting for something to happen. Nina walked next to them, but something was not right. She saw no birds, felt no wind, only a quiet hum around them. It was like magic was in the air, but not the kind from storybooks. This felt heavier.

The old stones beneath their feet lit up with each step, soft and quiet, as if they were breathing. Tessa hardly noticed, but the way the light followed them felt just a little too precise. People hurried past, each lost in their own world. No one stopped or noticed the strangers who did not belong. Well, thank God for that.

A woman in an orange hat walked by, the flowers on it shifting as if they were alive. Tessa was not sure. Nina quietly watched pigeons with flower necklaces. It was strange, but whatever it remained hidden. They turned to go back, but the library and the back door were gone. With no answers, they sank to the ground, exhausted.

Tessa looked up, her breath catching. The sky was alive with light. Blue, purple, and pink flashes streaked across it.

'What do we do now?' Tessa was about to cry. 'We have no money, we are stuck in some fantasy world, nowhere to go. We will die here!'

Asim was begging them to stay brave. He reminded them why they were here, the search for truth, and the books they could not forget now. He walked up to a gentleman in a shiny suit and hat, with orange hair sticking out. The man spoke to them kindly, but Asim did not waste any time and quickly explained that they were lost in an unfamiliar place.

'You are in London, young man, on the main street,' said the gentleman, as if it was nothing, and then walked off.

'London?' Nina gasped.

Tessa completely lost control, screaming, shouting, and carrying on like she had just found out tea was banned forever.

'Everyone, calm down, okay? We do not want to attract attention!' Asim said.

They looked around. Luckily, no one seemed to notice them, or maybe people were just pretending not to care. They took a deep breath, let it out, and tried to calm down. They saw a shop on the corner with black doors and a shining window. Inside, they found a small, tiny, and empty room with a reception desk. Only a man with long grey hair stood behind it. Asim told him they were looking for a library. The man chuckled, as if he could tell they had no idea where they were.

'Where are you lot from then?' he asked.

'Bradford,' Tessa replied.

'Ahhh, right,' the man laughed, as if that explained everything. Then he said, 'Right, so you go straight, right? Then take the second left, right? Right, and then it is on your right-hand side, right?'

They ended up confused. But the man noticed, grabbed a sparkling glove from his drawer, and pointed at the door. A trail of yellow sparkles appeared, lighting the way. They all stood there, stunned, trying to hide their reactions, and followed. That was where they would find what they were looking for.

'What is this?' Tessa whispered to Nina, still confused by it all.

Nina just shrugged. She had no idea either. In this strange world, nothing looked normal. The sky started turning a deep purple-black, and the stars flashed as if they were glitching out. Many random people wandered past, half blending into the fading light. Out of nowhere, a bus pulled up at the side of the road. But this was not an ordinary bus. Its bright orange body was covered in fruit and vegetables, as if they were growing straight out of the windows and roof.

Asim and Tessa froze. The young driver, wearing a tilted hat, smiled at them without a word. He tossed a few pieces of fruit into a basket in front of them. Apples, oranges, and even some vegetables. Then he nodded, flashed another smile, and before they could react, he drove off, vanishing into the distance without a sound. Asim scratched his head. Tessa let out a quiet laugh.

Meanwhile, Nina had just about seen what was happening. What she did notice, though, was the sudden absence of the pain that had haunted her for so long. Her legs and stomach, usually aching, were completely pain-free. She touched her legs in surprise but did not dwell on it.

'Hello? Nina?' said Tessa.

'Yes, nice bus. Anyway, let us move on. The dust is faster than us,' Nina said.

They moved a bit faster, and then the yellow dust vanished. Now they stood in front of the old museum, their mouths hanging open. Tessa stretched out her neck so high it started to ache, and the top of the massive building disappeared into the dark sky. When they reached the glass doors, they found them locked, and the place looked completely dead inside. Frustrated and exhausted, they collapsed onto the steps as strange lights swirled around them, spreading a hypnotic glow. Asim's stomach growled again as he glanced at the fruit the bus driver had given them.

'Can we trust this?' Nina asked.

She looked at the basket, nervously licking her lips but saying nothing.

'I do not know...' Tessa shrugged. 'But what if...?'

Asim did not wait any longer and grabbed an apple. Juice ran down his chin as he grinned.

'Flipping hell, this is good.'

Tessa and Nina stared at him. There was no way they were going to eat it.

'Anyway, where now? What are we going to do?' Tessa said.

Asim replied, 'Chill, Tessa, we have been here for twenty minutes!'

'Really? I can't even see a clock in here. We've got no phones or money, and we're lost, okay?' Tessa said.

'You're unbelievable, Tessa. You always make everything harder, you know?' said Asim.

'Harder? No, Asim, I'm the only one who uses her brain around here!' said Tessa.

'Shush, you two!' Nina jumped in.

She became stiff, hearing a whisper like it was coming from inside the museum. It grew louder, drawing her in.

'Do you hear that?' she asked Asim and Tessa, but they just shook their heads.

Nina moved closer to the main door, pressing her ear to the glass. Something was pulling her in.

'It's inside. The book is in there. I can hear it... feel it.'

Asim didn't think twice.

'Let's smash it!' he said, searching for a rock.

With all his strength, he threw the stone at the glass. But instead of breaking, it vanished.

'Wow, that was cool, innit?' Tessa said.

They slipped into the museum. There was no alarm, but their hearts were racing. Tessa switched on the lights, sparkling lightning pouring down from the ceiling. Glass cases were everywhere, each holding locked-up books displayed like hidden treasure.

Nina's ears caught something, pulling her toward a glass cabinet with a book titled *The Angel of Deaths*. It was locked behind green glass, unshakable. The moment her fingers touched the glass, it vanished, and the book flew open. The pages were blank, flipping rapidly by themselves. In a blur, a cloud of black dust exploded out from the last page and shot straight into Nina's chest. Tessa and Asim stood frozen like statues.

'Do you feel anything?' Asim asked.

'Are you alright, Nina?' Tessa asked.

Nina, shaken but trying to stay calm, said, 'No... I don't feel anything. I...' Her voice trailed off as green flashing lights filled the room.

Asim tensed up.

'Do you smell that?' he muttered to Tessa. The air smelled like old cheese. The stench grew stronger, nearly unbearable, and his head spun.

'What is it?' Tessa asked, pressing her temples as she shook. Her stomach knotted; something was really wrong.

'We need to get out,' Nina moaned, barely able to stay on her feet.

They had hardly stepped outside when flashing green lights and sharp sounds surrounded them. Sirens, police cars, it all crashed down on them at once.

'What the hell...?' Asim seized up. His gaze locked onto the gloves pointed straight at them. They sparkled in the lights. It was hard to say what unsettled him more, the strange smell or those gloves.

'Gloves?' he breathed. 'What is this, some kind of game?'

Tessa joined in, her eyes narrowing. 'Bloody hell, now I know where Jackson's from.'

'And now I know who Martin was. He had gloves just like these... and that hat,' Nina said.

The officer grabbed Asim by the head and roughly shoved him into the car, like he was tossing out an old piece of rubbish. Then he slammed the door behind him. Lovely.

Asim sat up, shaking off the rough handling, but something felt off. He glanced toward the front of the car, except there was no front. No steering wheel. No dashboard. No seats. Just a wall of dark, reflective glass, stretching from one side to the other. He turned to the windows, expecting to see the outside world. But they were pitch black, not tinted, just... empty. No movement. No sound.

It felt as if the car wasn't even real. Asim swallowed hard. His heartbeat picked up. He reached for the door handle, but before he could touch it—A deep *click*. The left door swung open on its own. Instead of a road, there was... nothing. No pavement, no city. Only a swirling mass of blue dust, twisting and shifting like a living thing. The moment Asim saw it, a force yanked him forward. He barely had time to react before it swallowed him whole.

Nina sat in the second car, pinching her nose against the overwhelming stench of sweat and damp leather. Something was wrong. She felt it before she even saw it. A deep hum vibrated through the seat beneath her. The air inside the car felt thinner, like it was pulling inward. Then, just like Asim's car, the door snapped open. A powerful vacuum yanked her forward, sucking her into the same swirling blue void.

Meanwhile, Tessa shivered in the third car, her arms wrapped around herself. 'I should've just stayed home. I'm such a stupid old cow,' she muttered. She barely finished the sentence before—Whoosh. The same invisible force grabbed hold of her, yanking her forward. And just like that, they were gone.

When they opened their eyes, they were in prison. Small cells. Simple. Grey walls. No windows. Each of them was alone, locked behind thick iron bars. At least there was a toilet in the corner.

Tessa frowned, rubbing her arms. 'Lovely. Just lovely.'

Chapter Thirteen
The Police Station

———— ⌗ ————

NINA WAS LED INTO A small room, the kind of room that shouted, *I'm here to make you uncomfortable,* complete with plain walls and the distinct smell of decayed sweat. Across the table sat an officer, dressed in a green suit and sporting lavender hair. Cunning, he was not. His eyes were trained on her, as if he could summon a confession purely through pressure.

'Why didn't you die when you opened that book? No one who's touched it has survived,' he said, as if casually remarking on the weather.

'I don't know anything.'

The officer's face shifted, like he was trying on emotions for size. Fear? Confusion? Hunger? Truly, who could tell? Something in him clicked still, and without a word, he slid a glass of blue, smoking liquid toward her. It had the look of something that should have stayed in a lab. It smelled worse, like sour milk left out in the sun for a week.

'Drink it. Now,' he said.

'I want a solicitor.'

'A solicitor?' He barely stopped himself from laughing. Dry, cruel—the sort that would have fit perfectly in a low-budget horror film.

'Drink it. Now!' he barked again.

But Nina didn't even get a chance to react—knock knock, someone was at the door. The officer looked properly baffled, like the universe had just glitched. With the grace of a cat that's seen some things, he slowly stood up and made his way over. He opened the door... and boom—instant eyebrow crumple. Yes, classic what-the-hell face.

There was no one. He frowned, standing in the doorway, then he looked down and a small man in a green hat appeared. No explanation, no dramatic flair; just there, like a magician who couldn't be bothered with tricks. Before anyone could react, he blew blue, sparkling dust into the officer's face and—poof—vanished. Gone as quickly as he'd come, leaving only confusion in his wake.

The officer blinked, and it was as if his whole attitude suddenly changed, like someone had pressed a reset button. The harsh look on his face softened, turning into a smile so friendly it seemed almost suspicious.

'Would you like some coffee, darling?' he asked, like they'd been discussing the latest BBC drama, not life-threatening potions.

Moments later, Nina, Tessa, and Asim were outside.

Free. And yet, freedom felt... off. Tessa threw her arms around them, bawling her eyes out, going on about how awful it had been. Meanwhile, Nina and Asim just exchanged one of those *Can you believe this?* looks. Finally, Asim couldn't hold it in any longer.

'We were in there for, like, ten minutes, Tessa. Ten bloody minutes!' he snapped.

Tessa wiped her tears so fast it was like they had offended her, then whipped out her trademark *I'm not having this* face.

'Oh, really? You were checking your watch again, were you? Go on, show me. Oh, wait, you don't bloody have one! Well, it felt like ten years to me, okay?'

'Will you two shut your mouths?' Nina cut in, rolling her eyes. 'There's someone, or something, waiting for us out there. Probably. Just look!'

She pointed dramatically into the distance. A shiny limousine sat parked, the kind that typically carried wealthy and important people. It was dark, dangerously elegant. Next to it, a man in a green hat stood motionless, with the air of someone who had seen it all and could not be bothered anymore. He nodded toward the open door, offering no further explanation. Because apparently, in this world, people just got into strange limos without asking questions.

Their hearts pounded like a drum and bass track, but there they were, sitting down like it was teatime at Granny's. Asim couldn't help himself; his hands ran over the soft leather seats as they climbed in.

'Bloody hell,' Asim muttered. 'Posh as anything.'

The ceiling glowed with a soft blue light, stars scattered across it like someone had decided to bring a slice of the Milky Way inside. It was a world away from the cold, damp jail they had just left behind. They all were, if they were being honest. Free, but now deeply confused. And scared.

The limo came to a stop, the windows still dark and unhelpful. Then the door opened, and they stepped out to find themselves in front of a palace. Not just any palace. A glowing, icy blue monstrosity, with spires so sharp they looked like they could stab you if you got too close. Asim paused, staring. The driver? Oh, he stepped out too... from the passenger seat. Because, why not? Who the hell was driving? Asim wondered about it, but the question stayed unasked, lost in the strange situation they were now facing.

The air hissed with something Nina couldn't quite name, like magic or danger hanging just out of sight, waiting for the right moment. They stepped inside the massive entrance, welcomed by the type of luxury that was so over the top it made you think, *ah, so this is where the tax money goes.* White and green leather everywhere. Diamonds and gems stuffed into vases that probably had no business being that sparkly. And the flowers? Yes, they were alive, shifting slightly, like they had opinions on the decor.

Before they could take it all in, the man in the green hat returned, soundlessly leading them deeper into the palace. No words. Just that lingering feeling of What have we gotten ourselves into? They were led into a room decked out with purple gems and enough luxury to make Buckingham Palace look like a Travelodge.

Right in the middle, someone sat on a throne. Not lounging. Not slouched. Sitting like he belonged there. When he finally lifted his head, his tone came out strong, confident—like he was used to running the show.

'Welcome. I've been expecting you,' he said, calm but carrying a power that felt just the wrong side of dangerous.

Nina, Tessa, and Asim traded glances, their anxiety now firmly settled in. But of course, Nina, ever the brave one, took the push.

'Who are you?' she asked, trying to sound far less intimidated than she felt.

The laugh that followed was sharp, almost too sharp, like he enjoyed the power shift.

'I'm known by many names, but you can call me Noah,' he replied, as if he were granting them some great privilege.

Noah continued as though he had been preparing for this meeting his whole life, declaring the palace as his own like it was something they should have already known. His words were heavy, each one landing like a warning they could not quite put their finger on. He suggested they freshen up in their rooms before dinner. Exhausted and hungry, they weren't exactly in a position to argue. As they were led away, Asim couldn't shake the feeling of unease, though he stayed careful. Tessa, ever the wildcard, winked at Noah.

'Finally, something interesting,' she said lightly, before turning to Nina with a smirk. 'See, that's the way to do it.'

Chapter Fourteen
The Magical Room

EVEN THOUGH NINA COULDN'T help but stare at the magical room, her heart gave a little wobble. She wasn't scared for herself; it was Asim and Tessa she worried about. This world felt like her one chance at answers, and for once, it looked like she was close.

Sure, it all felt strange, maybe even ridiculous, but she couldn't let that stop her. She had to be brave. This was what she'd always wanted: to leave the pain behind and finally uncover the truth she'd been chasing her whole life.

Then the thought crept in—what if she wasn't just a visitor here? What if this was where she truly belonged? She didn't know her parents, hadn't since childhood, just fragments of memory from nursery school. Every attempt to find them led to nothing.

Her head swam under the weight of it all. It was too much, but she wasn't alone. Asim and Tessa were here, and their presence made the madness easier to take.

And now she was so close. Nothing, not prisons, not some man named Noah with his palace, was going to stop her.

Tessa then slipped out of her room, her short white dress shimmering, a yellow scarf wrapped around her head. She knocked once on Nina's door, then entered without waiting, a wide smile on her face.

'Have you seen my room?' she started jumping. 'It's like a palace. Red bed, shiny furniture, a massive wardrobe full of clothes and jewellery, and the bathroom? Oh, no comment.'

She was talking nonstop, words pouring out so quickly it was like they couldn't keep up, hardly pausing to take a breath. But then she clocked Nina's room, and she froze, wide-eyed and amazed, like she'd just walked in on the Queen having a naughty kebab.

'Bloody hell, it's almost the same,' Tessa said.

Nina smiled, though there was a flicker in the corner of her lips.

'We need to get ready for dinner,' she said, calm and walked over to the large wardrobe. But something in her face was different.

'What's up?' Tessa asked, noticing the quick shift in Nina's mood.

Nina slowly turned around. 'Tessa, something has happened.'

'What! He's a murderer? Bastard I knew it!' Tessa said.

'Gosh, no. My lumps... they're gone. I had hundreds of them, and now... zero. No pain, nothing. I feel like I'm alive again.'

'That's... no way! How's that possible?'

Nina laughed, tears welling up in her eyes, but they were tears of joy. 'I don't know! But Tessa, I have no pain. After years. It's like I can fly again!'

'It's this magic, Nina... Lovely... Anyway, let's go, I'm hungry!'

And they stood in the hallway, waiting for Asim and voilà. He stepped out, sharp in a grey suit, his hair styled like he meant business.

'Wow, look at you, boy! You look cracking!' Tessa flashed him a grin.

'I know Tessa, thanks, but you are looking good yourself!' then he looked at Nina. 'You look fresh, Nina. Different. In a good way.'

Nina's face lit up. Then Asim added, 'Let Noah eat first, just in case.'

Tessa's eyes flicked to Nina's; no words needed. Nerves crept in. But what choice did they have? At least they'd landed somewhere half-decent.

Tessa, feathers bouncing in her dress, every step saying, "Yeah, that's right, look at me." Nina followed behind, looking like an absolute star in heels she wouldn't have dared to touch before, her pain clearly a thing of the past, and it showed in the way she moved. Asim stayed cool as ever, swagger on point, like he'd just stepped out of a GQ shoot. Golden dust drifted down from the shiny staircase, lighting the way to the dining room like the earth was rolling out the red carpet for them.

Their jaws nearly crashed the floor. The ceiling above poured out purple rain light, disappearing into lavender-scented dust as it hit the ground.

The table? It was loaded. Chicken that looked so juicy it might drip, bread stacked like a work of art. Fish pie, bangers and mash, and, because why not, a massive chocolate fountain. Fresh fruit piled high like they were trying to impress the gods.

The drinks glimmered in the light, shining like diamonds ready to be enjoyed. The entire room looked like something straight out of a gangster drama. Waiters dressed in black suits moved gracefully, their gloves shining, smiling on the outside but carefully observing every action.

Noah? He was already there, relaxed, waving them over like he'd been waiting for hours. Tessa's eyes were sealed to the food, drooling. Asim opened his mouth to say something, something about being careful. But before he could, Noah stood, smooth as silk, and started picking at the dishes. No words. Just action.

With Noah digging in first, they all relaxed and dived into the food.

'I love how the candles move, almost like they're real,' Tessa said, bits of food falling from her lips.

Noah belted her a mischievous grin. 'They are magical and real.'

Everyone was trying to act normal, like they weren't absolutely bricking it inside, hiding that horrible mix of fear and cluelessness.

Tessa chuckled, wiping her mouth. 'Lovely. I could eat a whole horse. This is unreal!'

Noah's charm was doing its work, but it wasn't just him, it was the food. The man had a taste, no doubt about it.

'Who cooked all this?' Nina asked.

Noah looked thrown. 'Err... cooking? There was no cooking.'

Nina just smiled, eyebrows raised. Was *he for real?*

Tessa found herself falling for him a little more with every bite, sending playful looks across the table, even pulling faces. But Noah? He didn't notice. Or, at least, he pretended not to.

Nina couldn't hold back any longer. The question had been burning inside her. 'How did you find us, and why bring us here?'

Noah set his fork down, eyes meeting hers.

'Because I know who you are,' he said softly, with a calm that troubled her.

Nina, still on edge, leaned in slightly and sniffed. It was faint, but purposeful, her sense for souls kicking in. A warm yellow glow filled her senses. Good, pure. The tension in her chest eased a little.

Noah didn't react. It was as if he didn't notice this strange action from Nina at all. He simply carried on that same easy smile.

Nina, intrigued, leaned in again, pushing for more.

But Noah smiled. 'Let's enjoy the meal first.'

Something still didn't sit quite right, but at least that yellow glow had taken the edge off.

She peered at Noah. 'Something feels... wrong.'

Noah smiled again, like he'd heard it all before.

'Your sense of smell is sharper than most,' he said, leading them into the living room.

Nina's eyes flickered. The place was massive, light everywhere, soft cream furniture, and marble floors that gleamed like glass. The staircase floated, literally hanging in the air. Everything looked polished, expensive, like it belonged right here in this world they were already part of.

They sat down, bounded by sunlight, feeling small in all that greatness.

Tessa hummed softly.

'Where are we?'

Noah leaned in, voice low.

'Welcome to the real world.'

Everything went dead silent. Noah's grin turned wicked. 'Time to find out who you really are.'

He suddenly changed, lowered his head, ego gone, eyes open.

'Welcome back, Nina. I'm so glad you're here,' he said quietly, as if making a confession.

Nina darted her eyes, confused.

'What are you talking about? Have you lost your mind?'

Tessa went still. Asim's jaw dropped. Noah calmly continued, 'Let me explain.' He reached for a small box on the table. Cigarettes. Her favourite. She then took a drag and immediately felt relief. Noah began, 'There was a potion in the food.'

Asim exploded. Tessa yelled. Everything they thought they knew wasn't fully true. The potion? It wasn't a trap, more of a test. A trial of their true nature. He wasn't a wealthy man, but a servant. And this palace? It belonged to Nina.

'The fact that you didn't change,' Noah continued. 'Means you're not ordinary humans. The potion would have stripped you of your magic, but you... you stayed the same. You're not from here.'

According to Noah, they weren't humans. They were something far greater than they could have ever imagined.

Nina didn't blink. Asim's fists clenched, and Tessa was tense, ready for action.

Asim's voice came out hard and confused.

'What the hell are you saying?'

Noah sighed, like he was finally letting go of a secret he'd been carrying for too long.

'Nina, you're an angel. The Guardian of Hell, but I guess you already know some of this.'

'Yes, I know, I mean, we all know...,' said Nina.

'Follow me downstairs,' Noah said in his calm, reassuring voice. Initially, they were doubtful and unsure of him, but now they trusted him completely. His soul was yellow and good, after all, according to Nina. They descended a grand staircase like they were entering a secret place.

'This place is full of history, your history, Nina,' Noah said, pointing to ancient manuscripts behind fragile glass. As he recounted the story of their world, Noah revealed a basic truth. Hell was like a weak copy, devoid of the magic that was part of their reality. He went on to describe their world, where magic could be bought, potions, charms, things that defied the laws of nature.

'Those in Hell lose their magic, memories and suffer as punishment. Hell is your world, not the real one, Nina,' Noah said.

Tessa was having a right hard time wrapping her head around it. And it wasn't just her. Asim and Nina were clearly in shock too, though they were trying to play it cool, emphasis on *trying*. Their acting wasn't exactly BAFTA-worthy, as Noah clocked it straight away.

'I see, yes, Hell it's where you just came from, copy of our real world and it's a punishment,' said Noah, 'People suffer greatly, and they have no free will, their fate is already written and unheard by God.'

Nina, Asim, and Tessa just listened quietly, trying not to show anything. Inside, though, everything was churning. Their heads were spinning from the news, and they were excited with the urge to ask questions, to press for answers. But somehow, they managed to hold it all in.

He continued that in this real world, they had the chance to live a long, good, and happy life with the help of angels and God himself. Nina struggled to understand this huge revelation as Noah gave a knowing smile and guided them to a golden door with a detailed key.

'Come inside,' he said.

A stunning light wrapped them as they walked into a room filled with gold, diamonds, and countless treasures. 'This is all yours, Nina.'

Tessa relaxed, pushed Asim's arm and whispered to him, well, whispered as much as Tessa ever could. 'Now Nina's got more than me. Check out the sparkle.'

Asim just gave her that strict look, the worldwide sign to shut it and not make a scene.

While Nina was trying not to lose her marbles, it all felt like a dream, these assets unreal. It was everything she had saved up over the years. Every guardian had a secret wealth they protected, and she was no different. Her memories, along with other abilities, were locked away in books, and Nina had to get them back, whatever the cost. But that was all coming from Noah. Could she really trust him?

Noah promised to help them bring to light their lost memories and grant them immortality. With full loyalty, he'd help the trio discover and control their new abilities. And bloody hell, they were hungry for it.

'Noah, how can we trust you? This all sounds like proper bullshit to me,' Tessa said.

But Noah ignored her and carried on.

'This whole world knows your story now. They want the books and the power they hold, Nina,' said Noah.

Tessa couldn't resist Noah's charm, even in the middle of a serious conversation. She blinked at him.

'But I really love this all around you, you know, your new world, lovely,' she teased with a slight smile.

Ignoring her again, Noah turned to face Nina.

'Listen, Nina,' he shook his head. 'Some people, especially demons, are terrified. They don't want to go to hell, and they certainly don't want you here.'

Nina stared down, cigarette hanging from her fingers. The mess in her head was a messy wreck. *Bloody hell, what's going on?* Her mind was fixated on the cash. She could grab it all, vanish back to the library, and live the high life. But the thought of her pain creeping back hit her hard, freezing her in place. She couldn't risk it. That's what stopped her, dead in her tracks.

'Oi, Nina, you alright?' Asim asked.

'Yes, I'm alright, was thinking.'

'We need to get some magic for all of you,' Noah said. 'You can't survive out here without it,' he added.

Asim's grin split his face, a wicked spark lighting up his eyes. Tessa was already on her feet, ready to move. Nina? She tossed her hand dismissively, her eyes glazed over as if she couldn't care less.

Noah's eyes locked onto Nina's. 'The demons can smell you, Nina. They know you're here. And trust me, it's not just them, your presence is stirring things up.'

Tessa jumped in: 'Look, you're really starting to pissing me off, yeah? Just hurry up and show us the books so we can get out of here. Something stinks.'

Noah didn't even look her way. Tessa was about to grab him, but Nina and Asim stopped her, cutting off her move.

'Calm down, I can feel Noah's soul and it's yellow,' Nina said, holding her back. That seemed to take the edge off, just a little.

'Drink this, all of you,' Noah said sternly, shoving green glasses at them. The stuff inside smelled rank, thick enough to choke.

Tessa's nose crinkled, her lips curling as she pulled back. 'You taking the piss?'

Noah's eyes locked on hers with a steely look. 'Tessa, you've got to trust me. If you don't drink it, they'll find us quicker. This potion masks your scent and buys us time,' he pleaded.

Tessa swallowed the stuff, her face a picture of disgust.

'No fucking way tastes like shit. Why the hell am I even doing this?' she grumbled, glaring at the vile brew.

Asim? He knocked it back like it was a craft pint. 'Mmmm, tastes like a strawberry milkshake.'

Nina watched the spectacle, pinched her nose, and chugged it down. 'Hell, that's what I call a Hell.'

She held her stomach, expecting the worst, but kept it down.

'We've bought ourselves time. Just one day before these wear off. No more faffing about,' Noah said.

He then savoured the last drop, smacking his lips as he finished off the bottle.

The bitter taste of the potion still stayed on their tongues. As they sat there, stunned, trying to take in what Noah had just told them, the silence in the room felt like it had been charged with the weight of a very large, very unwelcome elephant.

Before anyone could say anything, the big doors opened. A servant appeared, slid in like someone who'd practised the art of "mysterious entrances" far too many times. He whispered something to Noah, who nodded, then turned back to them with all the urgency of someone announcing they needed to get the takeaway.

'I've got something to take care of. Wait here,' Noah said, disappearing as quickly as he came.

Tessa blew out a loud breath.

'So, our world is really Hell. Just bloody brilliant, innit? Everything we thought we knew was a lie.'

Nina traced the edge of the table.

'I always felt something was off, but this...' She glanced between them. 'Sounds like it's the truth. We've been fed nonsense our whole lives. And now this?'

Asim crossed his arms.

'Yeah, well, it makes sense now. Life in our world... pain, suffering...'

Tessa's hands shook slightly.

'My son... he died. I watched him suffer. Everything fell apart after. So was he punished? Was I?'

Silence.

Tessa wiped her eyes and forced a smile. 'Well, this has been cheery, wait. Does that mean we're *dead*? We just came from Hell, right?'

Nina rolled her eyes. 'We are not dead, Tessa! We're very much alive.'

Chapter Fifteen
Johan's Market

Part One

IN A SHADY CORNER OF a far-off town, tucked away in a pub that had seen better days, the red paint peeling like old promises, Jonathan sat in silence. His sharp suit, all black and crisp, gave off the feeling of someone who didn't belong in a place like this. But that scar on his face? That said he'd seen things, done things, things that made sense in a joint like this. His blue eyes, cold as winter's first bite, didn't flinch. He didn't need to. His crew, like they had slipped out of the gloom, hovered nearby, ready for whatever kicked off.

The door groaned open, and in waddled a little round man, stinking like a soaked ashtray. He wasn't here for drinks. No, he was here for business. Without waiting for an invite, he dropped down next to Jonathan, shifting his sweaty, crumpled hat onto his lap.

Leaning in, the cheese-smelling man muttered, low and greasy, 'Everything goes well, my lord, as planned.'

Jonathan stayed quiet. No dramatic reaction. Just a slow exhale, like the information was already old news. He slipped a hand into his pocket, pulling out a fat stack of cash. He didn't toss it or flash it. Just slid it across the table with the same nonchalance you'd give a used napkin.

The man grabbed it, fingers twitching with greed, lips twisting into a satisfied smirk before he shuffled off. No thanks, no goodbyes. Jonathan leaned back, eyes narrowing just a fraction. His game was in motion now, the pieces moving whether they knew it or not.

AT THE SAME TIME, MILES away from the pub, stood a grimy old house in a knackered street, infested with rats and spread out with garbage. This place wasn't just another drop-in. It was wriggling with demons. The kind of place where even the air felt odd. Their presence soaked the area in an almost real sense of fear, a weight that pressed down on anyone unlucky enough to leg it about too close.

Their leader, Shad, a ruthless murderer and a thief, got wind that Nina and her lot were in town. That news lit a fire in him. Fuming, he stood there, surrounded by his crew, a mismatched group of about ten, all itching to make some serious trouble for Nina. They weren't just after your standard dodgy pranks. They wanted to turn her life upside down, proper wreck it.

Their bodies were falling to bits, chunks of decayed flesh peeling off like leftovers gone bad. Green, stinking, and crumbling away, but they didn't give a toss. The stink of rot and mildew filled the room, but it was just another day for them. They looked like they were barely holding together, but inside? Pure rage, hungry for power. They'd do anything to stay in this world, to keep out of Hell. Sure, they couldn't possess a body without permission, but when they found a host here? That bought them more time. Yes, the bodies would rot eventually, but it was worth it for the strength.

'What's the plan, boss?' one of the nastier ones croaked, itching for a scrap.

Shad didn't bother to look. He turned and slapped him so hard, half his face dropped off like a rotten piece of meat. The rest of the crew went still, fear in their eyes, while something darker than the grime on the walls flashed in Shad's look.

'I've got a plan,' he sneered. 'But first, we need fresh bodies. Can't get anything done in these bloody rotten meat sacks.'

AND AT ONCE, FAR FROM demons, far from Jonathan, back in the palace, Noah Nina, Tessa, and Asim walked into Johan Market, and the place was absolutely buzzing—green stalls lined up neatly, music bouncing off the chatter, and people moving like they'd been told the world was ending but only after they finished shopping. Asim couldn't help but feel it. The energy was infectious.

Then, out of nowhere, a woman with beautiful red hair shouted from one of the stalls. 'Magic mugs! Come and get your magic mugs!'

Nina slowed down, narrowed her eyes.

'What kind of mugs are we talking about, then?' she asked, her tone relaxed but sharp enough to make it clear she wasn't about to fall for any old rubbish.

The woman's grin stretched wider as she held up one of the mugs.

'Not your average cup. You'll never go thirsty for the next five years with one of these.'

Tessa, ever the curious one, reached out and let her fingers brush the mug's smooth surface. Before she could blink, it filled to the brim with her favourite tea. Her face lit up, and she giggled like a kid who'd just found an extra Christmas present.

Nina, caught up in the excitement, grabbed another. But instead of tea or something fun, a thick, dark red liquid poured out in a rush. She pulled her hand back, her face scrunching up.

The surrounding chatter died in an instant. The crowd turned with those eyes fixed on the overflowing cup like it might bite. The shopkeeper's smile faded, her earlier confidence slipping.

'Faulty one, just leave it,' she said.

Noah, close by, leaned in. 'Don't worry, Nina, it happens; it's just these magic rubbish mugs.'

They gave each other a quick look but didn't hang around. With a shrug, they slipped back into the flow of the market, eyes roaming, hands ready to grab whatever caught their eye.

Asim and Tessa wandered down one side, soaking up the sights and smells. The warm lantern light mixed with the scent of cinnamon, stopping Tessa in her tracks.

'God, that smells like Mum's cinnamon cake,' she said.

Asim smiled, but was lost in thought.

'I love it here. Wish my dad could see this.'

Tessa shot him a look that screamed, "I wish I could kill you right now."

'What? Your dad?' she said.

Asim just shrugged, not saying much more. They kept walking, getting pulled deeper into the market's pulse.

MEANWHILE, ON THE OTHER side of the market, Nina walked with Noah. The mood felt lighter, but she still sensed a tension in Noah's movements, like he wasn't fully relaxed.

Just then, a voice sliced through the noise.

'What a lovely afternoon, isn't it, Mr Noah?'

Nina and Noah turned to see a man in an expensive suit, flanked by bodyguards. The man's presence immediately shifted the energy, making it sharper.

Noah forced a polite smile.

'Lovely, indeed,' he replied, but there was a stiffness in his tone.

The man eyed Nina up and down.

'You've got a charming companion there. Care to introduce me?'

Noah paused for a split second before obliging.

'This is my cousin, Nina. She's just visiting.'

Leaning in toward Nina, Noah whispered quickly, 'That's Mr Jamal. He's well-connected, big in government circles.'

Mr Jamal grinned, his look lingering in Nina's hair.

'Didn't know you had family, Sneaky... Nice hair, anyway,' he added, tipping his fancy hat before striding off, bodyguards in tow.

As Mr Jamal walked away, Noah sighed.

'He's an old man who stays young using a magic hat and potions and trust me, you don't want to see him without it...He even owns a healer.'

'Own a healer?'

'Yeah, I'll explain more later.'

They wandered further into the market, where the food stalls looked more like neon-lit spaceships than anything earthly. One stall stood out. A bearded chef in leather and goggles was grilling something massive. He wasn't using his hands. Glowing magic sticks flew over the grill, flipping burgers and stacking buns as if following invisible commands. Behind him, a line of sizzling patties, glowing faintly like they were charged with electricity, lined the grill.

Noah stopped, his eyes brightening. 'Shall we try something?'

Nina raised an eyebrow, taking in the scene. This was a galaxy away from the tinned food and stale bread she'd been stuck with in the library. The chef caught her eye and flashed a wide grin as he held up a burger stacked high with everything. The sauce was dripping, the burger basically sparkling with freshness.

'Best bite you'll have today,' he said, cheerful and confident.

Nina hesitated, but grabbed the burger. The first bite was an explosion of flavour, juicy, spicy, and with just the right kick of heat. She hadn't tasted anything like this in years. She almost laughed, thinking about the cardboard sandwiches she used to choke down.

Noah took a bite of his own burger, chewing thoughtfully. 'Much better than whatever punishment they put you on before. No more biscuits and regrets.'

Nina didn't answer, just nodded, focused on the next bite. The chef's grin lingered in her mind.

The surrounding air was thick with smells: spices, roasted meats, and something sweet she couldn't place. It was both comforting and overwhelming.

'How does he use those sticks?' she asked, glancing at the chef. 'What are they?'

'Magic sticks,' Noah said. 'Quite a few people have them, but only if they've got the right kind of blood. Magical blood, that is. Connection, you know... the sticks follow what their body tells them. That's why every burger tastes slightly different.'

'That's... interesting. And a bit weird,' Nina said, eyeing the glowing burgers.

'Why? Oh, yes. I forget sometimes. You're from Hell, no memories, and no clue how things work here.'

'Thanks for that,' Nina said dryly.

Then they walked on, their stomachs heavy, but it was a good kind of heavy; meaty, satisfying, and rich. It was the kind of experience Nina probably wouldn't forget anytime soon.

'How old are you, anyway?' Nina asked.

'That's a personal question... but fine. I'm 88,' Noah said, a small smile tugging at the corner of his mouth.

'What? No way. Is that a hat, or are you just ridiculously healthy? You look 30!'

'Thanks. I'll take the compliment,' he said, tipping his hat. 'But no, it's not just a hat. I use potions too.'

Noah was grinning at the people around them, like he was in some kind of friendly sitcom, all while they strolled along, chatting about whatever nonsense came to mind. Classic slow-walk banter vibes. 'You don't look too wrinkly yourself, love,' Noah said with a cheeky smile. 'In fact, you're a rather stunning woman.'

Nina went full tomato face.

'Uh, thank you,' she said, suddenly very interested in the flowery plates nearby, as if they held the secret to world peace. Anything to dodge the heat of the conversation. But, of course, Noah wasn't about to let her off that easily.

'Pretty plates, sure, but why so shy? Don't tell me you haven't got a boyfriend?' he teased, leaning ever so slightly closer.

'No, well... I had one, once. Ages ago,' she admitted, her eyes darting between the plates and literally anywhere else but Noah's smirking face.

'Well,' he said, with a twinkle in his eye. 'Maybe we could grab dinner later, just the two of us?'

'Sure,' she said, managing a small, awkward smile. 'I'd like that. It'd be nice to get to know this place a bit more.'

ON THE OTHER SIDE OF Johan Market, Asim and Tessa wandered, taking in the endless variety of strange and magical items. They passed stalls showcasing self-writing pens that scribbled on their own, chatting candles that talked like they had something important to say, and enchanted tables that promised everlasting satisfaction to anyone willing to take a seat. There were books with pages that turned themselves and animated pictures that winked at passing customers, trying to grab attention.

'Those candles... they're talking?' Asim muttered, squinting at them. Before he could even process it, Tessa was already up close, crouching beside the display.

'Oh, your cutie little pie,' she cooed, reaching out to touch one of the candles. But the candle snapped at her finger.

'Oi, you little basta...!' but before she could finish, Asim quickly grabbed her arm and pulled her away. People were starting to stare.

'Let it go, Tessa. It's just a candle.'

They moved on, but what really caught their eye next were the glowing pillows lined up like precious jewels. They stepped closer, drawn in by the soft, warm light. The shopkeeper, who looked like he'd stepped out of a forgotten fairy tale, smiled with intent at them.

'Ah, the dream pillows... These are no ordinary ones,' he said, his voice lyrical, like a poem in the breeze. 'Made by the King of Dreams himself. Lay your head upon one, and it'll dive deep into your thoughts, weaving dreams beyond imagination.'

'Wait, what? It reads your mind?' Asim raised an eyebrow.

The shopkeeper nodded. 'It becomes one with your desires, your fears... everything. Whatever you wish to dream, it'll make happen.'

Tessa's eyes lit up like she was seeing a treasure chest. Without thinking twice, she grabbed four of them.

'I'll take these! One for me, Mum, my sister... and maybe another for myself!'

Tessa, looking like she'd just hit the jackpot, pillows spilling from her arms, beamed. 'Omg, can't wait to see Mum's face.'

Asim sighed and grabbed a pillow to help out, muttering to himself, *'Oh, bloody hell...'*

Like a strike, the air shifted. A loud bang shattered the market's rhythm, and Asim felt a searing pain shoot through his hand. He dropped the pillows and yelped, 'Ouch, that bloody hurts!' Blood started to ooze from the fresh cut. Looking up, he saw two men in torn, ragged clothes, their gloves crackling with fire.

'Oh my God, Asim!' Tessa screamed, grabbing his arm and pulling him behind a nearby shelf. 'Quick, let's hide here!' Her voice shook, eyes wide as they crouched low.

Fiery blasts ripped through the market, stalls burning as the attackers moved forward. Noah and Nina, who had been browsing on the other side of the market, heard the commotion and sprinted through the panicking crowd.

'Tessa, Asim!' Nina shouted, pushing people aside as Noah flicked his gloves on.

'Stay back!' Noah warned the attackers, raising his gloved hand as a burst of blue flames shot towards them. They barely flinched, the fire licking their bodies as if it wasn't enough to slow them down. They retaliated with fiery blasts of their own, turning stalls into blazing wrecks.

Tessa and Asim stayed hidden under the shelf, their hearts pounding. But Tessa, even amidst the madness around her, spotted one of the pillows they'd bought lying on the ground. Without thinking, she slithered out, grabbing it like it was gold.

'Tessa, what the hell!' Asim hissed, but she paid him no mind, clutching the pillow like it was a prize. 'Bloody hell! We are not on holiday, ok?' Asim added.

Noah threw more blue flames toward the attackers, but it wasn't enough. These two weren't just random thugs; they were trained, their firepower far beyond anything he expected. Sirens blared in the distance, but the attackers pressed on, tearing through with raw power.

Out of the corner of her eye, Nina caught sight of the fireball, blazing, wild, heading straight for her like a bullet. Too fast. Heart pounding, there was no time to think, just raw instinct. Her hands shot up, her voice more like a desperate plea: 'STOP!'

And the world... halted.

The flames went still midair, hanging there like they'd been caught in the grip of something invisible. Everything stopped, the noise, the destruction, all of it, gone in an instant. The air felt thick, heavy, as if the very essence of time had slowed down.

Nina stood there, hands trembling, heart thudding. What the hell just happened? She could feel the heat of the fire, but it didn't move, suspended inches from her, locked in place.

Everyone around her went still. The attackers, people around. Noah, his gloves still burning, paused in the middle of a fight. Asim's face, crimped in fear, and Tessa, mid-dive to protect her bloody pillows.

But Nina? She was still moving. Her breath came in sharp, eyes dilated, hands still. The entire world had stopped, and she was standing in the middle of it.

Nina's breath hitched. She then rushed to Noah, heels clacking on the still ground. Grabbing his arm, she shook him.

'What's happening? What have I done, oi, wake up!'

Noah gasped awake at her touch, blinking fast.

'Calm down, Nina,' he whispered, trying to steady her. 'Not now. Be strong. Look into my eyes.'

She nodded, still shaking, as Noah directed her to wake Tessa and Asim. The moment her hands brushed theirs, they snapped back into motion, wide-eyed and confused.

'Hide. Now!' Noah urged, pushing them toward a corner just as the market boiled over back to life; screams, fire, chaos everywhere.

One of the attackers growled, 'Let's go!' as police sirens wailed closer.

Tessa's voice shook.

'Why are they after us?' She glanced at Noah, but his attention was on getting them out.

Nina took a quick look at Asim's burnt hand, worry in her eyes.

'Who were they? Why us?'

'No idea. But we need answers.' He muttered, half to himself. 'Useless. Bloody useless.' Asim said.

Noah's gaze flashed to Asim's wound.

'You need a hospital. Now.'

Part Two

In the Hospital

TESSA TOOK IT ALL IN, the floors spotless like they were polished daily, walls so clean you could eat off them. The hallway stretched out forever, doors lining both sides like some kind of maze.

The nurse didn't mess around, no forms, no clipboard. 'Wait here,' she said, then was back in less than a minute, ushering them through.

The healer didn't waste time either. He just placed his hand on Asim's arm. The wound? Gone. Just like that. Asim stared blankly in shock. The healer handed Asim a glass filled with yellow liquid.

'Drink it. Three times a day, for three days.' No extra words, just instructions.

Asim nodded, still taking it all in, but Nina's eyes flicked around the room. That's when she saw it, a massive birdcage tucked in the corner. It looked out of place, too random for a spotless room like this. But she let it slide; it didn't seem worth thinking about.

Noah chimed in, 'These healers, they're born with it. Magic in their blood.'

Tessa's grin faded as her mind drifted. She looked at Asim's healed arm, but her thoughts were on her son. *Could've changed everything if we had them at home.*

Just as Asim was about to leave, Nina went still. Something was off. Her senses kicked in, sharp, and then it hit—a smell, green. She smelled green. It was always a sign of a bad soul. And then her nose started bleeding. She staggered back, shocked.

The healer's face went white. His fingers twitched, and for the first time since they'd met him, he looked scared. 'Illness?' he muttered, stepping back like she'd just triggered something dangerous.

'I had a rare disease,' Nina blurted out, almost without thinking. 'It disappeared when we came here; I don't know how, but it's gone now.'

The healer's eyes widened. He took another step back, as if she'd just turned into a monster.

'What's going on?' Nina asked, but he was already motioning them out, faster now, like he couldn't wait to get rid of them.

Noah then grabbed Nina and steered her toward the door.

'We're done here,' he muttered, nodding to Tessa and Asim. As they stepped outside, his voice dropped. 'In this world, there's no illness. Magic takes care of that. What you said in there freaked him out.'

Nina's stomach dropped. Asim and Tessa said nothing, but they'd drawn more attention than they should have.

'It's alright, just be careful next time,' Noah said.

Suddenly, birds flew out of the hospital, just ordinary pigeons. One of them landed right in front of them on the curb.

They were just about to turn away, heading toward the shop where Noah needed to pick up some hats and a few bottles. But then, suddenly, the pigeon started growing.

They flinched, startled, yet Noah barely reacted. He didn't even slow down. Instead, he just looked at them and said, 'What's the big deal? Let's go.'

But they couldn't, because the pigeon was no longer a pigeon.

It was a man.

He was wearing pants and black shoes, and before they could even process what had happened, he casually pulled a set of keys from his pocket, pressed a button, and got into his car like it was the most normal thing in the world.

Except he didn't start the engine. Instead, he just shut his eyes, sweat dripping down his face, completely drained. Within seconds, he was snoring so loudly they could hear him through the window.

Noah finally spoke up, saying that healers had a special gift, but they were also half-animal. Healing took a toll on them, so they slept a lot.

And Nina, Asim, and Tessa? They just stared, wide-eyed, not sure what to say.

They kept walking, but none of them looked particularly thrilled.

Asim walked with his head down, lost in thought. He kept replaying what had happened at Johan Market, and the more he thought about it, the worse he felt. He knew he had acted like a coward, and honestly, a part of him was ashamed.

He hated humiliating himself, especially in public. Even if no one else thought it was funny, to him, it was. Because, of course, his father had always told him that a man isn't weak. A man takes the hits. A man shows respect but doesn't hide. A man is strong, fearless, and tough.

And that had always haunted Asim, because deep down, he knew he wasn't that kind of man.

Even as a kid, he had been bullied at school.

They walked slowly, taking in the odd scene around them. The shops didn't look like anything they were used to. No signs, no names, just blacked-out windows, with no hint of what lay behind them. It was spooky, as if the shops didn't care if anyone knew they existed or not.

'This is it, this is the shop I was talking about,' Noah declared proudly, as they stopped in front of one of those jet-black windows.

'What's so special about this shop?' Asim asked, disappointed, giving the blank exterior a sceptical once-over.

They stepped inside, finding a small room with plain blue walls and nothing but a desk shoved in the corner.

Tessa snorted. 'We've been in a place like this before.'

Noah, keeping his cool, gestured for them to stand in the middle of the room.

'This is a magic shop,' he explained with a smooth voice. 'Just wait.'

With a cheeky smile, the three of them stood where he told them, eyes darting around, wondering what was about to happen. Like a flash, the floor under them lit up, buzzing with this electric-blue neon glow. Before they had a chance to even process what was going on, they were dropping fast, properly fast. Their chests tightened with each rapid thud. While Noah? Cool as ice.

In a blink, they were in the real shop, massive, pumping with life magic. Glass shelves stacked with colourful dust sparkled, and the floor littered with shimmering marbles that crunched softly underfoot. Ornate furniture dotted the place up for grabs. Racks packed with gloves in every shade and style imaginable, and hats, flashy, unique, like they had their own life. But maybe they really did.

'Why's the shop under the room?' Nina asked.

Noah chuckled, shaking his head.

'It's not under. It's the same room. Magic's funny like that, keeps things hidden. Protects it from thieves and worse.'

They really liked it there; it was something different, new, and even a bit extravagant. Asim and Tessa went over to the corner and tried on the hats—not just ordinary ones, but magical ones.

'How do I look?' Asim asked, trying on a black hat with sparkles.

Tessa sneaked a look at him with a warm smile and said, 'Oh, you should definitely buy this.'

'It is a special hat, Asim. All of them here are for sale because they contain magic. Even the gloves, the furniture around, and the dust in the glasses too,' Noah said softly.

'What magic?' Asim asked.

Noah leaned in a bit. 'The hats. They've got a spell on them that makes you look younger. Works best for the older lot.' Then, lowering his voice as if sharing a secret, he added, 'There's another shop, you know. Those hats don't just make you look younger. They can make you a whole new person, just how you want. But for now, this should do.'

'Er... Aww, I get it now,' Tessa jumped in, missing nothing.

She had picked out this right posh hat, proper fancy with this orange flower stuck on the side. Didn't quite do the job of hiding all her wrinkles, but she looked well chuffed, and fair play to her.

'Maybe you should splash out on a pricier one?' Noah piped up.

And then she did it. She put one on, a purple one, and just like that, she wasn't a 42-year-old blonde with a few wrinkles anymore. She was young. When she looked in the mirror, she started jumping around like a little kid. Well, she actually looked like one, too.

Asim saw her and nearly jumped back. He just shook his head and rolled his eyes. Meanwhile, Nina came over and started trying on the hats too, but nothing happened. So she tried another, then another, but she stayed exactly the same. She huffed, stomping her foot in frustration.

Tessa just smiled and took off the hat. She didn't need it. If it didn't work on Nina, then she didn't want one either. She cared about Nina and knew she would be jealous, so she just let it go. And just like that, she wasn't the young girl anymore. She was Tessa again.

Noah was somewhere up front, too busy with something else to notice. When Nina finally walked up to him, he saw the look on her face before she even spoke. She told him the hats didn't work on her. Noah just shrugged and said they were cheap junk, nothing special. Some of them didn't even last more than a few days, and then you'd have to buy a new one again and again. Waste of money, really.

'Oh yes, that's what we need,' Noah said, grabbing three glasses filled with orange dust that looked suspiciously like something you'd find under a couch. Then he snagged three pairs of gloves: one white with black dots, another a blinding shade of orange, and the last one classic leather.

Nina shot him a confused look, wondering why on earth they'd need any of this. But Noah just gave her that knowing grin, the one that seemed to say, *there's a reason, and it's going to be much too complicated to explain.*

They were done, so he tossed some golden coins.

The shopkeeper, who had bright green hair that seemed to glow, eyed the coins with open suspicion, muttering under his breath about whether they were real gold or "just fancy chocolate." Noah didn't flinch, but the whole exchange was starting to make Nina feel slightly off-kilter.

Tessa shifted nervously, glancing around as if looking for the quickest exit. She was clearly wondering how they'd get back upstairs. Noah, though, wore his usual smug smile, like he'd planned every detail down to the type of lint in his pocket. He led the way, and as the big glass door slid open, they found themselves outside... the exact same shop.

They all stood there, utterly baffled. Noah, of course, couldn't help but enjoy their confusion. He knew precisely what was going on, and the fact that no one else had a clue was half the fun.

Chapter Sixteen
The True Side

———⟡———

IN THE MIDDLE OF THE garden, Asim let out a laugh, while Tessa gave him a small smile. But Nina's eyes were locked on Noah as he held up the Deman Gloves, shiny and sleek, like they had a soul of their own—because they did have a soul. Noah was buzzing as he laid out what the gloves could do. They hooked straight into your skin, picked up what you were thinking, and locked onto your feelings.

Nina slipped them on, and her fingers twitched as the gloves tightened around her, syncing with her pulse. A shock shot up her arm. These weren't just gloves; they were buzzing with energy, consuming her thoughts. She could nearly feel them humming, like they were alive.

Asim and Tessa watched, glued to the spot. Noah stepped back, letting her try them out. All she had to do was point, focus, and whatever popped into her head would shoot straight out through the gloves. Nina aimed at a tree, her mind racing with ridiculous ideas. Fire? Lasers? Something completely mental? She barely had a second to decide before, in a flash, blue flames blasted from her fingertips, tearing through the air and smacking right into the tree.

The poor thing never stood a chance. The gloves pulsed with heat, growing stronger as she kept her mind locked in, feeding off her focus. Asim took a step back, impressed, while Tessa stood there, eyes wide as smoke curled up from the tree. Noah's grin spread wider, happy with what he saw.

'Oi, these gloves are sick,' Asim said, watching Nina's little fire show. He flexed his own pair, a bit too eagerly. 'What else can they do?'

Noah chuckled, clearly enjoying the moment. 'Depends on the gloves. Quality's everything here. Some last for months, others... well, they can turn on you if you don't handle them right. They're alive, after all, and like any living thing, they can get a bit... moody.'

'Moody gloves?' Asim asked.

'Yeah,' Noah said. 'Use them too much, and they'll bite back. Quality ones stick around, but eventually, all of them die. They're not forever, mate.'

Nina's hands tightened into fists, the gloves gripping her skin like they were becoming a part of her. 'I can feel them,' she said, half amazed, half freaked out. 'It's like they're reading my thoughts.'

'They are,' Noah replied. 'They lock onto your emotions, your intent. The stronger the feeling, the stronger the magic. But you've got to stay focused, or...' He mimicked an explosion with his hands.

'So, what, we're walking around with ticking time bombs on our hands?' Tessa asked, crossing her arms.

'Only if you're sloppy,' Noah said. 'They won't drain you, but don't mess around. Try summoning something they're not made for, and it'll backfire. Hard.'

Asim fiddled with his gloves, looking like he was trying to figure out a magic trick. 'Oi, Noah, how'd you know we were at the police station? You showed up like you had us on speed dial.'

'Ah, well, that's a bit awkward. You lot... smelled. Sorry, but it's true.' Noah snorted, a hint of embarrassment creeping in. 'Coming from Hell tends to do that. Magic, especially Hell's brand of it, sticks to you like a bad perfume. Enforcement can smell it a mile away.'

'We smelled... because of Hell?' Asim asked.

'Yep,' Noah replied.

Nina raised an eyebrow. 'So, magic is tied into the government here?'

'Of course,' Noah said with a casual wave. 'Invisible alarms, magical surveillance. It's all around you, but only enforcement can see it. The museum? That place had more magical security than Buckingham Palace, trust me.'

'Lovely,' Nina muttered. 'So, we're not just in a magical world; we're in a magical police kingdom.'

Noah chuckled again. 'Magic here's all about money. It's a product, and those who have it are in charge. It's not about being born powerful; it's about buying the right tools. But once magic fades, so does your life. You can't live without it.'

Tessa frowned. 'So, if your magic runs out, you're... what? Dead?'

'Not immediately,' Noah said, leaning back against a tree. 'But without magic, life here gets very short, very fast.

It's why some people pay a fortune to keep themselves going. You've seen those hats, right? The ones that make people look younger? Same deal. Everyone's trying to hold onto their magic.'

Nina flexed her fingers again, feeling the gloves hum. 'So, people buy power... to stay alive.'

'Pretty much,' Noah said, giving her a knowing look. 'And the powerful ones, the ones born with magic? They're the real players. But even they can't live without it.'

Asim glanced at his gloves, then back at Noah. 'What about you? You got magic?'

'I've got what I need.'

TESSA GROANED, HER legs aching as she dropped onto a massive silver sofa that felt more like a trap than comfort, pulling her down into the cushions.

'Energy boost,' she muttered, sounding more asleep than awake.

Noah, not even paying attention to her moaning, grabbed a yellow glass bottle from the bookshelf, the liquid inside spiralling like smoke.

'Well, this will do the job,' he muttered, looking more smug than a cat that just nicked a Sunday roast.

Tessa didn't need an invitation. She popped the cork like she was opening a bottle of cheap wine, took one deep breath, and—whoosh—dust straight to the lungs. Lovely. Within seconds, it hit her like a double espresso on an empty stomach. ZAP. Energy blasted through her like she'd been plugged into the mains.

Her body? Oh, it went full reboot. Snapped back to life like a dodgy old telly someone smacked on the side. All the heaviness? Poof. Gone. She practically vibrated.

'Wow,' she muttered, eyes wide, 'this stuff's mental.'

Noah just smirked, satisfied.

Tessa had no idea the potion she'd just knocked back came with strings attached, but Noah did. Oh, he definitely did. Leaning against the wall like he'd just solved world hunger, he watched her with a smirk that could power a small town on smugness alone. The first sign came when her stomach growled. Not a little rumble, either—this was a full-on, earth-shaking roar that made her freeze. She clutched her belly, confused, as the noise echoed around the room like an angry bear trapped in her ribcage.

That's when Noah's grin turned into a full-blown smirk. Of course he'd known. Of course he hadn't said anything. Because why warn her when he could just sit back and enjoy the show? The potion, apparently, came with a bonus side effect: uncontrollable hunger. The kind that could turn a person into a fridge-raiding maniac. And, obviously, Noah had chosen to keep that little nugget of info to himself because, let's be honest, winding her up was his favourite hobby.

Tessa groaned, throwing herself onto the sofa with all the grace of someone who'd just realised they'd been played. Her stomach growled again, even louder this time, as if Noah's little secret wasn't bad enough already. She glared at him, but he didn't even flinch. If anything, it made his grin wider.

He eventually let her know the fridge was fully stocked, as if that somehow made up for not warning her in the first place. Tessa rolled her eyes, already plotting revenge, but she couldn't help laughing. He was impossible. Annoying. Smug. But he was also kind of funny. And Noah? Well, he just leaned back, utterly pleased with himself, knowing full well he'd live to wind her up another day.

MEANWHILE, NINA AND Asim noticed Tessa and Noah inching closer, sharing a look that said they'd best leave them to it. Quietly, they backed off, giving the two some room.

Asim, for his part, headed straight to bed, took his meds with the practiced efficiency of someone who'd long since resigned himself to the nightly ritual, and was out like a light. He sank into his new pillow as though it were specifically engineered for weary souls who'd seen one too many strange things in a single day. It did the job admirably, and he didn't give it another thought.

Nina was knackered too, but sleep wasn't happening yet. She walked over to the wardrobe, running her fingers along the dresses hanging there, each one perfect, exactly how she'd imagined. She felt a flicker of warmth, grateful to Noah. Her eyes strayed to the bed. There was a new pillow waiting for her too, and something else—a letter on top. She touched it, and the letter floated up, unfolding itself.

"Sweet dreams," it read. Signed, Noah.

A warm feeling ran through her chest, softening her a bit. Even though Nina wasn't exactly thrilled with how Noah had flirted with her at the market earlier, because now he was downstairs, flirting with Tessa—it wasn't jealousy. Not at all.

She didn't have that kind of interest in Noah. It just felt... a bit unethical, if she were being honest. She'd never liked men like him, and she definitely wouldn't have pegged him as that type. But then, she knew Tessa. And, well, Tessa deserved a bit of happiness. So, in the end, she just shrugged it off with a little huff, letting the thought drift away like smoke. And she slid into bed. The moment her head hit the pillow, she was out, drifting into a deep sleep.

MEANWHILE, DOWNSTAIRS, Noah had shown Tessa how to work the fridge, the kind that could summon any food she could think of. He opened it, focused, and food appeared perfectly cooked. Oh, Tessa loved it. She started thinking up all sorts of food, from burgers to milkshakes, and the fridge delivered every time.

Noah watched, chuckling at first, pleased at how easily Tessa got hooked. She looked like someone who'd stumbled on the world's best-kept secret. Then the landline rang. Noah froze mid-smirk, his expression flipping faster than a sticky pancake.

The pleasure drained from his face, leaving something far grimmer in its place. His hand waited for a moment before he grabbed the phone, an old, clunky thing with a coiled cable that looked like it hadn't been untangled since the '90s. He picked it up like it might explode, the corners of his mouth twitching in a grimace.

Whatever this call was, it wasn't good. And judging by the way he held that phone, it might as well have been a viper he'd just dared to pick up.

Tessa, ever the opportunist, clocked the shift in Noah's behaviour and decided this was a moment worth snooping on. She moved like a cat on a mission, slipping behind the door.

Pressing her ear closer, she leaned in, bracing herself for whatever secrets were about to tumble out of this clearly not-normal conversation. And, of course, because it was Tessa, she'd convinced herself she wasn't snooping, just strategically collecting intel.

The landline clicked off with a sharp, final sound, the kind that makes your stomach drop. Tessa stayed frozen behind the door, heart thudding so loud she was sure he could hear it. What the hell had she just overheard?

Noah. Bloody Noah. He'd been charming, cocky, a pain in the arse most of the time—but this? His voice on the phone wasn't the Noah she knew. It was cold, cutting, every word like a slap.

'Everything's as planned, so why now?' he'd snapped, sharp as broken glass. 'Fuck! We had a deal. They trust me already!'

Her stomach had flipped at that. *They? Us?*

'What do you mean, that the palace will disappear now? Shit... It was supposed to last three days.'

The palace? It wasn't sinking in properly. None of it made sense, but every instinct told her one thing loud and clear—Noah wasn't on their side.

She'd tried to move, to slip away quietly, but her legs weren't cooperating. It was like her whole body was caught in a fight with itself: *run or stay, scream or keep quiet.*

'Fine. I'll do it now,' Noah had growled, like a man being forced to clean up his own mess.

Then silence.

She turned, ready to bolt, but it was too late. He was already behind her, moving faster than he had any right to.

'Where you off to, Tessa?' His voice was now icy.

She froze, eyes wide. Every instinct cried at her to run, to fight, to do *something*, but before she could even think about it, his hand clamped around her wrist like a vice. Not playful, not teasing, just hard, cold control.

And then he grinned. Not his usual smirk. No, this was something darker, sinister, like he'd been wearing a mask all along and finally let it slip.

Noah wasn't Noah anymore.

By she could scream, his tongue shot out. Not a normal tongue; this thing was long, slick, pink, twisting into a monstrous tail. She gagged, stumbling back, but his grip didn't move.

'You bastard!' He spoke in a weak, croaky voice before his sharp, wet tongue slid across her cheek, leaving a stinging mark behind.

The bite came fast, nasty, tearing into her shoulder. Pain exploded through her. She gasped, turning wildly at him, but it was like hitting stone. His tongue pinned her in place, wrapping tighter, her strength draining fast.

It was over. She could feel it. He wasn't just betraying them; he was ending her.

Noah had played them all. The jokes, the smiles, the loyalty — it was all fake, a perfect act. And now, standing there with his monster's grin and coiling tongue, it all made sense. He wasn't just a liar. He wasn't human.

Chapter Seventeen
Sand

ASIM AND NINA WERE scanning the horizon, heart thumping. Nothing but sand. No palace, no rooms, no sign of life.

Asim's face turned as he pulled himself up. 'Where's Tessa? Where is everyone? Are we... are we dreaming?'

'No, Asim. We woke up. This is real.'

'It was that fucking bastard, Noah. I knew it.'

'How can you be so sure?'

'Oh, come on, Nina. You're still playing dumb? He set this up. Motherfucker... He put us under, made sure we were sleeping, and did whatever he wanted with Tessa.'

They sat in silence for a beat. Just them and the sand, stretching out like it was waiting to swallow them whole. Asim dropped his head, voice turning low and bitter. 'Maybe my dad was right. I'm useless. Always have been.'

Nina's breath tied, and her hands balled into fists, trembling. She stared down at the sand beneath her with tears coming, and she couldn't stop them.

'Tessa's gone. She's... she's gone, Asim.' She shook her head. 'I don't know what's happening. I don't.' She choked on the words. 'What now?'

Asim sat beside her with a hard face.

'This is all wrong,' he said, scanning the lifeless desert. 'We wouldn't even be here if it wasn't for you.'

'What?'

'You heard me. You're the one who trusted that bastard, Noah.'

'I... I didn't know it would end like this. I thought.'

'I, I... Well, you thought wrong!' He stood up, pacing in front of her. 'Now look where we are. Tessa's gone.'

'I didn't want...'

'You didn't want? Well, neither did I, Nina!'

'This is not my fault!'

'No? Oh, right. I don't know who kept saying, "Oh, he has a good soul, yellow, nice smelling"... blabla... You probably smell some shit, not souls.'

She wanted to whack him, honestly, but she held back, biting her tongue and stewing in her anger. Her teacher always told her not to argue with someone on edge—just let it go. She tried to stick to that advice.

She knew Asim was just losing it, probably more by himself than herself. He was just taking it out on her a bit. Didn't make it less annoying, though.

She sniffed, reaching out with her ability, desperate for any trace of life. But when she stretched her senses, pain flamed through her head like a spike. Blood dripped from her nose, and she wiped it away, shaking, a bit surprised to feel blood dripping from her nose. That sort of thing had only started happening after they'd crossed the threshold into this world. But now wasn't the time for messing about with stupid details.

There was someone, no, something, coming. They couldn't see it yet, not with the sun blazing high, scorching the sand and their skin. Both had to raise their hands, shielding their eyes from the harsh light.

Nina's heart raced. She wiped the blood from her nose, trying to sniff out who or what was approaching. But her head spun. She stumbled slightly. And then she knew.

Her stomach did a full-on nosedive. When she spoke, her voice was hanging on by a thread, just about.

'Asim, run. Now!'

Asim shook his head, his brow furrowed.

'What? No. What's wrong with you?' His voice was too calm. 'That's my dad.'

Nina grabbed his arm, fingers digging in.

'Asim, I'm serious. Run. Now.'

'Stop it, Nina. Calm down. My dad might have had his secrets, but he's not—he's never hurt me.'

He wasn't afraid. Not even a little. In fact, something like relief crossed his face as he looked briefly into the distance. Nina's heart sank. She could see it in his eyes; he was glad. Happy to see him. Samir. Close now, his silhouette cutting through the haze of heat and light. Tall. Broad-shouldered. He moved with purpose.

'Stay back!' Nina yelled, stepping in front of Asim, arms stretched out.

Samir kept walking, ignoring her. 'Nina, calm down. I'm here to help. I'll explain!'

She didn't trust him. Couldn't. But Asim? He pushed past her, walking straight towards his father.

'Dad.'

That's all he said before he stepped into Samir's arms. Samir pulled him in tight, gripping the back of Asim's head. Asim's shoulders tensed at first, then dropped. His fists curled into his father's shirt, and his head dipped. One tear slid down, wiped away quick before anyone noticed.

Samir didn't let go. His arms stayed locked around his son, holding on like he was afraid to lose him again.

Nina stood a few steps back, her throat tight. She didn't say a word, but inside, something broke. She'd never had that. Watching them was like looking through a window at a life she'd never be part of. Her mind dragged her back to that place she hated, to memories she never wanted to revisit.

She was so young back then. A little kid, maybe four or five years old. Alone in that cold orphanage room. Her knee bloodied, scraped raw from the fall, but all she'd wanted was a hug. Someone to tell her it was okay. But instead, the caretaker stood there, arms crossed, face crooked.

'Stop that crying,' the woman had snapped. 'I don't have time for this nonsense.'

Nina had stood there, tiny and trembling, her arms outstretched, begging for something, anything. But the caretaker just shoved a worn-out teddy bear into her hands.

'Here,' the woman said. 'This is your comfort now. Don't expect anything more.'

Nina hadn't cried after that. She'd just clung to the bear, holding it like it could fill the hole that no one else would.

Now, watching Asim in his father's arms, she blinked hard, pushing down the flood of memories. She wouldn't let it rise, couldn't. She wouldn't give in to that bothering ache that had haunted her since childhood. Not here. Not now.

Samir finally pulled back, his eyes scanning Asim like he was making sure he hadn't disappeared.

'I thought I'd lost you,' Samir said.

'No, Dad. How did you find us?'

'It was the "Freedom" flask. When you drank it, your smell disappeared. But it fades. And that's how I found you.'

'How did you know we drank it?' Nina asked.

'That's part of what I need to explain,' Samir said.

He stepped forward, hands raised slightly. Nina stepped back, not buying it.

'You don't need to fear me,' Samir said. 'I've been trying to protect you both from this world. It's dangerous, Nina. Asim, I didn't want you caught up in this mess.'

Asim glanced at Nina, unsure but wanting to believe him.

'We don't have time for this. Tessa is missing. We need to find her. Now,' Nina said.

Samir nodded, his face softening, though something unreadable glistened behind his eyes.

'I'll help you find her. I promise.'

Nina crossed her arms. 'And why should we trust you? After everything?'

'Because the truth's coming. And I'm not the enemy. I'm here to protect you from what's next,' Samir added. 'Let's get somewhere safe, and I'll explain later.'

He then pulled a small green cloth from his pocket. Without another word, he stepped one foot onto it, holding out his hands.

'Grab on. Tight, and don't you dare let go!'

'And what would happen if we did let go?' said Nina.

'You don't want to find out, trust me! Come on already, time's ticking!' said Samir.

Nina and Asim shot each other a proper "are you serious?" look, but, like the mugs they were, did as they were told. The moment they grabbed his hands, BOOM—bye-bye solid ground. The whole world went full-on tilt-a-whirl, and down they dropped, faster than you can say "bad idea." Nina's stomach? Well, that had packed its bags and relocated somewhere near her throat. Lovely.

Before they could even scream or regret all their life choices, BAM—floor. Hard. Painful. And where were they? Oh, just a dirty pub that smelled like a festival's worst day: stale beer, a splash of guilt, and a lot of pisses. Lovely.

They stumbled out into the street, blinking like moles in a floodlight at the full-on sensory assault that was London. The city didn't do subtle, and this was no exception. Passersby threw them side-eyes, muttering under their breath with faces sick in looks ranging from "ugh, what is that smell" to "should I call the police?" They looked exactly like they'd crawled out of a place nobody talks about in polite company. And, let's be honest, they kind of had.

'Why are they staring?' Nina whispered, looking around.

'Ignore them,' Samir said, keeping his pace steady. 'Stick close. And don't make eye contact.'

Asim's brow furrowed. 'Why? What's going on? Why are the police after you, and how do you know your way around here? You've never been here before.'

'Now's not the time for questions,' Samir said.

'Where are we going?' Nina asked Samir.

'A mate's place, not far.'

They walked a few blocks through the backstreets of London before stopping at a silver door placed behind a shabby shop. Asim and Nina stayed close behind Samir, eyes broad.

'Three tickets, please,' Samir said to the door, as if it were the most normal thing in the world.

Asim looked at Nina, eyebrows raised. *Dads lost it*, he thought. But before he could say anything, a hand slid out from the door's surface, holding three gleaming gold tickets. Samir took them without flinching.

'Thanks,' he said, as the door opened.

'Wow,' Nina whispered, her eyes running around as they stepped inside. The station felt like a whole other world, the sort of place that made your jaw drop whether you wanted it to or not. Overhead, massive glass arches curved up like they were trying to hug the sky, reflecting light in a way that shouted "fancy." The floor was so shiny it could've doubled as a mirror, throwing back the image of the tracks like some arty Instagram post.

The place was full of energy, with the sound of rushing footsteps, people talking at the same time, and the occasional noise of luggage wheels.

Samir turned. 'Stay close.'

The train waiting for them was a beast, sleek, glowing silver, lit up like it was ready to take on the world.

They stepped on board, handed their tickets to a white-haired giant of a ticket collector, his fur brushing the ceiling. No words, just a nod as he took Samir's gold coins, and they were in.

The cabin was plush, no fuss about it. Deep blue velvet seats, gold trims here and there. Just enough comfort to make you forget what was waiting outside.

A woman in a matching green suit appeared at the door, smiling brightly.

'Shall I get you anything?'

'Food and drinks,' Samir said, slipping more gold coins into her hand.

She handed over three small, empty plates and glasses. Asim frowned, looking at Nina. Confused? Yes, very much so, and Samir noticed.

'Those plates are bloody expensive,' Samir said, leaning back like he was auditioning for a posh sofa advert. 'If you've got the coin, you can buy one. No food ever needed. They read your mind, link up with your stomach, and give you exactly what you're craving, right there.'

They decided to give it a go.

First, Nina and Asim shot each other a look, the type of look that says, "Let's pretend we don't still want to throttle each other from that argument earlier."

'Ladies first,' Asim said with a smug little grin, basically handing her the spotlight.

'Oh, thank you. How kind of you, now,' Nina said.

She stepped up, closed her eyes, and thought about food with the intensity of someone manifesting a lottery win. Her stomach growled loud enough to startle nearby wildlife, and she even sniffed the air, nearly drooling as she visualised her perfect meal.

And then the plate filled.

But it wasn't right. Not even close. Her food didn't just look bad, it looked like it had been dragged through a swamp, left to rot, and then invited to a mould party. Green slime dripped over the edges. And the smell? Oh, just your daily mix of dead rat and public toilet. The drink wasn't any better, bubbling with a neon-green glow that yelled toxic waste but make it fancy.

Everyone froze.

Asim stared at Nina, wide-eyed, like she'd just summoned the devil himself, which, honestly, wasn't that far off.

And Samir? Calm as ever. Too calm.

'It's alright,' he said with a shrug. 'This happens sometimes.'

But Nina wasn't having it. No. She knew that tone, the same tone Noah had used when he'd lied about the mugs filling with blood back at the market.

'Why does this happen to me?' Nina asked with her voice cracking under the weight of frustration and fear. 'Something similar happened at the market with those mugs. Tell me the truth.'

Samir sighed, his shoulders dropping like he'd been dreading this conversation.

'As you already know, I guess... because you're the Guardian of Hell,' he said with a steady but blunt voice. 'You came from there, Nina. This world knows it, and... there's more I'll explain later, not here Nina.'

And there it was. The answer.

Nina's head dropped, her hair falling forward like a curtain to hide her expression. It wasn't exactly the uplifting pep talk she'd been hoping for.

Samir, deciding to be useful, picked up the plate of horrors and walked off to chuck it in the bin.

Meanwhile, Asim decided to play the role of *a guy who fixes everything.*

'All right, my turn,' he said, stepping up to the plate. Literally. He closed his eyes, concentrated for about two seconds, and voila—perfection. His plate filled with a glorious spread: juicy steak, creamy mashed potatoes, a touch of veg, and a fruity drink that smelled like sunshine in a glass. Nina's stomach growled again, louder this time, like it was personally offended by her rotten plate incident.

Asim smiled and handed her a fork.

'There's enough here. You're knackered. Eat,' he said with a bit of a softer voice now.

Nina hesitated for a moment, guilt prickling at the edges of her mind. But she was starving, and hunger won the battle.

'Thank you,' she said.

They dug in together, their forks clinking against the plate as they shared the meal. Samir eventually sat down with them, and for a few quiet moments, everything felt... okay.

But then Nina's hand froze mid-bite. Her mind flew to Tessa, poor Tessa. How could she sit here eating when Tessa might be starving? Or worse, what if she wasn't even alive?

The thought hit her like a punch to the gut, and she felt her appetite vanish.

Samir noticed immediately. He leaned forward, his tone steady but softer this time.

'Don't worry, Nina,' he said gently. 'Everything will be alright. Eat. Drink. We're nearly there. She'll be okay.'

Nina wanted to believe him. Desperately. But deep down, the worry in her chest wouldn't shove.

There was something in his tone, something solid, that made them believe him. For the first time in what felt like ages, the tension in their chests eased. Asim and Nina sat back, letting the weight of everything slip away, even if just for a moment.

Then Asim then made his way to the toilet but stopped dead in his tracks when he caught sight of himself in the mirror. A scream tore out of him, loud enough to shock the train. Heads popped out of cabins, people covering their ears, eyes wide, trying to work out what the hell was going on.

Samir was on him in a second.

'What's wrong?'

'Can't you see?' Asim's voice shook, and he pointed to his ears.

Samir looked, and without missing a beat, fizzed out, laughing. Asim's ears had ballooned, massive, like something of a baby elephant.

Samir, still chuckling, patted him on the back. 'Better get back to the cabin before you scare the whole train.'

Asim, still clutching his oversized ears, trudged back down the corridor, Samir following behind with a grin. Onlookers swapped strange looks as they passed, some hiding smiles behind their hands, others just gawking.

Nina's eyes dilated when she saw Asim. 'What the hell happened to you?'

'Everything is fine,' Samir said, waving it off. 'Side effect of some medicine. Should wear off in a few days.'

Asim didn't look convinced, still sulking in his seat, his ears trembling awkwardly. Meanwhile, a man with a large chin sat in the corner of his cabin, his eyes locked on Samir. Without a word, he tapped something on his watch, his face unreadable.

Nina leaned back, the sound of the train speeding, roaring in her ears. She could feel it, the vibrations deep in her bones. The food, still fresh on her tongue, tasted like a burst of flavours she couldn't even name.

The train came to a sudden stop, with sirens blaring loudly as if from out of nowhere.

'Shit,' Samir hissed, eyes darting. 'They're here for me. We've got to move. Now!'

Nina's with Asim looked completely lost, but there was no time for questions. They ran down the carriage, but before they knew it, officers were waiting at both ends, trapping them like rats.

Samir noticed the man with the prominent chin poking his head out of his cabin awkwardly, like an unpleasant odour. Samir noticed it briefly, but he didn't care at all, not right now. The policemen weren't messing about.

'Hands up! On your knees! Move it!'

Samir and Asim hit the deck, hands up. Nina went still, heart hammering. Her hands inched upwards.

'Stop!' she screamed.

And just like that, the lot of them went still, officers' mid-step, demand gloves still aimed, faces locked in place. They weren't gone though, still watching, eyes sharp but helpless.

Nina wasted no time touching Samir and Asim, snapping them out of it. Samir blinked, thrown off, but he knew better than to stand around staring.

'Move!' he cracked.

They legged it off the train, not looking back.

The police were nothing but a blur. Rain smashed into their faces, but there was something electric about it, like the thrill of getting away, of being untouchable.

'I didn't know you'd got your powers back,' Samir called out, glancing at Nina, surprised but impressed.

She shrugged, still running.

'Yea, found out by accident not long ago.'

Samir's eyes darted around.

'Anyway, we're close enough to use the cloth again.'

Asim, puffing hard, threw him a look.

'Why didn't we just use the cloth in the first place?'

'Distance limits, my son, and the weight of us, too risky,' Samir said.

Without wasting time, he whipped the cloth out, dropped it to the ground, and stood one foot on it. Asim and Nina grabbed his hand, and they were gone.

They landed in the middle of nowhere. Caravans were scattered around like someone had tried to set up a fairground, then quickly lost interest. Everything looked rough around the sides, held together by a combination of duct tape, rust, and a solid sense of denial. It was the type of place that felt like it came with its own horror story... or at least a tetanus shot.

'Travellers?' Nina whispered, eyes scanning the place.

'Where the hell are we?' Asim asked.

Samir put a finger to his lips, quieting them.

'Right place,' he said, eyes flicking around, his tone low and sure. 'We are back home in Bradford.'

Chapter Eighteen
The Magical Caravan

SAMIR KNOCKED ON THE door, and it opened just enough to reveal a massive man who looked like he'd been summoned from the land of "fashion doesn't matter." Short white beard, a yellow jumper that looked older than time itself, ripped jeans and slippers that whispered, *I've given up.*

'Come in,' he whispered, then gave Samir a tight hug. 'It's been ages! I'm so glad to see you, mate,' he said, almost with tears in his eyes.

Samir introduced him to Asim as his son and Nina as his friend.

'And this is my best friend, Finley,' he said.

Asim and Nina didn't look too thrilled as they stood in the cramped, smelly caravan that felt as small as a rocket inside.

Finley noticed their expressions and reassured them, 'Don't worry, let's go inside,' he said.

Asim and Nina didn't quite understand, while Samir stood there smiling, knowing exactly what was about to happen.

Finley took a deep breath and blew into the air. From his mouth came a swirl of purple dust, carrying a faint, pleasant scent. Suddenly, where there had been nothing, a door appeared.

Finley stepped forward, opened it with a casual flourish, and gestured for them to enter.

'Please, welcome,' he said with a smile that practically sparkled.

Nina and Asim just stared, wide-eyed. This was cool. Really cool. And they were absolutely loving it.

As they walked into the beautiful home filled with fresh flowers, they all had big smiles.

The caravan was just a gateway to Finley's hidden home, a place invisible to anyone without his permission. Finley reassured them it was the safest place in the world, a shelter where they could finally feel welcomed.

Asim kept glancing back at the door, still amazed it was there, solid and real. Finley explained that the door was only visible to those he allowed. For anyone else, it simply didn't exist.

Nina exhaled slowly, the tension easing from her shoulders. For the first time in what felt like ages, she believed they might actually be safe.

'Stay as long as you need,' Finley said with a warm smile.

He then stared out at his crew of servants, each one once just a fly, now full-on humans, ready to jump whenever he snapped his fingers. For all the talk about him being a top wizard, there was still that soft spot he kept for those who stuck by him. Loyal. Kind. The ones who knew their place. A small, almost secret smile crept onto his face.

'You lot aren't just servants. You're my dear friends,' he said.

His eyes flicked to Asim and Nina. Without a word, the servants knew the drill. 'Take care o' them.'

Treated with respect, Asim and Nina were shown to their rooms. It wasn't a palace, no, but it had that cosy, homely feel. Exhausted, Nina was out like a light. Asim lay awake for a while, questions spinning, but in the end, sleep took him too.

Later that night, Nina woke to a faint sound. The place was not bright, but easy to navigate. She followed the noise down the hallway until she found herself in a massive room filled with machines and vials, all humming with activity.

Frightened, she started as a hand touched her shoulder, turning to find Finley standing beside her.

'Forgive me for startling you. I heard you and thought I'd explain.'

Pointing to the robotic machines, he then revealed to Nina the inner workings of his magical potions production.

Breathless with wonder, Nina inquired, 'So the potions in the shops... they are from you?'

'Yes an' no. While I am a wholesaler, there's plenty like me. We provide magic for folk without the gift, offerin' a chance for everyone to experience its wonders.' Finley's look softened. 'Not all are born wi' magic like I was. Every path's different.'

'Or like you,' he said with a wink.

'Hmm,' said Nina with her head down.

Then Finley hopped around. 'Look, I'll show you something,' he said, rummaging, and finally pulled out a scruffy little bottle with some odd name on it. He opened it, glanced over at Nina, who was just watching with a sceptical look that said *a bit of a nutter,* but Finley only smiled. Then he blew across the bottle, and right before their eyes, a magnificent horse appeared, standing tall.

Nina jumped back. 'Flipping hell. Is it real?'

Finley nodded, motioning for her to come closer, but she took a few cautious steps back. He offered his hand, and she gave in, sensing the calm confidence in him. He placed her hand on the horse's side, which stood quietly, muscles rippling slightly.

'Yes, it smells a bit, but that's cause it's real,' he said with a laugh as the horse let out a soft snort, looking pleased with itself.

And then, just like that, the horse vanished. Nina flinched while Finley chuckled.

'Magic's real enough, but it doesn't last forever. It's here for a moment, then gone.'

But when Nina gazed up at him, her eyes brimming with tears, Finley gently brushed her fringe aside. In a low, calming tone, he whispered, 'Don't worry, Nina. Everything'll be fine.'

She felt comfort washing over her. There was something about him, solid, almost fatherly. And as Finley looked back at her, he saw it; the daughter he never had.

'I just feel like going home. I don't know who I am anymore,' Nina said.

Finley gazed into her tear-filled eyes, and it blindsided him hard.

'Nina, listen to me,' he said gently. 'Once you get thy memories, everything'll change. I'll be right by thy side, helpin' you through it all. Stay strong. You are not alone, I promise.'

He then turned and grabbed one of the yellow potions.

'Nina, drink this,' he said softly. She held back, so he touched her hand gently. 'It'll help you sleep, ease the pain an' fear for a night. Err, yes, might give you a bit of a headache, but it's worth it.'

Nina nodded slowly, trusting him, and took a deep breath before downing the potion. As it kicked in, a wave of relief washed over her, and she felt lighter than she had in ages. With a real smile, she headed back to bed and drifted off, peaceful at last.

Samir had been listening in from behind the door. He stepped up to Finley, knowing they still didn't have all the answers. His mind floated back to the strange incident with Noah in the desert. Something wasn't adding up. Finley wasn't one for keeping quiet, and he made it clear; secrets weren't going to save anyone. The deaths, the lost souls, it was all connected. They had to act now, no more waiting around.

Samir's shoulders dropped. He'd been trying to protect everyone, but instead, he'd messed it up.

'Well, I see not much has changed around here,' Samir said.

'Yea, you know me. Still same old goat, I am.'

'Old? Take a look at me.'

'Eh, you aged, lad. But what do expect? You have been stuck in Hell for twenty bloody years. Folk age down there, same as humans do.'

'Don't remind me. You know what, though? I missed this place and you.'

'I missed you too. Thought about comin' to see you, I did, but, well, weren't like I could find a way. Still not forgotten what you did. Tekkin' t'key, leavin' me here, barricadin' me in like that.'

'I'm sorry. You know I had to.'

'Yes, I know. Just hurt, that is all.'

He knew where Samir was coming from. They weren't just close friends, but family. He offered Samir another yellow potion. Without thinking, Samir knocked it back like it was nothing. A few seconds later, his head spun, and he nearly hit the floor.

Finley eased Samir onto the bed with the sort of care you'd reserve for an old book or a fragile bit of glasswork. Samir's breathing slowed, the potion doing its job, his thoughts drifting into the quiet shadows. Finley watched him for a moment, a flicker of something unspoken passing over his face. He then gently touched his cheek, his voice dropping to a whisper. 'Still love you, I do.' Then, noticing a shape hovering by the door, he turned.

'Asim,' Finley said, his tone sharp enough to catch attention.

Asim, wide-eyed and caught, offered a hesitant smile.

'Looks like you could use one o' these an' all,' Finley said, holding up a small, worn bottle.

'You're always giving out these potions,' Asim said, eyeing it. 'Don't they, well... take something out of you? Doesn't it use you up?'

'Magic doesn't work quite like that,' Finley said. 'Folk think it's like coal or oil, but it's more... knitted into you. It grows wi' you, changes as you change.'

'So, what, you don't need them yourself? You're always fine?'

'Oh, I need it, all right,' Finley said, slipping the bottle into Asim's hand. 'These potions aren't gifts. They're parts o' me I'm sharin'. They keep me here, let me do what I do, an' give me a bit more time to do it.'

'So... without it, you'd be...?'

'Let's say I'd've been gone long ago,' Finley said, meeting his gaze. 'Magic isn't a gift; it's a bond. An' like any bond, it comes at a cost.'

'A cost,' Asim said softly. 'Guess that makes you... stronger than most.'

'Stronger, maybe. But strength doesn't come free,' Finley said, resting a hand briefly on Asim's shoulder. 'Now, get some sleep. That potion will help you rest.'

Chapter Nineteen
The Menu

—◦∞◦—

MEANWHILE, ASIM WAS living large, his new car hugging the asphalt like it owned the streets. One hand on the wheel, the other now and then tapping to the pulse of the bass, he speeded through town. The time was his. The city stretched out like a neon playground.

But on his way back to the caravan, something caught his eye: a woman with a lightning bolt tattoo snaking up her legs.

She slipped into a plain, simple building, but something about it gave him a bell. Thirst for answers troubled inside him. With a smirk, Asim pulled over, killed the engine, and walked to the place. From the outside, it had that elegant, too-clean-to-be-legit vibe, but inside? A tired-looking room with a desk and peeling wallpaper. Still, his gut told him there was more hiding beneath the surface.

A woman appeared from behind the desk, petite, with wild, orange hair that screamed trouble. She beamed like she knew a secret.

'First time 'ere? Need a menu?' Her voice was teasing, almost daring him to play along.

Asim wasn't sure what the hell this place was, a brothel? Maybe. But he wasn't about to make a fool of himself, at least not yet. Cool as ice, he had threw a half-smile.

'Nah, just lost. Took a wrong turn.'

'Of course you did.'

She winked, fingers already winding a pen around her neck like she was born with it. One touch, and she sketched a door right onto the wall; a door that, five seconds ago, had no business being there. Asim's eyes practically bugged out as the drew lines shimmered, sick, and, oh yes, turned real. Solid as stone.

And beyond it? The music smacked him in the face, bass thumping so hard it felt like it was rearranging his internal organs. The room was alive: laughter, sloshing drinks, half clothed women dancing through clouds of neon lights.

Asim just managed a breathless, 'Wow.'

The receptionist leaned in, smiling like she knew exactly what she was doing. You're welcome, her eyes seemed to say.

'Enjoy, darling,' she waved over a young woman in a green hat, whispering, 'It's his first.'

Asim followed the woman, her sly chuckle setting off every warning bell in his head. But it was too late to back out now. They walked down a hallway that seemed to go on forever, like it had been waiting for someone foolish enough to keep walking.

'Room 2020,' she said at last, handing him a gold key that was so heavy it felt like it should come with a bodyguard. The payment was quick and ridiculously high, but Asim was already so far down this rabbit hole, he'd need a map and a miracle to find his way out.

The hallway still seemed endless, but finally, he reached room 2020. There was no handle. Just a door, staring back at him like it was daring him to try.

He scratched his head, frowning, as a woman—tall, with long red hair—walked past him like she'd missed her stop at Hogwarts.

'The key,' she said, raising an eyebrow like she'd been waiting for hours. 'Press it to your chest.'

Before he could even think about questioning her, he did as she said. The key melted into his skin. The door opened with a deafening bang, and before he knew what was happening, he was sealed inside.

The room was… a lot. In the centre was a huge, heart-shaped bed, covered in red velvet and lace, like it was trying to win an award for the world's most ridiculous décor. Everything was shiny and gold, the walls essentially glowing with it.

He had always secretly wished to visit a place like this. He remembered walking home from school, passing the house everyone whispered about. The rumours said it was a brothel. Secretly wondering what it was like inside. But he never dared, especially not when he was younger, and his pockets were almost always empty.

Asim's eyes ran around the room, skipping from one strange detail to the next. Golden walls, an overly lavish bed, glittering bottles lined up on the bar. He ran a hand through his hair and opened his mouth to say something, but no words came. The whole scene was simply too much.

Then he saw it.

A menu, lying on the table. It wasn't the fact that it was a menu that caught his attention. It was the way it seemed to draw him in, nearly as if it were waiting for him to notice. He carefully picked it up, the leather surface smooth under his fingers. The first page opened on its own and revealed a single name, written boldly at the top.

And then, a woman jumped out. She was tall and stunning, with a radiant red hat on her head, and she looked just as surreal as the rest of the place.

'Your desires?' she purred, her words flowing gracefully with a soft Russian accent as she came so close that almost nothing but her cleavage filled his vision.

His hand moved before he realised it and ran over the curve of her chest. Warm, firm—yes, she felt unreal. His fingers scrubbed her nipple lightly, and something hot shot through him. His body? Full green light. His brain? Completely shut down.

She came even closer, pressing his hand against her and biting her bottom lip. That look, that little smile. It lit him up in a way he couldn't explain, and for a moment, he didn't care where he was or why.

'What do you desire? Do you want more of us?' she whispered while her hands slid onto his thighs.

Asim swallowed hard, signalled for her to continue, and winked at her. Then he opened the menu and turned the page, his mind already impatient to see what, or who would come next.

The second woman jumped out, and her shiny blue hat sparkled in the light. Her lips were a little open, and her eyes looked like they could see straight through him. Every move she made was slow, seductive. A strand of hair slipped onto her face, and after tucking it behind her ear, she started to undress the first woman. They both turned to Asim, touching each other, waiting. But for Asim, it wasn't enough.

He turned the page. Faster now. Hunger drove him forward. Another page. Another woman. And this one was different. An emerald-green hat, glowing as if it had its own light. And her body? The very definition of temptation. Full hips, smooth curves. And when she stepped toward him, it was as if time had stopped. Her skin, dark, shiny like velvet, smelled sweet. She leaned in toward him, and without a word, he reached out. With one swift motion, he tore off her dress. He couldn't wait any longer.

'I'm all yours,' she said. Her voice was deep, low, resonating through his entire being. He grabbed her firmly. One hand on her neck, the other in her hair. He tugged gently. She closed her eyes, her mouth slightly open. He leaned in, his lips brushing her ear.

'Show me what you can do,' he said in a rough voice. She took his hand and guided it to her hips. His fingers gripped her skin, and he felt the heat rising between them. His body responded to every movement, every touch, as if it were instinctual. He wasn't thinking anymore. He was just feeling.

And the other two women joined in slowly, touching sensually. They began kissing while Asim's shirt hit the floor. Their hands and tongues were everywhere, burning him with every touch. Every movement was another wave of pleasure. As if they were leading him to the ultimate peak.

He paused for a moment; the key sealed in his chest started to burn. He tried to ignore it. *Not now. Not now.* But the feeling wouldn't stop.

Then he reached out and tried to take the green hat off. But she pulled back sharply.

'No,' she hissed. 'That's not allowed.'

He grabbed her hands, pressed them back to her body. And then, as if none of it existed, he forgot. About the key. About the hat. About everything. Only her skin, her scent, her touch. *Was it a dream? Reality?* He didn't care anymore.

He turned her around, pulling her against him, and then her green hat simply fell off. At first, Asim hardly noticed, his mind was clouded, yet something was different.

The texture beneath his hands changed. That smooth skin, well, it wasn't smooth anymore. He stopped and looked down, just to make sure he wasn't imagining things. And then he saw it.

On her back, wrinkles were forming at an incredible speed. Small, fine lines. Then more. And more. As if her body were drying out right in front of him. Her hips were no longer firm. Her skin sagged like an old, worn-out fabric.

'What the...' he started, but the words caught in his throat. Slowly, he stepped back, not believing what he was seeing.

She turned to face him, and her face was completely different. Wrinkled. Shrunken. Her hair, once glossy and smooth, was now grey and limp. Her breasts, which had driven him mad just moments ago, now hung loosely on her chest like old rags. Her eyes were empty. Dead.

'This... what the fuck is this...?' He wasn't sure if what he was seeing was real or if he was losing his mind. But then he remembered the hats. The ones Noah had shown him at the shop. Those magical hats that could change a person or make them younger.

Meanwhile, the other two women stopped their passionate kissing and touching. They just stood there, watching. No shock. Just quiet, as if this was totally normal.

The emerald woman bent down slowly to pick up the hat, moving carefully as if she might break in half at any moment. She even held her back as she bent over. Asim stood frozen, watching as she placed it on her head. And then, just like that, she was back. The same stunning beauty. Smooth dark skin, firm curves, perfection.

But Asim was done. All the excitement, the desire—gone. Replaced by nothing but disgust.

'This is just sick,' he said. His hands trembled as he quickly pulled his pants back on.

'Where are you going?' one of the women asked in her Russian-accented voice. 'You've paid for the whole night.'

'Keep it,' he said. 'And do one.'

The woman laughed in a prideful tone.

'At least we don't have to work too hard here. That was exhausting,' she said, then turned toward the menu, opened it, and before Asim could say a word, all three of them disappeared. Just like that, they jumped inside as if the menu were nothing more than a usual door.

And then there was muteness. Asim dropped into a chair. All the tension drained from him, but instead of relief, he felt empty. Offended.

He looked around and saw the shower—shiny and luxurious, sure, but even the water wouldn't wash away the feeling that held to him. The memory of what he had just seen. He grabbed his things, pulled his shirt over his head, and headed for the door. He needed to leave and right now.

But the door had no handle. Again. He leaned against it, banged on it, kicked it until it hurt, but nothing. And then he remembered. The key. He touched his chest where it lay, and it was hot, searing. And then, with a click, the door opened on its own.

'Brilliant,' he said. Without another thought, he ran. Not walked, ran. He didn't look left or right, just bolted straight for the main exit.

The hallway was full of people, all watching him. Some laughed. They knew. Of course, they knew. Why else would Asim be running?

A first timer. A fool who didn't know what he was doing. And now? Now that would be written all over his face for a very, very long time.

BACK AT THE CARAVAN, the living room was warm and cosy, a safe little corner where the troubles of the world seemed far away. Samir, Nina, and Finley sat peacefully, sipping their tea, the soft sound of cups against saucers the only thing breaking the quiet. It was 5:30 pm, and although the sun was fading outside, there was no sign of Asim. Still, they tried to stay calm, as if something bigger than the ticking clock weighed on them.

Nina leaned forward.

'Samir, how did you really find us? How do you know about this world? And who are you, really?'

Samir squirmed in his seat, throwing Finley a look like he was hoping for a last-minute assist. He seemed ready to drop some serious info, but didn't know where to start. Then Finley? Straight in, no hesitation.

Nina, he explained, was an angel, the Guardian of Hell. Not just any Angel either; she'd had the whole power package. But, as things tend to go, she'd got a bit greedy, reached for more power than she was meant to. Death itself had stepped in, quite unimpressed, and stripped her of the lot: powers, memories, the works, and locked it all up neatly in a set of mysterious books. If Death ever wanted someone out of the way, Nina here was the perfect case study.

Nina's eyes went wide. Sure, she'd pieced together some things, remembered little pieces, but Death calling the shots? That was news. Seemed like her past life was a lot messier and way more intense than the half-remembered bedtime story she'd been fed so far.

Time, as usual, had turned the truth a bit.. Asim was a wizard through and through, magic born and bred. Tessa, meanwhile, was still the big question mark, her fate shrouded in mystery. And as for Finley? He wasn't just some mystical friend; he was Asim's uncle. Oh, and Samir's brother-in-law too, thanks to his marriage to Finley's sister. The family tree was complicated, like a soap opera, only with more demons.

Unmoving, Nina sat there, the weight of these revelations pressing down on her. Her past, her powers, and now this growing threat? The pieces of the puzzle were falling into place, and the picture they formed wasn't a pretty one. It seemed like her forgotten life wasn't just her own little mess; it was turning into a full-blown disaster, and she was stuck right in the middle of it.

But Nina was shaking her head as tears brimmed in her eyes. She didn't feel like the Guardian of Hell, not in the slightest. In that moment, all she could recognise in herself was an afraid woman who loved books and appreciated the quiet life she had lived as a librarian. That life, simple, peaceful, that's all she wanted. She didn't ask for any of this, didn't want the weight of responsibility or the madness it brought. More than anything, she just wanted to go home. And she needed Tessa there with her.

Samir lowered his head, regret heavy on his look. This was his fault; he knew everything from the start and told no one. She had been cruel before, and when she found out about his marriage, she took his wife's powers, then killed her. Nina's mind reeled. She'd killed Asim's mother? *No. Impossible. Bullshit.*

Finley smiled. 'And my sister.'

Nina stared at him, lost. She left the room, went to her window, and lit a cigarette. The air was cold. None of it helped. She couldn't shake it. She had been cruel.

Samir was ready to go after her, but Finley held up a hand.

'Give her time,' said Finley.

Chapter Twenty
Brand-New Melons

---⟨∽⟩---

SAMIR CHECKED HIS WATCH. It was 6:30 pm, and still no sign of Asim. He was starting to worry, but Finley just shrugged. What Samir didn't know was that Finley had already slipped a tracker on the kid.

'Relax,' Finley said with a smirk.

Samir leaned back, relieved. 'Phew, that's a load off my mind. But what happened to all that talk about trust?'

'How can you trust a lad with money in a world full of magic?'

'Good point. Where is he, then?'

Finley didn't answer. Instead, he grabbed a bowl, filled it with water, and added three drops of a strange yellow liquid, blew in. The water rippled, and a brothel shone into view. Both stared at the image, speechless.

'Should I take a peek inside?' Finley asked.

'No, he's just a kid.'

Finley waved him off, but Samir felt a strange sense of relief. He'd never seen Asim around women, and for some reason, which put him at ease. They both turned away from the image, satisfied with what they'd seen.

'Listen, I'm not dumb. Why are you here, Samir? Truly,' said Finley.

'I... I can't tell you, but I have a job to do. I need to get Tessa and...' said Samir.

'No, I understand. I get it...'

'It's just... it's not safe here for you. You're not immortal in this world.'

'I know, but don't tell anyone, OK?'

'No, I won't. I promise,' Finley sighed and headed towards Nina's room.

He paused outside the door.

'I know it's tough, but you've got to face it. Be strong. Keep moving forward.'

Nina's voice broke back from the other side. 'What do you know about how I'm feeling? You don't get it.'

Finley stayed by the door, his hand resting on the frame.

'Maybe not. But talking might help. Maybe I'd understand if you let me in.'

'It's not about the woman I obviously killed. It's all of it. My life, Tessa, this whole mess. I can't do it anymore. Why me?'

'Just... stop hiding. Come out here. It's a past, Nina, you are a new person now... There's something I want to show you,' Finley said.

The door opened slowly. Nina stood there, eyes empty, heavy.

'Fine, show me.'

She followed Finley into a room where he picked up two pairs of old shoes from a shelf. He handed the orange ones to Nina while he slipped on the green.

'Why these?' Nina asked, frowning.

Finley explained the shoes were magical and would allow them to feel each other's emotions.

'You said I don't understand, and I want to.'

'Close your eyes,' he said, and some kind of magic shoe voodoo kicked in. Suddenly, Nina felt like she was connected to Finley's emotions, like emotional Wi-Fi. Fire running through her veins? Definitely. Intense but not "help, I'm dying" intense? Also true. She was sweating like crazy, but nobody's perfect.

When they opened their eyes, there she was, hugging him like they'd been best friends forever. No big deal, just casually ignoring all personal room rules.

'You know what? Let's go to the living room. I've got something else,' Finley said.

Nina followed him, deep in thought, already wishing she hadn't worn the shoes. Finley held up a glittering bottle. 'This is even more magical than the potions.' He winked at her. 'Finally, I see you smiling; it suits you.' Nina took a sip and loved it. It was better than any whisky she'd ever tried. 'I call her my Old Lady. She's 44 years old,' Finley said with a chuckle and kissing the bottle.

'Oh, cool, so you're drinking the Old Lady without me, huh?' Samir walked over with his empty glass, ready to join in.

Just then, there was a loud bang on the door. Finley hurried through the magical door to an old caravan to investigate. He found Asim there, looking shocked and half-naked. The sight was so ridiculous, Finley couldn't help but laugh.

They made their way to the living room, where Samir and Finley lounged, their faces lit up with that knowing 'we saw it all' look.

'Ha, I remember my first time running like that,' Finley remarked. 'So, how was it? Did you meet Hannah? She's my favourite,' he added.

Nina was bewildered. 'What's going on? What are you all talking about, and what happened to you, Asim?'

Asim laughed, brushing off Nina's worry with a low-key, 'Just out and about.'

He chucked Samir and Finley a knowing look, eyebrow raised in usual style.

'How the hell did you two figure out where I was? Seems like you know this place better than I do!' Asim said.

Samir chuckled.

'Ah, yes, a famous place with younger, err... ladies donning stylish hats. Quite the sight, isn't it?'

Nina covered her eyes, slowly sipping her whisky, and then inhaled the devil. Oh yes, it was a hell of a lot of smoke. She leaned back in the chair and let the testosterone do the talking. She had other thoughts, probably more apathy.

But Finley was certainly obsessed with the key. He knew that once he stepped out of the brothel room, that little bastard would disappear faster than a magician's rabbit. So, he leaned in.

'Asim, what the hell happened?'

Asim's story was wild. When the women ripped off their hats, it was pure horror, sagging skin and deep wrinkles, a sight that slapped him awake. So, he grabbed his pants and ran. But the door wouldn't open, so he shouted and banged on it. And then it just opened. And he legged it. Fast. No way was he looking back.

'That's mad!' Samir barked, turning to Finley, who looked just as surprised.

Asim stood there, hands on hips, shaking his head like he'd had enough.

'So now I've got a key stuck in my chest and ears like an elephant. Fantastic, isn't it? Really buzzing about it. And thanks for offering me that whisky you're drinking.' His tone dripped, eyes rolling.

Without a word, Nina tipped the bottle, pouring the whisky like it was any other day. No fuss. The amber liquid hit the glass, and Asim grabbed it, downing half of it in one swallow.

They all took a sip, the alcohol blurring the mess around them, even if only for a moment. Nina's fingers twitched as she set her glass down. She couldn't stop thinking about Tessa. Her lips trembled, barely holding back. Samir noticed, but he looked far away, staring into his whisky like it might have the answers he needed.

After a long pause, he finally spoke, reflecting on the morning. He had gone to the bank, checked out a few pubs, and asked around. His gut feeling had been confirmed. Those snakes had Tessa. The weight of that realisation settled in as he thought about how hard it would be to get her back. It wasn't going to be easy.

Nina leaned forward, pressing for more. Where was Tessa? Who had her? The questions came one after another, rapid-fire in her mind. Samir sighed deeply, rubbing the back of his neck, as if the weight of it all sat there.

He didn't hold back the ugly details. It was bad, far worse than she'd imagined. Tessa was locked up somewhere, a place no one was talking about. And they were running out of time, fast. The call to action seemed clear.

The word *snakes* circled in Nina's thoughts. Samir's explanation rebounded in her head. These creatures were half snake, complex and aggressive. They were dangerous, and getting Tessa out from under their control wouldn't be simple.

When Asim thought about everything that had happened, his anger ended up slightly under his skin. Why had Tessa been taken? Who was Noah? How had they ended up stranded in the middle of a desert? There were still too many unanswered questions.

Finley had offered some explanation earlier. They still didn't know who Noah really was, nor what had gone down exactly. It looked like magic had been used, a whole palace built around them just to get closer to Tessa. The magic, though, was cheap and wouldn't last. It was all temporary, a tactic to buy time.

Nina had remembered the moment at the market when someone had been about to kill them. Noah had stepped in and saved them. But Samir's dry chuckle at the thought cut through her memory. It had all been part of the act. Snakes were crafty, playing people with smoke and mirrors, all just to gain their trust. The more she thought about it, the clearer it became. This was a game they'd been caught in, and Tessa was the prize.

An idea crossed Finley as he sat up. His words were fast, almost desperate, as he drew in.

They had to get Tessa out. Who knew what those snake things wanted with her? They could hurt her for all they knew.

Samir cut in, raising his hand. If they'd wanted Nina, they'd have taken her too. They didn't. It was Tessa they were after, not her.

Finley laid it out, plain and simple: he and Samir would down some potion, turn into snake hybrids, and slither their way in. The goal? Blend in, find Tessa, and bring her back before anyone noticed. Easy, right?

Asim nodded like it was no big deal, like they were planning a quick trip to the shops. But Nina? She was already feeling that knot of fear in her stomach. Her nerves were kicking in hard—this plan sounded like the type that could go very, *very* wrong. What if the potion didn't work? What if they got caught? She couldn't shake the feeling something was bound to go sideways.

Samir comforted her. They'd also drink a tracking potion, so Nina could keep tabs on them. If they didn't come back in two hours, she'd know where to find them. Nina may have thought there were flaws in the plan, but that was all they had. All she could do was cross her fingers and pray it would work.

Finley grabbed the potion and gave them a quick, 'Here's how it works, kids,' demo. Shake, sip, wait for the magic. Easy.

'So, this is how you tracked me, huh?' Asim smirked.

'Yes, all for safety,' Finley replied, like it wasn't totally an invasion of privacy.

'Sure, it was...,' Asim muttered, raising an eyebrow.

Then came the moment of truth. Finley and Samir took their drinks, and the transformations kicked off. Finley's body stretched like an elastic band, his face sharpening into someone who looked like they could sell dodgy elixirs in a back lane. His new lean frame basically shouted mysterious rogue.

Samir, though... Samir got the short end, or should I say round end, of the stick. He looked down, confused, and saw two very large, very surprising chest extras.

'What the?' he stammered, staring at his brand-new melons.

Cue everyone losing their minds. Asim doubled over laughing, tears in his eyes.

'Ooh, looking sexy there!' Asim teased, still just able to breathe.

Samir, ever the showman, smiled and gave his chest a playful shake.

'Oh yes, so tender.' He struck a dramatic pose like he was trying out for a calendar. 'Alright, ready, my hubby?' Samir asked Finley, flashing a flirty grin and flexing his tall, elegant new frame.

That's when the vibe changed. Asim stopped laughing, his face clouding with worry. Nina caught the mood too. Samir, clearly unfazed, hugged Asim tightly in a 'let's not make this awkward' way, then vanished alongside Finley.

Chapter Twenty-one
Lifeless Minds

'IT'S ALREADY BEEN HALF an hour.'

Asim was walking like a caged animal. Nina's words didn't reach him. He looked like he was seconds away from exploding.

'Did you hear that?' he asked one of the servants, but they just made buzzing sounds, pointing at the door.

They stepped through, and bang, the door closed behind them. Nina looked around like she needed to hit something. 'Oh shit, how do we get back in?'

Asim kept cool, like the door was nothing. The servant would handle it, no questions asked. Asim and Nina looked through the small window, their hearts beating fast. The man outside was ripping into caravans, throwing belongings into the dirt like they were worthless. They could hear people screaming inside, begging for it to stop. But it didn't. The gang went from one caravan to another, destroying everything and ruining lives.

Asim tightened his hands into fists, knowing it wouldn't be long before they got closer. 'Shit, they're looking for us,' he whispered. 'Let's go back inside.'

The door was no longer there. Their trembling fingers desperately searched for a way out as they banged, hit, and scratched the walls. Outside, the bloody screams of innocent people rang out, but they kept moving. Running felt wrong. Leaving others behind felt worse. But fear pushed them forward. They didn't look back.

Then, out of nowhere, the door showed up. They stepped through, thinking they were back at Finley's place, but something didn't sit right. It was too quiet. Too still. No servant. Nothing.

Asim and Nina exchanged a look, but they pushed on, blind to what was coming. They sat down, watching the clock, every second dragging slower.

'Who were those guys outside?' Nina asked, but Asim just gave her a blank look and shook his head.

'You know, I wish we could go back home. We shouldn't have come here. All this, it's bullshit.'

Nina told him to stay strong. She had thought the same once but had changed her mind since.

Asim asked what had changed. She softly said that she used to feel sorry for herself and focus only on her own problems—until she noticed she'd left others in tears.

'You mean, like the people we just left outside? The ones screaming while we ran back here?' Asim said.

'I didn't run. I did what you told me to do.' But deep down, it was eating at her. Watching people suffer and doing nothing—no matter the reason—hurt more than she cared to admit. She realised it was time to stop hiding and face things head-on.

Asim took this personally, like a whack he didn't see coming. 'Are you saying I'm a coward?' he asked.

Nina reassured him that she didn't mean that, trying to cool the heat rising between them. 'Don't move. Just stay calm,' she told him as she eyed up behind Asim's back.

Asim had already clocked Nina's face—like she'd just strolled into a midnight graveyard and seen her own name on a tombstone. 'What the hell is going on?' he shouted, quickly turning around just in time to see dark shadows circling like police around a suspicious car.

'Fuck me!' Asim yelped, nearly pissing himself, heart thumping like mad. The shadows were alive. And hungry.

'Do something, Nina!' His voice broke, his eyes filled with tears as he stepped back. But Nina wasn't moving. Couldn't. Her body was betraying her, like it had given up.

Asim's heart crashed. He saw it. They were sucking the bloody life out of her. And fast. He ran for the door. Too late. Those bastards had him too. Slammed into the ground. Shadows all around.

But just as darkness threatened to swallow them whole, the door opened. A servant stormed in, grabbing Asim and Nina like they weighed nothing. The shadows screeched and disappeared, like roaches under a torch.

Breathless, they came to—back in the real Finley's house. Their bodies felt weak, like they'd been wrung dry, but after one stiff drink, they started feeling human again. Nearly.

'What the bloody hell was that?' Asim cried out, shaking like a leaf. Poor servant wasn't much help. He just flapped his arms around like a headless chicken, pointed at the door, and made some weird buzzing noises.

'Well, this is just brilliant,' Asim wheezed, his voice growing louder. 'Proper chat we're having here.'

But Nina gave him a sharp look. 'Calm down, Asim. Finley's not here, yeah? The doors, the house—they're protected from magic. It's probably just... because he's not around.'

Before they could argue more, everyone froze, even the buzzing servant. There it was—that strange thudding sound. Bangs. Like a drunk guy trying to knock over dustbins. They all glanced around, but there was nothing to see. Servant, bless him, shuffled toward the door like he was going to check it out. And then, dust and chunks of ceiling started raining down, filling the air like someone had decided to hotbox the place with plaster.

Coughing and hacking, they all looked up. The ceiling was... moving. No, not moving—breaking. Like someone upstairs was throwing a proper tantrum, trying to punch their way through.

'Oh, for f—RUN!' Asim shouted, grabbing Nina by the arm.

The two of them jumped aside, with servant trailing behind, still looking like a confused toddler. And then—boom—the whole bloody ceiling came crashing down, together with Tessa, Samir, and Finley smashing into the floor like dead weight. There was no time to think.

Finley was pressing his hands into Samir's wound, trying to keep the blood from pouring out. Samir's shirt was soaked, and the black veins from the magic glove crawled up his neck, the curse spreading faster than they could act.

'Towels. Potion. Second shelf. Now!' Finley barked.

Nina moved without a word, just pure action-hero energy. Meanwhile, Tessa? Oh, Tessa. She was doing her best impression of a doll, face-down on the floor. Nina dragged her onto the sofa like a champ. Good news: Tessa was no longer collapsed out like roadkill. Bad news: still unconscious. Bless her. You win some, you lose some.

Asim rushed back in, sweating heavily, as if he had run a 5K in extreme heat, holding a potion and towels.

'Press the towel down harder!' someone yelled.

Blood seeped through like this was the world's worst Slip 'N Slide. Asim poured the potion into Samir's mouth, and his body thrashed about, coughing as the liquid went down his throat. It was the sort of reaction that made the whole room freeze, hoping it wasn't his last move.

Finley locked their hands on Samir, all business, their face a mask of concentration. 'Get the travel cloth, now!'

Asim nearly tripped as he quickly grabbed for it. They were at the hospital in no time. The lights blinked worryingly overhead, the type of glow that cried, *Hope you paid your magic insurance!* Samir was on the bed before anyone could catch their breath. The healer's hands moved fast and shone as they ran over him.

'I'm sorry,' he said, sweat leaking down his forehead.

Samir's pulse was faint, his skin cold as ice. The healer handed over some medicine, wiped his hands clean, and stepped back, looking very much drained out. 'That's all I can do.'

And just like that, they used the travel cloth and dumped Samir back into his bed. Asim just stared. Samir's chest looked fine, perfect even, not a scratch in sight.

'What is going on?' Asim asked, his voice shaky.

Finley looked at him with a sharp eye. 'He's not waking up anytime soon. He needs rest now.'

They left him there and made their way downstairs. Tessa was still lying on the sofa, looking more like a thrown-out mannequin than an actual person, but Nina sat next to her and held her hand. And that was it. One bleeding out. One comatose. The others hanging by a thread. Just another night.

Finley dropped into the chair, breathing hard, knocking back two shots of *The Old Lady* whiskey, and finally began to speak in a heavy tone. 'So, yep, we found Tessa in the room. Just like that. And then our bodies started changing back to normal. Right there, in front of everyone. Total circus. But,' Finley continued, 'there were too many of them for us to handle.' Translation: they got their asses handed to them, though it sounded cooler this way.

'And then, Tessa, well, she was tortured. By Noah. Yep, Noah. That sick bastard.' He shook his head. 'Why is it always someone named Noah? You can't trust a bloke with a biblical name.'

'But she doesn't look hurt,' Nina spoke up, tilting her head to the side like she was in a shampoo commercial.

Finley sighed, long and heavy. 'That's because it wasn't the type of torture that leaves bruises, darling. Got inside her head, messed with her mind, you know... I stopped it—or at least I think I did—but... who knows what it's done to her? She might wake up with her head all mangled or not wake up at all.'

'What?' Nina nearly collapsed.

Then Finley shot to his feet. 'I'll mix some potions,' he announced, heading to his shelves like a wizard on a mission. 'It might help. Might not. But it's better than sitting around doing nothing.'

'Why would Noah do this?' Nina asked.

'Good question,' Finley said. 'But I can't answer. We'll find out if Tessa wakes up and tells us.'

Before he could take his potion kit, Asim spoke up. 'Finley, someone's breaking into the caravans outside.'

'They're demons. Sniffing around for Nina.' Finley glanced out the window. 'And soon, there'll be more. And when they come, it'll be a bloody nightmare.'

His hand ran over his face. 'Right, listen up. You lot need to stop mucking about and actually learn how to use your powers. Properly.'

'Noah already taught us,' Nina said.

Finley shook his head. 'No, darling, he taught you party tricks. Real magic? That's deep.' He tapped his chest. 'It's in here.' Then his temple. 'And here. Takes knowledge. Practice. Work. No shortcuts.'

Asim, quiet up to this point, finally spoke up. 'But I don't have any magic,' he said.

Finley turned to him so fast it might've broken physics. He stared at Asim. 'What kind of bullshit is that? Of course, you've got magic. You're half-angel, half-wizard.'

Asim froze. 'Wait—what?'

Finley sighed. 'Yeah. Your mum, my sister, was a wizard from our world. And your dad, Samir? He's an angel. Serving in Hell, no less. You've got magic in you, lad. You just don't see it yet.'

Asim stood there, stunned, as Finley turned back to his shelves. 'Right then,' he mumbled to himself, 'demons outside, a tortured miss upstairs, and a half-angel wizard who thinks he's got no magic. Bloody perfect day, isn't it?'

Asim hadn't seen that coming. Finley, his uncle? It knocked the wind out of him. But Finley didn't waste time. Asim's powers weren't hidden in books. They never developed because Samir had taken him to Hell when he was just a baby. His powers didn't get lost; they stayed here, in this world. And soon, they'd come to him. No need to search for them. They would find him. It was only a matter of time.

'So, I belonged here the whole time?' Asim's world felt like it had flipped upside down. His whole life, everything he thought he knew, fell apart in front of him. Finley saw the look on his face but didn't hang back. He switched his attention to Nina without missing a pulse.

'I know where another book is. It's with Jonathan. He's holding your book.'

Jonathan wasn't just some old wizard pushed away with his spells. He was dangerous, cruel, and getting that book? It wasn't going to be an easy walk in the park, more like walking through a rainy park in flip-flops, with all the puddles around. But Finley didn't care. He would walk in flip-flops, no matter what.

He said he could teach her how to use the powers she already had for now. Finley explained it to her. She could sense human souls and even freeze time. Nina broke in, saying she could only freeze people around her for a few minutes. But Finley wasn't having it. She had no clue what she was capable of. She just needed to learn how to control it.

'Why can I smell souls? What's that all about?'

Finley didn't answer right away. He stared at her for a second... two... then nodded, like something clicked in his head. 'Right, come with me. I'll show you something.'

He led her down a tight hallway. At the end was a door, old and heavy, like it hadn't been touched in years. When Finley opened it, the room was empty. Just bare walls. *What is this? A joke?* Nina thought to herself.

Finley put his hand into his coat pocket, acting so laid-back it looked like he was about to pull out something usual. Perhaps a tissue, perhaps a crumpled receipt he'd forgotten about weeks ago. No, it was the small bottle he actually pulled out—a vial filled with a liquid that sparkled in exactly the way magic would shimmer if it decided to take a break from being ominous and mysterious and try being a bit unusual for a change.

And then, without any fanfare, he blew its contents into the air, and it rippled like an old television struggling to tune into the right frequency. It was disturbing, but fascinating, and just a little bit annoying. Nina caught a smell she could only describe as old books—dust and leaf, but also something deeper, something not quite definable, something full of silent promise. Then the lights blinked, and the books started to appear. They simply began to form in midair, as if they'd always been there and were just waiting for someone to notice them.

Nina stood motionless, eyes wide, watching as the room came alive around her. Shelves began to grow along the walls with a certain respectable care. Hundreds of books floated gently through the air, sliding into place on the newly formed shelves, each one fitting perfectly, like a puzzle piece falling into place. Somehow, it all felt natural. Not flashy, not overdone, but like this was exactly how things were always meant to be.

Finley, still standing there with his hands in his pockets, gave a small smile. It wasn't smug, exactly, just the sort of smile someone gives when they've done something impressive but don't want to make a big deal out of it.

'Well,' he said, with the tone of someone who's just finished making breakfast, 'a bit of improvisation, but I think it turned out quite well. Has a bit of flair, wouldn't you say?'

Nina looked at him. She wanted to tell him that *flair* was an understatement when describing something that would likely leave even angels and demons a little stunned. But instead, she just smiled. Lovely.

'These,' Finley said, waving a hand like it was nothing, 'are about the Guardians. About you.'

Nina's feet hardly moved as she stepped forward, eyes darting across the walls. Handwritten notes, drawings. *Guardians.* Her heart was banging.

Smelling souls wasn't just a random ability; it was how people were sorted after death, sent to Heaven or Hell. How else would God or the Guardians know who was good or bad? That was the whole point. Her fingers brushed the rough edges of the page as she stared at the drawing of a Guardian. This wasn't some rough story, or the fake ones Noah showed her, it was real. Too real. She was never meant to blend in. This was her purpose.

'But... the Bible, the Qur'an, they say people who sin go to Hell. Isn't that how it works?'

Finley let out a sharp laugh. 'That's the rubbish they want you to believe. It's all smoke and mirrors, made up by the ones down there.' He tapped the floor with his boot. 'There's no rulebook. No list of sins. It's not about what people do. It's about who they are inside.'

He stepped up to the wall, finger poking at a passage. 'People can look clean on the outside, but they're rotten underneath. And you? You see through the act. You feel what's really there. That's why you've got this ability.'

Nina's throat tightened.

'That's why you're here. You're not judging what people do, but their soul. That's why you've got this power. You know who belongs where. Heaven, Hell. It's in your hands.'

But Finley wasn't done. He motioned to the room. 'There's more. A lot more. But not now.'

He turned to the door. 'Samir and Tessa need us. This'll have to wait.'

Chapter Twenty-two
The Three

---⚬---

In a corner of Snahum

NOT FAR FROM THE CARAVAN, Noah choked on the thick, soupy air. He leaned back against his purple throne, looking as if he'd been carved out of granite, eyes colder than a bank manager's handshake. Beneath the calm exterior, anger boiled quietly, waiting. His people moved quickly but carefully, crawling to clean up the mess Finley and Samir had made when they'd freed Tessa. Their footsteps sounded like they knew exactly who was to blame, and they weren't planning on sticking around for a second round. Oh yes, it must have been quite the show—explosions, chaos, maybe a little blood for good measure.

'Oi, you. What's your name?' His stare and tone were a razor, cutting through the trembling man in front of him.

'Charlie, my Lord,' the man stammered, just about able to hold himself together.

Noah leaned forward, his words like poison. 'You're going to find Shad, the demon leader. Tell him I want to make a deal he can't refuse. And Charlie...' He grabbed him by the neck. 'If you mess this up, I'll peel your skin off and eat it while your family watches.'

Charlie's face drained of colour. He nodded like a broken puppet and ran out of the room, heart hammering.

He walked into that messy street, trembling all over and quietly praying to the God who had never answered him. Poor man, he knew Noah all too well and knew what that bastard was capable of. But now it was too late to escape—not when his family was waiting.

When he found Shad, the demon hardly looked at him. Charlie struggled to deliver the message, his voice shivering with fear.

'Whatever he wants, fine. Tell your master I'll meet him at 8 p.m. tomorrow. Now get the hell out of here.'

Charlie rushed back, sweat slick on his skin, practically collapsing at Noah's feet. The tyrant smiled for the first time that night.

But still, his plan had gone to hell, and now someone had to pay for it.

Charlie didn't stand a chance. The man stood there shaking, eyes far-reaching, knowing what was coming. Noah didn't say a word, he didn't need to. His hand shot out, clamping around Charlie's throat like a vice. Charlie's eyes bulged, feet shuffling as he struggled to keep standing.

'I did what you asked,' Charlie choked out. 'I swear.'

Noah's grip tightened, and then he went to work. Slow, mindful. His fingers dug into Charlie's skin, peeling it back like he was unwrapping something. Blood poured, hot and thick, but Noah didn't care.

Charlie's scream ripped through the room, raw and desperate, but it didn't stop Noah.

'I'm hungry... and angry,' Noah growled, leaning in close.

He kept peeling, working faster now. He wasn't punishing Charlie for screwing up, he was letting the rage pour out, and the poor man just happened to be in his way.

Charlie's family went still, eyes wide and wet with tears, too scared to move or make a sound. The disgusting odour of blood thickened in the air. People turned away, unable to handle the sight, the sound, the cruelty.

Noah? He was just getting started.

MEANWHILE, FAR FROM the bloodshed, Jonathan lounged in his palace, totally detached from it all. His cane tapped the floor like a slow trigger being pulled. The bowl in front of him shone, dark liquid rotating until it settled, showing him Noah's sick little world. Blood dripped from Noah's hands. Charlie's scream. Jonathan's lips hooked into a devilish half-smile.

'Bring me a whiskey!' he barked, not even bothering to look at the servant who rushed forward, shaking.

Jonathan sipped it, eyes still locked on the bowl. It was like watching a show, a messed-up one, but oh yes, he enjoyed it. Noah was doing his part, but Jonathan's mind was already miles ahead. He saw the lies, the moves being made. Nina, Tessa, and Asim were all caught in the web. Noah was pulling strings, but Jonathan was the one holding the whole thing together. The only problem was the caravan. Where the hell was it? His grip tightened on the cane, knuckles white as bone. He hated not knowing. That gap chewed at him like a crack in his mind. The poor servants sensed it first, shrinking back as if they could feel the storm growing. He tapped his cane again, harder this time. Being kept in the dark was unacceptable.

Then he remembered Asim at the brothel, the way his eyes had lingered on that redhead. That was when the plan slid into place. Jonathan, ever clever, made sure the woman knew exactly what she had to do. Desperation does wonders for people's willingness to agree to things, and she was broke, drowning in debt. So Jonathan dangled the cash right in front of her nose, offering just enough to make it impossible to refuse. She did not even hesitate. It was perfect. Jonathan knew exactly how to pull Asim's strings. He knew every weakness. His plan was not just smart. It was cruel.

CARAVAN

KNOCK, KNOCK.

Finley, thrown off, opened the door. Standing there was a red-headed woman, her eyes darting, impatient.

'Asim,' she said, breathless. 'I'm looking for Asim.'

Finley played dumb. 'Never heard of him,' he said, starting to close the door.

But she jammed her foot in. 'I know he's here. Just pass on a message, would you? Tell him I'll be waiting for him tonight. Ten o'clock.'

Slowing down, Finley nodded, stepped back, and gave them room as Asim, already behind him, stood there with a smile on. He wasn't expecting this, but he wasn't complaining.

She threw out an invitation, relaxed, like it was no big deal, and Asim, laughing like an idiot, accepted without a second thought.

She slipped him her address. 'Ten o'clock, don't be late.'

Asim buzzed as he shut the door, already thinking about the night ahead. He hardly noticed Finley watching from the corner.

'You sure about this?' Finley asked, tone flat, like he already knew the answer.

Asim just waved him off. But Finley knew, deep down, something was wrong.

Asim didn't give a toss about anything else—not his dad, still unconscious in bed, not even Tessa, cursed and trapped in her mind. He had forgotten it all. The books, Nina, magic, the whole bloody world. The redhead was all he could think about.

Polished up, dressed like a gangster, he didn't bother with goodbyes. He just jumped in his car, engine growling low, music thumping. The address burned in his mind.

Her place wasn't in the nice part of town. No, it was rough. Real rough. As he rolled up, it shocked him. This street was belted. Houses crumbling, rubbish everywhere, rats bold as brass, people hanging about like ghosts. But he had come this far. No turning back now. He stepped out and knocked on the door. A moment passed, then she opened it, standing there like she didn't belong in this dump. All done up. Lovely.

'Where are we going then?' she asked, offhand, like the dirt around them didn't exist.

He shrugged, playing it cool. 'Could just drive. Or grab a bite.'

At the word *food*, her eyes lit up. That was it. Her stomach even let out a growl, sealing the deal. He didn't know the area, but she smirked, already ahead of him.

'I know a place.'

Soon enough, they were pulling up to this elegant spot, completely out of place in the town. Fancy crystal tables, posh chairs, the works. And the weirdest part? No waiters. Just food, already on the table like it had appeared out of nowhere. Piano music drifted through the air, though there was no player in sight. As Asim headed to their table, a sharp scent hit him—women's perfume, strong and overpowering. He tensed.

They talked for ages. Her face lit up as she shared her story of growing up poor, living with her aunt, and just about making ends meet. Finding a job? Impossible in a world where magic had taken over everything. Asim listened, though he was more hooked on her looks than her story.

'Are you a wizard?' she asked.

He shook his head. 'Nah, errm. Just human. Visiting, really. Staying with my uncle.'

Their chat got cut short.

'Oh, hello there. Hope I'm not interrupting. I'm Jonathan, owner of this fine place,' he said, all charm.

Asim exchanged a few polite words, but Jonathan's eyes were locked on something else. Peeking through Asim's slightly loose shirt was the key embedded in his chest.

Jonathan leaned in, voice low. 'That's an angel key. It can unlock gates. Only someone powerful could carry that.'

Asim went still. His mind reeled. What the hell had he gotten into?

Jonathan, still smiling, revealed himself as a wizard. He offered his help, casually throwing in an invitation for Asim to learn more about the key. The name *Jonathan* hit Asim sharply, like he had heard it before. Somewhere. But where? Still, he nodded, agreeing to swing by the next day, playing it cool.

Later, night draped the streets as Asim drove the redhead home. No words, just the hum of the engine and the quiet of the town. She stepped out of the car—no kiss, no *see ya*—just walked. Asim sat there, fingers tapping the steering wheel, a curse slipping through his teeth. *Shit. I forgot to ask her name.* Before he could even wind the window down, she turned around, already on it, like she could read his bloody mind. 'Nicole. Nicole, it's my name,' she said, eyes flicking up. She blinked once, and then she was gone, swallowed by the night, just like that.

Asim pulled away, the streetlights flashing in the mirror as Nicole disappeared from sight. His thoughts drifted, but the smile stayed. Something about her stuck around, like a song he couldn't shake. He still couldn't get her sexy dress out of his head. Or was it the dress? Maybe just her figure? She'd look good even in a pair of wellies, Asim imagined as he sat behind the wheel. But the second he pulled up to the caravan, that smile dropped like a stone.

Finley and Nina sat on the couch, looking like they'd just seen a horror movie where they were the main characters. Pale, haunted, serious in a way that made the whole room feel like it was holding its breath. Asim walked in, tension filling his chest like it knew something he didn't. 'Alright, what's happening?' he asked, even though he wasn't sure he wanted to know. Nina didn't answer, just stared at the floor as if it could tell her what to do.

Finley finally spoke in the type of voice that tells you whatever he's about to say, it's going to hurt. 'I'm sorry, Asim. We did everything we could. Your da...'

Asim didn't need to hear any more. He ran to his father's room, heart pounding. And there he was. Gone. Just gone. Holding his breath as if time had stopped, Asim clenched his fists. Then everything collapsed. A scream tore out of his throat, raw and rough, shaking the whole room. Poor Asim was in shock, unsure whether to go closer, to leave, or just to scream again. But no. Instead, he turned, his eyes red, and headed downstairs. He didn't look to the sides, just grabbed the car keys and slammed the door behind him. Finley and Nina stood there, their faces drained of life, not saying a word. There was nothing left to say.

'Let him go, Nina. He needs his own time,' Finley said softly, taking her hand, his eyes urging her to sit.

'I'm sorry, Finley,' Nina said, staring at the floor. She was trying to ease his pain, knowing Samir was like a brother to him. But emotions weren't easy for her; they never had been. The sadness didn't cut as deep as it should, and she hated that. Carefully, she hid her detachment, hoping no one would notice.

It was impossible to fully understand what this must be like for Asim. Losing someone close was an experience she had never faced. Still, one thing burned clearly in her mind: an ever-growing fear for Tessa. The worry loomed larger now than ever before. Selfishly, she hadn't brought it up with Finley. Samir deserved their focus right now. But the thought stayed. What if something happened to Tessa, just as it had with Samir?

The idea was unbearable, something she couldn't even bring herself to imagine. Quickly, she pushed the thought aside, forcing her mind to something lighter, something safe. Her books. Yes, her books were better. But now, in this situation, it wasn't really working.

MEANWHILE, ASIM WAS drowning in sorrow, his father's death tearing at him. Tears blurred his vision as he sped through the streets, screaming, his voice breaking, and driving wildly. Then, a crash. He hit a wall. Or at least, he thought he did. The car had stopped, and the sound of the engine was gone. He opened his eyes and looked around, confused. Then he glanced at his hands, his legs, and breathed a small sigh of relief when he saw that nothing had happened to him. But how was that possible? No pain, no blood. He was absolutely fine.

'What the hell? How am I still alive?' he shouted.

He got out of the car and looked around. The car? Not a scratch, no sign of an accident. As if it had never happened. He looked up, and the sky above him was dark, streaked with an odd purple shimmer, which only made the situation worse. Was this the afterlife? His heart was racing as he stood there, scratching his head. Nothing made sense—this stank of something strange.

And then he saw Jonathan. Calm as always, just sitting on a bench, tapping his fingers on his cane, whistling, as if this whole thing were perfectly normal and he was just waiting for a bus.

'Bit chilly, isn't it?' Jonathan remarked, then glanced at his expensive black suit, brushing it off as if there were dust or dirt on it. Then, in the same breath, he added softly, 'My condolences.'

He raised his head and ran his hands through his polished hair, the scent of his expensive perfume reaching Asim from afar. Asim just stared at him, more confused than before. Jonathan stood up and walked closer, cane in hand, as though nothing had happened, and started explaining that cars in this world were protected from damage. That gave

Asim some relief, but his thoughts kept circling back to one thing: maybe death would have been easier.

'So, you're alive, no one was hurt, and you're just on another street. The car didn't crash; it vanished and teleported you here,' Jonathan said when he was finally standing right next to Asim.

'Brilliant,' Asim muttered.

'Come on, boy. You look like you need a drink.'

They ducked into a bar nearby, and it was drinks all around. Asim was a wreck, one minute talking like nothing had happened, the next breaking down in tears. The weight of his dad's death was crashing down on him, and Jonathan could see it plain as day.

So, while Asim downed drink after drink, Jonathan stayed sober, pretending to sip along but keeping his mind sharp. When Asim finally gave up for the night, though it was more like passing out than a decision, Jonathan settled the bill, helped him up, and brought him out of the pub. Asim was a mess, completely pissed, hardly knowing his own name or feeling the ground under his feet.

'Aimono loko,' Jonathan said, tapping his cane on the sidewalk twice.

Right on cue, his shiny limousine sped up, almost as if it had come out from the underworld. No driver, no fuss, just the smooth hum of precision machinery. The door opened by itself, standing like a beast ready to attack. Jonathan gently helped Asim into the soft leather seats as the car smoothly sped off toward the palace, moving so fast it could embarrass the devil.

Leaning back, Jonathan let out a soft sigh of relief as he watched Asim pass out, hardly awake. Alcohol had done its job. Asim was just surviving, reeking of booze. Jonathan, though, just smiled. Everything was falling into place. This was going better than he'd hoped, almost insultingly easy.

The limousine stopped gently in front of the palace. Jonathan's servant crept in, whisper-like, a shadow in motion, and with ease lifted Asim as if he were weightless. Jonathan followed, a dodgy smile playing on his lips, watching as the servant carefully carried Asim and placed him in the "ready" room with the same caution as sheathing a sharp blade—still deadly and dangerous, but temporarily at rest.

Chapter Twenty-three
Is She Real?

'IS IT MORNING ALREADY?'

But just as Nina let herself sink back into the pillow, something ran into her. A smell, somewhat faint but sharp, like white roses, except these white roses had their own scent, a scent Nina knew well. Her heart was racing. She opened her eyes and ran downstairs, and yes, her nose hadn't deceived her. She saw it.

Tessa, dancing around with a plate in her hand, singing out, 'Do you feel it? Oh yeah, I can feel it, baby, feel it!'

Nina stood there with her mouth open. And then she just started screaming. 'Oh my God, you're awake!'

Tessa screamed too when she saw Nina and rushed in for a hug, tight, like she'd been waiting forever. Nina stopped worrying and felt filled with hope.

'I can't believe it! You can finally see me!' Tessa's voice was shaky. 'I thought I was going to lose my mind all alone here.' She clung to Nina, who pulled back, confused.

'We've been here with you the whole time,' Nina said.

Tessa's eyes sparkled, almost teary. 'Oh, I know. But before, you didn't see me. I've been here the whole time, you just couldn't...'

Nina, still unsure what was happening, tried to play it cool. 'It's okay, you just need some rest.'

'Rest? No way! Let's have a drink!'

Behind them, Finley held his potions like they were the only thing keeping him upright. His eyes were wide, mouth hanging open as he stared at Nina, wondering if she'd lost her mind. He asked gently if she was alright, trying not to sound too alarmed, but Nina, riding high on joy, waved him off and insisted she was fine. Tessa was awake.

Finley wanted to sit down and talk it through, but Nina wasn't having any of it. She waved him off again as Tessa disappeared to grab the glasses. Finley then moved in close, his eyes dead serious, his hands gripping Nina's shoulders. He told her that Tessa was still out cold upstairs.

Nina shook her head like he was mad. She had just spoken to Tessa, who was wide awake. She avoided Finley's eyes, looking around like she was searching for something. Tessa walked back in, two glasses in hand, smiling like she owned the place. At first, Finley didn't sit. He just stared at Nina, then slowly moved to the sofa, eyes still locked on her.

Tessa slid in next to him, too close, throwing easy-going compliments his way. But it wasn't funny, not this time. Finley felt a strange, disturbed wriggle in his stomach. Nina stood there, frowning, her eyes shooting between them. She snapped at Tessa to pour her a whiskey, like she was trying to keep control of something slipping away.

Finley forced a smile, keeping his tone light, telling Nina that she was imagining things. Tessa wasn't here. Nina pointed sharply at the sofa, her voice tense as she insisted Tessa was sitting right next to him, looking like she was ready to eat him alive. Finley swallowed hard, leaned in, and lowered his voice, telling Nina to look around.

There was no one else here. Just them. But Nina couldn't accept it. She walked upstairs to Tessa's bedroom. And there she was. Tessa, stretched out, dead to the world.

Nina went still. This couldn't be real. Finley stood behind her, arms folded. He had told her all along—Tessa was still unconscious.

Tessa chimed in, winding her up. Nina spun, heat shooting up her neck.

'Oh, for hell's sake,' she muttered and stormed outside. The sun smacked her, but it didn't help.

Tessa followed, smiling, loving every second of it. Nina paced, her boots kicking up dust. She could see Tessa, plain as day, but Finley couldn't. And what was with Tessa lying there, passed out upstairs?

Tessa shrugged, still relaxed. 'No idea, but I've been bored stiff. Like a ghost wandering about, no one to talk to.'

Nina stopped mid-step, her fists tightening. 'Ghost? Seriously?'

Tessa just shrugged again, like it was all a laugh. 'Maybe. Who knows?' She leaned in, grinning. 'I've been here the whole time, listening, walking around, even saw Samir when he died.'

Nina narrowed her eyes, slowly starting to believe.

'I even clocked Finley's red boxers today!' Tessa added with a smirk.

Nina burst into laughter, doubling over. 'Oh my God, it really is you! This can't just be in my head.' She grabbed Tessa and pulled her into a tight hug.

'I missed you, Tessa. It's been hell without you.'

Tessa's face lit up, her smile wide. For a second, it felt like the old days—easy, like nothing had changed.

'I was scared at first,' Tessa said, 'but you know what? Being invisible had its perks. Though...' She wiggled her eyebrows, chuckling. 'Watching Finley naked gets old fast.'

They both laughed, the tension finally melting away. Tessa pulled Nina in again. 'Oh my God, I missed you,' she whispered, a warmth in her voice that hadn't been there before. Nina felt a weight lifting off her chest. The tight knot inside her loosened, and for the first time in ages, things felt right again.

Nina walked back inside, head high, and told Finley straight up, 'I'm not mad. I can see Tessa.'

'Yeah? Well, what else can you see, then?'

'You're wearing red boxers.'

Finley went still, eyes widening. 'Err, that's not cool, Nina. Staring at me while I'm getting dressed? Didn't think you had it in you.'

She rolled her eyes. 'It wasn't me. Tessa's been watching you, even in the shower.'

Finley snorted, waving her off. 'This is bullshit. I'm calling the healer.'

Just as he reached for the phone, Tessa leaned in, smiling, and whispered to Nina. 'Tell him... Zara was here.'

Nina threw it out there, casual. 'Zara was here.'

Finley stopped dead, his face draining. His eyes sparkled with something Nina hadn't seen before. 'What does she want?' he asked quietly.

Tessa wasn't done. She leaned in again. 'She's been coming a lot, loves him, regrets not having kids.'

Nina repeated, 'She's been coming around a lot. Still loves you. She's sorry you never had kids.' Finley's tough front crumbled. Tears welled up, his breath shaky. He couldn't speak, just stood there, letting it crush him.

Nina relayed Zara's message. 'She wants you to be happy, move on, forget about her. She's stuck here... and when the gates open, she's heading to hell.'

Finley's eyes pinched. 'Hell? Why hell?'

Tessa leaned in close to Nina. 'Tell him. Zara was cheating, and she wasn't the best soul as he thought.'

Nina sighed at Finley, feeling that knot in her stomach tighten. Could she even tell him? Finley clocked it immediately, asking what could possibly hurt him so badly.

She swallowed hard and, finally, let it out: Zara had been cheating.

For a second, Finley froze, gripping the chair like it was keeping him upright. But then... he just nodded. He already knew. Well, that threw Nina off her stride. She hadn't expected that. But Finley just swept it aside like it was yesterday's news and shifted back to Tessa.

Then came the question: how could Nina, in fact, see her? Relief hit Nina like a warm cuppa after a long day. He believed her. He said he'd known about her little magic power but couldn't work out how she could see Tessa without finding her book, the one that actually contained her abilities. That gave Nina pause.

And then the lightbulb moment hit—oh, right. The pills. She'd been on them since she was a kid, sometimes skipping a day, but never for this long. Finley's eyes widened as the penny dropped. Her power had never actually been taken away, just buried under all those years of meds. He trailed off, stunned.

Nina straightened up, remembering the dream she'd had about Samir, where he'd told her she could talk to the dead. Though, to be fair, she wasn't sure if it had been a dream or... something else. Finley, still piecing things together, said it had been a dream but admitted she really had spoken to Samir. The pills were the problem, or rather, the lack of them wasn't.

Finley's hands stilled, his brain doing that one plus one equals oh crap thing. He leaned in quietly, asking what else Samir had said. Nina thought back—Samir had mentioned someone stealing a book and a key, slipping through the library gate. And then Finley froze again, his brow furrowing like he'd just stepped on a big, juicy uh-oh.

Before he could even react, Tessa piped up, whining that they were boring her half to death (if that was even possible) and claiming she was already tipsy. Finley leaned closer, whispering like he was passing national secrets, asking what Tessa was saying. Nina gave him the look. No need to whisper. Tessa could hear just fine. Finley nodded like he'd known that all along, then coolly mentioned he'd met someone who could talk to the dead before.

Tessa, clearly not thrilled, snapped that she wasn't dead. Nina corrected her quickly, and Finley smirked, apologising to the empty air where Tessa sat. Oh, she was pleased. Teased him nonstop and even gave him a kiss on the lips. He, of course, had no clue. Nina just looked away, hiding her smile behind her hand. Then came the obvious question: why wasn't Tessa dead but still acting like a ghost? Finley explained that being unconscious probably had something to do with it. Typical in-between limbo rubbish. But he added he knew someone who could help, and Nina didn't even hesitate before agreeing.

Meanwhile, Tessa took another swig of whiskey, because why not? Nina raised an eyebrow, thinking the same thing anyone would: how the hell could a ghost get drunk? Tessa just chuckled, saying she could still feel things, yes, even needing to pee sometimes. Nina relayed the message, and Finley laughed. Honestly, at this point, nothing made sense anymore, but at least they were all in the same ridiculous boat.

MEANWHILE, FAR AWAY from the caravan, Asim was awake, sitting across from Jonathan in his palace. He thanked him for the room last night; Jonathan had been unusually kind. Asim glanced around, taking in the place. Jonathan's palace gleamed, every corner dripping in luxury, the sort of place you'd only see in films.

'I wish I could live like this one day,' Asim said.

'You're closer than you think,' Jonathan replied, reminding Asim of the money his father had left him.

Asim nodded, knowing about it. 'Still not enough for all this.'

Jonathan let out a laugh. 'Life could be easier for you, Asim.'

Asim frowned, not getting it.

Jonathan leaned back, calm. 'You're a proper wizard. Your dad was an angel. Your mum, a wizard by blood.'

Asim stared at the floor, muttering, 'Doesn't feel that way. No powers, no magic.'

Jonathan watched him for a second, then said, 'The powers are there. You just need to wake them up.'

Asim mentioned how Finley had told him his powers would show up on their own.

Jonathan snorted, brushing that off like rubbish. 'Probably just something Finley said to keep you down.'

But Asim wasn't having it. 'Finley isn't a liar.'

Jonathan's smirk hung around, hinting that Asim would see the truth soon enough. He offered him a deal—stay, and he'd show him how to unlock his powers, teach him real magic. Asim liked the sound of it but shook his head. He had to bury his dad first. Give him a proper send-off. Jonathan didn't shy away, saying he'd help. He knew Samir well and wanted to be there. Asim felt the pressure in his chest ease a bit. Jonathan had a way of making things seem possible.

MEANWHILE, FAR FROM the caravan and far from Jonathan's palace, Shad and Noah sat down for lunch in a vast hall, servants watching quietly from a distance.

'What's the plan?' Shad muttered, his mouth full of chicken.

Noah shot him a look of disgust but said nothing. He still needed him.

They were planning an attack on the caravan, but Shad shook his head. 'The caravan's protected by a spell,' he said, spitting bits of meat. 'Can't get inside.'

Noah leaned back, thinking it through while Shad tore into the chicken like he hadn't eaten in days. Noah suggested they find a hidden spot nearby, wait it out, and attack once the caravan moved.

Shad let out a loud laugh, wiped his mouth, and leaned in, suddenly serious.

'I thought you were clever, but you're a proper joke.'

Noah didn't like the jab, but yes, he knew the plan wasn't perfect.

Shad's smile became sneaky. 'Jonathan. That's our plan. Let's stick with him.'

'I tried that. I failed him. Not sure it's a good idea now.'

'Don't care. There's no other choice.' He sat back and looked at Noah. 'How'd you work with him anyway?'

Noah's jaw tightened, clearly hating the mention of old failures.

Jonathan had given him magic, a palace, everything he needed. They'd trapped Nina, Tessa, and Asim, but it had all gone sideways. The magic hadn't lasted long, and he'd been forced to rush, managing only to grab Tessa. Jonathan hadn't been happy about it and hadn't returned since.

Noah figured that was a sign Jonathan had finally let it go.

'Like I said, you're a proper joke,' Shad sneered.

Chapter Twenty-four
Grandma

'WHAT DID NOAH DO TO you?' Nina asked while looking straight at Tessa as they sat in the garden. She didn't want to be too intense but needed an answer.

Tessa's face grew tense, and a hint of something troubling flashed through her. 'He did what I deserved,' she said quietly, keeping her eyes on the ground. Her hands drummed as if grasping something beyond just words. 'Probably deserved worse.'

Nina, confused, stayed quiet as Tessa's voice broke. 'I caused the death of our child while we were in this world.'

Nina didn't say a word, watching as tears spilled down Tessa's face.

'He was my husband, Nina. Can you believe it? That cunt,' Tessa sobbed, wiping at her cheeks. 'I was one of those snake-like humans.'

The words came out broken, heavy. 'I sacrificed my own child to gain his power,' she whispered, tears slipping onto her lips. 'But once I absorbed it, it killed me. I ended up in Hell.'

Nina peered down, speaking softly to the grass. 'It's all in the past, Tessa. You've been through a lot. You've changed, and I can smell the good in you.'

'Hm. Noah haunted me. In my thoughts. It felt real, like living those moments over and over.'

'I'm really sorry.'

'I've been wondering why you all bothered to rescue me.'

Nina reached out, trying to comfort her, but Tessa pushed on, revealing more. 'Noah tricked us all. Even the market, it was a setup, just to get our trust.'

She turned back to Nina, her voice hardening. 'That bastard is coming back for me.'

Then Nina jumped, crushing a flower underfoot as a woman in a purple dress and a sunhat appeared out of nowhere, waving her hands like she was swatting invisible flies.

'Ugh, I hate traveling. Can't you see me? Go get Finley, now. Shoo, shoo,' she snapped at Nina, her voice properly irritated.

Before Nina could say a word, Finley rushed in, breathless. 'Grandma! How many times have I told you to use the door?'

The old lady kept waving her hands around, her gestures lively, like her words needed more room to come alive. Then she gave Finley's cheek a pinch. 'Oh, you're still my little cutie pie. Missed you.'

Nina just stared, trying to smile, but it didn't quite stick. Finley and his grandma hugged.

'Um, sorry, Grandma. This is Nina, my close friend. She's staying in the guest room.'

Grandma looked Nina up and down. 'Oh, well, I thought you had better taste, my cutie pie.'

Finley winced, turning to Nina. 'Sorry about that.'

But Nina waved it off.

As Finley followed his grandma inside, Nina glanced around, looking for Tessa. After a moment, she spotted her by the purple tree, flirting with some bloke.

Nina shook her head, smiling to herself. 'Gosh. What a woman. Even as a ghost, she's still at it.'

She stepped back, giving Finley and his grandma some room. Just then, a knock at the door.

Asim.

'Oh my God, you're back! What took you so long?'

Asim smiled. 'Hello to you too, Nina,' he said, throwing her a playful look.

They made their way to the living room when Grandma chimed in, eyes gleaming. 'Hmm. What a handsome young boy,' she said, winking at Asim.

Finley's face contorted in shock. 'Grandma! He's Samir's son! You're his great-grandmother!'

Grandma went still. A bead of sweat rolled down her temple. Then she moved fast, hugging Asim tight. But oh, he didn't mind.

'You look just like your mother,' she whispered, her voice shaky, fighting back tears.

Asim stood there, hit with a strange mix of emotions—anger for not knowing her, but warmth in the moment.

'I need to head upstairs and get changed,' he said, slipping out.

Nina followed him, asking, 'Have you made any arrangements for the funeral?'

'Yeah. I'll take care of everything. That's why I came.'

Nina was relieved. Finally, he was stepping up.

As Asim opened the door to his room, Nina walked past him toward hers. 'He's just downstairs with his grandma,' she said, smiling at the wall. 'No problem.'

Nina smiled again, like she was talking to someone invisible, and reached for her door.

Asim stared. 'What was that? What's wrong with you?'

Nina, still confused, pointed to the stairs. 'He just wanted to know where Finley was.'

Asim stepped closer. 'Said who? There's no one here. You were talking to thin air, like a madwoman!'

'Oh my God, it was a ghost. I thought he was human.'

Nina revealed that she could now see Tessa, who was outside, flirting with another ghost.

'What? She's a ghost? Why is this happening? And wait... flirting? What the hell?' He felt like the world had moved on without him.

Nina shrugged, telling him he'd just been out of the loop. 'Go get changed,' she said, brushing him aside.

Asim went inside his room, slamming the door. Typical. Nina stood there for a moment, wondering when he'd finally grow up. But her thoughts quickly shifted back to the ghost's strange question about Finley. Something wasn't sitting right. Heading downstairs, her face stretched. There, in front of her, Grandma was deep in conversation with the ghost.

But Finley explained that Grandma was the one he'd been talking about. She had the ability to interact with spirits.

MEANWHILE, SHAD AND Noah pulled up to Jonathan's palace in their limo. Jonathan welcomed them, but they could feel the fake warmth. They stayed on edge. Shad felt nervous, a bit scared, knowing who Jonathan really was, while Noah sat back, confident, proud.

'Nice place,' Shad muttered with a trembling voice as Jonathan gave him a cold, suspicious look. Jonathan didn't respond, just sipped his wine, leaving the two of them sitting there, waiting for something, anything, to be offered.

Noah spoke confidently, 'We're gathered here to stand together against the angel, a powerful enemy. We all know how important she is to you and...'

'Oh, shut the hell up!' Jonathan said, and with a flip of his cane, Noah's tongue was torn clean from his mouth. Searing pain ripped through him. He tried to scream, but nothing came out. His hands shot to his mouth, blood pouring between his fingers.

Jonathan slowly got to his feet, a derisive look shining in his eyes. 'Are you pissed? How dare you speak to me like that, you little shit. Don't you know who I am?'

He flicked the cane again, restoring Noah's tongue. Noah's hand shook as he touched it, still trembling with fear.

'Now, explain why you're here,' Jonathan hissed, pacing the room, his expensive shoes clicking against the floor, each step louder than the last. 'You've already messed everything up. I told you what to do, and you took Tessa? Now you come crawling back to me like nothing happened?'

Sweat pooled on Noah's forehead as he fumbled for the right words. Before he could spit anything out, Shad dropped to his knees in front of Jonathan.

'Forgive us, my Lord. We're here to ask for your help and offer whatever you need,' Shad said, bowing his head.

Jonathan smiled, slow and satisfied, taking another sip of his wine. 'Hmm. I like your demon friend, Noah. Smart. You should take notes and thank him—he just saved your life.'

Noah could only nod, fear gripping his chest.

'Killing her won't do anything,' Jonathan continued, cool and collected. 'She'll just be reborn in hell. Endless cycle. We need to trap her soul.'

He turned to Noah, eyes cold. 'As for your Tessa? I don't care about her.'

With a twist of his cane, Noah was gone. Jonathan chuckled. Noah had been sent home. Shad was alone. Shad looked scared as hell. Jonathan leaned forward, eyes narrowing. 'Do you understand the situation? If you want my help, you need to be completely loyal.'

Shad nodded again, firmer this time. 'I'm aware. You have my loyalty.'

'I need her alive.'

His voice dropped lower. 'I'm offering you wealth, immortality, eternal life in this world.'

Shad's eyes agreed.

'We need Asim on our side. Get close to him. Be his best friend. Show him the best this world has to offer.'

Shad nodded again. He understood what needed to be done.

'Now go,' Jonathan ordered.

BACK IN THE CARAVAN

ASIM LEFT WITHOUT A word, neglecting his duties to arrange his father's funeral. Nina fumed, but Finley stepped in, telling her to give him space. He promised to handle the arrangements himself.

While Grandma spoke to the ghost, Nina and Finley sat down for dinner, with Tessa beside her. The magical table did its usual— a lavish feast appearing before them. Nina pointed at the glasses, filling them instantly. Everyone went still, stunned, except Grandma.

'Really? A kid can do this?' Grandma thought, eyes narrowing.

Finley leaned in, explaining Nina had only recently learned it but was already skilled. Grandma waved it off. But something else caught her interest. Nina's ability to see ghosts. That was rare. Too rare. Grandma had only known one other person with that gift, a long time ago. Since then, she'd believed she was the only one left.

'Finley told me you can see this woman who probably hasn't eaten in ages,' Grandma said, pointing at Tessa, who was too busy devouring chicken to notice.

'Tessa's unconscious upstairs. How can she be a ghost if she's still alive?' Nina asked.

'Every person in a coma walks in their soul. They stay close to their bodies, but if they drift too far, they die. Lucky for Tessa, she's stayed close,' Grandma said.

Tessa grinned, still tearing through her food. Oh, but she was listening.

'What I'm more curious about,' Grandma continued, her gaze landing on Nina with a hint of pity, 'is how someone like you can see ghosts.'

When Finley dropped the bomb that Nina was a Guardian of Hell Earth, Grandma's whole appearance changed. Her eyes widened, and she leaned in with a respectful apology.

Nina gave her a nod, taking it in. Getting respect from Grandma? That was something.

'Yeah, and she's my best mate,' Tessa threw in, bits of food flying as she spoke.

Grandma smiled, but she lobbed Finley a look. Then she hissed, 'Why didn't you tell me this, you idiot?'

Then, just as fast, she smiled sweetly at them both like nothing had happened.

Finley lurked, eavesdropping on Nina and Grandma's chat, catching every word. Grandma then threw a look at Finley. 'I'll be sticking around for a few days, teaching her everything she needs to know. And more.'

Feeling a bit worn out, she then stood up, waving a servant over. 'Oi, you. Take my bags to the room.'

The servant looked around. There were no bags. He started shaking his hands. 'Bzzzzz, bzzzzz,' completely lost.

'Oh, silly me!' Grandma chuckled. She vanished for a second.

Reappearing in a flash, she stood there, arms full of eight pink cases. The servant's face dropped. Her room was on the second floor. Grandma just grinned, beaming, and whipped off her hat like she was ready for a holiday.

'What the heck? How old are you?' Tessa blurted, looking like she'd just seen something out of a nightmare. Nina just raised an eyebrow, scratching her head.

'What? Not used to a little magic around here?' Grandma shot back, grinning like she was holding all the cards.

Finley, clueless, took a gander around. He hadn't heard Tessa say a word. Grandma leaned over. 'She's asking about my age,' she said to Finley.

'Oh, right,' he muttered, glancing at the empty chair where Tessa was supposedly sitting. 'Magic hat keeps her young. Potions keep her ticking,' he added, his energy drained. Without another word, he trudged upstairs.

Nina, still buzzing, was itching to dive deeper into magic. She had a real knack for it. The spark was back, especially with Tessa at her side again. The possibilities? Endless.

Tessa leaned over to Nina, whispering, 'She looks hundreds of years old, but I thought she was younger than me.'

From upstairs, Grandma's voice boomed, 'I can hear you, Tessa!'

Tessa whispered again, 'Does she have magic ears too?'

They both exploded with laughter as they headed off to Finley's magical workshop, where Nina was busy soaking up everything she could about potions and spells.

As they sat down, Nina leaned in closer, dead serious, and asked Finley about thunder and rain. She mentioned this gentleman, Alfie, a really strange fellow from the library. It was as if he was somehow connected to the rain, as if he was part of it. She figured he might be from their world. It was even possible that he himself was Death. Nina approached it slowly but surely, not wanting to reveal what had happened in the library or how they had found that painting of Death himself, waiting for Finley to speak up first.

But he only frowned, looking a bit confused. He didn't say much, got up, shuffled over to the cabinet, and pulled out an old, thick book.

'I think I know something,' he said, flipping through the pages, but he wasn't sure. The book was full of things about controlling the weather, about how to manipulate it, but nothing about someone being connected to it like Alfie. And Death doesn't have a name, nor had Finley ever met it personally, so he didn't know much about it.

Finley pinned down his eyes at the pages and rubbed his temples. He was one hundred fifty years old, very old, and his memory wasn't as good as it once was. At the same time, Tessa kept a close eye on him, staring at him closely.

'He's lying. He knows,' Tessa said.

Nina smirked but kept her cool, pretending she hadn't heard a thing. She tried again, mentioning that Alfie was actually a pretty decent guy, hoping to get more out of Finley. But he changed, visibly uncomfortable, mumbled something about an early morning, and slipped out before she could push him further.

Tessa narrowed her eyes as he left. 'I told you. You can't trust him,' she whispered to Nina.

'Calm down. His soul is yellow, pure.'

'That's the same shit you said about Noah, remember?'

'Yes, you're right.'

'These bastards use some kind of potion so you can't sense their real souls. They're scum, all of them.'

'Hmmm,' said Nina.

Chapter Twenty-five
Finley's Choice

FINLEY STOOD AT THE edge of a spindly garden path, where the breeze boldly shook the bushes like an overly eager cheerleader. This was their spot, his and his wife's. A place where they'd walk at sunset, hands held, talking about everything and nothing. He tried to hear her laugh, that light, free sound that used to fill this place, but all he got was the rustle of leaves and the reminder that he was now quiet, pathetically alone.

He tightened his hands into fists. The loss wasn't graceful; it was harsh, eating away at him all the time. And the words— *She'll go to Hell*— had been doing laps in his mind like a bad pop song he couldn't shake.

'Really, mate? You'd give up anything for her?' came a voice, calm and nearly too calm, like someone asking if he'd prefer tea or coffee.

Finley turned, half-expecting to see some nosy gardener. But there stood a man, looking... ordinary. Boringly so. Simple coat, windswept hair, and a face that said he was probably that guy who always gets in front of you in the queue and orders the most complicated coffee ever. But his eyes, no, those didn't fit. Way too old, way too knowing, like they'd seen too many centuries and kept all the receipts.

'Who the hell are you?' Finley snapped, his temper already frayed.

The man's mouth twitched into a smile. 'Just someone who can't help but notice a guy in pain. And wow, you've got it bad. That heart of yours? Weighs more than the stones around us. You're looking for answers, aren't you? Maybe a miracle or two?'

Finley's skin prickled, but this guy carried on, like he was narrating a sad documentary.

'She's waiting, isn't she? Lost, stuck in this world, and heading straight for a one-way trip to Hell. Bit harsh, don't you think?'

Finley's mouth went dry. 'Why... why do you care?'

The man shrugged, like it was a stupid question. 'I'm a sucker for lost causes, I guess. Second chances are sort of my thing. But...' He lifted a finger, as if this part was important. 'Every gift comes with a catch.'

Then he looked around and pointed to the bench, which was now glowing. They sat down.

'The question is, what would you sacrifice to save her?'

Finley felt a knot in his stomach. This garden, once so beautiful and sacred, suddenly became cold and off.

'A... a catch?' he repeated, sounding like an idiot even to himself.

The man moved closer. Too close. That worrying kind of movement, like his feet didn't quite touch the ground.

'Yes, a price,' he said, his smile growing just a bit too wide. 'Souls aren't cheap, you know. But lucky for you, I'm open to trades.'

Images of Nina, Tessa, and Asim flooded Finley's mind. They were his people, his team, the ones he'd sworn to protect. But the thought of his wife— her laughter, her tears— God, the need to save her clawed at him, desperate and brutal.

'What are you saying?' he choked out.

The man leaned in, voice dropping to a conspiratorial whisper.

'Three souls for one. Your wife gets a golden ticket to Heaven, and I take the three keeping you company these days. Simple.'

Finley's breath caught, pain wrapping around his ribs. He knew exactly who the man meant. Nina, Tessa, Asim. The very people who trusted him. And yet, the vision of his wife's face, the way she used to light up his world... it tore him apart.

'That's madness,' he whispered, hating the way his voice wavered. 'I can't... I can't do that.'

The man raised an eyebrow, his gaze sharpening.

'Can't do it, eh? Funny, considering one of them is the reason your wife is headed for Hell in the first place.'

He paused, letting the words sink in.

'Don't tell me you've forgotten what Nina really is. Well, her job is to make sure lost souls, like your wife, stay right where they're meant to be.'

Finley's heart skipped a beat.

'So why, exactly, are you protecting her? Why side with someone who's basically a walking, talking lock on the gates of Hell? Think about that, mate.'

Finley stood there, feeling like he'd been kicked in the chest. His mind was a storm, a mess of guilt and grief and impossible choices. He couldn't breathe, couldn't think. But the ache of losing his wife forever... that might just kill him.

Chapter Twenty-six
Many Names

THE FUNERAL ARRANGEMENTS, Asim's job, now fell straight on him. No excuses, no delays. He'd take care of it. Finley had the misfortune of running into Asim at the bank. The tension hit instantly, like accidentally walking into your ex at a wedding. Asim's whole vibe screamed defensive, the kind of look you give when someone asks if you've paid your overdue bills and, well, you definitely haven't.

Finley went through the motions, explaining he needed money for the funeral, making sure to mention he was handling everything. All very proper, all very civil, except it felt about as comfortable as wearing wet socks. Something was clearly off and Finley felt it deep in his gut, like the uneasy feeling you get when you realise you've walked into a room full of people you owe money to. He took a cautious step back, not wanting to set Asim off any more than he already was, and leaned in, trying for a whisper that said, *I'm totally calm,* but sounded more like, *please don't punch me.*

He asked if Asim even knew how to withdraw the money, as if it required a secret handshake or elite training. Asim's reply shot out loud and cutting, making half the bank turn to look. Finley felt the judgemental stares burn into him, like he'd just yelled "free drinks" at a pub and then admitted he'd made it up. The heat of all that unwanted attention made him decide retreating was the best option. Yep, time to back off before this little fiasco turned into a full-blown spectacle.

Then Finley saw her, the redhead making a beeline for Asim. His gut twisted; she had that unmistakable look of someone who knew exactly how to charm a wallet out of a gentleman's pocket. But with Asim already wound tighter than a cheap watch, Finley wisely kept his mouth shut. He adjusted his rumpled travel clothes and slipped away, trying to be as inconspicuous as a giraffe at a tea party.

Nicole sidled up to Asim, sliding into his space just close enough to make his pulse pick up. She leaned in, whispered something with just the right amount of mystery to hook him, then pulled back, leaving him wanting more. She knew the game—dangle the bait, keep it just out of reach, and watch them chase. And Asim? Poor thing didn't stand a chance; he was already starting to fall for it.

'Next, please,' called the voice from the desk, sounding fully uninterested. Asim stepped up and told the hairy gentleman he needed to withdraw a large sum. The man handed over a small silver box, looking like it held some sort of secret, and waited.

Asim gave the box a quick blow and passed it back. The hairy man nodded, pulled out a large key from inside, and with a sound of effort, said, 'Follow me,' leading them down the hall, stone-faced and silent, like he was guarding the Queen's jewels.

They arrived at a door with no handle, just a threatening piece of metal. Asim blew on the key, and the door unlocked with a soft click, swinging open like it had secrets it didn't want to share. Inside, the floor was a flat, uninspired grey, lined with floating handles that whisked them along at a pace that felt somewhere between magical and mildly upsetting.

When they arrived at the destination, only Asim was allowed to step through. Nicole tried to follow, but the hairy man stepped in front of her, blocking her like a bouncer who'd just recognised a fake ID. Asim offered him some coins, and with a nod of approval, the man let her through. Once inside, the room was small but packed with gold. Asim pulled out his special wallet, known as a wallet-spacer, which could hold as much money as needed. Nicole tried to play it cool, but her surprise was obvious.

Asim gave her a wink. 'Don't worry, we've got more than enough.'

As they left the main entrance, Nicole asked, 'Why did you have to breathe into the box?'

Asim explained it was his identification, surprised she didn't know. Nicole shrugged, saying only the rich had accounts at that bank. Her family had always been poor, so she'd never been inside one before. Asim pulled her into a tight hug, giving a soft kiss on her neck.

'Don't worry, I'll look after you,' he whispered, like a fool.

AT THE SAME TIME, BACK at the caravan, Finley showed up with news about Asim. He laid it out for Nina, who glanced over at Grandma.

'As long as he's sorting the funeral, we're fine,' Grandma said, coffee in hand, before walking out to the garden.

Nina turned to Finley and asked when they would start looking for the books. He told her it would be after the funeral, and she nodded, looking mildly satisfied, like someone who had just been promised cake but had to wait until after the speeches to eat it. Sensing the need to brighten the mood, Finley suggested she get out for a bit and even offered to show her around. Nina, always a touch cautious, asked if it was safe. Finley shrugged, like safety was just a suggestion, and pulled out a potion.

'This will disguise you,' he said.

Nina drank it all in one go, but she did not feel any difference.

'You won't notice anything, but trust me,' he added, with the confidence of someone who had tested it on his mates and probably laughed at the results.

To everyone else, she now had blonde hair and looked like a completely different person. But to herself? Nothing had changed. Finley also drank a shot of the potion. His looks changed a bit, and now he appeared as a red-haired boy, but he still felt like the same person inside.

'Ready?' he asked, offering her his arm with a grin that suggested this was about to get interesting.

AT THE SAME TIME, ON the other side of town, Shad was working on a plan, but it was not something you would proudly share during a family dinner. The street he had picked was not a place you would take your gran unless she had a secret taste for a bit of danger. Even the lighting looked like it had enough and was ready to call it a day. It smelled like old beer and broken dreams.

Shad gathered his lot, a bunch of lads who looked like they had forgotten what the word "hope" even meant and made his way to a dirty side street where a group of teenagers hung about. You know the type: all bravado on the outside but with that impression in their eyes that said they never really stood a chance. Shad introduced himself, and the boys laughed at first because what else do you do when some guy waltzes in acting like he is the main character? People laughed at first but quickly stopped when he said he was a demon looking for a body. The joke stopped being funny all of a sudden.

But demons had been around for a long time. The kids knew how it worked, but none of them wanted to die for a few coins. Well, maybe one of them did. A blonde lad stepped forward, eyes weary like he had seen more than his fair share. He did not look scared. Just... resigned. Like someone who had long given up on surprises.

Shad offered a pile of coins, enough to mean something in a neighbourhood like this. As he did, he felt a blink of something unusual, like the boy's soul was not as simple or breakable as the others he had taken. But Shad shrugged it off; he had bigger concerns. The boy agreed, but not for himself. No, he was not looking for pleasure or a hero badge.

He did it for his mum, who was probably inside their dingy flat right now, lost in an addiction that had her tighter than a miser's grip on his last fiver. The coins might give her a fleeting smile, a temporary break from the endless cycle, and sometimes, that had to be enough. Because life is not fair, and sometimes, the best you can hope for is a momentary illusion that things are not completely messed up.

He slipped the money into her hand, and she hardly noticed. Her eyes were glassy, staring off into some distant universe, probably one where bills did not exist and happiness came in bottles. The boy sighed, the kind of sigh that said, *Bloody hell, life, you're relentless,* and dragged himself back outside. His steps were slow, heavy, like he had just been told he had to redo Year 11 maths, but his resolve stayed solid. He was doing it for her, even if she would never clock the cost. And yes, the world was a cruel bastard, was it not? Some mums spoiled their sons and got nothing but teenage trouble in return, while others, like his, had sons who would sacrifice everything for a scrap of love that never quite came back their way.

Before Shad made his move, the boy closed his eyes, whispering softly, 'Love you, Mum,' as if clinging to that last bit of humanity.

Shad hesitated for a fraction of a second, almost like the boy's defiant love left a bitter aftertaste. But he swept it aside. *Get on with it,* he told himself.

He stepped up, placed a hand on the boy's shoulder, and his mouth opened. Black, shadowy smoke poured out, streaming into the lad's body. It should have been smooth, like slipping into a well-worn coat. Instead, it felt awkward, like squeezing into a pair of jeans that were two sizes too small. The boy's soul refused to move, holding on stubbornly like an unwelcome guest who would not leave.

Shad felt a spike of irritation, seriously, what was with this kid? But he did not have time to settle on it. He had bigger fish to fry. Straightening up in his new body, he felt the power and energy of youth, clearing aside the boy's memories. A few sentimental moments tried to break through, happy moments, painful ones, but Shad shoved them down. He had a job to do, and Jonathan would not wait.

With this new body, he felt strong and ready, and he set off down the street, prepared to kick his plan into motion, no matter the cost.

NINA AND FINLEY WALKED toward the park. Ah, fresh air. Birds chirping, a light breeze, basically the sort of day you'd find on the cover of a wellness magazine. Finley's face tensed, though, when he snuck a look at his watch. A message flashed up, and he tried to play it cool. *Chill vibes only,* he thought, but it didn't quite work.

'Go on ahead,' he said, in a tone that was *trying* to sound calm but came out more like he was hiding a body in the trunk. 'I'll catch up.'

Nina wandered through the park, blending in like a proper civilian while quietly watching the world go by. People in odd clothes, kids playing like they were testing for a trampoline ad, parents pretending to enjoy the chaos, it was all a bit much. She let out a small sigh. Funny how just being here used to be impossible. Back then, a single step felt like walking on glass shards with a side of agony. Now? Nothing. No pain, no problem. It was weird, like wearing someone else's skin, but she wasn't complaining.

She sat down on one of those too-shiny benches, the kind that scream *'modern design!'* and took a deep, dramatic breath of fresh air. Nature. Better than the stale smell of old cigarettes any day. Her fingers twitched. Not because she wanted a smoke, those days were behind her, but because she was itching to try something... *special.*

Stretching her hand out like she was warming up for a magic show, she whispered, 'Stop.' And just like that, the world followed. People froze mid-motion, runners stuck in awkward poses, a dog leaping after a ball like a furry statue, and one poor man mid-sneeze. His face turned in eternal torture. It was strange. Beautiful. A proper *gallery of the absurd.* She leaned back and smirked.

So, do they breathe? Are they screaming internally? Is this weird? Nah, it's fine. She waved her hand, and time clicked back on. People moved again, unaware. She did it again. And again. Freeze, unfreeze, freeze, unfreeze. It was like flipping a cosmic light switch. But then, *oh no*, she noticed someone. A man. Moving. In her frozen world.

He wasn't just moving; he was strolling toward her like he had all the time in the universe. She froze the world again, hoping to stop him. Didn't work. He kept coming. Slowly, closer and closer. Like he wasn't walking through a frozen crowd but taking a Sunday Walk to the shops. Her stomach flipped. *Of course. Of course, this would happen.* She thought about running, but decided to stay put. Her best bet? Pretend she wasn't terrified.

'You don't need to run,' he said in a voice calm enough to qualify as a meditation app. 'You don't need to be scared. I'm not your enemy, Nina.'

Her heart was doing its best impression of a rock concert, but she kept her face neutral, giving him the kind of look you give a stranger who sits too close on the bus. He calmly waved his hand, and the park came back to life. People unfroze like nothing had happened, not knowing they'd just been the stars of her private experiment.

Oh, brilliant, she thought. *Who the hell is this guy, and why does he know my name?*

The man chuckled, shaking his head like he could read her mind and openly. He probably could. 'Nah, not quite,' he said. 'They call me many things: Light, Father, God... or Allah, if that's more your vibe.'

His words sank in, and the tension drained out of her, slipping away like last night's takeaway leftovers you wish you hadn't eaten. Curious, she sat back on the bench, mimicking his free and easy confidence. It was like she'd wandered straight into some silly episode where reality had decided to take a holiday, and anything—literally anything—could happen.

He shrugged, looking a bit helpless. 'Look, I don't have any say over Hell or its lot. Those angels? Yup, they answer to Death. Out of my hands.'

With a loud sigh, Nina pulled at her hair.

'Honestly, this all feels like some mad dream, and all I want to do is go home.'

He gave her a sympathetic smile, the kind that says *yeah, I've been there.* There was something about his expression, though. A fleeting shadow, or maybe a glint in his eyes, made Nina's gut tighten, though she didn't know why. A strange familiarity she couldn't place.

'I get it. Trust me. But first things first, let's get your memories sorted. Then your powers. Without those memories, it's like trying to drive a car without the keys. You get me, right?'

She nodded, though that odd feeling remained, like she was missing a crucial puzzle piece.

'So where are these books?'

'Ah, well... funny thing, that,' he said, scratching the back of his neck like someone about to admit they'd lost your favourite hoodie. 'Death's got them. Yep. But don't worry, we'll sort it.'

He gave her a nod, all serious-like. 'Tell you what, once you've got your memories back, I'll open the gates to heaven myself. There's another book up there, with your powers in it, held by Asim's mum. Real family business, you know now?'

Nina frowned, clearly not buying it just yet.

'Okay, but who's really Death? And why can't you just give me the book?'

He sighed, like he'd heard this question a thousand times.

'Even in heaven, there are rules. I'd love to explain, but we're short on time.' His gaze flicked over his shoulder, a hint of discomfort breaking through his relaxed front, like he really didn't want to be caught here. 'I've got something else to tell you first.'

'The third book's with Jonathan, it's all about immortality. The last one? Your other servants got it,' he blurted out, clearly racing against the clock. His tone was full of hurry as he spoke quickly. 'Oh, and listen, don't trust anyone, okay? Find a bookkeeper. There's a library in Hell, keeps track of every soul ever. That's where the truth is.' He threw another glance over his shoulder, more nervously this time. 'Right, I'm off, before Death clocks on I've been talking with you.'

'Wait, wait, just one more question!' Nina called, desperate.

He paused, turning back with a heavy sigh. There was a moment, so brief, she almost missed it, where his expression softened in a way that made her heart squeeze. Like he was seeing something he'd lost. But then it was gone, and she wondered if she'd imagined it.

'Why do you let everyone suffer?' she asked.

Sadness clouded his eyes.

'In your world, people see me wrong. It's meant to be a place of suffering. I've got no power there. But here? People know me. They listen, and I send angels to help. No one has to suffer if they don't want to. Free will, remember? Not everyone deserves my help, either.'

Before she could say another word, he gave her one last nod. 'You'll figure it all out soon,' he promised. And just like that, he disappeared, gone with the wind.

Chapter Twenty-seven
The Turn

Part One

'OH MY GOD, HE IS GORGEOUS.' Tessa pressed herself against the window, breath misting up the glass, her lips nearly brushing it as she stared at the gardener.

Nina had a cigarette hanging from her lips, the smoke hardly drifting upward. 'I spoke to God.'

Tessa's head whipped around, finger pointing skyward like she had just been told the Queen was dropping by for tea. 'Like God? The real God?'

Nina did not even react. She did not need to. She just started talking, while Tessa's mind drifted somewhere darker. The grief was always there, like a stone tied to her chest, dragging her down. Her son had died, and God? Nowhere to be found.

Nina ground the cigarette underfoot, taking her time. 'In our world, Hell, God's not showing up. But here? He's different, or so he says.'

Behind them, footsteps. Finley leaned in, catching the tail end of Nina's words. 'Ah, are you talking with Tessa?'

'Yes, and she's saying hello to you.' She was not about to tell him what Tessa had really said, how sexy she thought he looked.

Finley peeked out the window, muttering a greeting to the empty air. Tessa smiled. It made her feel noticed, and that was enough.

'God has always been by our side, helping us,' Finley started to speak, but his voice sounded... well, not very sure. The usual confidence weakened. He had repeated that line a thousand times, but this time, it felt wrong.

Nina gave him a look, sensing something. 'You don't believe that anymore, do you?'

Finley's jaw tightened. He exhaled slowly, leaning back against the wall. 'People think it's from God. That all the magic, the angels, the power.'

He paused. 'But it's not. It's all from Death. He gave this world the magic, not God. God's just a puppet, and only Death knows the full story.'

Nina's eyes darkened. Tessa stayed quiet, trying to understand it.

'But Death is the one who punished me.'

'Punished you? He was your lover, Nina. You know him better than anyone.'

Tessa could not believe it; she struggled to imagine Nina with anyone, let alone Death.

Nina shrugged like it did not matter. 'He holds my memories. If we want answers, we start there.'

She asked about the Hell bookkeeper. Finley seemed genuinely confused. 'I have no idea where that is.'

Knock, knock. Finley opened the door, but whoever banged was already running, hood up, vanishing into the distance. He looked down. A book and key lay on the floor in front of him.

'Someone left this at the door and then ran,' Finley whispered to Nina as Tessa made her way upstairs.

Nina's eyes widened, practically bugging out. She recognized that book immediately. It was the one from their library, the one holding the key to this world.

'Weird,' she muttered. 'Samir said someone nicked the book with the key. And now it just... shows up here?'

Finley looked just as surprised.

Nina let out a slow breath, her eyes narrowing as she pieced things together. There had been a break-in at their library, but nothing was missing. She was sure the thief had taken the book and the key, but the real question bothered her—why bring them back? And why hide them at the door?

Finley scratched his chin, clearly deep in thought. Samir had his share of secrets, no doubt. Nina nodded, her mind spinning with the possibilities. Then something clicked for Finley. His eyes lit up, and he suggested they ask Grandma. He was dead certain she knew more than she ever let on.

But Grandma? Nowhere to be seen. Typical. Always making these grand, mysterious promises, only to bugger off when things got interesting. Finley knew her better than anyone—she was not off baking scones or playing bridge, oh no. Her "business" ventures were more like the sort of dodgy deals you would expect from someone who kept a black-market contacts list in their knitting bag. Except, of course, she did not knit.

Meanwhile, far from the caravan, Noah sat on his throne, seething. Jonathan had pushed him too far, but it was not just anger clenching his fists; it was pure rage. Jonathan might have thought himself untouchable, but Noah had plans, plans that included getting his hands on Tessa and making her suffer. Revenge was a dish he planned to serve hot and as brutal as he could make it.

He rushed through the city streets, head down, fists shoved deep into his pockets. The Magic Law building loomed in front of him, ugly and smug, just like everything else getting under his skin today. The letters floated slowly over the entrance, showing off their magic as if they were something special. Noah could not have cared less. He was here to see Mr Jamal.

Inside, the air smelled bad—of desperation and power games—a place where deals were struck and souls maybe even traded. Mr Jamal sat behind an absurdly large desk, his eyes glinting like a predator's when Noah dropped Nina's name. The man was old, bitter, clinging to the last shreds of his influence, and Noah knew exactly how to use it.

'Go on,' Mr Jamal said, reaching for a bottle of whiskey at his side. He poured himself a neat glass and did not bother offering one to Noah. A tiny act of control that troubled Noah, but he chose to ignore it. He had not come here for a drink but to lay out the deal: if someone helped him punish Jonathan and win over Tessa, he would give them the book of immortality. That got Jamal's attention faster than a free round at a miserable pub. The whiskey glass froze halfway to his lips, like it suddenly remembered it had somewhere else to be. The man was filled with overwhelming desperation. Noah did not have to explain everything to him. Immortality was a hard thing to pass up when you were one missed step away from the grave.

Jamal's voice came out slow and careful, like he was trying not to spook a wild animal. 'How? I have heard about those books. People die when they try to absorb their power.'

Noah sighed and rolled his eyes, showing a touch of impatience. 'Not this one. Jonathan has got it all figured out. The bastard has been using it already; does not even need to hide under that ridiculous hat anymore to keep looking like he just walked off the set of an anti-aging cream commercial.'

Jamal's eyes lit up with a glint Noah recognized all too well. Desperation. The man had been shackled to that stupid hat for years, holding onto its temporary magic like a toddler clinging to a security blanket. And now here Noah was, dangling the promise of eternal youth like a carrot on a very cruel stick.

Jamal took a slow sip, but Noah could see the gears turning behind those greedy eyes. There was no way he would turn this down. Not when the prize was this sweet.

'Alright. I will help.'

Noah did not bother with pleasantries or thank-yous. Those were not his style. Instead, he went straight to laying out the plan. Samir's funeral was coming, and Jonathan and Tessa would both be there, reasonably gift-wrapped for the taking. Jamal just nodded and gestured toward the door, the universal sign for 'get lost.' But then, as Noah was turning, Jamal added, 'Getting Tessa is the easy part. She is here without a permit, illegal as hell, literally. It is not like her papers are in order. And I know her story. Straight out of the underworld, is she not? Your ex-wife, the one who kicked the bucket forty-two years ago.'

Noah stiffened for a fraction of a second, but he swallowed it down. 'Yeah, but that is none of your concern.'

Jamal shrugged, chilling in a way that only someone with a warped sense of power could manage. 'Maybe not. But do not forget, you are still wanted. Criminal on the run, remember?'

Noah, running out of patience, told him to hurry up and get to the point. Jamal's eyes sparkled with a familiar charm. 'You cannot take Jonathan alone. You need someone stronger. Someone who hates him just as much as you do.' He leaned in, sharing a juicy little rumour about Jonathan that even Noah had not heard before. Something about that scar. Proof of something nasty.

Noah brushed it off with a smirk. Rumour's? Yeah, right. He did not have time for that kind of rubbish. Facts were what mattered, and the fact was, Jonathan had the book. That was the only thing worth his time. With an arrogant nod, Noah left.

As he stepped back into the cold, a malicious smile shaped his lips. This was not over, not even close. But things were finally starting to swing his way. The plan was rolling, and for the first time in what felt like forever, it seemed like he just might win.

ASIM IN NICOLE'S HOUSE

ON THE OTHER SIDE OF town, well away from Noah's mess, Asim was drowning under the grief of his dad's death. It felt like carrying an invisible anvil strapped to his chest, one that refused to budge no matter how many deep breaths he took. But with Nicole? Oh, with Nicole, that crushing weight magically lifted, like a dodgy magician making an elephant disappear. She was his solace, his little pocket of peace, and naturally, he stuck to her like superglue.

'This is my brother, Shad,' Nicole introduced with a smile so sweet it could give you cavities. Asim, blissfully clueless, shook Shad's hand, not realising he was basically offering himself up on a silver platter.

Shad and Asim ended up slouched on an old, creaky sofa in Nicole's house, a place that smelled like damp and disappointment. It was the kind of place that might have given up on itself long ago if houses could feel existential dread. Nicole had swanned off with her aunt on some shopping expedition, leaving the two of them alone. Shad, ever the Oscar-worthy performer, played his role as Nicole's kid brother with a charm so thick you'd need a chainsaw to cut through it. Every grin, every easy gesture was finely crafted to make Asim feel like he belonged, like he'd finally found that brotherly connection he'd missed growing up.

Asim, poor sod, was buying every bit of it. Sitting there, he felt a warmth he hadn't felt in years, like he'd found a family he didn't know he needed. Nicole's strange little world wrapped around him like a comforting blanket, and he had no idea he was being played like an out-of-tune ukulele. Shad wasn't what he seemed, and Nicole? Oh, she had her own game going, but Asim was happily ignorant.

Later, they went out, with Shad leading Asim through a maze of introductions: shady club owners, rich fellas who looked like they'd sell their own nan for a laugh, and other unsavoury types Asim had never dreamed of mixing with. It was a parade of excess and privilege, the kind of life that felt miles away from anything he'd ever known. And for the first time in forever, he felt a thrill, like he was finally living. But beneath all the warm fuzziness, there was a razor-sharp edge he couldn't quite feel. Love, that tricky bastard, had a few plans of its own, and none of them involved happy endings. No, love was about to hand Asim a bill for all the temporary joy he'd been sucking up.

'What's this?' Asim asked, frowning slightly as Shad handed him a small, sparkly pill.

'It's a happy one. Come on, bro,' Shad said with a wink so exaggerated it should've come with a flashing warning sign.

And Asim? Oh, bless him. He popped that pill right into his mouth without a single pause, chased it down with a drink of something that smelled like old cheese and tasted worse.

Immediately, the room began to warp, the edges blurring like someone had spilled cheap whiskey all over reality. Suddenly, he was surrounded by women and men who fawned over him, like he was the king of everything or at least the prince of questionable decisions. They showed him respect, and it filled him with a comforting warmth he hadn't known he was longing for. He felt like heaven had opened its doors just for him in that moment.

But this "heaven"? Oh, that illusion was the worst thing you could think of.

'What about Nicole?' His thoughts drifted to her. Hadn't she been the one grounding him, keeping him steady through grief?

Shad leaned in close. 'This is life, bro. You deserve to enjoy it. Nicole wouldn't mind, trust me.' He gave Asim a firm pat on the back. 'You're my brother now,' he added, wrapping an arm around Asim's shoulders, hardening the lie that held him captive.

Asim, who was already excited, nodded along as if the world were a big, soft blanket. Shad's words were the lightest part. He felt like he really belonged for a short, bright moment. He finally had the secret handshake to join the small group of "People Who Matter."

It felt like someone had pulled the plug on reality when Jonathan walked in. The music stumbled for a beat, like it wasn't quite sure how to keep going, and every head might as well have turned his way. Jonathan had that effect—making even the air feel a bit nervous. His eyes focused on Asim, standing right in the middle of the neon-lit chaos, holding him there like a trapped insect.

'What a small world,' Jonathan drawled, with the kind of charm that always had a hidden razor blade. 'You deserve this, Asim. Being treated like royalty for once. Not like the coward Finley makes you feel when you're with that sorry lot.'

And then, just as casually as you'd hand over a pub quiz flyer, he slipped Asim a sleek card. Black and shiny, with a time and date printed in neat little letters. Samir's funeral. The reminder hit Asim like a cold gust of wind, and he found himself scratching his head, his brain desperately trying to catch up.

'How? What is this?' he managed.

Jonathan smiled, all easy charm. 'I've sorted everything out. No need to worry.'

Asim let out a long, shaky breath, feeling overwhelmed but weirdly relieved. Deep down, a little alarm bell was probably trying to get his attention, whispering that there was always a catch with Jonathan. But tonight? Ignoring that irritating voice seemed so much easier. So he let it slide, let the night carry him away, and tried not to think too hard about the man who'd just pulled his strings.

BACK IN THE CARAVAN

JUST AS NINA WAS ABOUT to drag herself upstairs, a bell rang. She froze. Finley, still in his tatty dressing gown, dragged himself downstairs with that look, he knew exactly what this was. No need to ask. Funeral card. Then, like it had its own set of wings, a fancy card floated into the air, spinning slowly before zipping past Nina and heading straight for Tessa's room, like it had business there.

'Tomorrow. 11 a.m.? Well, this is interesting,' Nina babbled, feeling both a bit impressed and a bit weirded out. Cards didn't just float around. But inside, Finley clocked it right away. Asim wasn't pulling this show solo. Did he say anything? Of course not—how typical Finley. Just a nod. 'Be ready, Nina.' And with that, he sloped back upstairs.

Then she thought of Tessa, who'd been missing for hours. That knot in her gut tightened. She went to her room and found Tessa there, legs tucked up, staring at her own body like it wasn't hers. Not moving. Just... stuck.

'You've been here the whole time?' Nina asked, not used to seeing her like this. Tessa, the tough one, now looking like she'd been hollowed out.

'I just want to go home.'

Nina's heart did this weird flip, something she didn't like. She tried to shrug it off with a smirk. 'You miss your boring job that much?'

'I miss all of it.'

Then Tessa started going off, saying how sorry she was that they'd ever come to this shit world. She thought magic would be fun, like the movies—exciting, something good. But no. It was all bollocks. She didn't give a toss about it anymore. Wished she didn't know anything about it. 'Broken' didn't even begin to describe it, like none of this crap was her life.

Nina stood there, a bit lost. Emotions weren't her thing—all that messy stuff. But whatever this was, it hit deep, and she hated it. For once, she tried to tap into something close to empathy.

'You know, with you holed up in here, it's been pretty shit for me. Lonely. Boring. Feels weird without you around.'

Tessa smiled, just a little. It wasn't much, but it was there. She held the funeral card tightly, crumpling the edges.

'I can't even go to the funeral. Grandma says I need to stay close to my body.' Her eyes clouded over. 'I can't even talk to Asim. Where is he, anyway?'

'Asim? Off somewhere, like always. Lost in his own ego and anger. Doesn't give a shit about his dad dying.'

'He's a man,' Tessa said, softer than usual, like she was letting Nina in on a secret. 'This is how they show pain. He's broken inside, that's why he acts like he doesn't care.'

'So, what? All that angry front? Just... stressed? Depressed? Completely devastated?'

Tessa's gaze drifted, landing somewhere Nina couldn't follow.

'Every man's different. But Asim? He's just a young, lost boy. Trying to act tough, trying to hide that mess he's got going on inside.'

The room changed before Nina could reply. Something didn't feel right. Looking at Tessa, her heart skipped.

'No... no, you're disappearing!' Nina's voice shot up in pure panic. 'What's happening?'

Tessa looked down at her hands, her fingers turning transparent, like she was being erased. Her eyes found Nina's, wide and filled with sadness.

'I don't know,' she whispered, her voice trembling as her body thinned out right in front of them.

Nina screamed, stumbling back, her chest tightening with fear. Just as everything seemed to spiral out of control, Finley burst into the room, wearing nothing but his boxer shorts, eyes wide, breathless.

'What the hell's going on?'

But no one answered. Tessa, almost gone, her eyes pleading for help none of them could give.

'Oh my God, I'm me again!' Tessa suddenly shouted. Tears ran down her face, hands grabbing at her body like she had to check it was real. 'Feels bloody amazing!'

Nina stood there, her pulse hammering. 'What the hell just happened?'

Finley, rubbing his face, said, 'Right, I'm calling a healer.' He turned to leave but stopped, glancing down at his shorts. 'And probably finding some trousers first.'

Tessa, still wiping tears, half-laughed through the mess of it all. 'No need, Finley.'

Nina was still reeling, blinking hard, caught between wanting to scream or laugh.

'Oh my God, I thought you were dying. I can't imagine living without you. Really.'

Tessa's tears flowed even harder, the unexpected honesty hitting her deep. 'Nina...'

Before anything else could be said, Finley walked in, now fully dressed, with the healer beside him.

'Oh, that was fast,' Tessa said, wiping her face with the back of her hand.

'I'm a quick-call healer,' the man replied with a calm smile that suggested he had a subscription to *Chill Monthly*. 'I'm going to touch your body now, check everything from the inside.'

'Oh, please, touch me everywhere,' Tessa shot back, flashing a grin that could've powered a small city.

Nina rolled her eyes and slapped Tessa's arm, laughing. 'Tessa, really?'

The healer smirked but kept it professional, doing his check-up routine with all the seriousness of someone auditioning for a medical drama. He stood up straight after a minute.

'Everything is fine, even the brain. No abnormalities,' he said, as if he were giving over an A+ test.

After shaking Finley's hand, he bent down and held onto his legs. His skin started to change, turning grey and even slightly hairy. It happened unbelievably fast. Wings grew from his back, and instead of a mouth, he now had a beak. Then, just like that, he was a bird. He whooshed out the window and didn't even say, 'Ta-ra.'

Tessa collapsed back onto the sofa, letting out a breath. 'And I thought disappearing into thin air was the weirdest part of my day.'

Part Two

AS NINA LAY SLUMPED in bed, her body begged for rest. Her head sank into the pillow, tension easing now that Tessa was safe and alive back in her body. Then came a knock, soft but enough to bite her awake. She blinked and saw Tessa standing in the doorway. Nina looked, flipping on the light, and couldn't help but smirk. Tessa was floored out in a tight white dress, heels, hair done like she was about to walk straight into a club, not a caravan.

'What the hell, Tessa? You're not seriously going out. Noah's looking for you. And minutes ago, you were a bloody ghost!' Nina said, half-irritated, half-confused by her friend's absolute lack of chill.

But Tessa wasn't listening. She dug around in her bag, taking out two small blue potions with a naughty smirk.

'Do you really think I'm that shit? And you, my love, are painfully boring,' she teased, tossing Nina a wink that said she had this all under control.

Nina couldn't stop herself from smiling slightly. Tessa always found a way to turn the situation on its head. 'Alright, fine. One drink won't kill me. But we're broke, and we've got no clue where to go.'

Tessa, of course, had already thought ahead. She pulled out a fistful of coins. 'Don't worry, money's sorted. Plus, there's a taxi waiting outside.' Her smirk said it all, this was a Tessa plan, and her plans never went halfway.

'Let's see the magic in action,' Tessa said, dragging Nina to the mirror as they drank the potions.

Moments later, their reflections started to wobble and warp, like someone had just thrown a rock into the universe's most unreliable puddle. Tessa's hair darkened to a shade of black that screamed drama, and her legs stretched out like she'd made a dodgy trade for supermodel proportions. Nina blinked at her own reflection: blonde hair, curves turned up to eleven. But instead of shock, she just let out a dry smirk. Typical magic. Couldn't even muster a proper wow anymore.

'Bloody hell, I love it! You see that?' Tessa yelped, spinning around like a kid who'd just nicked the last biscuit from the jar and gotten away with it.

Nina snorted, giving herself a half-hearted once-over. 'Alright, alright, I'm ready.'

On the way, they were cracking up, throwing jokes back and forth, the kind that knocked sharp and fast. The energy was buzzing between them, nothing heavy, just that cheerful edge.

Tessa pointed at Nina's lips. 'You know what? Red lipstick would look fantastic on you.'

Then, bang, out of nowhere, it happened.

'Oh my goodness, how?' Tessa stared down at her finger like it had just betrayed her.

Nina, not wasting a second, took out a pocket mirror. Red lipstick—bold, perfectly lined—sitting right there.

'Did you do this?'

But Tessa shook her head, just as lost. Nina barely reacted. In a world like this, surprises lost their bite. She threw the mirror back in her bag, and Tessa, after a beat, just went with it, shoulders relaxing like it was all part of the ride.

Now they stood in the club, their jaws dropping to the floor. It was as if the pulse of adrenaline in the air coursed through the music, seeping into their very veins. They didn't drink a single drop, yet they were completely absorbed in the dance, caught up in each other's movements and the wild energy of the moment.

'Okay, but now I need a drink,' Tessa shouted at Nina.

'What? No, you don't stink!'

Tessa grabbed her hand and headed to the bar. There were no waiters, and they both were confused about how to order drinks. A guy behind them noticed their lost expressions. Intrigued by Tessa, he approached her, dropped a coin in the box, and the drinks instantly appeared in their hands.

'Just think about what you want to drink!' he shouted, the music eating his words.

'Thank you!' Tessa turned to Nina.

'What'd he say?'

'He said all you have to do is blink!'

They had a great time, dancing a lot and enjoying the atmosphere.

Sparkling rain fell from the ceiling, turning into sandy dust as it hit the floor. The whole place had that wild, raw energy, just enough to keep things unpredictable. Tessa? She was booming, enjoying the attention of men, their eyes stuck to her like she was the only thing worth looking at. Nina? A different story. No one winked her way, but she moved with confidence, owning her new body as the music took over. Head light, this night out gave her exactly what she needed, no strings, no stress, no pain.

'Don't you dare leave me alone!' She knew the drill; Tessa usually abandoned her the moment some guy flew a smile.

'I'm not a hero!' Tessa shot back. 'They just love this new body!'

Neither could hear a bloody thing over the music, but this time, Tessa didn't leave her. The guys? No. Tonight wasn't about them. She stayed right there, locked into the moment with Nina, the rest of the world fading out. Then the crowd shifted, parting like something big was about to happen. Nina and Tessa found themselves dead center, the only two left standing as every pair of eyes locked on them. Confused. What the hell?

Out of nowhere, the DJ grabbed a mic, his voice dripping with theatrics. 'Just close your eyes, girl. Let me feel you, your soul all alone,' he crooned, dancing his way straight to Tessa like she was the only thing that existed.

'Omg, this can't be happening!' her voice wavered between shock and laughter.

Nina slid out, blending into the crowd. She left Tessa to deal with the DJ's full attention, the lights spinning wild patterns around them. He leaned in, singing in her ear, 'Pull me close, let me feel you, touch my soul, just lose control.'

Tessa's moves were electric, hair pulled up, body syncing with his like they were two wild birds locked in. The tune shifted.

'I keep looking for something I can't get, I just died in your arms tonight...'

The energy was intense, spinning faster and faster.

She stiffened, stepping back. Her face had gone pale.

The DJ noticed immediately, the vibe crashing. He stepped back, looking confused, and as if on signal, the entire crowd did the same, pulling away as though an unseen force had broken.

'Why did you stop? It was so good; I thought you were enjoying yourself!' Nina shouted.

Tessa didn't say a word, just grabbed Nina's hand tight and led her straight out of the club.

'Shhh, just keep walking and don't look back,' she whispered in a fearful voice, not looking back as they walked into the night.

In the car, Tessa blurted out dramatically, 'I saw Asim with some girls and guys.' Her voice trembled like it was the end of the world.

'So what? It's just Asim. And look at us—we've got different faces anyway.'

But with wide eyes, Tessa shook her head.

'He was with Noah's friends, I'm sure of it. I saw them, I remember. We need to warn him, but how? I'm a coward. I'm sorry, Nina,' her words collapsed into a meltdown.

'Oh no, don't worry. Finley will help. You did the right thing,' Nina said. 'It's normal to be scared—he's a son of a bitch!'

'Yes, but Asim...'

'Don't worry about Asim. Everything will be fine.'

But inside? Nina was falling apart. Her mind raced, and she couldn't stop worrying about Asim.

She even found herself silently praying, *please, God, help us.* And bam, there was a bang, like a gunshot, except there was no shooting. God simply appeared, no lights, no drama, just sitting there across from them in his beautiful black suit, smiling and inspecting his nails as if he were looking for dirt under them.

But Tessa couldn't handle it; she totally smacked down onto the leather seat. A shame, really, she missed the show.

Meanwhile, Nina just sat there, looking at Tessa, then at God, unsure whether she should deal with her or him.

'What the heck? I don't get it.'

God, with a chilled shrug, replied, 'I told you, I listen. You prayed for help.'

Still speechless, Nina was met with a grin from the serious, the whole situation somehow getting even more unreal.

'I just wanted to show you that I hear and listen to my people,' God said, easy-going, like it was just a typical chat. 'But you used potions to be someone else. So, yes, now you are human, but actually, you're an angel, and Tessa... well, she belongs to Hell. I can't do much for you because of the rules, you know.' He gave a little shrug. Then, seeing her face still frozen, he added, 'Calm down, okay? Noah's friends? Trust me, they're not Asim's biggest enemy.'

Before Nina could ask what he meant, God dropped a blow about Jonathan and Shad's plans. 'You just need to warn him. I can't do it myself without breaking the rules,' he said. And with that, he vanished.

She, still in shock, slapped Tessa across the face. 'Wake up!'

Tessa, like a shot, sat up straight, eyes wide, confused. 'Oh my God, was he really here?'

'Yeah, but we're outside the caravan now. Let's just go inside.'

As they stepped in, Nina filled Tessa in on the message from God.

'Bloody hell, Nina. We really need to start charging an entry fee for all these celestial drop-ins.'

But the humour hardly hid the worry on her face. Her thoughts darted straight to Asim, and she pulled at a loose thread on her dress.

'Tomorrow,' she spoke in a voice that was a little louder than a whisper, 'we'll sort it out. Finley will help. Everything... it has to be alright. Right?'

Chapter Twenty-eight
The Funeral

Part One

'WHY AREN'T YOU EATING? You look stressed,' Tessa asked Finley, eyeing him over the rim of her glass.

But Finley wasn't in the mood for conversation. He grabbed his travel cloth, gave her a quick nod, and disappeared without a word.

'Oh, men!' Tessa waved her hand dramatically, then she screamed, 'Help!' and rushed over to Nina in a flurry of panic.

'Oh my God, the kitchen is full of men! I mean, handsome men, of course, but...'

'What the hell, Tessa!' Nina shot up, in a moment wide awake. 'What about Finley?'

'He went somewhere!'

Nina didn't think twice. With her heart racing, she quickly grabbed some potions and put on Demand Gloves from Finley's workshop. Tessa followed closely as she rushed to the kitchen, both prepared for whatever was inside and ready to face it.

Inside, they found a scene. Men in sharp suits stood around, looking just as confused as the two of them, pointing at each other like they had no idea how they'd ended up there.

Before they could understand, Finley dropped in. 'Get the purple glass from the third shelf, now!'

Nina grabbed it, her hands steady, and as soon as the men inhaled the purple dust, they vanished into thin air like they were never there at all.

'What on earth just happened?' Nina asked, still catching her breath.

Finley pointed at Tessa. 'Ask her.'

Tessa shook her head. 'I didn't do anything! All I said was, "Oh, men."'

Finley sighed, rubbing the back of his neck. 'Your magic found you. But Tessa, you need to be careful. You haven't mastered it yet, and things could get... dangerous.'

Tessa's eyes widened as she blinked. 'Wait, hold on, magic? I have magic?' Her confusion instantly turned to excitement. 'This is incredible!'

Nina gave her a sharp look. 'Incredible? You just summoned a room full of strange men in suits, Tessa!'

'Right, right, of course.' Tessa nodded, but the grin crept back. 'But still, magic! I mean, how?'

'Because you forgot. You're not supposed to remember,' Finley said.

Tessa's smile faltered. 'What are you talking about?'

Finley's gaze softened. 'You once died, Tessa. Your memories were wiped, your magic stripped. You don't belong here. You're... dead. You forgot you came from Hell?'

Tessa opened her mouth, but she couldn't say anything. Her heartbeat sped up, and her excitement gradually turned into something different. Nina stepped closer, eyes narrowing.

'This is a bit scary. Are we even safe?'

'Well, Hell never forgets, Nina. It's alive. Hell knows,' Finley responded in a serious tone. 'And the world knows it too. It looks like the world is confused.'

'So, what? I'm a walking death trap now?' said Tessa.

Finley glanced at her. 'I've never met anyone like you. No one has. That's why it's dangerous.'

There was a moment of awkward silence. Tessa took a deep breath and forced a weak smile. 'Well, I mean, sure, that's... terrifying. But also, kind of cool, right?'

She shot a look at Nina, as if hoping for backup.

Nina just sighed. 'Oh, brilliant. She's excited she might accidentally trigger the apocalypse.'

Tessa couldn't help but smirk. 'I mean, a little.'

Nina then launched into her story with the enthusiasm of someone who clearly didn't realise today wasn't the day for her personal dramatics. Something about meeting God in a club, as you do, with plenty of unnecessary detail. Finley, meanwhile, sat with his head in his hands, the international sign for please stop talking.

Today was about Samir, not any of the mystical stuff Nina kept talking about. Finley's quiet pain eventually became a small, weary plea, asking for everyone to stay focused on remembering their friend. Tessa and Nina exchanged a look—a doubtful understanding on both sides. Finley was aware of the moment. Quite predictable, to be honest. But given the circumstances, they decided to agree. Though Tessa, in a final act of defiance, threw an eye roll in Nina's direction. The type of roll that said, Men, with all the energy of someone resigned to dealing with them.

Nina nearly laughed. Even on a day like this, some things just never changed. As Finley and Nina got ready inside, Tessa slipped into the garden. She knew Finley was upset about the funeral, but she didn't feel the same weight. Right now, she couldn't resist testing her new magic.

She pointed at her ears, concentrating hard. 'Headphones,' she said, and just like that, they appeared.

'Oh yes!' Tessa squealed. She pointed again. 'Now, proper music.'

The music started, blasting through her headphones. She danced around, excited and completely lost in the moment.

'Tree,' she said, trying to summon one. Instead, leaves swirled. She scowled. 'Tree, shit, come on, tree!'

And poo smashed into her face. Wiping it off, 'Lovely, just lovely,' she muttered, rolling her eyes.

What she didn't realise was the ghostly gardener watching her, laughing. Nina, looking out the window, spotted him as she saw Tessa from inside. Something about the scene—Tessa dancing like a maniac, the silent ghostly figure looming nearby—made her feel uneasy.

Watching the ghost, Nina felt a sharp, sudden pang inside. It wasn't just one ghost, it was all of them, stuck here because of her. The gates to hell were closed, and somehow, she was the reason. She wasn't sure how, but the thought dug in deep. People are suffering, she thought. And I'm just sitting here, wallowing in my own mess. Useless.

She glanced at the ghostly gardener, his laughter almost mocking. I've got to find those books. Not for me; for them. The souls waiting for her to set things right. Once she got her memories and powers back, she'd be the Guardian of Hell, the one who could finally open the gates and let them move on. But right now? She was stuck, just like them. Then Nina's mind drifted. Watching Tessa muck about in the garden, she thought back to when they first got the library. Tessa, always the scrappy one, stepping in when that bully had a go at her—no doubt, like a proper sister. She was the protector Nina never had. And life without her? Couldn't even imagine it.

The smile disappeared. The idea of sending Tessa back home was more difficult than she had thought. Glancing down at the library key in her hand, she flipped it over again and again. Could this really be done? A deep exhale followed as doubt threatened to overwhelm her. Right, time to get on with it, she thought, tucking the key into her purse. Her mind, however, kept spinning. Sitting on the bed, her face wrenched as if she'd just spotted a spider. No spider was there, just thoughts, lost in the mess of her mind. Over and over, the same questions echoed: What the hell am I doing? Why is this all happening around me? It almost felt like a dream. Life had already put her through hell, and sometimes it seemed like she didn't pity herself enough. Hmm.

Her primary school teacher's words came to her. Once, he'd told her, "Don't feel sorry for yourself, and don't expect pity from others. Remember, there's always someone out there going through worse. If you wallow in self-pity, you'll never stand on your own two feet." Those words had stayed with her, guiding her through life, especially during the darker moments. They gave her strength now, too. Standing up, she steadied herself and shook off that "spider face." This wasn't going to beat her.

AT THE SAME TIME, IN THE HALLWAYS OF JONATHAN'S PALACE

ASIM BENT DOWN AND pulled his laces tighter than they needed. His reflection stared back at him from the mirror, tired eyes, a little sad. He whispered to himself, 'One day, Dad, I swear... you'll be proud of me.'

The words stuck, dragging him back to a memory he didn't think still had power over him. A long time ago, when he was just a kid. He could see it, clear as day; the park, the bench, the feeling of being too small for the world.

He sat there with his feet dangling, watching the other kids. They were everywhere, laughing, running, calling for their mums, or chasing their brothers. It was full of life. And him? Just there... alone, no one calling his name, no one waiting.

That's how it always felt. Like he was on the outside, looking in.

His dad had shown up, quiet as always, and sat beside him. Asim didn't say a word, just kept his eyes on the kids, feeling like he didn't belong in that world. His dad didn't push, waiting. Then finally, he spoke.

'Why you just sitting here, Asim? You don't want to play?'

Asim shook his head, kicking at the dirt. 'They've got people, Dad. Mums, brothers, sisters... I'm just here by myself.'

His dad sighed. Asim could feel his eyes on him, heavy, like he was trying to figure out what to say next. After a beat, his dad's voice came, quiet but sure.

'Asim, you're not always going to get what you want. Sometimes, you're going to be alone. That's just how it goes. And you got to be okay with that. Learn to stand on your own. It'll make you stronger.'

Asim frowned. 'But I don't want to be alone.'

His dad chuckled, but it wasn't light. It had weight, like he understood more than he let on. 'No one does. But there'll be times when you are, even if you don't want to be. And when that happens, you can't let it break you. You got to be able to hold yourself up. No one else will.'

Asim blinked, still watching the other kids, hated hearing it. He didn't want to be strong but wanting someone to tell him it'd be alright. That he wouldn't always be on his own and lonely. But that wasn't the kind of thing his dad said.

'You'll be strong, Asim,' his dad added, softer now. 'One day, you'll have your own family. You'll make your own happiness. But you can't let the loneliness chew you up. You'll get through it. And one day, you'll look back, proud of what you've done. Proud of yourself.'

Asim hadn't said anything back then. Just nodded, pretending to understand, but all he really felt was small. Small and alone, watching the world carry on without him.

The memory slammed into him now, hitting harder than he expected. He tied his laces tight, staring at his reflection again. His dad had been right, hadn't he? He'd been preparing him for this all along, for being alone.

I can't do this, Asim thought. *I'm not strong enough.*

But his dad's words came back to him, those ones about not letting it break him. About finding his own way. And maybe he had. Maybe he'd held himself together all this time. But being strong didn't stop the loneliness. It just stayed there, chewing away bit by bit, always haunting, 'One day, you'll be proud of me.' His voice was rough as he hissed to the mirror, as though saying it out loud would somehow make it real. 'And maybe then... maybe that'll be enough.'

Meanwhile

JONATHAN STOOD TALL in his own room, watching his servant kneel and polish his shoes like they needed it. He glanced at his reflection. Unlike Asim, there wasn't a hint of doubt, just pure, electric arrogance. Touching the scar on his face, he felt a surge of something dark.

Now it's my turn, my brother.

The words stirred something in him, pulling him back to a memory that still clawed at him.

He'd been a kid, standing in this very room, hiding behind the door when he heard the shouting. His mother's voice tore through the house like a sharp slap to the face.

'Where you going? Huh? Off shagging her again, making another bastard?'

Something slammed. Well, that couldn't be good. Jonathan froze, the wood of the doorframe cold under his fingers.

'You fucking bitch, I'm not shagging anyone!' his dad spat back. Charming, as usual.

'Of course you're not,' his mum shot back. 'Not even me!'

Jonathan's heart hammered, his palms damp with sweat. Lovely. Nothing like overhearing a bit of marital bliss. He didn't dare breathe.

His father's voice, low and dangerous, the kind that makes the hair on the back of your neck stand up.

'Maybe if you'd given me a decent son, I wouldn't have to go shagging anyone else. Look at him—what you gave me. Useless. No magic. Weak. A bloody poof.'

Ah, there it was. The punchline. Jonathan's breath caught in his throat. He'd run that day. Couldn't blame him, really.

He was back in the room now, fingers still pressed against the scar on his face, the hidden darkness boiling underneath. Always this room, always this memory, lovely.

His jaw tightened, glancing at the servant, still kneeling.

'Oi, do it properly! I'm paying you, aren't I?'

The servant pulled back. It's great when they actually pay attention. Jonathan smiled at his reflection, his eyes shine with confidence. *Now it's mine.*

Part Two

BACK IN THE MAGICAL CARAVAN

'LIMO'S HERE! HURRY up!' Tessa's voice broke her out of it. Outside, Tessa and Finley were already waiting.

Nina stepped out, her eyes catching Tessa's sharp look. Black sparkling hat, long dress, all done up.

'You look good,' Nina said, though the occasion made it feel all wrong. Her eyes roamed to the limo. Sleek, too extravagant. 'Nice limo, Finley.'

Finley glanced at her, scratching his head. 'I didn't order any.'

He tried to play it cool. Maybe Asim had set up this spooky surprise. Clever, but he had no idea Jonathan was pulling the strings on this one. Tessa gave Nina a playful touch, smiling. She mouthed, *wow, I love it*, clearly more excited than freaked out. A violin started up, slow and sad. Then the door opened on its own, like some invisible butler had just waved them in. No one was driving. The seat was empty.

Finley, pretending to be the gentleman in control, waved them toward the limo.

'Ladies first,' he said, doing his best impression of someone who was not completely weirded out.

Nina gave a nod, a little stiff. Strange, but not out of place for them. She glanced at the empty driver's seat again, unease gnawing at her. But *what the hell*, she thought. There was no turning back now. She climbed in, with Tessa practically bouncing in behind her.

Inside, the violin music was still going, making the whole thing feel like they were heading to some gothic ballroom, not a funeral. As the car moved, no one said a word.

Nina felt it first. This weird, lurking sense of something not quite right. Finley and Tessa were quiet too, and for once, it was not comfortable. It was that uneasy silence, the kind that sticks to your skin. The shivers? They were real, and they were going nowhere. Their emotions whispered the truth. Something was seriously off. Just then, their voices were gone, like an invisible force had wrapped itself around their throats, squeezing tight. They could not speak. Not a sound.

Scared, they started gesturing wildly with their hands, trying to communicate, but soon enough, even that was taken from them. Their limbs felt heavy, stuck in place, like someone had hit *pause* on their bodies but left their minds open. They sat locked in place, like lifeless dolls. A single tear slid down from Tessa's eye, her face showing the dead scream. Nina squeezed her eyes shut, trying to fight it, but the more she struggled, the more powerless she felt. Finley, next to them, looked as though he was trying to calm them down, his eyes speaking where words could not, as if willing them to hold on just a little longer.

But whatever was happening, it had them, and it was not letting go. After what felt like hours of terror, the car stopped, and the violin finally cut off. Tessa wasted no time, jumping out.

'Fuck me, to hell with this shit!' she shouted, only to step straight into poo. Looking down, she groaned. 'Excellent!'

'WTF... shi—' She was about to scream again, but Finley clamped a hand over her mouth.

'Shhh, don't say anything,' he whispered, eyes darting around like they were in a horror movie.

Nina stepped out next, wiping the sweat dripping down her face.

'What the hell was that?' she gasped, leaning on the limo for support.

Finley seemed a bit anxious but tried to play it calm. 'I tried to warn you with my eyes, didn't I? This is Jonathan's thing. Used to be a normal part of funerals ages ago—respect for the dead and all that. It was the violin.'

Tessa was not impressed. 'Respect? That was torture!'

Before she could launch into another rant, Finley silenced her with a finger to his lips, motioning for her to look around. The scene was anything but comforting, a creepy atmosphere pressing down on them.

They weren't just at a funeral. Oh no, this was something else. Something darker. Like a funeral on a bloody sugar rush. And honestly? They were nowhere near ready for it. As they turned back, a line of limousines pulled up behind them, each one carrying passengers who looked just as shaken. People stepped out, swapping tales of their rides like they'd all just survived the same screwed, ghost-driven Uber Pool from hell. While Tessa was still wrestling with the mess on her heel, muttering curses under her breath, Asim and Nicole exited their limo. Both looked sharp in their elegant outfits, but their faces matched the upset looks of everyone else.

'That was torture!' Asim yelled, running a hand through his hair, clearly still trying to shake off whatever they'd just been through. Nicole, ever calm, was checking herself over, making sure no strange residue from their ride had followed them out.

The door to their limo remained open. Then, he stepped out.

Jonathan.

Tall, with sleek blonde hair that flowed, he looked like he'd just walked out of a magazine. Dressed in a white suit, he strode into the scene as if he owned it. His confident grin, paired with the way he seemed to toy with his surroundings, only added to his dangerous charm.

Nina couldn't tear her eyes away from him.

'Who is that?' she whispered to Finley.

'Jonathan,' he replied, his face like someone had just ruined his pint.

Before Nina could respond, Tessa stomped over, still wrestling with the poo on her shoe. 'Oh my goodness, Finley, any ideas on how to get this shit off? Or maybe a little magic, for once?'

Nina and Finley didn't blink. Their eyes were still glued to Jonathan.

'Hello? Anyone? Help with crap on my shoe?' Tessa waved her arms in their faces, but then she caught sight of Jonathan. Her mouth parted as if the words had been stolen from her.

'Omg, ooh la la.'

Nina snapped out of it. 'Shh, don't say the word *God*. You know why!' She rummaged in her bag. 'Here, just wipe your shoe.'

When Nina turned back, Jonathan was suddenly right there, standing way too close.

'Oh, you scared me!' she squeaked.

'Nice to finally meet you,' Jonathan said, his smile almost too perfect. 'The rumours were true.'

Nina blinked, half-expecting him to mention the Guardian of Hell, but instead...

'You're beautiful,' he said smoothly, kissing her hand, his eyes never leaving hers.

'I... uh... thank you,' she stammered, her palms starting to sweat.

Jonathan turned to Finley, giving a short nod. 'Finley,' he said, in that smug, too-cool-for-school way.

Finley nodded back, all business. 'Jonathan.'

The tension hung heavy, but before anyone could say anything else, Jonathan moved to Tessa. Taking her hand, he kissed it, and then... he sniffed. His eyebrows shot up. His face twisted in disgust the moment he caught the shoe's smell. Without a word, he turned back to Nina, offering her his arm like a proper gentleman.

'Ready?'

Nina slipped her arm through his like it was the most natural thing in the world. Fear? Gone. She was ready for whatever madness came next. Tessa stood outside, with Finley looming behind her.

'You should go to the bathroom and wash your shoe,' Finley said to Tessa.

She ignored him, her eyes scanning the surroundings. It wasn't the funeral anyone had expected, not Nina, not Tessa, and definitely not Asim.

Jonathan led the way, walking ahead with all the grace of someone who'd just ordered death to suit up.

The others jumped out of the limos, still trying to shake off the strange feeling that stuck to them like a nightmarish dream.

Overhead, a group of seagulls flew in circles, but weirdly enough, instead of their normal annoying squawks, they sounded more like someone playing a harp. Lovely. As if the day needed to be any more unsettling. Nina half-expected the birds to break into a chorus of *Ave Maria* at any moment.

Jonathan guided them toward the graveyard, where rows of identical purple marble graves shimmered in the light. It was strangely gorgeous, like it belonged in some sort of posh gothic catalogue. Nina couldn't help but think, *well, at least the dead get a decent view. Shame they can't enjoy it.*

Jonathan leaned in close to Nina. 'This is how we grieve, with respect and celebration.'

Then, louder, for everyone to hear, he declared, 'There's no need for pain and sorrow. Our bodies may die, but our souls live on.'

Asim stood beside Nina, with Nicole at his side, watching as the others gathered around. His face was stone-cold, revealing nothing, but underneath, he was a mess of emotions. Seeing Samir's casket, so bright and almost cheerful, didn't really make things any easier. He couldn't see the body, and that little blessing helped him stay calm.

Tessa didn't give a toss about the seagulls or the mess on her shoe. *Oh, Asim,* she thought, glancing at him, *I'm so sorry.*

Nina peeked at him, sensing his pain even though he kept it buried deep.

Tessa gasped loudly, drawing everyone's attention.

'What is he doing here?' she blurted, her eyes locked on Noah, who had just swaggered in with his crew, positioning himself right across from where Samir's coffin lay in the middle of the gathering.

Then, Noah caught Tessa's eye, giving her a cocky wink.

Finley leaned in close and whispered, 'Don't worry, nothing can happen at funerals. They're protected by magic.' He took her hand, squeezing it gently, offering her a reassuring smile.

But Nina and Asim? They weren't buying it. Nina's jaw tightened, and Asim's fists clenched at his sides.

Jonathan noticed the tension and took a step forward.

'Noah was a close friend of Samir's,' he said. 'But don't worry, the funeral is under magical protection.'

Still, all eyes were on Noah.

Nina gave Tessa a quick, reassuring pat. 'It's fine, nothing's going to happen.'

The birds above were still singing, strangely cheerful, like they hadn't got the memo this was supposed to be a funeral, not a sunny day at the beach. More people dropped in, shuffling awkwardly in their somber outfits, as if they too wondered if they'd taken a wrong turn.

Then, like an uninvited comedy act, Shad strutted in with four demons, each one decked out in matching green suits. The kind of suits you'd expect at a wild garden party or a stag do gone horrifically wrong. The demons' grins were just a tad too wide, the sort that made you question whether they were there to mourn or to audition for the next supernatural fashion show.

Asim's face lit up. 'Glad your brother and his mates could make it,' he whispered to Nicole.

Her smile was calculated, perfectly hiding her true intentions.

Tessa elbowed Nina. 'What's with the green suits?'

Nina just shook her head, looking as clueless as she felt. *What a bullshit.*

Jonathan, always on cue, overheard and swooped in with a wink at Nina. 'We're not here to be sad, remember?' He said it like he was announcing the start of a party instead of, you know, a funeral.

Then, two more women joined the scene, both looking like they had stepped straight out of a salon. Late thirties and rocking orange hats that made them stand out even more. They walked right over and stood next to Shad's group, like they were part of the crew.

'Who's that?' Nina mumbled, loud enough for Finley to hear.

He leaned in, keeping his voice low. 'That's my grandma, with her friend.'

'What?'

Finley, as if it was the most normal thing in the world, whispered, 'She's wearing a magical hat.'

Tessa jumped in. 'Oh, alright. I should start wearing one too.'

'You don't need any, you are perfect,' Finley whispered. Tessa couldn't help it. Her cheeks flared.

Right after Grandma's arrival, Mr Jamal showed up, lined by two men in suits and green hats. They positioned themselves right next to Grandma's young friend.

Finley, clearly not impressed, muttered, 'What is he doing here?'

Jonathan, picking up on it, quickly added, 'I didn't invite him.'

Meanwhile, Mr Jamal stood there, scanning the scene with a strange, almost knowing smile, like he was in on a joke no one else got.

'Right, we're all here,' Jonathan began, but just as he spoke, another group arrived. A young woman, probably in her twenties, immediately caught Asim's eye. She moved with quiet confidence, accompanied by an older woman without a hat and two men.

They nodded at everyone and stood next to Finley.

'What are you all doing here?' Finley whispered to one of the men.

'Mind your own business, Finley,' the man said.

Then Jonathan stepped up, and like a conductor silencing an unruly orchestra, the birds fell silent, mid-chirp, as he raised his cane. 'Asimo Nar,' he announced, voice dripping with authority.

Fireworks exploded above them.

Nina, Asim, and Tessa stood there, unsure what to make of it. At the peak, the sparks broke off, floating down. They landed on Samir's coffin.

Each spark turned into a candle, now alight. They circled the coffin, throwing a strange light over everything.

'Wow, that is beautiful,' Tessa whispered to Nina, her voice hardly clear over the scene, as if they were at a sunset picnic and not in the middle of... whatever this was.

Nina nodded. Her nose wrinkled as a weird smell snuck in, like the peaceful vibe had just been crashed by a fart. The atmosphere? Like an old movie. Oh, and those eyes.

Noah's were bonded to Tessa, and that creepy gleam wasn't exactly slight. The rest of the group? All eyes on Nina, like she had a neon sign flashing 'EAT ME.' Suspicion, fear, rage, who knows what else, but they weren't hiding it. Asim stood there, arms crossed, not moving.

Jonathan stood before them, all serious. Wizards, magical beings, everyone was waiting for him to get on with it. His voice had that mysterious edge, but you could tell he was enjoying the attention a bit too much.

'Friends, today we say goodbye to a special soul who touched us in ways we may not fully understand,' he started, then glanced at Asim, who looked like he'd rather be anywhere else. 'Samir, my half-brother, has passed.'

And there it was. The part where everything got weirdly heavy. The crowd stilled, eyes wide, jaws clenched. Masterpiece. Even Asim had the look of like he'd just been slapped. No one knew about this, no one. Jonathan, clearly loving the shock, kept smirking and went on like he hadn't just said something shocking. 'In our magical world, we all know death isn't the end, it's just a beginning,' he said.

Jonathan let the moment hang. 'Let's honor Samir's journey.'

The crowd stood there, taking it in. But with Jonathan, there was always that feeling he was waiting for applause, or a curtain call. Nina was stuck in her own head, just about hearing Jonathan's words. Too many faces, too many people, she couldn't tell who was real and who was a ghost. Tension, like they were all waiting for something to go wrong. Jonathan finally stepped back, and Asim took his place. He started slow, a cold shiver running through him as he faced the crowd.

'Ladies and gentlemen, today, we're here to remember and honor my dad.' He paused, feeling every word. 'He taught me never to give up, to fight for the best, and to hold tight to those we love.'

'Bullshit,' Tessa said quietly.

Asim's words faltered. His eyes locked onto a young man walking up with an older woman, and something about the guy threw him off. He dragged his gaze back to the coffin, replaying his father's voice in his head, telling him to hold it together.

'Though my heart aches, I'm grounded in the memories we shared,' Asim continued, his voice finding strength again. 'Thank you, Father. Rest in peace, knowing you'll always be remembered by your only son, Asim.'

He ended.

'Well, well, well, wow, nice speech,' the young man said and clapping his hands. 'Your only son... I love it.' Everyone was on edge now, eyes darting between him and Asim.

He moved in, calculated, like he owned the ground he walked on. Jonathan's eyes narrowed as he tightened his hold on his cane. It felt like something could break at any second.

'Who are you, and what do you want?' Asim's voice hardly held back.

The young man's evil eye tangled, darker. 'Oh, my dear brother, I'm here to pay my respects to our father. Oops, sorry, should I say, my half-brother?'

Everyone stood there, slack-jawed and wide-eyed, as if collectively thinking, *What the hell just happened?*

Jonathan stayed still, eyes locked on him, cane tight. Asim clenched his jaw, fists at his sides.

'Would you mind?' The young man gestured for Asim to step aside. It wasn't a question; it was a push.

Asim stepped back. Everyone went still, except... Grandma, who looked like she was enjoying the show. Nina's gut coiled, sniffing, catching the unpleasant smell of his soul, green, rotten, like garbage. Her nose bled, just a drip, but Jonathan handed her a tissue. What a gentleman.

'I'm Samir's bastard. His blood's in me,' the man said, 'and I'm here to take what's mine.'

He locked onto Asim. Every word aimed to hurt. None didn't dare move.

'What do you want?' Jonathan asked, sounding more confused than scared.

The young man turned, a dark smile on his face. 'Asim's magic is mine. I'm Samir's first-born.'

Jonathan stayed quiet, yes, he knew the rules.

'Anyway,' the man added, 'my name's George. Your beloved nephew.'

Then his eyes went black, veins pulsing. With one motion, he ripped his wand from his jacket and thrust it skyward. 'Isonima dole!' he shouted.

And the barrier blew apart like a bomb. The noise was intense, like metal crashing against metal, making the ground shake with the impact.

Shards rained down, tearing through flesh, bone, whatever stood in their path. Screams cut through the air. People bolted for cover, though there wasn't much left.

Asim cowered behind a pillar and covered his ears. Too loud. Too much. Curling up, he looked completely helpless, his eyes wide with fear and trembling.

Tessa yelled over, 'Where's that magical protection now, huh?'

'Get the hell down!' Nina pulled her along, the smell of burning flesh hitting her like a whack to the face.

Jonathan barked over the madness, 'Get back! Cover yourselves!' A sharp slash of his cane and he snapped, 'Samiro deko!' The shards broke apart and turned into dust.

But Grandma wasn't giving in. She put on her Demand gloves, cracked her finger sharply, and black lines shot out like bullets. Still, George was quicker. His wand broke, and the blast hit Grandma's arm, leaving a burn on her skin. She tripped, but her eyes weren't giving up.

'Grandma!' Finley crawled through, dragging his coat, shielding her. 'We've got to move,' he babbled, pulling her to hide behind a broken pillar.

'It's nothing. Just a scratch. Get down, will you?' she bit, not letting a minute of pain slow her down.

George turned toward Asim, wand raised. But Shad was quicker, springing forward and throwing a kick to George's chest, whacking him to the ground.

They locked eyes—Shad steady, George seething. This wasn't over.

Spitting blood, he whipped his wand toward Jonathan. 'Otamaro sino!' Fire roared from the wand, shooting straight at him.

Noah bolted, dragging his crew behind him, leaving Mr Jamal bleeding out in the dirt. Flames licked at the ground. The air full of smoke.

Jonathan, sturdy, raised his cane. 'Apolono serus!' The sky split open. Heavy rain poured down, smothering out the fire. Jonathan released his shoulders beginning to droop under the weight. A stray blast smashed into Samir's coffin, breaking the wood. Asim's face went pale. His breath caught.

George stared at Jonathan with intense, hateful eyes. 'This isn't over,' he growled.

With a sharp flick of his wand, George hissed, 'Osime sa,' and bam, he and the woman beside him vanished.

Shad's demons rushed to Asim, dragging him onto the travel cloth. The healer was waiting. Asim, barely holding on, his scorched skin and lodged shards a reminder of how close it had been.

Sirens screamed closer.

'Get everyone to the healers, now!' Jonathan barked.

Finley smashed a potion to the ground. Smoke swallowed him, Tessa, and Mr Jamal, and they were gone in a blink.

Jonathan ran to Nina, who was still on the ground, breathing hard, mud streaking her clothes.

'You alright?'

'Yeah... I think. But Tessa...'

'She's safe, with the healers,' Jonathan said, as the sirens drew closer. 'Let's get out of here.'

Before Nina could reply, Jonathan slammed his cane into the ground. 'Asomoro endomo.'

The air cracked, energy flowing through, and Ta-da, they were gone.

Chapter Twenty-nine
The After

Part One

MR JAMAL AND GRANDMA sat together, both looking a bit tired. The funeral had been a mess. They talked quietly, each trying to cope. Grandma had lost her hat, and now she looked older. Mr Jamal wasn't better off. His hat was gone too, and without it, he seemed drained, deeply unhappy. He'd probably lost something important.

So, he mentioned his plan—capturing Jonathan for his crimes and taking the book, the key to immortality. Grandma's interest was piqued. Immortality was one thing, but Jonathan was another. She chuckled.

'You're a funny man. You think you can put Jonathan in prison? The man's untouchable.'

'We've got evidence. Magic violations, kidnappings, murders. This isn't small stuff, is it?'

'Oh, Mr Jamal, you fool. That's not enough. This won't be easy, no, no,' Grandma muttered.

'That's why I need you, my love. Do you remember our good old times?'

'Of course, I remember. Lovely times...' She trailed off before shaking her head. 'Anyway, we're both useless. But maybe, well, just maybe, with someone else's help, we can.'

The idea was dangerous but tempting. Then, with a wicked laugh, she admitted to tipping George off about the funeral. She had hated Samir and didn't think he deserved any respect. Mr Jamal's reaction was quick, and they both shared a dark smile—the beginning of something new and dangerous. They clinked their glasses, sealing the agreement.

They bumped into Noah outside a small pub. Noah, being his usual trouble-stirring self, flashed a smug grin and threw out a comment like he'd been waiting all day just to annoy someone.

'Well, well, Grandma, you're looking positively charming,' he teased. 'Quite the match, isn't it? Two old birds.'

'Mind your manners, snaky man. We're here for George,' Mr Jamal said.

'Funny you mention it. I've been looking for him too. A waiter said his mum shows up here every Tuesday at 10 pm for a drink,' Noah said.

With a nod, Grandma and Mr Jamal agreed to join.

As Noah left, that creepy feeling slipped up his neck—the type that screams *someone's watching you*. He whipped around like a paranoid ninja, only to see a hooded figure legging it. He shrugged it off. Bigger things were on his mind. Like his looks.

He stopped by a shop window, checking the hats on display. His reflection laughed back, still wounded from the funeral attack. *Thanks, healer. Great job, really.* His fingers skimmed over the choices until one screamed at him—bright orange, bold, loud, and obnoxiously perfect. He slapped it on. Even so, that unsettling feeling clung to him like a fog that refused to lift.

JONATHAN'S PALACE

'NINA, YOU'RE AWAKE. Welcome.' Jonathan's words came from behind.

'I'm so confused. What's happening?' She turned back, but the ghost had already vanished.

'Let's get you something to eat. You must be hungry,' said Jonathan.

He led her to the dining room, eyes sneaking glances at her. He had tried—and failed miserably—not to stare. That dress: hell, it looked incredible on her. And he wasn't even trying to hide how much he loved it. Like a proper gentleman, he pulled out a chair, and Nina collapsed into it, her mind still spinning from everything, not even noticing the food in front of her.

'You've only been napping for an hour,' Jonathan said. 'You had a couple of burns and cuts, but my healer took care of it.'

Nina sat there, ignoring her plate, as worry started to take over. Even though Jonathan kept trying to reassure her about Tessa, Asim, and the others, his smile seemed a bit forced, and there was something weird in his eyes. He wasn't used to getting close to people, but Nina was different. Somehow, it made him feel things he wasn't comfortable with.

She kept her eyes on him. It was a bit tense. Jonathan's usual confidence wavered for a moment. George had just been a name, but the disaster at the funeral had shaken him. His fingers tapped anxiously on the table. The use of magic to hurt and mess with funeral protections was serious. He knew the officers would deal with it. Well, whoever was behind it was facing real consequences. He asked Nina why she had been hiding in the caravan. And she laid it out; demons could smell her. Noah was on her back. And Finley had practically forced her to stay hidden. Even now, she wasn't sure what to believe.

'Well, you can stay here. I can protect you.'

'No need to act, Jonathan. I've heard things about you... and you're hiding one of the books.'

'Nope, rumours are just noise, Nina. I thought you were smart enough to know what's real and what's not.' Jonathan leaned in a little. 'But I use my powers for good. I don't hurt anyone.' He reminded her how he'd saved everyone at the funeral. Nina had seen it with her own eyes.

'I'm sorry... it's just, ever since I got here, I'm lost, confused.'

Jonathan gently pressed a finger to her lips.

'Shhh, don't apologise. I get it. I know your story, Nina. I know who you are. Ok?'

While he was talking, something kept pulling at her heart the whole time.

'I can help you,' he continued. 'I've never seen a guardian as vulnerable as you.'

Nina's eyes dropped. Jonathan wasn't letting go. No matter how hard the truth smacked, he promised her straight-up honesty. Strong as steel, he said that would be their bond. She agreed but inside, she stayed sharp. God's warning still echoed: *don't trust anyone.* And it wouldn't leave her—that nagging sense of something wicked in Jonathan.

'Do you remember me from when I was an angel? I mean, the guardian?'

'Not really, no. I only know what everyone else knows, but I wish,' said Jonathan.

The weight of the moment sank in when he locked eyes with her. Something stirred deep inside, something he couldn't ignore. His face stayed steady, like nothing had changed, but it had. Her eyes searched his, like she was trying to figure out something just beyond her reach. She didn't recognise him, not really. But there was familiarity. It made his chest tighten. He knew her better than she'd ever guess right now. Shame this wasn't the time to let it show. Well, not yet.

Pointing things out with a relaxed air, he took her around the place. He was probably trying to shake it off. Nina followed, taking it all in, amazed by the beauty around them.

'Is that you with your family?'

'Yep, that's me, my father, and my mother,' said Jonathan.

As they walked past a gallery of hand-drawn pictures, Nina went still. She'd seen this picture before. Not just similar—the exact one she had found in the library, tossed among broken glass after the break-in. Her pulse quickened. What the hell was it doing here?

Keeping her face cool, she pushed it down. Luckily, Jonathan didn't notice, too caught up in his memories.

His mind slipped back to that day. His mother, eyes red, tears silent, holding everything in as his father walked out the door. The betrayal, the lies. It had broken something in her. It had cracked something in him too. He had sworn to her then, a vow he couldn't break, to fix it, to protect her from everything, even if it meant becoming someone else entirely.

'That picture...' His voice softened, distant. 'It's... old. Very old.'

Staying quiet, Nina hummed. That picture carried weight, the same strange pull it had when she first saw it. A connection... And now, it made even less sense. She tucked the thought away, but it clung to her. Something bigger was going on here. And she needed to find out what.

Jonathan watched her for a moment, then shrugged.

'Okay, just do it,' he said.

'Do what?'

'I know you're dying to sniff me, so go ahead. I've got nothing to hide. I prefer trust between us.'

She went still, unsure how to react. But bloody hell, he was right. She loved sniffing people's souls; it was like second nature. So, she leaned in. Sniffed him like a dog. But something went wrong. As she breathed in, her nose started bleeding again.

Jonathan moved quickly, handing her a tissue. Gently, he held her nose and tilted her head back.

'It's fine.'

'No, it's not. How long has this been happening?'

'Since we got here.'

'That's not good,' Jonathan said, his voice serious. 'You need to find your book. You know, without your full powers, it's like you're living without a soul, and that's... well, that's impossible. This world knows who you are.'

Before she could even process that, he hit her with a question.

'And how's the leg pain?'

Like he'd just dropped a bomb, she went still, staring at him. 'How the hell do you know about that?'

Too carelessly, Jonathan blew it off. 'Rumours, Nina. I hear a lot, like everyone else.'

Inside, alarms were blaring. She nodded slowly. How did he know about her illness? Since arriving in this world, yes, she hadn't felt the pain, but still... it was kind of weird.

'Erm, it's gone,' she finally said. 'Ever since I got here.'

'Of course, of course,' replied Jonathan. 'No illnesses in this world. You know that, right?'

Suspicion bit at her, but Nina nodded again. How did he know so much? Was he working with Finley? Was this all some kind of trap, like what Noah had pulled? Who could she trust anymore? What the hell was really going on?

In the caravan, at the same time.

FINLEY STROLLED TOWARDS Tessa, tea in hand. He blew on it, sending a sparkling bubble up before it popped with a faint hiss.

'Oh, what magic have you done?'

'I've infused your tea with love and healing energy, to soothe not just your body, but your soul as well,' said Finley.

'Lovely.'

But Tessa's concern for Nina grew. She'd been gone for over an hour. Finley tried to keep it cool, reassuring her that Nina was with Jonathan and would hopefully be fine. Tessa's worry deepened.

'Hmm, excellent. What do you know about him? Why did he take her, and why can't you go get her?'

'Jonathan's a Lord. He won't hurt her. Don't stress, she'll be back soon.'

'Yeah, Lord my ass. Same as trusting the protection at the funeral, innit?'

'I'm sorry, Tessa, that you feel that way. Trust me, everything will be okay.'

Though Tessa eased up slightly, something didn't sit right with Finley. His mind wasn't on Nina; it was on someone else. Asim was now in the firing line. Looking at the floor, he sipped his tea.

'Oh gosh, everything's so shit now. What's happening, Finley? I feel like I'm in a movie, but I kind of hate it.'

'Well, yeah, we've got a bigger problem than I thought. I didn't know about George, and that worries me. His powers are strong. We need to find Asim.'

'You mean the boy who acts like Harry Potter?'

'Harry what?'

'For God's sake, this world... Do you even watch movies?'

'Of course, but we have a big issue now, Tessa, okay? Asim, remember? He's definitely with Nicole.'

She looked at Finley with a furrowed brow, waiting for answers. He explained quietly, tension in his words. Samir's old crew—Raj, Lorenzo, Margot, and her daughter—had been at the funeral. Criminals. Seeing them there had unsettled him, and he admitted they might be after Asim for the money Samir still owed. Tessa's face fell, realising the deeper trouble Asim was in.

The two of them were growing closer, really close. Then Tessa smiled, and so did Finley, though he went a bit red. They leaned closer, and closer, and then it happened. They kissed. But Finley pulled away and moved back a bit, then a bit more, until he was sitting right on the edge. He didn't fall, but he was looking down.

'I'm sorry. I don't know what just happened. That's... not me.'

'It's alright,' said Tessa. 'We didn't do anything wrong, did we? Did you not want to?'

'I like you, like, a lot. Since the moment I saw you. But... I've never been good with women, you know.'

Tessa leaned back, her mind racing, but she didn't want to push him. Hurting him wasn't the point, and honestly, she got it. But the whole marriage thing? No kids? Was that the reason?

She smirked to herself. So what if he likes men? He likes women too. I don't give a shit.

'Errm... You know... I actually grew up in a caravan, probably not far from here.'

'This is Bradford Four.'

Tessa jumped up like a kid. 'No flipping way! Yes! That was my home!'

'Yeah, don't forget, this world is a copy of yours. I mean, Hell...'

'I know, I know... Anyway, what do you know about me? Can you help me figure out this magic, like, in my words?'

'I'm not sure, Tessa. You know, magic here... it's always tied to something. A wand, a cane,' said Finley, 'potions, wood, whatever. It's in our blood, and we're connected to it. You... you just spoke, and it happened. That's different, and to be honest, I've never seen that.'

He led her downstairs, grinning as Tessa laughed.

'A basement? Really?'

'Just trust me,' Finley chuckled.

The room was tiny and empty as they stepped down, the kind of place no one bothered with. It was the same room where he had taken Nina. He did the same thing, turning the emptiness into a beautiful library.

'Omg, that's something I love about this place.'

'Yup. How the hell do you survive without magic in Hell?'

'We got TikTok, you know, and all those tech stuff.'

'I've heard about that. But let's stay on track. We've got something to find,' said Finley.

At the same time, but far from the caravan—though not too far from Jonathan's palace—Asim sat in Nicole's warm, snug home. Not that the warmth did much to help. The healer had done their bit, and now Nicole was pushing him to drink the medicine. He eyed the cup with suspicion; the last time he'd taken it, it had left him with elephant ears. Nicole waved away his hesitation, firmly reminding him the injury was creeping back.

Asim heard her, but his mind was elsewhere, tangled up in thoughts that felt far more important than whatever mixture was in that cup. He dropped his gaze, a heavy weight settling on his shoulders, feeling painfully useless, as usual. She moved closer, believing that he just needed to trust Jonathan more. She reminded him that Jonathan had saved them and that he was now his uncle. Asim reacted sharply to this, wondering why Jonathan had never told him. Nicole suggested that he should ask Jonathan himself. She warned him that George was dangerous and that this wasn't something to take lightly.

Asim gave a nod. Nicole pulled him in for a hug, but just as he was starting to sink into it, Shad barged into the room without so much as a knock—full-on stormed in, like subtlety was something he'd never even heard of.

'Shit, sorry, didn't realise...' said Shad.

'It's fine, mate,' Asim said and pulled back from Nicole.

Shad stepped closer. 'I've got your back, mate. We're in this together.'

Asim gave a slight nod, finding comfort in Shad's words.

He then shoved a drink into Asim's hand, practically forcing him to take it. Asim didn't fancy it, but he knocked it back anyway. It was rough, the type of taste that made you wince, but he kept quiet. Then he felt it—a searing pain shot through his eyes, ripped down his throat, and left him gasping, like he was being strangled from the inside out.

Shad and Nicole clocked it straight away and rushed over. But Asim looked like he was done. Couldn't talk, couldn't move. Nicole and Shad didn't waste time. They knew what to do. Jonathan. Now.

'Quick, grab his feet,' Shad said, already tying Asim's arms.

Nicole's hands were shaking, but she managed to lift Asim's legs. Shad grunted as he dragged Asim's limp body to Jonathan's door. It wasn't how he planned to spend his day, but here he was, pulling dead weight and hoping for the best. Sweat dripped from his forehead as he rang the doorbell again and again. A servant inside shuffled toward the door, slow, like nothing was happening outside.

'For heaven's sake! What took you so long? Get Jonathan. Now!' said Shad.

Without waiting, he dragged Asim again, laying him on the grand sofa. He stood over Asim's pale face—there was something he couldn't name.

Jonathan rushed in, Nina right behind him. 'What happened?' His fingers pressed against Asim's wrist, steady, but he was unconscious.

'Get the healer!' Jonathan barked at the servant.

Shad's hands trembled, and Nicole stood watching.

'What's happened to him?' Nina shouted.

Shad dropped the details, but his eyes locked on Jonathan.

'I swear, my Lord, I didn't do anything,' Shad shot back, a bit defensive. But something felt fishy, and Nina felt it too.

The healer made his way to them, scanned Asim's body, then looked at Jonathan. 'It's dark magic, my Lord,' he said.

Jonathan's pulse was hammering as he waved him away. Nina's voice trembled as she tried to get answers, but Jonathan's mind was already drowning in memories of his mother's curse.

'It's a spell. Recall. It traps you, body and mind,' said Jonathan.

Shad and Nicole looked at each other, knowing more than they let on. Nina's confusion deepened.

'Do something! Will he be alright? Who'd do this, and why?' she said.

Jonathan's pale face said it all. 'We need Finley's potions... but only the one who cast it can truly undo the spell. It was that bastard, George! Go get Finley now!' he shouted at Shad, who took off, heading straight for the car.

'Get blankets and fresh water!' Jonathan then barked at his servant.

Nina collapsed into a chair. Meanwhile, Jonathan told Nicole to leave, and she did, not that she looked like she wanted to stick around anyway.

BACK IN THE CARAVAN

IN THE MEANTIME, FINLEY and Tessa, completely unaware of what had happened to Asim, wove through the shelves, hunting for that one book. Tessa's mind drifted back to her first day—Nina showing her around the dull library. She had hated it. The books, the quiet, everything. But after her son died, it was the only place where she could hold it together.

'Ah, got it!' Finley pulled an old, weighty book off the shelf, smirking like he'd cracked a code.

'You know, this smells just like our place back home.'

Finley noticed the shift in her. Homesick. She didn't need to say it. 'Let's sit down.'

Tessa looked around. Nothing to sit on. Finley pulled out a tiny glass flask and blew a fine mist into the air. In an instant, two armchairs appeared, a small table between them.

Tessa blinked like she'd been slapped with a wet fish. 'That's mad! Didn't know you could do that.'

'I can do a lot more than that,' he said, winking.

Tessa's heart kicked up, buzzing. But a sharp, rough shout tore through the air.

'Oi, Finley! Oi! Open the bloody door!'

Being in the basement, they couldn't see who it was. Finley dug out the vial and blew. A small window shimmered into existence, letting them get a proper look at whoever was outside the caravan.

'It's that young lad from the funeral,' Finley muttered.

'That's Nicole's brother,' Tessa said.

BACK AT JONATHAN'S PLACE

WHILE THEY WERE WAITING for Finley, Jonathan sat stiff, staring ahead as if he were watching the past play out in front of him.

'This is exactly what happened to my mother, you know,' said Jonathan.

Nina stayed quiet, watching him while he carried on. 'I didn't know what was happening, and my father was off on some business trip. The healers were completely useless. She died, Nina. After three days. Three bloody days of agony.'

Nina's eyes flicked to Asim, worry creeping in. She didn't want to make this about him, but the fear snuck in anyway. Like an annoying little itch she couldn't quite reach, the thought popped up. Could this happen to Asim too? But she bit it back, not wanting to throw it in Jonathan's face, not when he was still drowning in his own pain.

'I... I don't know what to say, Jonathan. I'm sorry,' she murmured, her voice softer now. Her eyes went back to Jonathan, watching him tense up. 'So you're saying there was no one? No one could save her?'

Jonathan's eyes were full of rage as he clenched his fists. 'I tried everything, Nina. Trust me, the best healers, wizards. Hell, I even called on God himself, but no one came,' he spat. 'There was help, of course, but no one lifted a bloody finger.'

The silence stretched, thick and heavy. His mother's death stuck to him, deep and raw, a scar that never faded. And that anger sat there, festering.

'People hunger for wealth, fame, power. Hell itself isn't enough punishment for our greed, Nina,' Jonathan whispered, his stare hollow.

Nina felt the weight of his misery, the scars running far deeper than she had ever imagined. She finally saw how the world had screwed him over, not just with pain, but with all the so-called good people who bailed on him, turning him into this unrecognizable mess of who he used to be. Jonathan moved to Asim, carefully wrapping him in a blanket. His touch was gentle, and it made Nina's heart flutter. Beneath all of it, she saw a good man. Someone still capable of care and kindness.

Then, the same haunting whisper came again. 'Find me, Nina. Find me.'

She looked around, scratching her ear. 'Did you hear that?'

'Hear what?' said Jonathan.

The doorbell rang.

'Where is he?' barked Finley.

Nina pointed to Asim, who lay unconscious on the sofa. Finley rushed over, Tessa right behind him, worry written all over her face. Nina, Tessa, and Jonathan stared as Finley opened his suitcase, and it morphed into a full room of potions. Only Finley could make this happen. He was the potions wizard.

Finley turned to Jonathan, sweat dripping down his brow.

'I'm not sure, Jonathan. I...' he stammered, hands shaking.

Jonathan stepped closer, eyes burning. 'Listen to me now. You have to do it this time, you asshole! Or are you going to let history repeat itself, huh?'

Tessa and Nina watched, confusion flickering across their faces.

Finley finally exhaled into the potion. A shimmering blue. Then a fiery red. He blew into each one, colourful dust drifting toward Asim, but at first, nothing happened.

Then, Asim coughed. He was still unconscious, but stirring.

'Stay back!' Finley barked. He dropped to his knees, blowing more dust into Asim's face. The coughing kicked up a dark, muddy hue.

'Shit, I need a jar or a bowl. Now!'

Jonathan brought one without hesitation. Finley wasted no time, mixing a potion with the murky substance and exhaling into it again. Dark dust exploded from the bowl, swirling toward Finley.

Tessa, worried, moved to help, but Jonathan held her back.

'Let him work, no one moves!' Jonathan said.

Finley's eyes now had this creepy, full-on black glow. He gasped for breath, but then he saw it—Nicole wasn't who she seemed. She was George's fiancée, and her mission? To poison Asim with a Recall spell.

When Finley took a deep breath, or whatever you'd call it, because it felt more like gulping down a mouthful of burnt marshmallow—the world around him disappeared.

His eyes rolled back until they vanished under his lids, and then that bloody dust... yes, the dust that would ruin even the world's best vacuum, flew right back into Asim. It was a magical navigator into the cursed, black world where Asim was trapped. Sounds like a cool way to help someone, right? Except it didn't always work. Of course, why would it ever be simple? Black magic was banned, not from some strict moral stance, but because it had consequences, dark ones.

Finley stood up, and suddenly his face... well, it changed. Like, really changed. Wrinkles carved into his skin like some wicked carpet designer had gone to town, and within a second, he looked like a grandad from a fairy tale. But he didn't care, as long as it helped Asim. Noble, sure, but Nina could see this magic was serious business, and it scared her a little. Tessa, though, stayed calm. Yeah, well, I expected that, she thought to herself, like she'd just bought overpriced popcorn. She'd seen this kind of thing in a film, yes, magic takes its fee, but who wouldn't be moved when Finley practically sacrificed himself for Asim?

Jonathan, the ever sceptical one, stood off to the side, shaking his head. He knew the truth, creeping along like a lazy old cat: there was no guarantee Asim would be alright. Black magic—nasty, treacherous, and unreliable, like that dodgy insurance policy you'd never trust. And Finley just nodded, his silent look confirming it all. Tessa handed him water as he continued, heavy with dread. Asim was still alive, but only because his powers were tangled with the poison. He was fighting the spell from the inside, aware but trapped.

Jonathan went quiet, deep in thought. Nina lit a cigarette, working out their next move. They had to find

Nicole to break the spell, but it wouldn't be easy. She was likely already one step ahead. If she'd gone back to George, tracking her down would be a real pain.

'Shit, what do we do now?' Tessa yelped, and a piece of poo plopped right in her eye.

'For God's sake, Tessa, again?' Finley rolled his eyes, exhausted, completely drained after using the dark magic.

'Alright, where's the bathroom?' Tessa asked, but before she could move, Jonathan shot up, cane in hand, and pointed it at her.

'Asimila ante!' he said, and the mess vanished.

'Wow, brilliant! Thanks,' said Tessa.

'You? No way. How is that even possible? This can't be, no!' Jonathan's face twisted with disbelief.

Everyone traded blank looks, like a room full of people who had just realised they had shown up to the wrong party in fancy dress.

'Are you talking to me?' Tessa asked, lost.

'You... You're the Queen of Snakes!' Jonathan's voice dropped, laced with shock.

Finley jumped. Could she really be real?

Jonathan nodded, a knowing look on his face. Only the Queen of Snakes could wield the kind of magic Tessa had. It was odd, though; the last queen had vanished hundreds of years ago. How had she taken her place?

Tessa shook her head, rejecting the idea. Jonathan insisted that magic never messed up; it always sought its rightful master. Anyone trying to steal that power was asking for trouble, just like Nina's books—consume it, and you're done for. Finley turned to Tessa, connecting the dots. This was why George was after Asim. Samir was their father. After his death, his magic would flow through them. It was in their blood.

In a world of magic and mystery, Jonathan stood like a sage, his sharp mind drawing from great experience. Nina, watching quietly, knew that if they teamed up, they could find a way to save Asim. Jonathan realised there was a way to save him, and it was Nina—capable of giving or taking life. Finley admitted to hiding her book, but Jonathan denied having it, saying Nina would know if he did. He reminded them that the book's power was dangerous and that those who sought it paid with their lives.

Nina agreed, confirming the book was not nearby, and that was all she needed to know. Tessa's eyes blazed with fury as she faced Jonathan.

'You are a liar! Where do you hide the key for the basement? I'll go have a look!'

'None of your business. Look at you, stuffing your face like a fat pig!' Jonathan shot back.

'Oi, you bloody shithole! I will cut your dirty mouth!' Finley shouted, jumping in.

'Aww, look, so cute. Two little piggies!' Jonathan smirked.

Tessa scoffed, crossing her arms. 'Oi, you milkshake! Ugly as my ass! Come here, and I will show you how we do this at home. Come on, come here, you bastard!'

The insults flew faster, each one cutting deeper. Tessa had finally had it. She lunged at Jonathan, arm cocked back like she was about to deliver the punch of the century. Finley, bless his heart, was trying to hold her back, but let's face it, he had all the stopping power of a kitten in a rainstorm.

Then, bam. He lost his cool too and spun around, ready to clock Tessa like she owed him money. Jonathan? Oh, he was done pretending to be civilised. He tossed his fancy cane aside like it was an old takeaway box and squared up, fists ready, eyes burning with the *come at me, bro* energy of a man who had just been told his favourite football team sucks.

Finley, the poor old sod, threw a punch at Jonathan and instantly regretted every decision that had led him to that moment. His hand screamed in agony, and he nearly burst into tears, while Jonathan's eyes blazed with rage as he stood quietly.

Just as Jonathan lifted his hand, probably planning to turn Finley into a human pancake, Tessa barrelled in like a caffeinated squirrel, shoved him to the ground, and pounced. She rained down punches like she had been training with Mike Tyson, leaving Jonathan so shocked he probably could not spell his own bloody name.

'Enough! This isn't you, there's magic messing with your heads!' Nina yelled.

She knew she had to act fast, so she raised her hands toward them and froze everyone in place. But now what? Then she remembered, 'God, I need your help!'

And voila, he appeared, not in a glow, and asked why she called. Nina explained they were human and needed his help. After a quick look around, God said they were under a spell of anger and vanished.

Nina said loudly, 'he's a proper asshole.'

She grabbed the traveling cloth from Finley's pocket, not even a "sorry, mate" thrown his way, and transported herself to the caravan. Quickly, she took the potion labelled *Anger* and travelled straight back.

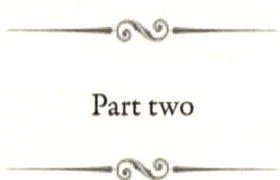

Part two

BACK AT JONATHAN'S, the scene looked like someone had pressed pause on a room full of drama queens. Nina dumped the potion over their heads, but nothing happened. The potion simply dripped down, as useless as a chocolate teapot. Then, a lightbulb moment. She needed Finley's breath to activate the magic. She shoved the potion under his nose, and that did the trick. Immediately, the room was filled with quiet, soft voices and the sound of spells dissolving like cracking plaster.

Nina spelled it out for them. They had all been under an anger curse. Jonathan's face turned red, and he exploded, shouting for answers. Tessa kept waving her hands around, moaning about how the spell had scrambled everyone's brains. Then came a big, dramatic cough from behind. Everyone turned to see Asim sitting up, clutching a gold key like he was about to knight himself.

Tessa hurried over, giving him a hug that probably bruised a rib or two, kissing him all over. Asim struggled, looking like he would rather be anywhere else, but low-key loving the attention. Jonathan's eyebrows nearly jumped off his forehead, while Finley's eyes locked onto the key. Jonathan stepped closer and barked orders for his servant to get the healer.

'No, this is impossible,' said Jonathan. 'What's going on? And what's with the key?'

Asim looked at the key as if it were his firstborn baby.

'This key saved me, uncle.'

Jonathan gave a slight smile, a pure and unexpected feeling surfacing when Asim called him that. Then, the key vanished from Asim's hand and stuck onto his chest.

Nina moved in, her brow furrowed. Before she could voice her confusion, the healer shuffled down the stairs in his pyjamas, looking like he had just fought a bear and lost.

'It's only afternoon,' Nina said.

Jonathan steadied himself. Healers were always exhausted from draining their energy.

'Well, he is fine, but drink this medicine,' the healer said.

Asim immediately shot him down, telling him to keep that disgusting thing to himself. He needed food and drinks, not some medicine with nasty side effects.

With a tap of his cane, Jonathan commanded, 'Atíme soltó!'

A massive dining table appeared, filled with mouthwatering dishes and drinks. Tessa helped Asim to his feet. The poor boy could barely stand. He attacked the food like a starving beast, so wildly that he seemed to debate whether to drink or eat first. Tessa leaned in, gripping his arm tightly.

'Slow down a bit! You don't want to choke, darling!' she said.

But Asim was too deep into his feast to care. Nina jumped back, feeling the hairs on her arms rise as she heard that strange whispering voice again, the one that kept haunting her. *'Find me, Nina. Find me.'* She was scared, but more afraid that she was losing her mind.

'Why won't this bloody ghost leave me alone?' she screamed, covering her ears.

'The whisper again? Oh God, what's happening!' said Tessa, waving her hands in frustration.

Then, with a sudden bang, God appeared right in front of them. Tessa's jaw nearly hit the floor.

'Why did you call me?' God asked, looking around.

Tessa threw her hands up. 'Nope, wasn't me,' she said.

Jonathan and God locked eyes, like a scene straight out of a Van Damme film, both just staring. It was the kind of dramatic moment where the invisible camera zoomed in for no reason... or maybe there was a reason. Jonathan ran his fingers over the scar on his face, as if it burned. But no, it did not. It was more like a memory, and not a pleasant one. Jonathan and God had their own history.

'Do one. She called you by mistake!' said Jonathan.

God paused, gave a quick, 'Hmm, strange, very strange,' as if he were judging some weird art project, and then vanished, probably off to deal with something more entertaining.

Finley leaned in closer to Tessa, and it was not for a relaxed whisper or a friendly suggestion. This was serious business. There were names you did not just throw around for fun, only when you absolutely needed something. Tessa, bless her impulsive heart, knew that rule well enough but seemed physically incapable of keeping her mouth shut.

Jonathan, forever the voice of reason, or at least the one keeping them from making stupid decisions too quickly—was not having any of her excuses. His scolding was calm but had a sharpness that commanded attention. Nina didn't like his whole *"I'm in charge"* act, but she stayed quiet about it, likely saving her annoyance for later.

Meanwhile, Finley was having his own mental adventure, flipping through an encyclopaedia of terrifying knowledge he had crammed into his head over the years. And then the puzzle pieces fell into place. The whispers were not just spooky background noise. It was the Hell Bookkeeper reaching out, like a dark librarian who really did not care for late returns. Nina was baffled and just trying to keep up. But Finley explained, because he was generous like that, and because the stakes were kind of high. Tessa, of course, took this moment to suggest the most disturbed plan possible. She wanted to storm right into the Bookkeeper's domain and shake the secrets loose. It was typical of Tessa, the kind of person who would run into a haunted house yelling, *"What's the worst that could happen?"*

Finley, feeling trapped in a corner with no better options, admitted he knew the way. That was when Jonathan cut through with a reality check. Oh yes, because Asim had just come back from, you know, *being dead*. And no one seemed to be giving a bloody stir. With an incensed gesture, he gave Asim the spotlight. Asim took a shaky breath, probably grateful for the chance to finally unload. His voice carried the weight of that haunting vision. Cold sand. A darkness that stretched forever. Shadows creeping in like a nightmare on steroids. He had been alone until those shadows surrounded him, hungry and relentless, draining every bit of life from him. It was not exactly a pleasant vacation story.

Then, just as things were going south, the key on his chest flared up. He grabbed it, felt its power, and wiped the shadows out. He took a sip, lost in the rush. For a moment, it felt like he was the key to the universe, as if he held a VIP pass to the cosmic club. A glance at Jonathan revealed the familiar exchange of knowing looks with Finley, both clearly in on something he was not. Typical.

Jonathan's voice became low and firm, his intense stare focused on Tessa and Finley, who stood still like deer caught in headlights. Nina was not messing about. She stood tall, signalling the others to move. Tessa and Finley got up slowly, doubt written across their faces. Asim, however, stayed where he was, staring straight into Jonathan's eyes. He was not budging. Staying with his uncle. End of discussion.

Asim could practically hear the dramatic music playing, adding an air of suspense to this family drama. Because really, who needed words when the tension was already growing? The next moment, they all vanished from the room, taken away by Finley's travel cloth. Jonathan threw a sly smile at Asim. It was a clear signal that they had work to do, and big things lay ahead. Asim looked full of life, his energy matching Jonathan's as they sat together. Family reunions were always a bit dodgy.

Shad waited by the gate, catching a glimpse of them through the window. They were laughing and drinking like everything was perfectly fine. It seemed real, but a distressing sense of worry settled in. Jonathan, noticing the sensation of being watched, lifted his cane, his eyes shifting quickly to the window. When Shad stepped into view, Jonathan walked outside as relaxed as ever, like it was just another usual day.

Shad felt a spin of confusion about Jonathan's recent actions. With Nina present and Asim near death, it looked like Jonathan was acting against their goals. Jonathan assured him they were sticking to the plan. Asim needed to be convinced. The real problem, however, was Nicole. She had even managed to pull one over on Jonathan, and that was no small feat. For a split second, something like genuine concern flashed across his face. It nearly, just nearly, covered up the sarcasm he had been throwing around earlier about Shad's performance. Nearly, but not quite.

As Shad walked off, a cold dread settled in his gut. Bringing Asim to Jonathan had done more than ruffle feathers. It had stirred something serious. And Jonathan felt it too, that uneasy sensation lingering just beneath his cool exterior. For the first time, Shad started to wonder if Jonathan was all he claimed to be. A typical day in the demon trade, right? With a deep breath of determination, he walked over to his demon crew, already planning his next step. Because in this business, you had to keep one eye on the game and the other over your shoulder, just in case.

Chapter Thirty
Just an Accident

———— ❧ ————

NINA RUSHED DOWNSTAIRS, still dripping from the shower, to find Tessa halfway through dinner. Finley was nowhere in sight. Tessa, just about pausing to swallow, mumbled that he had vanished without a word. Nina, now seated in her long gown, cleared off the food offer. She had bigger things on her mind. It was time to track down the books, even though exhaustion was pulling at her. Across from her, Tessa seemed worn down, lost in thoughts of home. The tension with Asim had started to weigh heavily, his behaviour making her feel like they were the villains.

Hell was home. It always had been. But now that they knew the truth, it did not feel the same. And what about God? Was he the good one here? Did that make her, as Hell's guardian, the bad one? She had not thought so. She was not exactly the spider-killing type. And Death... was he truly the terrifying figure she had heard about? Could he be the real Satan, the devil, like they had all feared? Or was he someone else entirely?

These questions hovered over her, making Hell feel less like home and more like some knotted lie. She felt lost, and as she looked at Tessa, she knew she was not the only one questioning what they had been told. Then Nina's nose started to grow—fast. Tessa, wide-eyed, spilled her drink in shock.

'Oh my goodness, what's happening?' she gasped, too stunned to even say *OMG*.

Nina's terror matched Tessa's as she stared at her absurdly long nose, only to see Tessa inflating like a massive, floating balloon.

Tessa screamed, 'Aaahh! What the heck is going on?'

Finley showed up just in time, rushing over with a potion in hand. He blew forcefully, which somehow stopped the strange growth.

Yes, it slowed down, but the aftermath was not much better. Nina's nose now looked like a scruffy shrub, and Tessa? She was shaped like an Atlantic pumpkin.

Finley could not help but laugh, but oh no, Tessa was having none of it.

'Yeah, very funny! Come on, do something! It was Jonathan, the bastard. I knew he was evil!'

Nina, still in shock, kept touching her now shiny, long nose.

'Chill out, both of you!' Finley said, trying to keep things under control. 'It's just a temporary side effect of that medicine you took after the funeral.'

Nina and Tessa looked at each other, then, remembering the healer's potion, clearly were not thrilled about it now.

'Great. So now I can't even swear, I can't move, and I'm a bloody giant pumpkin!' Tessa yelled.

Ah, the joys of word magic. And just like that, she was one.

Finley let out a heavy sigh. 'Right, now we've got a problem.'

Nina peered at Tessa, who was now sitting there, round and orange.

'Shit, what now? Can you fix this?'

Finley nodded, though not too confidently. 'I'll try, but I need to check a few books first.'

He buried himself in the books, hunting for a way to turn Tessa back into a human. Nina sat beside the pumpkin, sadness slithering in. Her long nose kept jabbing Tessa, but she did not notice, still talking, convinced Tessa could hear her somewhere inside. Her mind wandered back to that one Halloween when they were making pumpkins together, laughing like kids. The memory brought a brief smile to her face. But what Nina did not realize was that the pumpkin next to her was not Tessa at all.

'Nina, are you ready? You won't believe what I've found,' Finley said, stepping out of his office.

'Tessa isn't actually this pumpkin. She's inside,' he continued with a serious look.

Nina shrugged, already confident. 'Yeah, I know. I've been talking to her. She can hear us, even though she's a pumpkin.'

Finley shook his head. 'No, you don't get it. This pumpkin isn't just her form. It's a whole other world. Tessa is inside, living in the pumpkin world.'

Nina stood there, confused. Finley revealed the strange truth—pumpkins had their own world, with living humans, and Tessa had somehow crossed over into it. The worst part? Finley had no idea how to get her back.

'Wait, you mean Tessa's in a world full of living pumpkin people?' Now it was no longer a joke. Nina was bloody terrified, her heart thumping. 'Shit, what now? Is she even safe?'

Knock, knock.

Finley, already on edge, wasn't expecting visitors. When he opened the door, there they stood, two detectives in green suits, white hats tilted just so. They didn't look like they belonged here, and that made him, well, uneasy. Still, he let them speak without a word of invitation.

'Got a report about some funny business down at the pumpkin area,' one of them said with sharp eyes. Finley's gaze dropped to their boots, muddy, like they'd been somewhere they shouldn't have.

'You don't look too chuffed to see us,' the other one remarked, but the tall detective wasn't in the mood for small talk. He pushed his way in, sizing up the caravan.

'Well, you're not looking too fresh yourself. Anyway, no one's here but me,' Finley muttered, trying to keep things on the level.

But no, the second detective wasn't buying it, his eyes locked on the glistening sweat on Finley's brow.

'You're the potion wizard, aren't you? Living in this dump, hmm?' he said. Then he leaned in, too close. 'Fancy a dose of truth serum? That might clear things up... you know what that means, do you, Mr...?'

Finley said nothing, his silence louder than any denial.

The tall detective cut in, 'We're also sniffing around a kidnapping. Noah? Anything familiar? And that mess at the graveyard. Where are they? And what about the use of dark magic, huh? Nothing? No?' His voice had a hard edge to it.

'Errrm, shall I see your ID?' Finley finally shot back, flipping the situation. They weren't expecting that.

'Very well, Mr... We'll be back,' one of them sneered, walking out like they already had the upper hand.

Finley filled Nina in—how strange they'd acted, how something about them felt wrong. Magic police, he explained. They had their ways of knowing things, especially when it came to crossing forbidden lines. The thought of the consequences struck a deep nerve. Prison and death were the price for breaking magic laws here. Well, maybe Finley's gut was right. Those detectives were strange, no doubt about it. The truth? They really were detectives, just not from this world. But Nina's mind was elsewhere. She wasn't particularly interested. Some detectives, apparently. Completely useless, in her opinion, causing trouble instead of helping. That's what Nina still thought about the officers. How were they going to get Tessa back? That was the only thing she cared about at the moment.

Finley seemed confident. He'd handle it, he'd get Tessa back safely, but she'd only slow him down. The words stung, even though she knew he didn't mean it that way. While Finley was in his workshop, sorting himself out for the trip to the Pumpkin world, Nina sat off to the side, feeling like everything had collapsed in on her. She felt this heaviness on her chest, useless, like she couldn't do one bloody thing right.

'Oh, Nina! Look at your nose, it's shrinking!' Finley said.

He packed a small suitcase, Demand Gloves on, potion in hand. She sat there like a statue, dead inside, not even giving a toss about her nose. Like it bloody mattered now. Finley looked over at her, trying to reassure her. Someone had to stay back in case things went sideways. He handed her a bottle and a battered old book.

'Listen, after 55 minutes, no sooner, no later, use this potion and say these words.'

Nina gave a nod, the kind of half-hearted, 'Yeah, sure,' gesture you'd make when you're too pissed off about not getting your way to actually care.

Finley blew into the potion, and just like that, he was gone in a puff of orange dust, leaving her sitting there, all alone.

Chapter Thirty-one
The Bookkeeper

Nina sat at the table, feeling properly emptied, and the fly servant seemed to sense it. This whole new world, all these riddles, and people who appeared to have more secrets than a crime novel. It was all doing her head in. The servant poured her a whiskey, then dumped himself down beside her, watching in that silent, concerned way of his. She clinked glasses with him, because, well, at least she wasn't drinking alone.

He gave her a kind look, buzzed a bit, but she didn't understand a single bzzz.

'Errm... You know, you're actually quite sweet... for a fly,' she said with a tired grin. 'Can't really picture it... and honestly, I don't even want to, yep.'

He buzzed again, and she rolled her eyes. 'Lovely, isn't it? Here I am, sitting around talking with a bloody fly while everyone else is off saving the world. What a cool Guardian of Hell I am, right? Total bullshit.'

He buzzed harder, like he was telling her to stop being so down on herself. She caught his drift and sighed. 'Alright, alright, I mean... you're a good lad, anyway... thanks for trying.'

She leaned back, thinking out loud. 'Sometimes, though, it feels like Finley doesn't even want me to find those books, you know? But... It's the whole reason I'm here.'

The servant buzzed again, like he was agreeing.

'It's not that I don't like him. Oh no, no...,' she added quickly. 'I do... he's a decent man. It's just... sometimes this whole thing feels weird, you know what I mean?' She threw back the whiskey and set the glass down. 'Here I am, sitting around, doing nothing.'

The servant gestured again, trying to reassure her that Finley was alright, that she could trust him. She nodded, lifting her glass. 'Yeah, you are right,' she said. 'It's not everyone around me that's the problem, it's me, useless... waiting for some miracle... but I just need to get off my arse and do something about it myself, you know.'

And then that dark whisper came. *'Find me, Nina.'*

Nina screamed this time. 'Where the hell do I find you?!'

The whisper shifted, turning into a normal man's voice.

'Oh, finally, you took ages! Cranmer Road. Find the last house with no number and hurry the fuck up!'

Nina shot up, startled. *What the hell was that?* The fly servant waved his hands, shaking his head, but Nina wasn't having it.

'Well, I just heard a creepy whisper, and now it's some *funny* voice telling me to go there,' she explained, pacing. The servant motioned for her to leave, pointing towards the door. But Nina? 'No, I'm waiting for Finley,' but the truth is, she was scared.

The servant held up the potion Finley had given her, his silent reassurance that she'd be fine.

Nina sighed, reminding herself that he couldn't speak, but he still managed to guide her towards the travel cloth. She stood there, torn.

'But... what if something goes wrong? What if it's a trap?'

The servant placed a hand on his chest, signalling courage with steady eyes. He believed in her, and finally, she felt it too.

'You know what, you are right, I'm not weak,' Nina said, squaring her shoulders. 'I'm not a coward.'

The servant smiled, a rare thing, and handed her the Demand gloves. Nina then took a deep breath, ready and stepping onto the travel cloth. In an instant, she vanished and reappearing on Cranmer Road.

She had checked every single house on this street. None missing a number. She was over it.

Spotting an older woman strolling by, no hat, Nina decided to give it one last go.

'Errm, excuse me, have you seen a house without a number?' she asked, trying not to sound desperate.

The woman gave her a deadpan look and shuffled off like she hadn't heard a thing.

Nina rolled her eyes. 'Right, cheers then,' she muttered, scratching her head. This was getting ridiculous. Just as she was about to throw in the towel, this little orange cat wandered over, like it had somewhere to be. Now, Nina wasn't a fan of cats, but something about this one was... weirdly calming.

It stopped a few feet away, didn't come too close, just sat there, staring her down like it had a point to make.

'Oh, brilliant,' she squatted down, shaking her head at how absurd this had become. 'Listen, cutie, well, I'm kind of... losing the plot, but you wouldn't happen to be one of those talking cats, would ya? Know where I can find a house without a number, no?'

The cat just stared, didn't move, sitting there like it was judging her entire existence.

'Brilliant, very well Nina,' she said to herself, standing up. 'This world just keeps getting better. I'm talking to cats, going mad.'

And then, clear as day, 'Meow.'

Nina went still. 'You what?'

The cat's eyes flashed, glowing yellow, and then they weren't cat eyes anymore. They belonged to a man—curly hair, blue suit, standing where the cat once was.

'Errm, yeah, you've definitely lost the plot. Talking cat? Flipping hell!' He laughed.

Nina, mouth wide open, stared at him. 'Wait... I know that voice. You're the one who whispered to me. So, you're... a cat?'

'Well, yeah. Who else, love?'

He gave Nina a once-over. 'Rumours were true, then. Didn't think it'd be this bad, though.'

Nina frowned. 'What's that supposed to mean?'

'You've changed, haven't you? Used to be... well, different. But look, let's save it. Can't be asked with this bullshit. Anyway... Neighbours are nosy as hell. Let's get inside.'

He stepped back, his eyes glowing yellow again, and out of nowhere, a large door without a number appeared, revealing a full house.

'Come in, bloody hell, why're you standing there?'

Nina looked around, then stepped inside without a word. He, though, wasn't the quiet type.

'Right, girl. Didn't expect you to be like this. Sit down,' he said, handing Nina a cup of coffee.

'How... how do you know?' Nina asked.

'What, no sugar, no milk?' He smirked. 'Oh, come on, that's how you used to drink it. Looks like that's the only thing left of the old you.'

Nina stared down at her cup, feeling a pang of something, but stayed quiet.

'Anyway, I'm Tommy,' he continued. 'Bookkeeper, librarian, whatever they're calling me these days, don't give a shit, really.'

'Oh, ok, why were you whispering to me?'

'I can speak to you through your mind, silly you!' Tommy said coolly. 'I'm the only one who can. But seeing you in this new body, err... I didn't realise it was so bad. This isn't you. I know you, and you are defo not her.'

Nina flitted a look around, acting like she didn't hear it. 'Nice place, anyway. How are you a cat and then a man?' she asked.

Tommy shot her a dark look. 'What, are you trying to change the subject? Focus. I called you here because you messed things up for all of us!'

Nina opened her mouth to talk about her lost memories and powers, but Tommy cut her short.

'Stop talking, I know everything... I'm the bookkeeper, and I keep track of everyone, so don't play innocent with me!'

'Ok, listen, why are you so upset with me? What the hell did I do?'

'Well, Miss Goodone, while you were off doing your human bullshits in Hell, selling books or whatever, we were suffering... No pay, no work. The gates are closed. No one's coming or going, so no records to keep. I hope you understand now?'

But no, Nina didn't understand. 'Wait, what? Paid? What are you talking about?'

'Obviously, people get paid for their work!' Tommy snapped. 'Or you, Miss Goodone, think I work for free? What, because I'm a cat? Do I look like I don't need food, huh?'

Nina tried to calm him down, hands raised. 'Ok, ok, look, without my memories, I can't do anything! I'm a wreck and I fucking know! How am I supposed to help in this state?'

Tommy's anger softened a little. 'Alright, calm down, I get it. But we need to fix this. And you're going to have to pay up, Miss Goodone!'

Nina nodded, unsure what else to say.

'Good,' Tommy continued. 'Now, get the fuck up.'

He gestured for Nina to follow as they climbed the seemingly endless staircase. Nina was panting halfway up.

'How can you do all these stairs? Flipping hell, I can't breathe.'

'Oh, right, you're human now. Sorry, Miss Goodone, next time, I'll get you a lift! Now come on, stop moaning and hold my hand tight!'

A yellow glow blasted out of Tommy's eyes, and before Nina could even say, "What the hell just happened," they were somewhere else entirely. Nina braced herself for something horrifying, but instead, her heart started racing, and she cracked this soft, disbelieving smile. Seriously, she couldn't believe her eyes.

'Oh my God,' Nina whispered, taking in the sight. 'I love this place.'

It looked like a library, but not the boring kind you'd find in a sleepy town. No, this place had endless, spiralling stairs slithering around like colossal, lazy snakes. Books lined the walls, glinting and sparking as if they were alive—and knowing this world, they probably were.

'Great, isn't it? Welcome to my workplace. A world where every dead and ugly soul is recorded,' Tommy declared, with a look around that screamed, "Yeah, I run this joint. Deal with it."

Nina was speechless, caught up in the beauty of it all. 'Yes, but this... these books are like, really alive?'

'Of course they are. Each one holds a human soul,' said Tommy.

Nina absorbed it all, though it pulled at memories of her old life and her distant home, which she missed so deeply it felt like a whack to the stomach.

'You see, I don't even know who I am anymore... I feel lost, and sometimes I just want to go back home, and other

times I feel like I should be saving the world. I just feel...
weak, useless, and I...'

'I.I.I. blabla... I know. Ok? But listen. That so-called
"home" isn't where you belong. It's your workplace! You're a
flipping Guardian of Hell, and we can't walk away from that,
even if we wanted to. It's who we are! So, stop crying like a
little human, Miss Goodone!'

Nina just lowered her head, feeling a bit like an idiot, but
she played it off like nothing happened.

Tommy led her through this magical place, casually
dropping bits of history like it was no big deal, while Nina's
eyes kept darting around, still gobsmacked by everything she
was seeing.

'Guardians like you, Miss Goodone, are born every 500
years,' Tommy continued. 'Now, let me show you something.'

Nina couldn't ignore that nickname Tommy kept
throwing at her—Miss Goodone. It always dripped with
sarcasm, but then again, Tommy was basically sarcasm in
human form. Still, there was something about him that Nina
couldn't shake off, like maybe he wasn't as bad as he seemed,
just... pissed off at the world. And honestly, Nina kind of
got it. Tommy just wanted to set things right. For the first
time, Nina felt like something was actually moving forward,
instead of the endless feeling of being stuck in place.

Tommy took out a large, shiny golden book that
sparkled in his hands.

'Here. Open it. This book holds everything about
Guardians... everything about you, Miss Goodone.'

Nina flipped through the pages, but instead of words,
the book seemed to drain, like water spinning down a sink.

'What the hell just happened?'

'Oh, come on, Miss Goodone, you're funny, actually,' Tommy laughed. 'We are in the book; this is how history and souls are written. We don't read; we watch!' He winked.

Nina grabbed Tommy's hand, her head spinning as the surrounding letters twisted into a mad whirlwind, getting bigger and bigger, like some over-the-top magic trick gone wrong. Before she could even think, *oh, bloody hell*, they were pulled right in, the whole world around them crumbling into black dust, like a bad day in the middle of a sandstorm.

And then, just like that, they were inside the scene. Full of real air.

Nina didn't know where to look first, whether at the scene unfolding in front of her or at the living history surrounding her. She still wasn't sure if they were really in the past, because it all felt so vivid. She could feel the air, the stench, every footstep, even the slightest breeze brushing past.

It had an old-fashioned feel, a large four-poster bed with intricate carvings. The walls were panelled in dark, polished wood. There was a single wooden table, but the room felt cosy, though what was happening in it was no longer so cosy.

'Shhh, just watch,' Tommy said. 'They can't see us, Miss Goodone... This is a story from history that we can observe.'

Nina's nerves settled a bit, but what she saw next wasn't easy to stomach. A woman was giving birth in this dingy little room, screaming her lungs out. Two elderly women stood by, whispering prayers, while a third one helped deliver the baby.

A sharp cry broke through—a baby girl. The two older women beamed like they'd just witnessed a miracle.

But the mother? Her face wrangled in disgust. 'Take it away!' she screamed. 'It's a monster!'

Nina's shock hadn't worn off when another scream tore through. The mother gasped and out came a second baby. A boy.

The whole mood shifted instantly. The mother, who had been terrified moments ago, softened. She held the boy like he was made of gold, smiling through her tears, whispering to him like he was her prize.

The younger woman bolted into the woods, darting between the trees. Tommy grabbed Nina's hand, and they ran together, with Tommy determined to show Nina everything that had happened. What they were looking at wasn't just a scene; it was history, the place where the Guardians were born.

The woman knelt down and carefully placed a small woven basket on the ground, tucking the newborn inside with a quiet, unreadable expression. Without a word, she turned and disappeared into the woods, her figure fading into the night.

The baby remained still, peaceful, as though asleep. The surrounding air shimmered, soft golden threads weaving through the space above her like a quiet pulse of magic. Then, without warning, the energy wrapped around her like a cocoon, lifting her gently from the basket.

Nina took a step back, blinking. 'Uh... is this supposed to happen?'

The glow deepened, swirling with soft blues and golds, the light shifting and bending around the small body as if time itself was folding. Slowly, her form stretched, not with any sudden, painful snaps, but with a natural flow, like a river moving from one shape to another. The baby's tiny hands grew longer, fingers unfurling gracefully. Her hair lengthened in soft waves, dark strands forming into the exact same shade as Nina's own.

Her features refined, her jawline sharpening slightly, her nose taking shape, her lips full, her skin settling into a familiar warmth. It was subtle at first, but then, suddenly, it was obvious. Too obvious.

Nina's breath hitched. Her stomach flipped.

Because the woman standing there now, tall, fully grown, glowing with an eerie, quiet power, was her.

Same dark hair. Same high cheekbones. Same sharp, deep-set eyes.

Nina took a step back, shaking her head, her hands gripping the sides of her coat.

'No. No, no, no, that's not right. That's not me.'

Tommy, however, looked completely unbothered. He idly chewed his fingernail.

'Anyway, this is you, Miss Goodone. This is how you were born.'

Nina pointed, shaking, eyes darting between Tommy and her *other self*. 'That—that's not possible.'

'It's very much flipping possible. And now watch. This is the interesting part; how you got your powers, of course,' Tommy said.

'This is a bit scary,' Nina muttered.

'Oi, stop covering your eyes, Miss Goodone, and watch. You're worse than a kid!' Tommy said, pulling Nina's hands away.

The now-grown woman stood there, her nose twitching as she inhaled an overflow of rainbow-coloured dust. She sniffed the air, sharp and instinctive. Her fingers brushed her ears, and at once, a dark liquid shimmered through the space around her, seeping into her like ink dissolving into water. Her eyes brightened, reflecting the shift, a soft glow that pulsed with quiet energy.

She raised her hands, and everything around her stilled. The trees, the leaves, even the distant hum of the wind, all of it held in place, like the world itself was waiting. Another breath, and dark shadows circled her, spiralling gently before vanishing into her chest with a quiet ripple of power.

When she opened her eyes again, they held something vast, something ancient, but it wasn't violent or wild. It was just *there*, like the weight of an ocean, deep and steady. She touched a tree, and its leaves withered slightly before springing back, richer, fuller, bursting with apples.

Nina swallowed. 'Okay... that's something.'

'Scary, isn't it?' she whispered.

Tommy scoffed. 'For fuck's sake, I told you. I wrote it. We are in the book of history. Now, shush already.'

Nina tried to calm herself, but she couldn't shake the feeling that this wasn't just history. It felt too real, like she had stepped into another world, a world from the past. And the woman they were observing wasn't just some random brunette stranger, it was her.

The young woman, her past self, took a step forward and suddenly flinched, glancing down at her foot. A small, sharp twig had scraped her skin, leaving a faint line. But before Nina could even react, the mark faded within seconds, vanishing as though it had never been there at all.

Nina swallowed, still staring, barely able to comprehend what she was seeing. 'How the hell is this my power?'

'Stop whispering, I told you. We're not really in the past. It's just a book.'

'Alright, alright, calm down. I'm just saying, it's a bit eerie, you know? Feels so real.'

'Anyway, that was immortality.'

'Omg, that's cool. What else can I—'

'What did I say about whispering?'

'Ok, ok,' Nina muttered again. 'And listen, who was the baby boy then?'

'That was your brother, you stupid woman. God himself.'

'What?'

But when they turned back to the Guardian of Hell, the dark hair woman who had been the baby, something was off. She wasn't there anymore.

'No... this isn't right,' Tommy muttered, fear creeping into his voice, slowly stepping back. 'No, no, impossible. What the fuck? This isn't how it's supposed to go! That bastard tricked me!'

Nina frowned. 'What do you mean? I don't get it!'

Tommy kept stepping back slowly. 'There's something...'

His words were broken by a sharp gasp as the Guardian of Hell, Nina's own past self, appeared behind him, her fingers pressing lightly against his shoulders.

Just as Tommy's strength wavered, the past version of Nina locked eyes with her present self and gave her a knowing smile, as if to say, *there you go, figure it out yourself.*

Nina felt her stomach lurch. Looking into those glowing blue eyes, her own eyes, was like staring into something she wasn't supposed to see. Like meeting someone who knew all her secrets before she even knew them herself.

All Nina could see now was the flicker of something in Tommy's eyes, like he was trying to tell her something. But it was already too late. Both the past version of Nina and Tommy vanished together. And Nina was left standing there alone, not having a clue what had just happened.

'No, no! What just happened? Where did you go? Oiiii, come back, Tommyyy!' Nina cried out into the shady woods, but the only sound was her own voice bouncing back.

Now alone, lost in a lifeless place where only memories of the past remained.

Chapter Thirty-two
Click... Clack...

———⚬———

ASIM WAS BUZZING, ALIVE for the first time in... ever. His life had overturned, and he was loving every second of it. Fame, cash, fast cars, mental parties, women, the works. It was all a blur of excess, and he didn't care about Nina, Tessa, his dead old man, or whatever the hell 'home' used to mean. His power? Growing by the day. Jonathan was teaching him how to use it, and Asim was eating it up like it was nothing. The training? Brutal. But Asim smashed it.

Now, he wasn't just some wannabe wizard, he was the real deal. He could dive into dreams, slip through dimensions, even take a stroll through heaven or hell without breaking a sweat. And this was only the start. There was so much more to learn, and he was hungry for it. But the magic he had, the key in his chest that he had already mastered so well, wasn't given to him by chance. It had a purpose. And that purpose, Asim would soon discover, was far more serious than he could have ever imagined. No, this wasn't free, nor was it for nothing.

'Where you off to?' Jonathan called, eyeing Asim, who was suited up.

'Just out, Uncle. Won't be long.'

He snatched his black leather jacket, ready to head out when Jonathan yelled from across the massive hall, 'Oi! You forgot your keys!'

'No, I didn't!'

Standing by his flashy motor, the one Jonathan had forked out for, Asim placed a hand on his chest. The key materialised in his palm, smooth as you like, unlocking the car with barely a thought. He soaked it up, loving every bit of that power and using it whenever the mood struck him, whether he needed it or not.

Windows down, one hand draped over the steering wheel, music blasting out, sunglasses on, feeling like a gangster. Oh, he was loving every second of it. Pulled up outside the club, a towering building with sparklers shooting up the sides, so tall you couldn't even see the top. The line stretched around the block, but Asim was not part of it, walking right inside. Getting nods and handshakes all the way through. People treated him like royalty. Women couldn't keep their eyes off him, while his crew was already posted up at the VIP table, drinks flowing.

'Blonde or brunette tonight?' one of his bold mates smirked, but Asim didn't even bother with a reply. He just looked around the room, chin high, like he was sizing up his kingdom. Then his eyes landed on someone unexpected.

'Shad! What you are doing here, bro?!' Asim yelled, catching sight of him just a step behind.

Shad's face lit up when he saw him standing there. Stepping closer, he greeted him with a handshake and a solid shoulder bump.

'Your uncle asked me to be here tonight, make sure everything's all good, pal,' Shad said, leaning in.

Asim raised an eyebrow. 'Why didn't you come earlier?' he shouted over the music.

But Shad barely caught it, motioning for them to step outside. Drinks in hand, they slipped out through the back door into the warm night.

'I couldn't show my face after what Nicole pulled on you... Felt ashamed, bro,' Shad admitted.

But Asim waved it off, not interested, as if nothing had happened, while Shad looked a bit stressed, or at least he was pretending to be.

'What's up with you?' Asim asked.

In a sad, quiet voice, Shad said, 'Listen, I've got to tell you the truth. I might get in trouble for this, but... you don't deserve to be played. You're a good guy, Asim.'

Asim was confused but listening. Shad didn't hold back.

'Jonathan's using you. He wants to kill Nina. And you. He's the one who killed your father.'

'Are you fucked in the head? I thought you were a mate!'

'I'm serious, Asim! He's setting you up, playing you. Once he's done, you'll be dead too!'

Asim swore at him, turning to leave, but Shad grabbed at one last chance. 'Go to the basement. You'll see.'

Asim pushed him aside and went back inside angrily. However, Shad's words were stuck in his head, burning through the fun.

Later, with two women in his car, Asim drove off, yet his mind was far from the night's buzz. All he could think about was what Shad had said.

He was speeding, the two blondes not even noticing, too far gone on drugs and booze to care about anything. Shad's words kept playing in his head, louder and louder, until he hit the brakes.

'Do one. Now!' he barked at the girls.

They tried to argue, but there was no point. They stepped out, complaining as they tripped onto the sidewalk.

'You fucking asshole, don't come back begging for me to suck your dick!' the smaller blonde screamed.

But Asim didn't pay attention, just stepped right over it. Then he remembered, 'Oh, I'm proper dumb. What am I doing? I've got the key, fuck this.'

He grabbed the key from his chest and blinked straight into Jonathan's basement. It was almost empty, dark, and cold. But then he spotted a door. Locked, of course.

Touching the key on his chest, voilà, he was behind it. Cool. The room was tiny, barely anything in it. A chair and a table with an old lamp. But what drew his attention were the pictures spread out on the table. Leaning in, he stared at them—Nina, with her ex. The same picture he'd seen once at her flat. His pulse quickened. There was more. A watch, some British money, and a passport. But it wasn't Jonathan's face on the ID. It was Nina's ex-boyfriend. What the hell is this? It clicked. Jonathan wasn't who he claimed to be. He had to be her ex. Before Asim could grasp what was happening, the sound of footsteps reached him. No time to think. He ran back into the main room and hid behind a curtain just in time.

And then, Jonathan walked in, cane in hand.

'Apollo Siso.'

The room flipped in an instant.

Poof—no more cold, creepy basement. In its place? A full-blown supernatural spa setup. Lights flared on like someone was showing off, and right in the centre, a round bath appeared out of nowhere. Impressive. Then came the green mist, seeping through the air, spreading and spiralling like it was auditioning for a horror movie.

'Come in,' Jonathan said.

A tall woman in a red robe stepped inside.

'Take your robe off,' Jonathan instructed, his eyes scanning the woman from head to toe.

She let the robe drop. Now naked, she stood there, all quiet, the green mist wrapping around her legs like it was breathing. Asim, crouched behind the curtain, felt a wave of shame and regret for even listening to Shad. What was he doing here? Hiding like some fool, watching Jonathan bring women down for his fun. He wanted to leave. Nothing was happening. This was Jonathan, doing... whatever Jonathan did. Weird, arrogant, messed-up stuff. The woman slid into the bath, and Jonathan started taking off his own robe. Asim reached for the key, ready to disappear, but something made him stop.

Jonathan raised his cane.

'Isomnio Asolo Hato.' And just like that, it all went sideways.

The woman's neck split, just opened up like a zipper, blood pouring into the bath. Except it wasn't blood anymore. It turned green, thick, bubbling, sending up steam that filled the air with this heavy, awful smell. Asim instinctively froze. His mind was racing, struggling to make sense of what he had just witnessed. Then it struck him like a London bus, and he screamed in a way that could curdle milk.

He ran to the door as fast as he could, legs fuelled by pure fear. But, oh no, Jonathan saw him.

'Silly! It's not what you think! I can explain!' he shouted, chasing after him.

Asim was shaking like a leaf in a hurricane, clutching his key like it was Excalibur. His knuckles were tense, breathing quickened, and his eyes moved rapidly around the room as if expecting monsters to jump out of the walls.

'Stay back! You're sick! Shad was right. Stay the hell away from me!' he yelled, his voice cracking like glass under pressure.

Jonathan, completely naked, looked like a swamp creature that had crawled out of a toxic spa. Green mud dripped off him in thick, sticky streaks, and his face screamed mildly annoyed evil genius.

'Shad? That bastard! Listen!' he shouted, waving his arms wildly in a blend of anger and despair.

But Asim wasn't about to hang around for a TED Talk on Jonathan's villain origin story. No, he went full fight-or-flight—and spoiler: it was all flight.

Before Jonathan could take another step closer, Asim vanished in a fog, running for freedom while holding his grand key. Jonathan stood there, soaked and angry, left in the green haze, looking like a failed attempt at a low-budget horror movie. Asim got to the address Shad had given him and banged on the green door. No answer. He dropped onto the step, head spinning. What the heck had just happened?

He was still in shock. Then it smacked him in the face—just how much of a dumbass he'd been.

Seriously, he felt like the biggest fool in the whole world, and his heart hurt like he'd just watched the saddest dog movie ever. Thoughts of Nina and Tessa hit him hard, and he had this ridiculous urge to teleport back to the caravan and hug them like some emotional maniac. But he had no clue where they even were, or if they were still hanging around at all. Because, yes, genius move on his part, he never bothered to ask about them, or even Finley. No, he'd been too wrapped up in his own drama, blissfully thinking the universe was running smoothly, while in reality, he was living in a soap opera.

And now? Now he felt more crushed and messed up than when his dad had kicked the bucket. Which, by the way, was a memory he liked to lock away and throw into the ocean. But of course, when he felt like absolute crap, it always came back. If only his dad were still around, if only everything could rewind to the good old days... Asim was sure he'd never have ended up in this magical shitstorm.

Then the door opened on its own. He stepped inside, looking around. Hmmm. The place was brighter than expected. Shad came out from the kitchen. Asim collapsed onto the sofa, wiped out. He spilled everything, everything he'd seen, like he had to get rid of it, and Shad listened without interrupting once. He then handed him a cup of tea. Asim downed it in one go, staring blankly ahead.

'We need to call the police,' he said, almost like he didn't believe it himself.

Shad laughed a hard, bitter laugh. 'Call who? You think anyone's going to take on Jonathan? He's loaded, got everyone in his pocket, and he's a bloody Lord. Who's going to stop him?'

'But he killed her, he...'

'They know,' Shad jumped in. 'Everyone knows what he's done. No one's touching him.'

Asim felt like a complete idiot for even thinking the police could help.

Shad leaned in. 'Anyway, forget him. It's not only Jonathan, my mate.'

Asim looked at Shad, and suddenly, it all made sense. He knew now, realised this was all just a load of crap. His heart began to beat faster, footsteps reaching his ears before he could react. His eyes quickly looked at the stairs, and there she was—Nicole.

All he managed to say was, 'You bastard...' but he never finished the sentence.

Asim woke up in a different place, head spinning. His hands were trembling, and everything around him was black, blinking, couldn't see or hear a thing. Only the smell, sharp and sour, like something rotting. Feeling the pain inside his body, but he kind of already knew what was happening. He just couldn't, or maybe didn't want to believe it.

What the hell is this? Where am I?

He tried to grab the key from his chest, but his hand wouldn't work. No matter how hard he tried, it was like something was holding him down. Then he heard it.

Click, clack.

The unique sound of high heels clicking. A bright light shone on his face, making him wince. With one eye open, he saw her.

'Nicole? What the fuck is going on? Where am I?' His stomach coiled, churning like he was going to be sick. 'You... You bitch,' he spat out slowly in a weak tone.

Nicole pressed her finger against his lips.

'Shhhh, do you really think someone like me would ever be with you?' she sneered. 'Oh, you smelly bastard. I hated when you touched me. I hated all of it. Sucking your dick? Fucking disgusting!' Then she smiled, like a clown at a kid's party. 'Now I can finally breathe. Seeing you like this... yummy, it feels nice somehow, you know.'

She laughed, watching him struggle, soaking up every second of his helplessness. Meanwhile, Asim was suffocating from the inside, unable to move, but oh man, he had the strongest urge to punch her right in that overly made-up face of hers.

Then George stepped in.

'Go. Leave us.'

Nicole gave one last satisfied smirk and vanished as if she had never been there. Asim tried to rise, rage building inside him, but his body wouldn't move. He was stuck, weak, and powerless on the cold floor. He even backed away a bit, having neither the strength nor the will to fight. This was too much for him. His brain could hardly think straight anymore.

'Oh, little bro, feeling weak? Oh no, I'm absolutely heartbroken...,' George sneered, his voice dripping with fake concern, relishing every second of Asim's vulnerability.

He bent down, leaning in closer and closer. George sniffed Asim's skin slowly, enjoying the moment. 'Hmmm, lovely, smell that? That's fear... Love it. Always have. Makes you human. Makes you... pathetic...' He paused, breathing in deeply with a sick, gleaming eye.

Asim tried to move, but his body refused. But he felt it, that psychopathic desire coming from George. He knew this was no joke; this was serious, and he even started to think that this might be the end for him. George's grin widened as he circled with a voice full of venom.

'You really thought you were a king, didn't you? Thought you had it all: power, respect, people bowing down to you? This was too easy... You're a fool. Everyone was acting. Every single one of them was playing... But no one ever cared. Not Nina, not Tessa... They're dead, my little brother.'

Asim's chest tightened. The words punched hard, and despite everything, a tear slipped down his face. George saw it and licked it. 'Mmm, yummy... I've waited for this. You didn't know about them? Of course not, you didn't give a fuck... But, now this makes me happy, you know...'

Asim's mind was spinning, pain radiating from every corner. Now, all he could think about was Nina and Tessa. Not only did he feel like an idiot, but he blamed himself for everything, feeling a heavy sense of responsibility. He knew he had messed up badly, and at this point, he didn't even care what happened to him anymore. He even blamed himself for their deaths, convinced it was all his fault. George had got under his skin and was thoroughly enjoying every second of it.

George paced around and still enjoying feeding off Asim's misery.

'No one's coming to save you, my little brother... You're alone now, just like I was!' He bent down again, locking eyes with Asim, his sick satisfaction pouring out.

'Anyway, I kind of forgot to tell you... I'm the one who killed our dad, but I didn't enjoy it. It was just, you know, too quick! But now? With you? I'll take my time...' He stood back up, circling again. 'That tea Shad gave you? Yep, poison, stripping your powers, bit by bit. So, now, you'll die! But slow! Painfully!'

George stepped on Asim's face, pressing down hard with his boot as Asim screamed in agony, while George just laughed. 'Well, you can thank God for this. I'm sure he'll hear you out; he listened to me too, you know... But anyway, we've got all the time in the world. I'm not in any rush...', he smirked.

Then he wiped his boot on the ground, and Asim just stared up at him with tear-filled eyes, completely defeated. 'Alright then, time for lunch. Lovely, enjoy your stay here...' George said. And with that, George vanished into thin air.

Chapter Thirty-three
Pumpkin World

———⁓◦⁓———

FINLEY FOUND HIMSELF in the Pumpkin World for the first time, walking down a street made entirely of pumpkins. It was weird. As he walked along, minding his own business, he accidentally stepped on a tiny pumpkin.

'Oi! Watch it, mate!' screamed the tiny one, flailing its little arms.

Finley's lashes fluttered as he looked down.

'Oops, sorry, didn't see you there.' Then, trying to get back on track, he asked, 'You wouldn't have seen a blonde human about, would you?'

The tiny pumpkin stared at him, hands on its hips.

'A blonde human? Are ya takin' the piss? Look around, ya daft cunt!' It stomped off, or at least tried to, with its stubby little legs.

Finley, slightly stunned, gave a shrug. Humans and pumpkins were everywhere. Instead of traffic lights, pumpkins were hanging about on poles. Pumpkins were driving around as cars. Pumpkins were even walking down the street, chatting away like they were people. He had to admit, it was a bit too much. Noticing a man holding hands with a pumpkin, because why the hell not, Finley stopped him.

'Excuse me, mate, where do they take people who accidentally end up here... I mean, without a permit?'

The man gave him a friendly nod.

'Police station, pal. Just down the road, second block on the right.'

'Thanks.'

Then a loud siren blared as a line of pumpkin cars screeched to a halt, blocking his path. Police officers jumped out, their big pumpkin heads foolishly mismatched with their human faces. They had tiny toeless feet, no shoes, just bouncing along.

Finley couldn't help but chuckle.

'What's so funny, human?' one of the officers yelled. 'Show me your permit. Now!'

Suppressing a beam, Finley calmly opened his suitcase and pulled out a small orange ball. In his palm, it transformed into a tiny green pumpkin, blushing faintly. The officer's face fell. His annoyance was clear as he recognised the permit, realising Finley was a legit traveller.

'Right, carry on,' the officer grumbled, motioning for the others to get back in their cars.

As they loaded into the vehicles, Finley overheard one of them whispering, 'Cannibals. No wonder they're so fat. Fatties.' He shrugged, shaking his head with a simper, and continued his way towards the police station. Tessa had to be in there somewhere. He found her, but not in the way he expected. She wasn't locked up, upset, or hurt. No, she was laughing, flirting with the pumpkin police officers at their desks like she was at a party.

When she saw Finley standing there, arms crossed, she beamed.

'Oh, Finley! Come here! How did you find me? Oh, I love this place!'

Finley shoved a smile.

'I'm glad you're safe. We were worried. But erm, time to go. Nina's waiting, right?'

One of the officers raised an eyebrow.

'Hold on a sec, where's her permit?'

Finley flashed his own permit, but the officer wasn't buying it.

'No, no, her permit. You know the rules, mate.'

Finley, sweating now, rummaged through his suitcase and, to the officer's surprise, pulled out a tiny one for Tessa.

'Here it is. Anything else?' he asked, trying to keep it cool.

The officer frowned.

'How'd you get this when she arrived without one?'

'Her permit's right here, and we're leaving now,' Finley said.

Tessa, oblivious to the tension, giggled.

'Actually, can we stay a bit longer? This place is lovely!'

But Finley leaned in, whispering as they walked toward the door.

'Don't look back. Just keep walking.'

Something in his tone made Tessa stop, her laughter fading.

Then, boom. Finley's suitcase exploded.

'Stop them! The permit's a fake!' one of the officers shouted. 'Oi, you lot! Fat humans!'

Tessa and Finley bolted for the door, but it was too late. The pumpkins surrounded them. With their hands in the air, both stood there, caught.

'What's happening? Oh, I wish I could swear right now!'

Finley shushed her.

'Oi, not a word!'

Within moments, they were placed in separate orange rooms.

'Oh, again!' Tessa said to herself.

She wasn't scared at all. Tessa was tough. No, this place wasn't going to break her. But the other one? That was a different story.

Tessa sat in the cell, alone. No bed, no mattress. *But whatever,* she thought to herself, *at least I have a toilet.* Sure, it was made entirely of pumpkin, but that only made it more interesting. She moved closer, then a little closer still, and pushed the raw seat. Yes, it was soft and fresh, though maybe a bit sore. Then Tessa felt a bit sad. She gazed down at the orange floor. It was quiet, and there was a faint smell, like a nasty tomato. Her heart ached as she thought about leaving her mother behind, along with her sister. Her niece's birthday was coming up, and Tessa always managed to make her happy.

But now she was locked up. Not just locked up, but in another world. She felt lonely and regretted going anywhere at all. She sighed, her stomach rumbling. *Bollocks, what a life, really. Free will, huh?* she whispered to herself. Then she heard sounds, like someone jingling keys—purposely. That much was obvious. Tessa, of course, being experienced with films, knew exactly who was coming.

'Get up, fatty, come with me,' one of the cheeky officers shouted.

'Yeah, can't help it. Love to eat pumpkins, you know, they are so tasty, you know...'

'Whatever, move your fat arse and hurry up.'

As they walked down the hall, Tessa spotted Finley standing there, head down. He was free, eyes narrowed.

She yelled, 'Finley! What the hell are you doing? Help me!'

He didn't move, didn't even look at her. Finally, in a low voice, he mumbled, 'Tessa, I'm so sorry...'

This time, Tessa felt it. Still, she couldn't believe that Finley would ever actually do something wrong—no, not Finley. She knew this wasn't a joke anymore; that look on Finley's face told her everything.

Something heavy and merciless was about to happen.

'Sorry for? Oi, you bastard! What are you talking about!' she snapped, but the officer shoved her forward.

Tessa kicked back, reaching for Finley, but he just turned his back on her. The officer shoved her through the door. Inside, the lights were blinding. *Shit, this stinks.* She was about to shout again, but then she saw him.

Noah.

'No, no!' she screamed, but the officer slammed the door behind her.

Tessa wasn't so tough anymore. She was scared as hell. *No, no, this can't be happening.*

'Now, nobody can save you, my love.'

Noah was waiting, eyes full of sick pleasure. He stepped closer, grinning. His mouth opened, and his tongue shot out, biting her neck.

Tessa didn't even have time to react before everything went black. When she opened her eyes, her heart started pounding, and she trembled with fear. A windowless room. Lights without bulbs. Emptiness all around. *Bloody hell, what is this now?* she thought. She wiped her nose, and when she looked at her hand, blood covered it. *What? That doesn't make sense. Is this a bad dream?* She kept darting her eyes around, her head spinning. She swallowed hard. Tessa knew this was wrong. She'd been through something like this before. *Bloody hell, no, not again.*

Tears burst out as she realised she was about to experience it all over again. *Where's Nina? Where's Asim? And what about Finley? What the hell is going on? This can't be real.* I hate this freaking world! she screamed into the emptiness. And then she almost had a heart attack when Noah appeared out of nowhere. Just like that, he was there. Tessa slowly realised she stood no chance. She *had* a chance, but she hadn't taken it. She'd completely forgotten her power, the magic she could use. Every time she saw Noah, Tessa became a different person, so scared she almost forgot her own name.

'Look at you,' Noah said, licking his lips.

He leaned in, then sniffed—proper deep, like a psycho. While Tessa was terrified to death, she just stood there as if she wasn't even present. 'Yeah, I can smell the fear. Love it,' he said, voice low, enjoying every second.

Without breaking eye contact, he pulled out a little bottle and let dark purple dust shoot straight into her chest. Then pain slammed into her. Her body snapped back, arms flailing as she collapsed onto the ground, hard. Every muscle in her body tightened. Her veins felt like they were burning, her skin stretched tight, like it was being peeled from the inside out. Her mouth opened, but only a strangled gasp escaped, nothing more.

'Aaaa!' she tried to scream.

Then her bones started to crack. She could feel them snapping.

Pop. Snap. Grind. Like twigs being crushed underfoot. Her eyes, wide and terrified, now had tears streaking down her face, each one stinging like hell. 'Help! Someone, aaahhh!' Her body wouldn't move. She was trapped. Every movement, every scream, absorbed by the pain that ripped through her.

Noah watched, eyes gleaming, his grin spread wide, loving every second like it was the best thing he'd ever seen. He then knelt beside her, his lips close to her ear, voice dark.

'Nope, no one's coming to save you. Your friend, Finley? He sold you...' Then he stood up slowly, his toothy smile widening, like he had all the time in the world. 'Nina? Yes, that one... Well, she left you. Yep, she's back in Hell, your so-called home.'

He paused, enjoying the taste of her defeat. 'And now Asim? He kind of doesn't give a shit. He's living his best life. Doesn't even want to hear your name!'

He laughed, stepping back, eyes glittering with cruelty. 'But don't worry, you won't die, no, no, no... I won't let you, my darling. You were and always will be my first love, my life!'

And poor Tessa lay there, still. No more tears left to cry. Those words punched her harder than anything he'd done to her body. No more screams. No more tears. No, just an empty, painful chest, the kind of pain that made you wish for death.

But Noah, with that chilled grin, had stolen even that escape. He leaned down one last time, his voice dripping with pleasure. 'You know, I prayed and God finally listened to me. This is just the beginning, my darling. Yep, just the beautiful beginning.' And with that, he vanished, leaving her alone and broken. In a place of nowhere. While Tessa was being tortured, not just from the inside but from the outside as well, she lay in a room, in the light yet surrounded by emptiness, where the air wasn't really air. Noah had made sure that no one would find her this time. Of course, with some help.

And there it was. Nina, stuck inside the bloody pages of the past, where no one heard her, where no one saw her. Stripped bare of any strength or purpose, drowning in loneliness and fear. Asim, lying there at the mercy of his half-brother George. Betrayed and abandoned by those he once trusted. And Tessa, tortured by cruel Noah's hands. Her body and soul, broken. They were left isolated, trapped in a hellish agony beyond words, with no hope in sight.

Tick. Tock. Tick. Tock. Yes, for some, time moved. But for others, it no longer did.

Chapter Thirty-four
Meow... Meow...

TOMMY LAY THERE, COMPLETELY battered, slumped out on the street like rubbish nobody noticed. He closed his eyes, focused, and with a soft *Meow... Meow...* behold—he was a cat once again, licking his wounds. He couldn't quite piece together what had gone wrong with the landing, but he remembered perfectly well how Nina had ended up stuck in the book of history, while the other half of her had escaped. Tommy just didn't know where to. Not that it particularly bothered him—he was more worried about himself. His home had vanished, and he wasn't fully sure what to do next.

As a cat, he healed quickly enough to reach his grandfather's place nearby. *Knock, knock.* Back in his human form, he stood at the door.

Seeing his grandfather, he hugged him as if he hadn't visited in a hundred years. Grandpa immediately knew something was wrong. He closed the door fast, checked twice to make sure no one had seen them, then turned to Tommy with a stern look.

'So now, tell me what happened!'

Tommy stayed trembling, possibly putting on a bit of a performance.

'I'm scared. I don't know what to do,' he said.

Grandpa made him tea, a proper grandpa's tea, and Tommy swallowed it down as if it weren't still boiling hot. Then, finally, he started to spill everything, explaining from the beginning what had happened. Grandpa's eyes went wide, and he clutched his chest as if he might have a heart attack.

'You don't even know what you've done! How could you?' Grandpa shouted, his voice nearly breaking with fury.

Tommy tried to deny it all, saying it wasn't his fault. Nothing like this had ever happened before. He'd taken plenty of people into the history book before—it was just history, after all, just a book, nothing more. But Grandpa wasn't some clueless old man; he was far too clever for that. He had been the bookkeeper long before Tommy, and he knew the rules all too well.

'If you don't tell me the truth right now, I'll drag you to Death himself!'

Tommy put down his tea. 'You're my grandpa. How can you do this? I trust you! I need your help; I haven't done anything wrong!'

Grandpa sighed. 'Listen, Tommy, I'll help you, but I need the truth.'

And then Tommy finally admitted, 'I didn't know this could happen. I was tricked, I swear.'

Grandpa rolled his eyes. 'Alright, for God's sake, just talk!'

'God came to me a few days ago. He told me to do it, to take Nina in. He said it was safe and that it was the only way to save our Hell and our work. I did it for us, Grandpa, so we wouldn't have to suffer anymore! Look at us, look at you, you can't even buy a decent tea! We live like animals!'

Grandpa was far from impressed. 'You idiot! Animals? We *are* animals! Get used to it already! And you have no idea what you've done!'

Tommy started apologising, crying, but Grandpa's mind was elsewhere, trying to figure out what to do. He knew the situation was dire.

'You know the rules! You can't take a Guardian into history; that's the first rule! Every bloody bookkeeper knows it! God's a liar! Don't you know that? If only you'd listened to a word I taught you, you fool!'

Grandpa sat down, his face filled with dread. 'Now, we're all going to die.'

'What, Grandpa? What are you saying about God?'

'Don't you get it, you silly boy! God? Forget him for now. We have a bigger problem!'

'What, Grandpa? Just tell me!'

'You broke the line between life and death. The old Guardian in this world is... well, dead for us.'

But Tommy still didn't understand it.

'The world can sense it, Tommy. The world knows, and you've made a hole, a hole that's going to consume everything,' Grandpa explained.

But Tommy just laughed. 'Oh, don't be so dramatic.'

That really set Grandpa off. 'You foolish cat! Now we both must go see Death himself, and you're going to pay for your sin, while the rest of us will pay with our lives. You have no idea! You just did God a *favour*!'

But Tommy stood up. 'I'm not going, Grandpa. I've had enough of this bullshit. I want my freedom, and I'll have it. My life is mine.' He transformed back into his familiar feline form and bolted out the door.

Grandpa just sat there, staring into space, trembling from head to toe. He knew all too well. After all, he was the oldest bookkeeper. He understood that this couldn't be easily fixed. He was deeply afraid; this wasn't about cats or Hell anymore. This was about all the people, all the magic, and this world—well, this world couldn't survive without magic. A rift had formed, and it was going to cause madness. But Grandpa loved the world, and he loved its people. He had to do something; he couldn't just sit by and watch this world crumble.

But Tommy didn't look back. He'd led Nina into the world of books and survived, after all. As a cat, he had a few more lives to spare. Once his home and the world of books had vanished, he was finally free from his work. And oh, he loved it.

For a fleeting moment, a twinge of guilt surfaced, but it faded just as quickly. He would finally live the life he'd always dreamed of, and Nina? He didn't spare her a second thought.

But the consequences were coming. The police were after him, not just any, but the Saluhi detectives sent by Death himself.

How long could he hide from them, who neither sleep nor eat and are especially faithful to their mission?

Not long.

The Saluhi couldn't return to their own land until their mission was complete. And their job wasn't just to capture Tommy for his sin. It was to hunt down those who had meddled with Hell itself. And there were many. No one could run far, and no one could run forever.

But there was a catch, and that was the rift. The rift was dangerous, even for them. This world could make them disappear, vanish forever.

Chapter Thirty-five
Saluhi

SIP... SMACK, SMACK. 'Bloody hell, this is good,' one of the detectives said, mid-bite. Vito and Klad were tucked in a corner café, enjoying a fry-up like it was their last meal. They weren't just any detectives, of course; they were those Saluhi, Death's personal bloodhounds.

'So, what's the plan, then? We can't exactly head back without her. Death'd have our heads,' Vito muttered, eyeing his empty plate.

Klad shrugged, picking up a slice of red velvet cake.

'Oh, we'll think of something. Probably. She's out here running around, no permission slip, and we're stuck here working doubles. Well, at least the food's good. Love it.'

'You tried the red velvet yet?'

'Not yet. Hand it over.' But before he could take a bite, Vito's nose twitched. That sixth sense Death had warned him about kicking in. The world was thick with magic, and whenever it got turbulent, they had to answer the call. There was no escaping it.

'Nah, you're imagining things,' Klad grumbled, but Vito shook his head, already up from his seat.

'Mate, you don't sense that? It's trouble. Grab the cake, though. Death never said we couldn't eat on the job.'

Finally, the two of them rose, still chewing as they headed straight for their next target.

'We're here. I can smell it,' Vito said, dropping down on all fours and sniffing around like a police dog trained to find drugs. He stopped in the middle of a busy road, causing cars to slam on their brakes, drivers honking and shouting, but he didn't give a toss.

'So, what's going on?' Klad asked as Vito told him he could smell the torn fabric of history itself.

'It's burnt to shreds, mate,' he said.

'What on earth are you talking about?' Klad asked.

Vito explained that he could sense someone soulless—someone powerful—had walked straight out of history and was now in their world. He suggested they should go see the bookkeeper to find out what was going on. Drivers kept shouting; one looked like he wanted to kick them off the road. But the detectives ignored them all, carrying on with their task.

They climbed back into their car and followed the trail, which led them straight to Tommy's grandfather's house. He welcomed them in, offering tea, coffee, and of course, biscuits, which Klad and Vito devoured as if they'd never seen food before.

'So, Tommy's gone missing, you say? And the old Guardian's out, leaving Nina trapped?' Vito asked Grandpa, who nodded and told them everything. He explained that he'd served Death faithfully for a century and would never betray him; he meant everything to him and still did. He even said he'd cooperate, adding that he understood what could happen to the world with this kind of turbulence.

'Those biscuits are lovely, I mean... you do realise Tommy's going to be punished, don't you?' Vito asked. And Grandpa, of course, knew; he knew more than the two of them combined. He told them where to find Tommy, saying they should go to Jonathan and Finley.

But Klad reminded him that Death had instructed them that if anything like this happened, they'd have to vanish from the world. But nothing had happened yet, after all, so they could still enjoy playing detective for a little longer.

Back in the car, and off they went, straight to Finley's.

'That's the old caravan we were in a few days back, wasn't it?' Vito said, eyeing it like it had personally wronged him.

'Yeah, the wizard. Let's check on him. This old git better start talking this time,' Klad replied, sounding like a man who'd been on one too many disappointing visits.

'You don't mean... use the stuff? You know we're not supposed to, don't you?' Vito said, but Klad shrugged.

'What's the worst that'll happen? They'll pull us back a few centuries early? We're heading back soon enough anyway. Besides, something here stinks, mate.'

Knock, knock. And there, in all his messy glory, Finley opened the door, wearing a moth-eaten jumper and stockings pulled up to his knees. He looked ready to make excuses, but the detectives weren't in a listening mood. Vito kicked the door, and Klad followed with a swift shove that sent Finley sprawling onto the floor, thankfully cushioned, as it turned out.

'Right, old man, spill it. We know you've got your hands in this mess,' Klad said, as calm as someone asking about the weather.

Finley could only shake his head, but Vito was already on to something. He leaned in, sniffing with the focus of a bloodhound, catching a distinct whiff of something.

'Ah, guilt. Gotcha. So, what are you guilty about, then?' he asked, tone dangerously polite.

Finley's face went as pale as his stockings. 'You're... you're not from around here... you're not local officers,' he stammered.

Vito didn't even blink. Instead, he pushed a foot down on Finley's stomach, leaning in with a smirk. 'Saluhi. We're here for Tessa, Nina and Asim... and we know you've got something to do with it.'

When Finley kept denying everything, Klad's patience ran thin. He moaned under his snort, blew a quick puff of air into Finley's eyes, and, as if on cue, Finley froze. Time itself seemed to stop, like the whole scene stood holding its breath.

'Right, we've got sixty seconds before the spell wears off. Let's get this over with,' Vito said.

Klad leaned in, locking eyes with Finley, and in a moment, everything came into view, unrolling in his mind with all the detail of a punch.

'Got it. Let's go,' Klad said, and they left Finley slumped on the floor, back to the car in seconds.

Klad's head was spinning as they drove off; he'd seen everything Finley had. The Saluhi weren't supposed to pull stunts like this. They had rules to follow, after all.

Technically, they'd crossed the line. But then again, rules were more of a suggestion, weren't they?

'What's the worst that can happen? We're already dead,' Vito said with a shrug, and Klad couldn't argue with that logic. Death wasn't just their boss. He was... well, Death.

But time was running out for them. Sooner or later, their bodies would disappear, and back to Death's world they'd go, with or without answers.

'Right, coffee or burgers? That'll keep us going, yeah? Humans eat when they're weak, don't they?' Vito suggested, and Klad cracked a grin.

They stopped at a fast-food place, ordered through the machine, and came out with a bag stuffed full of burgers and coke. Heaven, if heaven was a paper bag full of fatty goodness.

'Mate, this is brilliant. You feel it hitting the stomach?' Vito asked, sounding genuinely impressed.

'Yeah, it's heavy, but it works. Drink up; we've got a job to do,' Klad said, chewing through his burger as he detailed what he'd seen in Finley's mind: how Finley had sold the lot to God, who'd promised him his dead wife would finally cross Heaven's gates.

'Poor sod thought he was doing her a favour. Honestly, if his heart doesn't give out from the betrayal, I'd be surprised,' Klad added with the sympathy of a man watching a trainwreck he'd seen a dozen times.

'Well, serves him right, don't you think? Heaven's gates? Like he even knows where he's sent her!' Vito scoffed.

'I've got energy now, but this stomach... bloody hell, what is this?' Klad groaned, clutching his middle.

'Mate, you're just getting fat, or you need poo. Now floor it, we're off to see Jonathan,' Vito said, finishing off the last burger with a smirk.

They got out of the car, taking in their surroundings with an air of annoyed dread. It wasn't every day you saw a palace like this, though neither of them seemed especially impressed by the magnificence. They both knew exactly who Jonathan was.

'Hmm... careful with this one. He's the gentleman Death told us about,' Vito muttered, eyeing the door with suspicion.

'I know... Let's check in quickly and get out. Maybe he'll be more willing to talk if we drop Death's name, yeah?'

They didn't even have to ring the bell; a servant opened the door as if he'd been waiting since last Thursday. Suspicious, Vito thought about it but stepped inside anyway, pretending not to be impressed by all the posh decor, even though it was hard not to stare.

To their right was a brunette woman they didn't know, and something about her made Vito's nose twitch. Was it a bad vibe? Or just way too much perfume? Either way, he had this dodgy feeling about her, and he just knew she was wrapped up in their case. Jonathan, with that smooth-talking smile of his, promenaded over and asked, all polite-like, what they were after.

Klad wasted no time.

'We're Saluhi,' he announced, just in case Jonathan needed a reminder that they didn't do small talk. Jonathan's polite smile shaken slightly, and Klad wasn't fully sure they were welcome, until he mentioned Death. Suddenly,

Jonathan was all warm smiles and hospitality, as if they'd just become his favourite guests.

They plopped down at the table, and Jonathan whipped up a feast so elegant it would make a royal chef hide in shame. They dug in with the kind of excitement you'd expect from people who hadn't seen proper food in ages, which, let's be real, was spot on.

'Death is my friend, and you're welcome in my home anytime. How can I help you?' Jonathan said, beaming.

Klad cut straight to it, explaining they were looking for Tessa, Nina and Asim and mentioning Finley's connection. Jonathan nodded, not seeming the least bit surprised, muttering that he'd always suspected Finley was a spineless coward. He'd never trusted the man, obviously. Jonathan then provided directions to find Noah, and Klad nodded in thanks, while Vito lined his face as if he were making up for a lifetime of missed meals. Which, technically, he was.

Jonathan watched them with pleasure. 'Death doesn't feed you lot well, does he?' he asked.

Klad smirked, shaking his head.

'Food's not exactly on the job description. We don't have stomachs, technically speaking.'

Jonathan raised an eyebrow.

'Of course. Anything else?'

Vito decided to press on.

'Know anything about that turbulence we felt?' he asked, but Jonathan claimed complete ignorance.

'And who's the woman over there, the one looking like she's watching paint dry?' Klad asked.

Jonathan shrugged, giving them a knowing grin.

'Oh, just a lady friend. Don't suppose you're familiar with that sort of thing? We men have certain... instincts, you see.'

'Ah, I've heard about those. Fascinating,' Klad replied, suppressing a smirk. 'Apologies.'

Just as they were about to leave, Jonathan offered one final comment. 'Asim's in danger. Help him if you can. I'm sure it's connected to his brother George and those demons, the Shad.'

The two detectives switched a look before responding that local authorities would have to handle it. Asim wasn't from Hell; he'd ended up there thanks to Samir, but he theoretically belonged to this world. They couldn't interfere, a fact Jonathan already knew but couldn't help pushing. Deep down, he genuinely cared about Asim. He'd lost his own family, and though Samir was far from his favourite person, Asim was still his nephew.

Back in the car, Klad and Vito were still mulling over Jonathan's uncharacteristic friendliness. Vito, although he couldn't shake his worry about the dark-haired woman. Something didn't sit right.

'Mate... your hand,' Klad moaned, eyes widening.

'What? Oh, great, where's it gone?' Vito said, nearly leaping out of his seat. His hand was simply missing. No blood, no pain, just... not there.

'It's happening. We're starting to fade. I'll drive,' Klad said, swapping seats with him, his tone filled with all the passion of a man facing a tax review. They set off toward Noah's place, Vito examining the empty spot where his hand used to be, like a child fascinated by a magic trick got wicked.

'This is hilarious. What if I lose my head next? Or my eyes? And what about the loo? How am I supposed to manage that?' Vito moaned.

'The loo? Brilliant. Haven't thought of that one... let's just get this done before we're missing anything essential,' Klad replied, hitting the pedal. They arrived at Noah's place in record time, only to find it absolutely abandoned.

Not a soul in sight. Noah was gone, and so were his friends. Even his throne looked like it had been through a brawl. The whole place was a disaster.

The Saluhi weren't thrilled, sniffing around for clues and coming up empty.

'Oh hell, my eye! My eye!' Klad suddenly yelped.

'Fantastic. How are we supposed to drive now? You're missing an eye; I'm missing a hand. Perfect,' Vito replied, sounding equal parts frustrated and pleased.

'It's time. Let's get out of here. Grab the powder before you vanish completely,' Klad said. Vito pulled out a small bag of powder, took a sniff, passed it to Klad, and just like that, they were gone, leaving only their clothes behind as a neat little goodbye. The Saluhi were back in their world, returned to Death.

Chapter Thirty-six
The Beginning

DAYS DRAGGED LIKE MONTHS. Months like years. Nina wandered, unseen, unheard. Hope? Gone. She'd stopped calling into the void, screaming for help that never came. Like a ghost now, sticking to scraps of memory, home, her past; but no longer questioning how or why. She didn't feel the air. The months rolled on, but her skin stayed smooth, untouched by time.

She always ended up here, a crumbling old cottage where a young man lived alone. She'd watch him, sometimes talking to him, acting like he could hear her and would respond. It made her feel like she was losing it, but there was something deep inside, something she couldn't shake, that tied her to him in a way she couldn't explain.

The gentleman had these brown eyes, gave off the vibe of about thirty. He played the piano, wrote songs, never sang, though. Nina would sit or pace around him, desperate for him to notice her, just once. But nothing. To him, she didn't exist. 'Sometimes I feel like you see me, hear me... or maybe that's just what I want,' she muttered. There was something about him that made her feel less alone. She knew his every move, watching him closely, but still, he was a mystery. He never ate, drank, left the house. No visitors. Always alone. He didn't speak, and Nina never even knew his name.

The man made her feel like she wasn't the only one suffering. Watching him was like watching someone slowly torture themselves, isolated, lifeless. His loneliness mirrored her own, and in that, there was some strange, bitter comfort. Yes, Nina had lost the plot. But who wouldn't? She even pretended to be his wife. He never reacted, always off in his own world, but to her, it was like they were living together, like they belonged to each other in some way. Days blurred together; sometimes she'd divorce him in her head, fighting with him, only to make up later. She'd pretend to make breakfast, pretend she was alive, pretend she was seen.

She often sat on the old wood, talking to herself, her memories spinning around. She had so much time now that she'd even uncovered things she hadn't realised she'd forgotten. Her ability to sniff out souls? She wasn't born with it—not like she'd thought. The memory came back to her. She was a little kid, running on the playground. A woman had approached her; young, kind, shaved head. She handed Nina a book, and when she opened it, a strange dust burst out, smashing into her. That's when it started. She remembered being so confused, holding her nose constantly because she couldn't bear the smells. Kids ran from her, called her a freak.

But then, in second class, there was a new teacher. Young, again. Kind. He saw her. He knew. He started showing her how to control the power, how to live with it. And then everything made sense. She wasn't alone. She'd forgotten all this, but now the memories came flooding back. Why had they faded? Was she too young? Or had something else happened? The teacher? Oh no, it wasn't a coincidence. She realised that now. Without him, she would've been lost. He knew all about her power, and soon, it wasn't even that hard to control. He made her smile, in a way no one else ever had. Someone who truly cared never hurt her.

But he didn't stay. Two months, that's all. It was during those rainy days. And then, one day, he didn't show up to class. She remembered trying to smell his soul, but she never could. He had told her once, 'You can't smell the souls of non-humans.' Yes, he wasn't human. But who was he? And that woman who gave her the book, who was she? Her mind floated back, back to the days in the library. The happy ones, though she hadn't appreciated them then. Now those memories only tortured her, especially during sleepless nights. It was like the weight of all those books, their histories, refused to let her rest. When she tried to close her eyes, it hurt.

The questions troubled her. She had ignored so many things, never thought twice about them. Had she missed something? Had someone known more than they had let on? Had she been played from the start? But who had been pulling the strings? And now, more than ever, she wished she could tell someone, anyone. She needed to piece it together, needed answers. She had spent all this time hoping someone would come looking for her. But with all the magic in their world, no one had. No one. Or had they just forgotten her?

TESSA WAS BATTLING pain, completely lost to time. She had no idea if it had been a month or a year and could not tell day from night. Every day repeated itself in a single room with no doors or windows. She had lost herself, just like anyone would in her place. No human could endure that and remain whole. The pain was part of the ordeal, but it was not the worst part. It was the silence that truly messed with her head. The fact that no one came, no one even bothered.

Nina, Asim, the people she thought would care, they were not coming. They had left her to rot here, and after a while, she stopped fighting it. And yes, that was what killed her inside. The realisation that she was not worth saving. Someone visited Tessa in her mind. She was not sure if it was real, but she felt something, as if she knew this person. She could not see a face. The voice was unfamiliar, but the feeling did not lie to her. For a moment, she even felt safe, but not completely.

The voice whispered to her, 'Do not forget, even though you died and went to Hell, your blood still comes from a royal line.'

Then there was silence, and Tessa just listened. She knew she had come from royalty before she died, and her memories had been wiped, her magic stripped away. The voice spoke again. 'Use your magic, Queen of Snakes, and save yourself,' it said.

And then, as if everything vanished, Tessa was back in the nightmare. But she understood. Whoever it was or why they were telling her this did not matter. She felt hope. The snake. That was it.

Tessa found a new purpose. It became unbearable, and that voice had given her a sliver of comfort, a trace of hope, without which survival might have been impossible. She buried the memories, buried the pain, and in the end, buried herself too. Names and faces all faded away. Even her own name slipped from memory. But she managed it, transforming into a snake and escaping the horrible death that had been waiting. Yet it came with a price. No more humanity. Tessa was no longer who she had once been.

The snake had taken over, turning her into a true predator, cold, dark, and venomous. She moved through this nightmare where she was both hunter and prey. But none of that mattered anymore. She could not feel anything, only a concerning hunger. It was ruthless and intense.

FOR ASIM, IT WAS DIFFERENT. He had hit rock bottom. George tormented him relentlessly, to the point where Asim lost all will to live. Time passed without him even noticing, aging him, but for him, the days seemed endless. Each time he was on the brink of death, George would bring him back, never letting him die.

Lost in a sea of painful memories, Asim lost track of time. Yet, through all the agony, there was one place he could escape to—his dreams. He could still think of Tessa and Nina. They kept him tethered to life. The regret was heavy, weighing on him until he finally let go, accepting his fate. But his dreams were different. They were alive, a strange comfort. In his sleep, he was still the young boy he once was, living the life he never had. No nightmares. Just peace. He could not sleep long, but it was enough to give him some rest.

Asim wished for death countless times, but in time, even that desire faded. He gave up completely, so much so that he no longer felt the pain George inflicted on him. No matter how brutal the torture, Asim was numb. Dreams saved him. But dreams were more than just an escape for Asim. There was an old man. Grey-haired, wise, and full of strength despite his age. He was kind, always patient with Asim, teaching him things that seemed so far from the horrors of his life now. The man treated Asim as if he were his own son, guiding him, moulding him.

It was not just about learning how to fight. The old man taught Asim how to be a man, how to hold on to his sense of self, how to survive not just in battle but in life. He would show Asim how to wield a sword with precision and grace, but also when to wield it and when not to. The old man would talk about honour, toughness, and the strength of the mind. Asim found himself not only growing stronger in the dream but also more centred, more at peace.

The strange thing was how much care the old man put into every lesson, every word. It was as if he knew Asim's pain, felt it too, and wanted to protect him from it, even if only in dreams. Asim found relief in these moments, the kind he had never known in the real world.

Asim became important, skilled with a sword, faster and sharper than he could have ever imagined. The old man pushed him, but never too hard.

He kept repeating to him, 'Asim, you are the future King of Dreams. Find the key, the key,' and he said it over and over again in every dream. He just had to find the strength, the courage, and the desire, which were buried deep inside. But Asim could not figure out what the hell the man was talking about. Maybe it was just because it was, well, just a dream.

AS TIME WENT ON, NO one remembered them anymore, or rather, they chose not to. Finley felt guilty. That much was true, but there was something, or someone, more precious to him, someone who meant more than anyone else in the world: his late wife. He could not come to terms with the thought of her going to Hell. In the end, he agreed with God and sold them out. Maybe he would not have done it, but God was a master manipulator. He knew how to get to Finley and how to get to people. He promised Finley that his wife would be allowed into Heaven, that she would not have to wander or suffer anymore, waiting for the gates to open, only to endure more pain.

But Finley did not really know what Heaven was truly like. What he did know was that he was also afraid. If Nina regained her books, her memories, and her power, she could reopen the gates, and people would suffer even more. Even though he knew Nina was not evil, there was still that feeling, the fear that she was the Guardian of Hell, and that was something that frightened him a bit.

Finley secretly loved men, and his late wife had suffered because of it. They could never have children, and the guilt tore at his heart. His wife had taken her own life when she found out, and ever since, Finley had been broken, eaten by grief and guilt. He thought he could make it right, but he only made everything worse. There were days and nights when he wanted to stand up and fix it all, or at least help Asim. But a deal was a deal, and it could not be undone, especially not when that deal was with God himself.

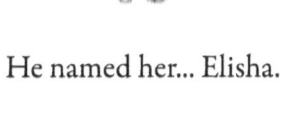

He named her... Elisha.

JONATHAN KNEW EXACTLY what had happened, but like everyone else, he turned his back. For him, things had worked out perfectly, even better. Asim? Nina? He did not care about them anymore. Nina was only useful for one thing: bringing his mum back from the dead.

His mother had died, gone to Hell, and had her powers ripped away, her memories scrubbed clean like everyone else. She had been reborn as a man. Jonathan had found a way to reach her with a little help from someone. And it had not been cheap. But it did not matter now. Nina was trapped, and his plan had gone to the toilet.

But he was not finished. Another Hell Guardian had crawled out of the book instead of Nina. He found her and named her Elisha, after his mother, and in no time, they were lovers. But Elisha was not the saviour he was hoping for. She was a cold, soulless monster, killing to survive. Jonathan helped her, and in return, she was his. But no matter how powerful she seemed, she could not open the gates of Hell.

She belonged to the past, and Hell was not fooled. Neither was the world.

Elisha needed to feed, and the body count started rising. One or two souls here and there were not enough. She was getting greedy. People started vanishing, and no one—enforcement, governments, whoever—could do a thing about it. Elisha was unstoppable, becoming one of the most wanted criminals around. Then it got worse. She started dragging people back from the dead, bending them to her will. Madness broke loose, and it was only the beginning.

The consequences were heavy. Cities started crumbling under the weight of fear. Whole towns vanished, swallowed by Elisha unleashed. The dead were not just back, they were weapons, tearing through the living. Governments were collapsing, order fell apart, and nobody knew who to trust. It was not just a bit of trouble; it was Hell spilling over, and the world was paying the price in blood.

Jonathan's plan had failed, and now everything was going down, hard and fast.

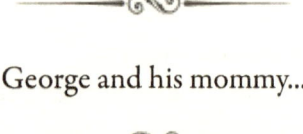

George and his mommy...

GEORGE WAS FIXATED on getting Asim's power, but it was not just for the power alone. The key inside Asim was what he really wanted. With it, George could travel between worlds—Heaven, Hell, anywhere. And that was the only way he could find Samir.

Samir, the angel who had wronged his family, was out there somewhere, hiding. And George needed that key to get to him.

He knew Asim's magic was not just your everyday magic trick, like, 'Ta-da, here's a rabbit!' No, he knew Asim was destined to be the future King of Dreams, and George was basically the walking Wikipedia of history. The man knew every single detail, which was both impressive and a little annoying. But George did not care about being king himself. What he did care about, though, was making sure Asim never got to wear that shiny crown.

And yes, George was a mean, ruthless son of a—you know what. Did he have his reasons? Oh, you bet he did, and some of them were kind of understandable. Asim's dad, Samir, pulled some serious villain-level shenanigans that neither George nor his mom could ever forgive. Samir forced George's mom, and voilà, George came into the world. He loved his mom like crazy, but let's just say his childhood was not all sunshine and rainbows. And maybe, just maybe, he would not have turned into such a cruel man if his mommy had not pushed him down that dark path.

So, George and his mom had been biding their time, just waiting for Asim to waltz out of those infernal gates and come back to the real world. Asim had not died, so he did not deserve to be roasting in Hell. No, his place was here, in the real world.

Twenty-one years ago, when he was born, his father, Samir, had to take him to Hell. Asim's mother was an angel working for Heaven, while Samir was an angel working for Hell. That made Asim some kind of illegal baby. But Death allowed Samir to take his son to Hell, where he had to look after Nina and always made sure she never got near the door to the real world. But the world knew. The moment Asim crossed that door, it recognized him. And that changed everything. He had this whole 'free will' thing going for him too. The magic inside Asim woke up, but the man was more clueless than a puppy chasing its own tail. He was busy with all sorts of other nonsense instead of wondering, 'Why the heck do I have this magical key?'

Anyway, George and his mom finally had Asim under their control. But revenge? Oh, lovely summer, they were just getting started. Together with Nicole, George had kept Asim captive, torturing him not just for the suffering. They had cut the key from Asim's chest, locking it away in a glass box protected by a spell. Asim had been awake when they sliced into him, and George always made sure to heal him, only so they could cut him open again.

The torture never stopped, like an obsession. Even Nicole, who had helped him, did not enjoy it anymore. She stopped asking after a while. She would watch him with narrowed eyes as he mumbled to himself, his fingers twitching as if itching to slice into Asim again. He was not sleeping much anymore, and it showed. His eyes were red-rimmed, dark circles forming under them. His hands trembled slightly when he thought no one was watching. The stress was eating him alive, though he pretended otherwise.

Nicole had grown tired of it all. One day, she packed her bags and left, abandoning George and their son. She was a "good mother." Of course. George hardly noticed; he was a "father of the year." Too. His focus had concentrated on one thing: the key. It consumed him. The thought of Samir haunted him. He needed to find him, to make him pay. But the longer it dragged on, the more it bit at George's sanity.

His mother remained by his side, but even she noticed the changes. The spark in her son's eyes was gone, replaced by a burning obsession that had worn him down over time. His body was showing signs of the toll, his frame thinner, his skin paler.

'My heart aches when I see you suffer, but son, do not give up,' she said, as if seeing her son suffer was not enough. 'Just do not end it. This is dragging you down, I know... but good will come of it.'

And George's eyes gleamed with that familiar, dangerous light. 'I will never give up. I will make him pay for what they did to you, even if it costs me my life.'

His mother gave him a kiss on the cheek.

'You are a good son,' she whispered.

Oh, Noah

AND THERE HE WAS, NOAH—INFAMOUS and on the run for years. He was only lucky because the poor Saluhi had to leave. Oh, they would have given him a hard time. But his time would come. The Snake Detectives were on his tail too. Yes, Noah was a half-snake, just like Tessa, and in their world, that meant trouble.

Tessa came from a royal bloodline, and their snake world had its own king. Word got back to him about what Noah had done to Tessa, and he was not having any of it. The King hated Noah's kind. He was not just a criminal in the human world—he had fled from their snake world too. He was a runner, and the Snake Detectives were sent to track him down. They were gunning for him, hungry to get their hands on him, and they were not stopping until they dragged him back to face the music.

But Noah knew better than to let them catch him. If they got him, it was game over. He was dead. So, he had found a hiding place, somewhere no one had thought to search for years. He had stayed low, biding his time. But Noah knew the truth. No one could hide forever. Time was running out. He could feel it. Forty-two years ago, before Tessa died in the real world, Noah was her ex-husband. Sure, Tessa was quite the lady, crueller than Noah himself. She had actually killed her own son just to gain the power he possessed. That was probably the cruellest act imaginable, but Hell sure put her through the wringer for it.

When she arrived in Hell, it was not just punishment, it was a complete reset. Her memories were stripped away, her powers erased. She was reborn there, forced to suffer like any other damned soul. Then Tessa changed. Her soul became good. But Noah found that laughable; he did not think she had suffered enough for her crimes. So, he took matters into his own hands.

EVERYONE HAS THEIR own story, and it can be good, bad, or something in between. But to be born and live in a world where you wake up one day and realise that everything is a lie? That can drive any story to madness.

This world, the real one, seemed different, but in reality, it was quite similar. Hell was just an imitation, where the wicked souls were sent to serve their punishment. Their memories were stripped away, their magic taken, and they were reborn into a new life, completely unaware that everything had already been written for them. No matter how hard they tried, things always ended the way they were supposed to, ensuring their punishment was fulfilled. But some had a chance—a rare one—to redeem their souls.

Tessa was one of those exceptions. She died once, served her time in Hell, and became a good person. Yet, the gates had been closed. Hell was not letting anyone out, nor anyone in. But should Nina, Tessa, or Asim have ever left Hell in the first place? Was Nina even supposed to be searching for her books? Nowhere was it written that Nina had to or even could find her books. Thirty-one years ago, Nina was punished; she was no longer the Guardian of Hell. Yet, she still chose to become one. Magic in this world now had a fracture that could not be easily repaired. Not even Death or Life themselves could interfere with the human world, where free will ruled. But that did not mean they did not care or were not watching. They were closer than Nina, Tessa, and Asim ever realised.

Rules were being broken, not just the rules of magic, but the very rules that governed Heaven, Hell, and the world itself. And unfortunately, that had consequences. People walked the streets in despair, shadows of their former selves. Magic was drying up, vanishing right before their eyes. It was not just a luxury; it was life. People did not know how to survive without it. They could not even buy food without magic; they had forgotten how to live like normal humans. Now? They were suffering. Poverty was everywhere, and with no magic left, the healers were powerless.

FINLEY COULD FEEL IT too. His magic used to hum through his veins like a live wire, but now? Not even a flash. His breath trembled like it wanted to do something, anything, but the power was not there. It was slipping away, day by day, and he could not stop it.

No magic, no control. Schools shut down. The whole system collapsed, spiralling down the drain. People lost it. Unrest broke out, streets turned into war zones, some folks looting for scraps, others just sitting down and giving up. The whole world was collapsing, and there was not a thing anyone could do about it. Instead of a bright sky, the world was now shrouded in darkness.

Finley felt the weight of it all like a knife to the heart. Now, with magic dying, his own powers fading, it was printed all over his body. He could not escape the memory of what he had done. Gripping his glass of whiskey, he swallowed it in one shot, but the bitterness could not drown out the haunting thoughts.

His servant buzzed mournfully, but Finley belted him a look. 'I know. You have got no idea how sorry I am.'

The servant nodded. 'Bzzz, bzzz.'

Those were the last words he spoke before the fog rolled in, swallowing the world in darkness. He stepped closer to the window, staring out at the thick mist. There was no more day, no more light, just endless blackness and sorrow.

Chapter Thirty-seven
The Stench

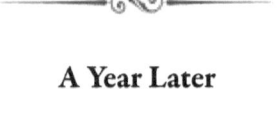

A Year Later

'DAD, MY HEAD'S SPINNING. I don't feel well. I can't do this today,' Leo said, his voice quiet, careful.

George barely looked up from his armchair. Then, without warning, he snapped his book shut and slammed it onto the table.

'Listen here, you little brat,' he growled. 'You think just because the world's gone soft, you get to be lazy? You'll study whether you like it or not. I won't have a son of mine growing up weak and useless.'

Leo dropped his gaze. He already knew there was no point arguing. But the words came out anyway.

'Dad... but the man downstairs. The one you're keeping locked up... he's weak. And he's your brother.'

Silence.

Then George's hand shot up.

Leo saw it coming. He always did. He ducked and bolted before the slap could land, feet pounding against the floor as he sprinted for his room. He barely got the door shut before his father could follow.

George stood outside, fists clenched. He wanted to go after him. He wanted to make sure the boy never spoke to him like that again.

But he wasn't alone.

His mother sat behind him, silent, watching.

'Leave him,' she said. 'We have other matters to deal with.'

George let out a slow breath, forcing the anger down. He turned his head. The cabinet stood in the corner. Solid. Locked. And inside was Asim's key.

His mother stood, straightened her coat, and adjusted the red hat perched neatly on her head. Then she stepped closer, placed a hand on his shoulder, and nodded.

'Soon, son... it will be yours.'

Without another word, they stepped out, shutting the door behind them.

Upstairs, in the silence of his room, Leo sat with his back against the door. He wiped his sleeve across his face, but it was too late. The tear had already fallen.

He had a beautiful, massive room. Luxurious, spacious—whatever word rich people use to describe a place they don't even appreciate. His father had more money than sense, owned properties, ran his own company, all that impressive nonsense. But Leo? He didn't want any of it. Not the house, not the fancy clothes, not the privilege that came with his last name.

He just wanted a family. A real one. One that didn't hurt him, one that didn't make him feel like a prisoner in his own home. His mother had left. Just walked away, leaving him behind to suffer alone. And now? Now he was trapped. He thought about the orphanage sometimes. Thought about giving up, letting go, just handing himself over. Maybe they'd be kinder, maybe they'd at least look at him like he existed.

Studying was supposed to be an escape. He used to enjoy it, back when it was his choice. But now? Now, it was a prison, a list of demands, a never-ending cycle of his father deciding what he had to learn, how long he had to study, and how perfect he had to be. Even when he was sick.

His skin had taken on a sickly green tinge, and his stomach twisted like it was trying to eat itself from the inside out. He forced himself to stand, dragging his feet to the bathroom. Splashed cold water on his face, but it didn't help. He needed food as his stomach was screaming for it, but the thought of eating made him nauseous. No, this wasn't just hunger, this was something else, something worse.

As he made his way downstairs, something stopped him in his tracks. A scent, like white roses. It didn't belong here, not in this house. But it cut through the sickness, easing the pain in a way nothing else had. And then he saw yellow smoke. It drifted from under a door. That door. The one Asim was locked behind.

His stomach settled, his head cleared, and suddenly, that scent was all he could focus on. It pulled him in, whispering to him in a way nothing ever had. His hand hovered over the handle. He wasn't allowed in there. No one was. If his father caught him, the consequences wouldn't just be bad; they'd be brutal.

But the scent... it wouldn't let him go. It had only started a few days ago, on his birthday.

His fingers tightened around the handle, and before he could stop himself, he pushed the door open. The smoke didn't stink. He'd expected something foul, something rotten. But no. The scent remained. The strange, quiet pull.

Inside, a corridor stretched before him. Empty. Lit. Silent.

His heart hammered. He knew what lay behind the next door. And yet, the scent... why? A voice in his head screamed at him to turn back. George could be home any second. He could be caught, dragged out, punished.

But he wasn't turning back... no... not now. His hand found the second door, pushed it open and stepped inside.

Asim lay there, eyes closed, fast asleep.

Leo looked around, stepping carefully, barely even breathing, so he wouldn't wake him. It was the first time he'd seen him today, and now he just stood there, unable to move any closer.

He swallowed, his palms suddenly damp. That sight wasn't right. But the room was clean, white, and so brightly lit it almost burned his eyes. One bed, no chains, no signs of violence. Just Asim, lying there, breathing.

And then he smelled it.

At first, it was faint, but then it hit him full force; a heavy, sweet scent that curled into his lungs. And that yellow smoke... he could see it coming directly from Asim.

He stepped closer and took a sniff.

And that rose... God, it smelled incredible. Something inside him loosened, like he could breathe more easily, just for a second. Even though fear still gripped him and none of this made any sense, that scent was... perfect. It shouldn't have been, but it was like heaven.

He edged forward, but his foot knocked against the bed frame.

Asim stirred and slowly opened his eyes. Leo flinched, his hand flying to the door handle, ready to bolt, but then he heard a voice.

'Don't be afraid of me. I'm harmless.'

Leo froze, but something in that voice made him stay. Slowly, he turned and narrowed his eyes.

'You... you're Asim? My... uncle?'

Asim sat up, still dazed, rubbing a hand over his face.

'Uncle?' His voice was rough, dry. 'You're... George's son?'

Leo then took a step forward.

'Yeah... they call me Leo.'

'That's a great name. How old are you?'

'Thirteen... um, actually... fourteen. I had a birthday and I even forgot about it.'

'I was fourteen once too. And I know that's an age you don't forget. Tell me... does George hurt you?'

Leo dropped his gaze.

'No... just sometimes... sometimes he's...'

Before he could finish, he heard the clatter of keys in the lock.

He froze. His dad was coming home. Leo's heart pounded as he spun around and ran, not looking back.

But...
He hadn't shut the door.

A few hours later...

LEO DRAGGED HIMSELF back to his room. George was in the study with his mother, door locked, because of course, they had secrets to whisper. Like always. His head throbbed, his stomach twisted. Every second near his father or grandmother felt like stepping into a rotting sewer. It wasn't just in his head. He could smell it. Thick. Filthy. Like something decaying under his skin.

He didn't know what to do anymore. He was tired, done. Collapsing onto his bed, he let out a shaky breath. And then... just like that... it vanished. The sickness, the nausea, the rot in the air.

Instead, he smelled roses. That scent, that perfect, golden scent, warm as sunlight, soft as a whispered promise. His heart clenched and he could breathe again.

And then, the yellow smoke.

His eyes snapped open. It drifted through the air, twisting like something alive. Not from his room. No, it was leading him, calling him.

Leo sat up, sniffing like a bloodhound. Then he was on his feet, following the trail out of his room, down the corridor, down the stairs, but slowly, carefully. His pulse pounded. The yellow smoke curled its fingers towards the kitchen.

When he tried to open it, he couldn't, it was locked. Weird, really weird. The kitchen was never locked, ever. But Leo was a bit of a mischief. No magic? No problem. Locks weren't exactly his barrier. A few clicks, a little twist; there.

The door swung open, and Leo froze.

Asim.

The man was devouring food like he hadn't eaten in weeks. Hell, because he hadn't. Chunks fell to the floor, and for a second, Leo thought he'd choke right then and there. But no, he was just... starving, desperate. Leo quickly shut the door behind him.

Asim stopped chewing, just stared, waiting.

'You're not gonna tell?' Asim asked, voice low.

'No. Should I?' Leo shot back.

'I'll be gone from here. And you better act like you saw nothing, or you'll be in trouble, alright?' Asim said, stepping towards the back door.

Leo's mouth worked faster than his brain.

'Wait! Your key. Don't you want your key?'

Asim froze.

His fingers slipped from the door handle. His body turned slow, careful, eyes locked onto Leo.

'How do you know about that?' His voice had changed.

'It's in the living room. In the cabinet. Can't open it—I tried. There's a spell on it,' Leo admitted.

Asim exhaled, slumping into a chair. His head dropped into his hands.

'I can't risk it. I have to go.'

'Then take me with you,' Leo said.

Asim lifted his head.

'With me? Leo, don't you see what I am? I'm nothing, you get that? I've got nowhere to go. My skin's covered in blood and... I don't even know if I'll make it more than a few steps.'

'Fine. Go, then. You're just as much of a coward as my dad. Can't hide being brothers, can you?'

That one hit. Asim had reached the door, one foot over the threshold. Then he stopped.

'Where's your dad now?' Asim asked.

'In the office, talking to my gran.'

'Fine. Come on. But I'm not promising anything good.'

'Trust me, there's nothing good waiting for me here,' Leo muttered.

They slipped out the door. Then Asim stopped again.

Leo swore under his breath. 'Now what?'

Asim's breathing had changed, shoulders stiffened.

'My key,' he whispered. 'My key is calling me. I can feel it, hear it.'

Then he staggered back, gasping, a hand clutching his chest. A burning pain in his ribs.

Leo watched him, sadness creeping into his gut.

'I know what that key is. I heard my dad talking about it.'

'Yeah?' Asim wheezed.

'You're the future King of Dreams. That key is everything and without it, you probably won't last much longer. That's what Dad said.'

Asim dropped to his knees.

'I've got no strength left, Leo. I can't.'

Leo stepped closer. His voice softened.

'Call it to you. Break the spell. Gran always said you could. That's why they've been watching you so closely.'

Asim let out a shaky breath.

'You're a clever lad.'

Leo smiled, really smiled. It had been a long, long time since he'd heard anything kind. Usually, it was more like:

'You little brat. You bastard. You idiot. You little shit.'

This? This warmed his heart.

But Leo hadn't expected Asim to actually do it, to actually try. But then he saw him. The way Asim trembled, how his fingers clenched tightly around the fabric of his shirt, how his breathing quickened and how everything around them started to change.

The air grew heavier, like the moment before a storm, when the sky darkens, when everything goes still for just a second, but you can feel something coming. Pressure, it was there. Not physical, but Leo felt it deep in his bones, in his stomach.

Asim closed his eyes, his chest rose in a deep, unsteady breath.

And then—a crack. Not outside, inside the house. Leo flinched. A click, glass, wood. Something shifted. something gave way.

Asim exhaled and then a sound escaped his lips. Half pain, half surprise. In that moment, Leo knew. The key was gone. It was no longer waiting inside the cabinet.

And then—impact. No grand explosion, no flash of light, just a sudden, invisible energy slamming into Asim's chest. A fire spread beneath his skin. Not real fire, no flames, but it burned like hell.

Asim's mouth opened, but no sound came out. Just a shaky, ragged exhale, while pain rushed down his bones, sharp and relentless. His entire chest burned, like something was being branded beneath his skin.

Leo could do nothing. Just stand there and watch as Asim's body trembled, as the fabric of his shirt stretched and tensed beneath his hands, like something underneath was settling into place.

And then, suddenly... it was over. The key was back, and Asim coughed a bit. Then, he looked fine, even better than before.

And Leo? He stood there, staring at him, completely speechless. But one thing was clear. This wasn't the same Asim who had barely been standing a few minutes ago.

Leo was still standing there, staring at Asim, watching his heavy breathing. Then he touched the key. And in that moment, something changed. As soon as his palm made contact, the key started turning red. Slowly, like an ember heating up and it appeared in Asim's hand, firmly clutched between his fingers.

Leo let out a breath. 'Okay... that was... cool?'

Asim just stared at it for a moment, didn't say a word. His thumb ran over it, almost as if making sure it was real. And then slowly, almost tenderly, he lifted it to his lips.

'I missed you,' he whispered.

And then... he kissed it.

Leo's eyes widened completely.

'Wait—did you just—? You're actually serious?'

Asim didn't even look at him. Didn't need to. He held onto the key almost protectively.

Leo shook his head. *This guy was nuts.*

'Let's get out of here before my dad finds out.'

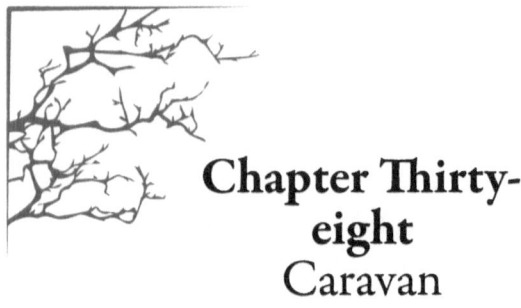

Chapter Thirty-eight
Caravan

ASIM WAS FREE. STRONGER than ever. A total upgrade. Except for the whole scar-from-George's-torture-still-burning-like-hell thing. But, yes, nothing was perfect.

Not that he was thinking about it. No, definitely not thinking about it. And if he managed to keep it out of his head, it wasn't thanks to his own mental strength or inner peace or whatever. No, the real MVP here was Leo, who had not shut his mouth for the past fifteen minutes.

They walked down the street; the city stretching out around them, and Leo kept talking. Talking and talking like he was afraid of silence, or maybe just allergic to it. Either way, Asim didn't mind. He was just relieved Leo wasn't in George's clutches anymore. The real problem?

He had no idea what to do with this kid now.

Asim glanced around, still trying to process everything. It was all still real, no sudden time to rewind. No, "just kidding, you're still locked up." They had actually escaped.

But standing around all dumbfounded wasn't an option. They needed a plan, and fast.

Then it hit him. Finley.

Maybe Finley could keep an eye on Leo for a while. He wasn't too far. His caravan was parked near the edge of the park. That could work, or it could be a disaster. Either way, it was a plan, and Asim was seriously running low on those.

He took a deep breath, stretching out his limbs as they walked. Moving felt... weird, not the "ow, my bones hurt" kind of weird. More like "why am I not a broken, half-dead mess right now?" kind of weird. His legs weren't shaking, his muscles weren't screaming in agony.

It was unexpected. The plan had always been to get out. Run. Never look back. And yet, something felt off. That nagging little voice, the one he usually ignored, was whispering in the back of his head. You messed up, man. You left something unfinished.

But what was he supposed to do about it? Where was he supposed to go? Home? That wasn't an option. Home didn't exist anymore. His father? Dead. That place? A Hell.

Nina was gone... Tessa was gone. There was literally nowhere left for him. And yet, somehow, he knew this wasn't over, not by a long shot.

'Right, wait here for me,' he said to Leo as they stood outside Finley's caravan. It was dark, and no one was answering. The only way to get inside was with his key.

With a heavy heart, Asim touched the key glued to his chest, and in a blink, he was standing in Finley's living room.

The shock hit Finley hard. His tea slipped from his hands, the cup smashing on the floor, shards flying everywhere. Lucky for him, he didn't spill it all over himself.

'Who the bloody hell are you? How'd you get in here? That's impossible!' Finley's lips trembled, unsure whether to run or pass out.

Asim stepped closer, the air familiar.

'Don't you recognise me? It's me, Asim.'

Finley's eyes locked onto his, blinking like he'd just seen a ghost. He edged forward, staring straight into Asim's eyes. Then his chest tightened, squeezing the life out of him. The tears came fast, like a bust tap.

'I didn't recognise you. Don't even know what to say.'

'Yes, got a few scratches. It'll heal. You're not looking any better yourself.'

Finley's chest tightened, breath shallow, pulse racing.

Asim stepped in and shoved him into a chair. 'Let's get you to the healer.'

'Healers aren't like they used to be. They can't help me now.'

Then, blunt as anything, he said it—he was dying.

Asim stood there, eyes locked on him, no words left.

Finley couldn't bring himself to talk about what had gone down. Instead, he switched the focus to Asim. He wanted to know everything, every detail.

Asim wasn't sure how much Finley could handle, so he kept it brief.

'I was locked up. Just managed to escape.'

Finley couldn't keep up the front anymore.

'I know everything,' he admitted, the words dragging out. 'I knew George had you kidnapped, tortured. I knew about Nina. But I did nothing. I betrayed her... I betrayed all of you. Just... kill me. Please.'

Asim didn't even flinch. No rage, no heartbreak, just disappointment.

'Hmm, I had my suspicions, but I wasn't sure. And no, I'm not killing you. I don't care enough about that. I'm here because I needed help, but I guess you can't help me...'

Those words shattered Finley. His breath hitched, barely able to speak. Still, he forced out his last:

'Nina is...'

And just like that, it was over. Those were Finley's final words.

Even after the betrayal, Asim grabbed him, carried him like he weighed nothing, and buried him in the garden. Head down.

The servants stood by Asim, faces heavy with sadness, a few shedding tears as they looked down at Finley's body.

But the moment didn't last. As Finley passed, his magical dwelling started to crumble. Everything around them: the flowers, the furniture, the house itself, began to fade into nothing.

Even the servants weren't spared.

'Bzzzz, bzzz,' were the last words of the fly servant before he shifted back into his original form, now buzzing aimlessly around Finley's grave.

That was all that remained of Finley. Just the caravan and the empty ground.

'Right, he was your grandad?' Leo asked Asim, standing behind him.

Asim turned to Leo. 'No, my uncle. And come on, we're going somewhere else. I've got an idea.'

In the last ten minutes, Asim had learned Leo's entire life story. He talked, and talked, and talked...

'Why don't you just use the key and teleport us?' Leo said as they walked down the street.

'I... I've never transported anyone before. I don't know how, and it could be dangerous,' Asim replied.

'You're weird, you know that?' Leo said, and Asim laughed.

'Hey, but you smell nice. I mean, not like you actually smell good or bad or anything. It's just... sometimes people stink to me,' Leo said.

'Stink? Look, I haven't had a bath in like a year, so honestly, I think you're the weird one here,' Asim said.

Leo smirked. 'Yeah, I know. It annoys me.'

'What annoys you?'

'The smell, you know? It makes me feel sick. But with you, I don't smell anything bad. I smell roses. Anyway, I'm starving. Can we stop somewhere? Like for a burger?' Leo said, looking around for a shop.

But Asim stopped him. 'What did you just say?'

'What? Burger? I mean, I'll eat anything, I'm starving—'

'No, not that. The thing about the roses. What did you say?'

'Oh... well, you smell like roses,' Leo said.

'And do you see anything with it? Is there something coming off me?' Asim asked.

Leo stopped walking. 'Yeah, I see something. Like a mist. Yellow. Do you know anything about that?'

Asim swallowed. 'No. I was just curious.'

They kept walking.

'We can't stop. It's not safe here. It's just around the corner,' Asim said.

'But my feet hurt,' Leo complained. 'And I can't take it anymore. I'm thirsty, and I really need the toilet.'

Asim just shook his head, but didn't stop walking.

'We're here.'

Leo looked up at the beautiful castle. But there were iron bars now, which was new. Jonathan had never had iron bars before.

Suddenly, the gate opened on its own. That was really weird.

Asim held onto the key, just in case.

'Is it safe here? Where are we going? Do they have food?' Leo asked.

Asim kept walking. 'Yeah. Stay close to me.'

He knocked on the door, and a servant opened it, inviting them inside. They stepped in.

Nothing had changed. The place shone with cleanliness.

Then Jonathan appeared. The moment he saw Asim, he just stood there and swallowed hard.

'Shall I come in?' Asim said.

'Yes, I... no, come in, I...' Jonathan said.

Leo cut in, 'Do you have any food? Also, I really need the toilet.'

Jonathan turned to him with sharp eyes. 'The toilet is upstairs. Wash your hands. You'll get food only if you come back clean!'

Jonathan then gestured at the chair, barely looking up as he poured the drink. The glass hit the table with a dull *clink*; the liquid swirling inside like it had better things to do. Asim dropped into the seat with the kind of energy that said he knew this night wouldn't be worth shit, but he'd sit through it anyway.

The room smelled like stale cigarettes and the kind of leather that had seen too many fights. Something metallic still clung to the air, like an old grudge no one had bothered to settle.

Jonathan spoke. 'So, you're free now?'

'Yeah. But not thanks to you.' Asim let the words drop like a sledgehammer, slamming his glass onto the table.

Jonathan exhaled, slow and measured, like a man who knew he was about to get chewed out but had already given up fighting it.

The silence between them sat heavy. Not the awkward kind, but the type that stretched before a storm, thick with the promise that something was about to go horribly wrong. Then Jonathan tensed. Not because of what Asim had said, but because of what was happening.

Something glowed beneath Asim's shirt. Not a soft, warm glow—nothing comforting. This was sharp, pulsing, like embers just waiting for an excuse to set the whole place alight.

'What do you need?' His voice was quieter now, eyes locked on the burning key like it might lunge at him.

'Look after the kid. Just for a while.'

Jonathan blinked. 'You want me to babysit some brat?'

And because the universe was an absolute bastard when it came to timing, a scream rang out from upstairs.

Both men exchanged a look, the kind that didn't need words.

They moved.

Upstairs, the hallway was all dust and tension. Leo stood there, caught red-handed by a furious cleaning lady who had his ear in a death grip.

'Mr Jonathan! This little creep was watching me while I was changing!' she yelled.

Asim dragged a hand down his face. Jonathan, ever the smooth talker, muttered an apology before grabbing Leo away by the shoulder and marching him downstairs. His boots hit the steps hard.

'That was bloody rude! You don't do things like that! Didn't your dad teach you any respect?'

Asim stepped in before things escalated. His voice wasn't raised, but there was something in it that shut Jonathan up.

'Don't talk to him like that. He's George's son.'

Jonathan froze. 'George's...' His brain visibly stopped. 'Wait. How old was he when he had him? And are you sure?'

Leo stayed quiet. Still. The kind of stillness that meant he understood more than he let on.

Asim ran his fingers over the burning key, as if grounding himself. He let out a slow breath. 'Take care, Uncle.'

Jonathan's mouth opened, then shut. He rubbed a hand over his face. 'Wait... Sorry, Asim. I'm being an arse. Let him stay.'

'No. I won't leave him with you. He's been through enough.'

But Leo, completely unfazed by the tension thick enough to choke on, looked at Asim and grinned. 'But he smells nice, Uncle Asim. Like you. Like roses.'

Jonathan's head snapped towards Asim. That look passed between them—the *oh hell* look.

'How is that possible?' Jonathan's voice was low. Careful. 'Is he... like Nina?'

'Maybe. But he doesn't know it yet,' said Asim. He crouched in front of Leo. 'Are you sure? What colour does he have?'

'Yellow,' Leo said, like it was the most obvious thing in the world. Then, with brutal honesty only kids possess, added, 'But that nasty woman upstairs is green and smells like a sewer!'

Jonathan burst out laughing.

Asim just sighed, dragging a hand down his face. 'Fine. He can stay.' He glanced at Jonathan one last time. 'Once I sort things out, I'll come back for him.'

Jonathan just nodded. No arguments this time.

Asim walked out, shutting the door behind him. But something annoyed him. Doubt.

Nina had never been sure if the souls worked the way they were supposed to. And Jonathan, of all people, having yellow? The colour of the good ones? That was a miracle.

Still, he paused for just a second, glancing back through the window. Inside, Jonathan was summoning food for Leo. The kid was grinning. And Jonathan—*Jonathan*—was smiling back. Maybe, just maybe, miracles did exist.

Chapter Thirty-nine
High Heels

———◦◦◦———

ASIM WAS IN TOWN, WALKING, but something was different. The kind of silence that made his ears strain, every faint breath of wind carrying an unpleasant smell, foul, like sour milk. His stomach growled. Also stunk. Yet, his mind kept circling back to Nina and Tessa. He needed to move, to find a lead, any, but where to start?

Standing in front of the old magic shop. Maybe the shopkeeper knew something, but as he tugged on the door, locked. He tried the next shop along the road, but hmm, same story. Just as he was about to give up, a single light sparkled on across the street. Odd... Asim felt a thirst of knowing and crossed over, eyes narrowed. The door creaked as he pushed it. Lifeless, the desk empty, no surprise. Shops like this often were.

He turned slowly, and there he was, an elderly man with short, curly hair, and a little rounder, standing there.

'We haven't had any customers for a long ages,' he said with a kind voice, but tired.

Asim gave him a faint smile. 'What place is this?'

'It's a restaurant. But magic's fading, food's scarce, but maybe there will be a little something. You look like you haven't eaten in years.'

Asim looked down at his ragged clothes. 'I don't have any money,' he mumbled. 'I'll just go.'

'Money's not important today,' the man said, giving him a sly wink. 'Come with me.'

He led Asim to a wall, touched it, and the wall shifted, sliding open to reveal a tiny restaurant behind it. It wasn't anything grand, but it had a warmth about it, cosy, with just a handful of tables. The sort of place that made you feel at home the second you stepped inside.

Asim sat down where the man pointed, feeling both humbled and strangely comfortable. His hunger was so overwhelming that he didn't care what was brought out. He just needed something, anything.

'I've got a small yellow napkin here,' the elderly man said softly, pulling it from his apron pocket. 'Like I told you, there's not much food left. Hopefully, this will be enough.' He placed it in front of Asim before sitting down across the table.

The napkin began to work its magic; toast with butter and jam, a steaming cup of tea. Asim's throat tightened. It was exactly what his dad, Samir, used to make for him every morning. Oh, he dived in, devouring. The taste was just as he remembered, but he was too hungry to appreciate it properly. He couldn't stop shovelling food into his mouth as if he'd never eat again. The elderly man watched him closely, his eyes full of quiet understanding. He could tell Asim had been through something.

'Slow down, son,' he said gently, his voice like a grandfather from an old fairytale. 'And have a sip of this,' he added, pushing the tea towards him.

Then a storm hammered down. Purple rain, thick and intense.

Asim blinked. 'What's this now?'

The man didn't move an inch. Just started talking like this was normal, like storms that bled purple were part of the deal these days. He broke down how the world went to hell. Everything flipped, nothing like it used to be. Then he dropped a name: Elisha.

'Who the hell's that?'

'Guardian of Hell,' the man said, straight-faced. 'She came here, feeds on souls. She's got everyone terrified. People tried to take her down, but no one's ever come close.'

'She feeds on soul?'

'The rumours say she came from hell, but she's weak. She is eating them to survive.'

'Hm...' Asim was thinking, how could Nina be her? Things got even worse than he thought.

'How come you don't know a thing? Who are you?'

'I'm just a guy trying to save the people I love... and get back home.'

'The world's about to end. No salvation. No happy endings.'

The elder's words carried a weight Asim didn't like. It wasn't fear, exactly, but the kind of certainty that made his skin tighten. He exhaled slowly, pressing his fingers against the table for a brief moment before standing. The wind outside slipped through the cracks in the door, steady and deliberate, moving more like a presence than air.

The elder's expression didn't change, but his eyes darkened slightly. He had seen this before. Lived through it. Knew what came next.

'You feel it,' he whispered. It wasn't a question.

'What's that?'

'She's somewhere nearby, probably eating souls.'

Asim placed a firm hand on the elder's shoulder. 'Go inside. Lock the doors. No matter what happens, stay there.'

The elder studied him for a moment, as if weighing the chances of arguing. He must have decided it wasn't worth it. Without another word, he stepped back, disappearing into the hidden passage. The door clicked shut behind him.

Asim stepped outside, and the purple rain fell upon him. He pulled up his hood and shoved his hands into his pockets because it burned. He crossed to the other side of the street. It was eerily quiet, but the sound of dripping was still audible. Then he heard hissing. *Sssssssss. Sssss.*

Where was it coming from? He saw a lot of blood on the ground, and at that moment, he knew this was no joke. Could it really be Nina? Had she truly become the cruel Guardian of Hell? Maybe it had always been in her blood? Had she found her books and power? Had she used them?

He shook his head and kept walking slowly, following the bloodstains. But soon, they weren't just stains—they were pools. Long, vast pools, like a slaughterhouse.

Asim's heart pounded when he saw a figure with long black hair kneeling on the ground, holding a person in their arms—someone unconscious. And he saw her pulling something from them... dust? Energy? When he took two steps closer to confirm what he was seeing, he must have disturbed her. She turned her head towards him so fast that it defied the laws of physics.

Asim flinched, stepping back. This couldn't be Nina. Maybe he had seen wrong as it was dark, purple rain was falling, and the mist was thick. But her? She stood up, discarded the person like rubbish, pushed her hair back, and smiled.

Then Asim saw her face. It was Nina.

But this Nina?

She wore high red heels. A tight, short dress with a deep neckline—white. Red lipstick. She looked so sexy that Asim swallowed hard, barely believing what he was seeing.

And the way she walked. Step by step, her movements were hypnotic, as if even the rain itself made way for her. Maybe it wasn't just the heels, maybe it was her power. But still, hell, it was a sight.

'Nina? Is that you?' Asim called from a distance, narrowing his eyes.

Then she spoke in a same voice as Nina's, but something was different. Her accent wasn't the familiar, practised Yorkshire accent. It was something posh. Pure.

'Hello, Asim. It's been a while. How did you find me?'

She kept walking slowly, the sound of her heels growing louder.

'You weren't hard to find. What's going on, Nina? This... I... this isn't you,' Asim said.

She paused, standing about three metres away from him. Just the two of them on the road. No people, no cars. Just them, under the purple rain.

And then the storm began.

'What do you mean this isn't me? Oh, I've simply changed my name. They call me Elisha now. Nina was boring, you see,' she said, winking at him.

No. Nina would never wink at him and she definitely wouldn't give him that look. This wasn't Nina.

'You look good. Changed your style?' Asim asked.

She laughed, looking even sexier now.

'Style? Are you saying I wasn't pretty before?'

'No! I would never say that. I just... you're different.'

'So are you, Asim.'

She smirked.

Asim glanced down at himself, then lowered his head.

She took two more slow, deliberate steps towards him, pulled out a cigarette, and lit it.

'Want one?'

Asim lifted his head.

'I don't smoke. I never have. You know that.'

He sighed.

'You know what? Forget it. I... I get it now. I'm not surprised they took your powers away, Nina. What have you done? Do you consume people's souls? Look at yourself—you're killing people. How can you? Who are you? Who the hell are you, really?'

'Me? I'm the Guardian of Hell, Asim.'

She exhaled smoke and stepped closer.

'And look, join me. We'll rule together. I know who you are. That key of yours—it's the key to our future.'

'Asim, look at what they did to you. Your own brother. Your uncle. Everyone around you betrayed you, tortured you. And yet here you stand, asking me what happened to me?'

Asim clenched his fists.

'Really? Then why didn't you come to save me? You forgot about me, and now you want my key? Now I'm useful to you?'

His voice wavered.

'And where is Tessa?'

'Who?'

Asim froze. For a moment, he said nothing. He just watched as her cigarette burned out. She tossed it onto the ground and crushed it under her heel. Nina would never do that. And more than that? She would never, ever forget Tessa.

'What is your full name? Where did you live? What is our history, Nina?' Asim asked.

And suddenly, Elisha's expression changed. She frowned, and there was no more grace on her face. She didn't even have to answer—Asim saw the rage in her eyes.

'You know what, Asim? Fuck you. I hate this shit, these games. Of course, I'm not Nina, you arsehole! Do I look like her? Look at me, Asim—I'm a sexy bitch. Do you get me? I'm the fucking Guardian of Hell. I came here to take back what's mine, and trust me—no one, no one will stand in my way.'

'So you'd better get the fuck out of my way. Keep your fucking key. I don't need it. I don't need you.'

'Nina's gone, Asim. Go get your life together. I'm giving you a chance. I'm being kind. Because I like you. I really do,' she said.

Asim took a deep breath.

'Where is Nina? What have you done to her? And who the hell are you? And try telling me again that you're the Guardian of Hell, and I won't be standing here talking to you anymore.'

'Haha haha—hah! You're funny, Asim. A shame, really. But you know what? Why not? Jonathan never told you, did he? Your own uncle?'

'Talk,' Asim said.

'Nina is in history. She got stuck there instead of me. And I'm here. She's gone, Asim.'

'In history? What the hell are you talking about?'

'Nah, it took me a while to understand it too, you know. But... you're starting to bore me now.'

Then she dropped to her knees, touched the ground, and lifted her head. She smiled at Asim and winked.

At that moment, not only did Asim shudder, but the entire street trembled.

And that wasn't enough for her.

She screamed, like some kind of psycho.

'AAAAAAA! AAAAAAAA!'

And then the street split in half.

Asim quickly jumped to the side.

'Are you fucking insane?!' he shouted, breathing heavily.

'I like your soul, Asim! I need it!' Elisha screamed.

'Go to hell,' Asim said.

Elisha laughed.

'I wish! But don't worry—soon, very soon, I will have my full power. Hell, too. And trust me, I will turn everything and everyone into flames, not into those stupid games you all play there.'

'Great. Good luck,' Asim said, turning away.

'Going somewhere?' she asked.

'Yeah. You're starting to bore me too,' Asim said.

Elisha smirked.

'You're not going anywhere, Asim. Your soul... your soul is worth thousands of others. It's different. It's powerful. You are not just some ordinary human. And you know what? How do I put this in a way you'll understand?' She took a step closer, her voice dropping to a near whisper. 'I need it. And I—I am not some pathetic Nina. I am powerful. And when I want something, I take it.'

'So go on. Take it. Please.'

Asim spread his arms wide, standing in the rain.

He pulled down his hood, lifted his head up, and stuck out his tongue.

'Thereee, take meee.'

At that moment, Asim was furious.

Furious with the whole world, with people, and even though it looked like he had given up, he hadn't. He knew Nina was still alive somewhere. And his rage, his fury was greater than ever before. Elisha almost believed him. She blinked at him and walked straight to him. She was so close. They were touching faces. Her face against his. Their eyes locked. Their bodies were not touching, but their faces were.

Then she sniffed him, just like Nina used to do. Like a dog.

Sniff.

Sniffff.

Then she whispered, 'Such rage... I've never felt this in anyone.'

She looked like she was about to lick him. But maybe she held back.

'Elisha?' Asim said.

'Yes?'

'Fuck you,' he said.

Elisha started screaming.

'You bastard! What have you done?!'

As she began inhaling Asim's soul, instead of a soul, instead of dust, Asim had tricked her.

He had whispered to the key, commanding it to imitate a soul and instead send choking dust. Elisha grabbed her throat. It burned. She couldn't breathe. Then she collapsed to the ground.

Asim took two steps back.

'I don't hit women,' he said.

And there she was, writhing on the ground. Asim turned to leave. But Elisha started coughing. Asim stopped in his tracks. He wiped the rain from his face. And he knew this woman was seriously powerful.

'I have to admit... that was a good move. You're not just a sexy guy, you're smart too.'

'Yeah, thanks for the compliment.'

But Elisha no longer looked like she just wanted to talk.

Elisha slowly pushed herself up from the ground. Her body was still trembling, and she gasped for air.

Asim took a step forward. 'Give it up, Elisha. You're losing.'

But she only smirked. 'I haven't even started yet.'

And then—BOOM.

She lunged at him with such speed that he barely had time to react. A direct hit to his chest.

Asim was thrown backwards, but while still in mid-air, he flipped and landed smoothly on his feet.

'Nice try.'

Elisha leapt at him again, but this time, he was ready. He had his key, and in an instant, he appeared right behind her.

She landed on nothing.

And before she could react—Asim pinned her down with his foot, holding her in place.

'I don't want to hit you. You're way too sexy for that, you know?'

She didn't like that.

Asim lifted his foot off her back. He couldn't hurt her. Something inside him just wouldn't let him. Because no matter what, he still saw Nina in her. And even if she wasn't Nina, she was still a woman. And hurting a woman? That was the greatest sin of all.

Elisha dropped to her knees, wiping the blood from her nose. Asim noticed something was off. She looked weaker. Her eyes flicked around as she sniffed the air, searching.

'Do you need a soul? Are you getting weaker? But you haven't even done anything yet.'

Asim laughed at her.

'What's wrong? I thought you were the Guardian of Hell.'

Elisha froze. She lifted her head. Her face shifted.

'You know what? I was saving this for the last moment. The perfect moment.'

'You want to see the real Guardian of Hell?'

'Then watch.'

Something inside her snapped.

And at that moment—Her gaze turned cold as ice. She closed her eyes. Asim stepped back. She spread her arms wide, lifted her head, and opened her mouth wide—And screamed.

'AAAAAAAAAAA!!'   Then   louder. 'AAAAAAAAAAAA!!'

Her body started shaking uncontrollably. And then from the sky a thick, red smoke began swirling downward. Clouds were black, heavy clouds, like they were being pulled from every corner of the world. Even the rain itself changed direction, as if avoiding them. The clouds remained untouched, gathering into a violent vortex above her.

And then, as if sucked by some invisible energy. They shot straight into Elisha, right into her body.

Asim felt it in his gut that this was no joke. This was something far beyond anything he had ever seen before.

Her skin started changing. Slowly, her fists clenched, her knuckles turning white. Her eyes were still closed, but she dropped her head forward. Her veins bulged, pulsing so hard that they showed even under her flesh. And then her skin itself started transforming.

At first, it melted, not like burning flesh, but like something unnatural was pushing through. Her body expanded. Her thin arms thickened, turning into massive, monstrous muscles. Her legs bulked up, powerful, almost beast-like. Like the Hulk, but not green. Black.

The darkness spread, consuming her entire body, stretching her into something far bigger, far stronger. She was no longer a woman, no longer even human. Her hair disappeared, burning away into nothing. Her body grew taller, nearly two metres high, her shape monstrous and overwhelming.

And then she screamed again. Her body twisted and trembled, as if the transformation was breaking her apart from the inside. But she didn't fall. She stood firm, bearing the pain like it was nothing more than fuel.

Then, the final horror came, her eyelids vanished, simply disappeared. Her eyes were gone. No whites, no pupils, but smooth, black skin where her gaze should have been.

From that pitch-black flesh, something began to seep out. A thick, slimy green liquid oozed from her body, slowly dripping over her like a second, sickening layer of flesh. It covered her completely, as if her entire being was melting into something worse.

Asim's stomach tightened. This... This was not Elisha anymore. This was... The Guardian of Hell.

'What the fuck?' said Asim.

Elisha, no, now the Guardian of Hell, laughed.

'This is the real Guardian of Hell. Nina can't do this, can she?'

'Now you can try hitting me. I'm not a woman, not a man either, you know. But I'll tell you one thing—I love this transformation. I can't wait to stay like this forever. You see, I'm sick of looking and breathing like a human. You cannot imagine what it is like to be what you truly are. It's...'

'Yeah, I believe you,' said Asim, swallowing hard.

What he was looking at wasn't just the Guardian of Hell, it was a monster. Terrifying, evil, huge, black, shiny, eyeless, and disgustingly slimy. That green, stinking sludge dripped off her, bubbling as it slid down. Her teeth were as long as human fingers. This was a true Guardian.

'Soon, Asim, soon. This form will stay mine. My power will be whole, and I'll take back my Hell. But believe me, flames and torture? That's only the beginning. I'll be nibbling on your little fingernails and decorating myself with you humans.'

She stepped closer, right up to Asim's nose. The stench was overwhelming, like tones of shit.

The Guardian of Hell blew, and a black liquid came from her mouth, surrounding Asim. It looked like a hundred snakes, wrapping around his neck, shoulders, stomach, legs. It twisted tighter and tighter until he couldn't move.

Elisha blew again, and Asim was flung backwards. The liquid splattered everywhere as he crashed through a shop window, shards of glass cutting into him. But he stood up. And now—now he was pissed off.

The rage inside him erupted. He needed this. He wanted this. The Guardian, despite having no eyes, saw him all too clearly. Asim ran at her, ripping his shirt apart and throwing it aside. His key shone so brightly it lit up the entire street, casting the Guardian of Hell in a stark black silhouette.

They stood there, facing each other.

The Guardian of Hell knelt, touched the ground, and sent black flames shooting towards Asim. They flared up from the earth like beams of darkness. Asim blocked them with his key, pushing back, holding firm, sending counter-flames in defence. Bloodied, but unyielding. And neither was the Guardian.

Both dodged and weaved through the flames, until suddenly, Asim vanished, only to reappear behind the Guardian. He grabbed its throat, but it was so slimy his hand slipped off.

In that moment, his key dimmed. He couldn't focus. The Guardian of Hell was draining his soul. A yellow mist rose from Asim as he stood there, eyes rolling back, powerless. The Guardian's mouth was open, arms outstretched, pulling, pulling, and Asim's life flashing before his eyes.

But he wasn't thinking about himself. He was thinking about people. He didn't want this monster in the world. This thing didn't even belong in Hell. It deserved to die.

Asim started screaming. 'Aaaaaaaah!'

So loud it called to his key. His muscles locked up, and then... he did it. He reached out. His key flared, and the Guardian of Hell was blasted five metres away, crashing into a car. The impact shattered the windows and crushed the vehicle under its weight.

Asim exhaled. His breathing was ragged, his mouth dry, his energy drained. But he pushed forward.

He stepped closer to the Guardian. It rose.

Asim lunged, kicking it twice. The Guardian struck back three times—right, left, and from below. Asim was knocked so high it felt like he'd fly straight into the sky. He landed hard, coughing up blood. Something in his ribs might have cracked.

But he stood up. He ran at the Guardian, key in hand, holding it straight out, sending beams of energy towards it. Asim stood his ground, struggling. He was sweating so much it washed the blood from his skin.

But the Guardian fought back. It opened its mouth, and darkness spewed out a thick, black dust.

Asim's beams couldn't break through. He couldn't hold on much longer. It was tearing him apart. He had to let go. The second he did, he was flung backwards, crashing onto the pavement. His head scraped against the kerb. He thought he wouldn't get up again.

The Guardian came closer.

'It's been an honour, Asim,' it said, pressing its foot onto his wound.

Asim started bleeding.

The Guardian pressed harder. It reached for Asim's key—Big mistake.

'What... what is this?' the Guardian howled as its hand burned.

'The key is mine. I'm its master, you idiot,' Asim laughed, watching as flames spread up the Guardian's arm.

It threw the key down, but the moment it hit the ground, it let out a loud chime and shot straight back into Asim's chest.

The Guardian burned.

And then, suddenly, George appeared. He looked around.

'This isn't over, bro,' he told Asim. Then he waved his wand. 'Asim's holeko be!' he shouted, and took the Guardian of Hell with him.

Chapter Forty
The Last Fight

———⟨∾⟩———

ASIM SAT ON THE BENCH on the same street, pulled up his hood, and wiped the blood from his nose. He felt weak, so weak that he just stared at the shop where the old man was, but Asim wouldn't even make it that far.

He still had that monster in his eyes, and now he knew why Nina's memories had been taken, along with her abilities. But he also knew that the real Nina was out there somewhere, and he had to find her. He leaned back against the bench, lifted his head, and let the purple rain burn against his face. He wiped his face on his dirty sleeve.

Reaching for his key, he kissed it and whispered, 'Take me to Nina, the real Nina, not this beast.'

The key flickered three times before a bright light surrounded him. Warmth spread through his body as the world blurred and shifted. His bones ached, but he held on until suddenly, there was silence.

He was standing on the ground. It was rough beneath his feet—sand, dirt, maybe leaves. Trees loomed above him, leaves were falling, and the rustling of branches could be heard. In the distance, flickering torches revealed faint outlines of wooden structures, ancient small houses, not the grand buildings he had expected.

His chest tightened. He had expected to see Nina immediately, for her to be waiting there, but she wasn't. Turning, he scanned the silent wilderness, listening for any sound. Nothing, only the whisper of the wind through the trees.

He clenched his fists. 'No. Not now. Come on, my key, where have you taken me?' The key on his chest flickered weakly. He pressed his palm against it, trying to make it react. 'Again. Show me where she is.'

The magic responded, but it was weak, shaky. Before he could brace himself, the energy pulled him sideways, and he hit the wet ground hard. Cold earth pressed against his skin, but he barely noticed. With a shaky breath, he lifted his head, searching for any sign of her. His hand buried itself in his hair. He could feel it... she was close, but still not close enough. He took a deep breath and called into the silence. 'Ninaa.' Then louder. 'Ninaaaa!' And even louder. 'If you can hear me, come out!'

Nothing. Just emptiness.

Then he saw an older woman. She wore old, dirty clothes, an apron, and a scarf over her hair, pushing an old cart. 'Madam, I'm sorry, but where am I?' Asim asked her, but she just kept walking, not even looking at him.

Asim just sighed, looking around, unable to believe where he was. Everything was so old—no cars, no roads, just that village air, the smell of burning wood, like someone was barbecuing right next to him. And then he heard a faint rustling. His heart stopped for a moment. He turned his head, looking left, then right. He took a careful step forward, then another.

From the shadows at the entrance of a small hut, a figure emerged. Barefoot, cautious. Her hair tangled, her clothes rough and worn, like she had been here too long.

Asim froze. 'Nina?'

She turned, her body stiffening, her wide eyes locking onto his in shock.

'Asim?' she whispered, as if she were afraid to believe what she was seeing.

Asim exhaled slowly, his hands trembling at his sides.

'Yes. It's me.'

For a moment, she just stared. Then she ran straight into his arms. He held her so tightly he feared he might hurt her and had to loosen his grip.

'How? What happened? You're alive... you found me? And how did you...'

'Shhh. It's okay. Everything's okay,' he soothed her as tears ran down her cheeks.

'I thought everyone had forgotten about me. You have no idea what it's been like,' she said.

Asim looked around. 'No, Nina, I didn't forget. What is this place?'

'It's history, some kind of book.'

'A book? Forget it. We have to go quickly. The key... my key is weak.'

'What? What key? And why are you covered in blood, Asim? What happened?'

'Not now. Just hold on to me. Tightly,' he said, and she did.

Nina now sat on the old wooden bench, elbows on her knees, staring at the ground. It felt strange to be back here after everything that had happened. Nothing was the same anymore. The world felt smaller, emptier, as if it was slowly collapsing.

The park was quiet, with no wind, no movement, just the steady sound of purple rain falling onto the cracked pavement. Asim sat beside her with his arms crossed, staring ahead. He looked different, thinner, and his face was sharp with exhaustion. The past year had changed them both.

'I thought you were dead, or you forgot about me,' Nina said quietly.

Asim exhaled slowly.

'I never forgot about you, neither did Tessa,' he admitted.

Nina shook her head.

'What happened to Tessa? Where is she? And Asim, why do you look so stressed out? I mean, look at you. Why do you have blood everywhere? What's going on? Did someone hurt you?'

His face was thin, his eyes shadowed, and his expression was empty.

'No, Nina, forget all this. We have to go back home,' he said. Asim clenched his fists. 'This whole year,' he muttered. 'My own brother.' He paused for a moment before shaking his head. 'How did you survive in there anyway?'

Neither of them spoke for a while. They both knew there was nothing to say.

Nina then let out a slow breath. 'Forget me. I'm fine now, thanks to you. We just... we were never supposed to come here, Asim.'

'I know, Nina. This is all my fault.'

'No, Asim, please stop it. What are we going to do now? And have you got any food?'

'Food? Shit, no, but I know where we can go to get something. It's just... I thought we could use my key and go home.'

'Home? Asim, our home is Hell, and it's been so long. And Tessa? I'm not going anywhere until I find her. You go, please. I don't want you to suffer. I'm not dumb, Asim. I mean, look at you. Who did this to you? George?'

'I'm fine, Nina. Don't worry about me, I...'

But he didn't finish what he wanted to say because he heard the sound of slow, deliberate footsteps on the wet ground.

Nina lifted her head and saw a woman standing a few feet away, watching them closely. The sight made her breath catch. The woman had her face, her eyes, her features. It was like looking into a twisted reflection.

It was Elisha, standing right in front of them.

'Aww, look at you two birds. How lovely,' Elisha said, then turned to Nina. 'Oh gosh, Nina, you look terrible, just like your friend Asim. Poor boy.'

'I can't believe how ugly I am. Did you do this haircut yourself?' said Nina, absolutely fearless.

'You bitch, you were never meant to come back here. I'm gonna send you back where you belong, together with your shitty boyfriend.'

Nina stood up slowly. Asim got to his feet beside her, gripping the key in his hand, ready for whatever came next.

'No, no, no one is going to mouth off to my friend. His name is Asim, and he is my family,' said Nina, while Asim watched. She looked brave, angry, and ready for whatever it would take. She was standing for him.

Elisha wanted to say something, anger in her eyes, but someone stepped forward from the back. This time, it was George.

He had changed too. His once-confident stance was slightly slouched, but the amusement in his expression hadn't faded. He twirled his wand between his fingers, watching Asim closely.

'Still alive, little brother?' George smirked. 'I thought you'd be tougher by now.'

Asim tightened his grip on the key, but before he could respond, Elisha made her move first. She raised her hands, and the surrounding air warped and twisted. Nina knew what was coming, but her body was slow to react.

For a split second, time itself stuttered, just long enough for Elisha to strike. A blast of energy hit Nina square in the chest, sending her stumbling backward. Pain shot through her ribs as she barely managed to catch herself before hitting the ground.

Elisha smiled. 'Is that all you've got? I expected more from myself.'

Nina gritted her teeth.

'You're not me,' she said firmly.

She lifted her arm, trying to stop time, but Elisha mirrored the movement. Their powers clashed, shaking the ground beneath them.

Meanwhile, George flicked his wand toward Asim and shouted, 'Asama lio!'

Asim teleported just in time, vanishing from view and reappearing behind George. Flames burned in his hands, and before George could react, Asim drove the key into his back, sending a surge of energy through him. George stumbled, but instead of fear, he laughed. He wiped his mouth, smirking. 'This is almost fun, isn't it?'

Asim clenched his fists.

'You won't win.'

George only grinned. He tightened his grip on his wand and aimed again.

'Asimono holooo!'

Nothing happened. Smoke curled from his wand, but there was no attack.

Asim smirked, even though he was barely holding himself up. George's eyes darkened in frustration. With a growl, he threw the wand aside and rushed forward. He kicked Asim in the ribs, sending him rolling across the ground. Asim coughed, blood splattering onto the floor. But he didn't stay down. He pushed himself up and threw a punch at George. George staggered back, wiping his mouth, then charged at him again.

Elisha turned sharply. She touched the ground, and in an instant, a pulse of energy shot toward Asim. He barely had time to react before it hit him like a lightning strike. Pain tore through him. His body locked up, his vision blurred, and he collapsed onto his knees. Blood dripped from his mouth, pooling onto the ground. George stepped back, watching in satisfaction. Nina saw everything. Her eyes widened, and she screamed his name. Without hesitation, she lunged at Elisha. But Elisha was faster. She was overflowing with power.

She struck Nina hard in the stomach. A sharp pain tore through her body as blood spilled from the wound. Her breath hitched. The world spun. Her knees buckled, and before she could even cry out, she collapsed onto the cold ground. Her vision darkened, her body growing numb. Her eyes fluttered closed.

Elisha stared down at her, then smirked.

'Now, I'm the only Guardian of Hell. No one can send me back.'

She turned to George, smiling. He smiled back.

Then, a sudden crack of thunder tore through the sky. Someone stepped forward from the darkness. It was Alfie. His black suit was perfect, untouched by the world falling apart around them. He didn't speak, but his presence alone was enough to make the air grow heavier.

Elisha's face twisted with fear. 'No, noo—'

Alfie raised his hand without a word. The air became dense, vibrating with an energy that didn't belong in this world.

Elisha let out a scream as an invisible power dragged her backward. She tried to resist, her fingers clawing at the ground, but it was useless. A door appeared behind her, shifting and changing like liquid ink. With one final, desperate cry, she was pulled inside. Then, the door vanished, and she was gone.

George stood frozen, realising what had just happened. His smirk disappeared, replaced by fear. 'Please, Lord, no, I haven't do...,' but he couldn't finish what he was about to say. Alfie waved, and George just—pff—gone, disappeared.

The silence that followed was almost deafening.

Alfie turned toward Nina and Asim and walked to Nina. She was lying on the floor, covered in blood, hardly breathing, hardly seeing. Blurry, but she saw him, yet couldn't move, couldn't talk. Alfie pressed his hand on her stomach, and her blood was coming back to her body, her skin healing. And in a moment, there was nothing. Nina didn't feel the pain anymore. She started breathing, relieved. A tear fell, yet she just looked into his eyes and didn't say a word.

'Don't worry, Nina, you're safe now. See you soon,' he said.

Then he walked to Asim, who was watching, holding his stomach, gasping for breath. Now he knew what was coming, and yes, Alfie did the same. He healed his body, and Asim felt like a new person. But Alfie had something inside him that Asim felt. It was respect, not fear. He didn't say anything, but he knew, he felt, that Alfie was a good soul, even if he didn't have one.

'See you, Asim,' Alfie said, then he turned back and disappeared along with his thunder.

Nina and Asim stood up, their mouths open. They couldn't believe what had just happened. It was too fast, too emotional, and they just sat back down on the bench.

She broke into tears.

'I just wish I could tell Tessa now... that she was right about him. He is—I mean, Alfie is... and Tessa...' she tried to say but couldn't.

Asim had a tear too, but he quickly wiped it away so Nina wouldn't see it.

'It's okay, Nina. We're alive. We will find her, and you will tell her everything. Don't worry...' He hugged her.

'I know, but this was too much, Asim. What the hell just happened?'

'Nina, be glad you didn't see her true form. She probably didn't have the power to change herself.'

'What are you talking about?'

'Nothing. It's better you don't know.'

Then he pulled out his key, but before he could do anything, an envelope came flying at them, glowing.

'What is this now?' Asim groaned.

The envelope opened itself in mid-air. An orange letter fluttered out, twisting like it was alive. It glowed, then snapped together. An invitation, their names in gold ink.

And then they saw it: the location.

Death's World. Invitation to the celebration party.

'Nooo, screw this. We're not getting dragged into more dirt,' Asim muttered, crumpling the letter.

But then the letters glowed red, fiery, like the letter itself was pissed off. They stared at it, feeling the weight of its message.

You don't have a choice!

Chapter Forty-one
Celebration Party

—⁂—

NINA WAS LOOKING AROUND, her eyes wide, trying to make sense of what she was seeing. Nothing about this place was familiar, yet here she was, sitting on a throne. A real one.

Her hands pressed against the arms of the seat, cold and solid under her fingers, heavier than she expected. She looked down, and everything about her was wrong. The dress, deep red, silky, it wasn't hers. It fit perfectly, clinging in a way that felt too precise, like it had been tailored for her, but she had never owned anything like it. Her arms, usually marked with small cuts and bruises from life being its usual mess, were completely smooth. No scars, no roughness, just flawless skin.

She took a slow breath, but the air felt thick, carrying the scent of roses, rich and almost too sweet. Then her eyes landed on Asim. He was next to her, sitting on another throne, dressed sharp, his face clean, his clothes untouched. Not a trace of everything they had been through. No blood, no exhaustion, nothing. It was like the last few days had never happened.

He turned to her, his expression tense.

'What is this?'

Nina shook her head, eyes scanning the room.

The hall was massive, packed with people dressed like they had money to burn. Fancy clothes, glowing drinks, fake smiles. The usual.

Above them, chandeliers hovered, candles flickering like they were on a dimmer switch. Waiters zipped between tables, trays steady, movements sharp. Efficient. Almost too efficient. Because, yes—turns out they weren't people. Just skeletons in tuxedos, striding around like serving overpriced drinks was their life's purpose. Which, considering they were literal bones, wasn't far from the truth.

The guests were even stranger. Some had green skin, others had golden eyes that shimmered under the light, and a few had wings neatly folded against their backs, as if that was completely normal. And then the applause started. Slow at first, then rising, hands clapping in a steady rhythm. Nina stiffened slightly, glancing at Asim. Every pair of eyes in the room was focused on them.

She leaned toward him, lowering her voice.

'Are we supposed to do something?'

Before he could answer, the crowd shifted. Someone stepped forward. A woman in white.

She walked with ease, like she belonged here more than anyone else. Her eyes locked onto Nina's, familiar in a way that hit immediately. It was Tessa. For a second, Nina just stared, her mind catching up with what she was seeing. Then, suddenly, she was on her feet.

'Tessaaa?' Nina screamed.

Tessa smiled. Her hair was neatly styled, her white dress untouched. No wounds, no fear, just standing there, waiting. Asim had already got up beside her, watching closely.

'Is it really you?' said Asim.

Tessa let out a soft laugh, shaking her head.

'Honestly, you two look like you've seen a ghost.'

Nina moved before she could think. One second, she was staring; the next, her arms were around Tessa, holding her tight. She was warm, solid, real. Asim followed, arms wrapping around both of them, his grip firm, steady, like he needed to be sure of it too.

When they finally pulled back, Nina kept her hands on Tessa's arms.

'Where have you been?' said Nina.

'Here. Waiting for you,' said Tessa.

'We thought you were dead.'

Tessa didn't even blink. 'I am.'

Nina's breath caught slightly, but Tessa didn't give her a chance to respond. She reached for a glass from a passing tray, lifted it, and took a sip like none of this was strange. 'Alright, stop looking at me like that. This is a party. Your party. Relax, have a drink. Trust me, you'll like it.' She gave them both a wink before taking another sip.

Nina turned to Asim, but before either of them could say anything, another voice cut through the noise.

A voice Asim knew instantly.

'Well, if it isn't my son.'

The shift in Asim was immediate. His entire body stilled. Slowly, he turned. A man stood a few steps away, hands in his pockets, watching him closely. Dark suit, sharp features, familiar stance.

Samir, Asim's father. He didn't move at first. Just stared, like his brain wasn't quite ready to catch up to his eyes. Then, before he even realised what he was doing, he took a step forward, lifting a hand slightly before pressing his fingers against his father's arm. Testing.

'Dad?'

Samir's lips tugged into a small smile.

'It's me, son.'

Asim swallowed, his throat moving.

'You were gone.'

'I was. But things work differently here.'

'How is this even possible?'

'Let's not do this now. Tonight is for you. Let's enjoy it.'

Asim hesitated, but then nodded.

His father was here. Tessa was here. For now, that was enough. The music kicked back in, and the chatter in the hall picked up like nothing had just gone down. Nina dropped back into her seat, clutching her dress like it was the only thing keeping her sane. A tray floated by—because of course, trays just casually fly around here—stacked with more of those weird glowing drinks. Without thinking (which, let's be honest, was becoming a bad habit), she snatched one up and swirled it under the candlelight, watching the liquid shift like it had secrets.

Screw it. She took a sip.

Warmth spread through her chest, melting the tension in her ribs. Maybe this was real. Maybe they had actually won. Or maybe she was about to wake up with a killer hangover and a whole new set of problems. And then Nina saw it. Not *it*, but *her*—Lisa, from the Chinese restaurant. Dancing like an absolute maniac. Arms up, arms down, maybe even slapping someone for fun. If there was a way to dance *wrong*, Lisa had mastered it.

Nina pinched herself. *Nope. Still here. Brilliant.* And then things got worse. Lisa was waving at her. She had a red feathered scarf, a gold dress... and socks. White socks. A crime against fashion. A crime against *life itself.*

'No, Nina, I didn't want to bother you. It's your party, after all. But I can see you're settling in.'

She sidled up next to her, not even looking, just observing the crowd like some undercover agent on a break.

'Yeah, this is a dream. Or actually, more like a nightmare. Fantastic.'

Lisa whacked her on the shoulder. Nina hated that.

'Oh, but you're hilarious! And so bold! Come on, what is it like? No, wait... don't tell me, I know. Have you tried the red bubbly drink?'

Nina just sighed deeply. She wasn't giving this nonsense any more energy than it deserved.

'Oh well, I'll get you one. Hold on. Oh, and by the way, it's ok Nina, the battle wasn't that bad, but obviously, you tried, at least you wanted, I mean... you weren't that bad, I'm sure of it.'

'What the hell are you on about?'

'Oh, nothing. Just heard something. You know, my heart attack won't leave me alone, not even here.'

'What? Heart attack? What the hell are you talking about?'

'Oh, Nina, still confused, even here? Anyway, don't use the word Hell in here. This lot hate it and hold on. I'll get you a green one instead of red. You'll see, *that's* the real deal.'

And with that, she trotted off across the floor, her socks working overtime to polish the place up like she was being paid for it.

Nina just shook her head, smiled, looked away.

Chapter Forty-two
The New Beginnings

Part One

Nina

NINA SAT IN SILENCE, knees pulled close to her chest. Across from her stood Alfie, Death himself, leaning against a table, a cigar in his hand. He looked calm, as if this was just routine for him. The fire crackled softly, and the place was posh, his office. It should have been safe, but right now, she could not trust anything.

'Are you upset? Disappointed? Or just tired?' Alfie asked, exhaling smoke.

Nina shot him a look.

'Are you joking?'

He smiled.

'I never know with you.'

She clenched her fists.

'What the hell is going on?'

'Do you want the truth? Fine. Plain and simple.'

With a wave of his hand, the place shuddered and disappeared. The battlefield appeared again, the park where Asim and Nina had fought Elisha and George, just before they arrived at the party. Alfie took her there to show her what had really happened. It was the past, recent, but true. Nina's stomach tightened when she saw herself in the mud, holding her wound. The rain fell, mixing with blood and dirt, and the smoke stung her eyes. Asim lay nearby, barely breathing.

'This is the moment you remember, right?' Alfie's voice was calm but firm. 'You thought I saved you, you and Asim, but none of that happened.'

Nina swallowed hard.

'No... I remember it. That is exactly how it happened.'

'Nina, so think, think about it. How could you fight? You have no magical power, nothing.'

'I... I...' said Nina and looked at her hands.

'You see? Elisha killed you. Once George showed up, this... this never happened.'

'No...'

Alfie looked her in the eyes.

'No, Nina. That is what your mind created. When a soul is about to leave the body, there is a moment, a limbo, where reality bends. You were trapped there, seeing only what you wanted to see. But the truth is, you and Asim did not survive.'

'No... that cannot be true.'

'I am Death, Nina. I only come for the dead. I do not have permission to walk this world freely. I have my place, my job, and this, this is my job.' Alfie gently placed his hand on her shoulder. 'You have to accept it. You lost the battle. Both of you.'

She closed her eyes, trying to breathe under the weight of it all.

'Then why are we here? Why did you bring us... wherever this is? And why are we not in Hell or Heaven? I do not understand!'

Alfie stepped back, patient.

'Nina, the gate is closed, and I would not let you wander in darkness, nor Asim. That fate never belonged to you. So I brought you here, to my world. To live.'

'Live? In Death's world?'

'It is not as grim as it sounds.'

Then he waved his hand and told her to hold on to him, that they would go to a quiet place so she could calm down. The air glowed gold, like an endless sunset. The scent of fresh coffee and vanilla wrapped around Nina. Soft chairs invited her to sink into them. Outside, the streets were quiet, the world as if it had stopped just for them.

She swallowed.

'Where are we?'

Alfie pulled out a chair.

'A place where I bring people when they need to breathe. No souls, no interruptions. Just you and me.'

A cup of hot coffee appeared in front of her. She wrapped her hands around it, focusing on its warmth.

'You lied to me,' she muttered.

'I did not. I let you believe what you needed to.'

'Yeah, that makes it so much better.'

'You are different.'

'Yeah, I have been through things, you know.'

'I know. Sorry. I could not do anything. Are you hungry?'

Nina clenched her jaw.

'Hungry? Do I even have a stomach? I do not feel anything, not even the coffee. And now what? Do we sit here drinking coffee in the afterlife? Or more like pretend to drink it?'

Alfie laughed.

'No, Nina. I brought you here to understand something important.' He leaned closer. 'You were never meant to rule Hell. But the new Guardian has not arrived yet, and soon they will be born. Now I am giving you a chance, a new life.'

She frowned.

'What?'

Alfie stood.

'Come. I want to show you something.'

They walked in silence through Death's world, the streets eerily quiet. The black sky above them shimmered with scattered lights, like broken stars. Nina's boots tapped against the pavement. The weight of everything still pressed on her, but beneath it, something stirred quietly.

'Where are we going?' she asked.

Alfie stopped before a massive wooden door.

'Go ahead,' he said, stepping aside.

Nina hesitated, then pushed on the doors. She held her breath. And when the doors opened, there it was. A library. Not just any library, but it looked exactly the same as her library, her baby.

Wooden floors, towering shelves, and the worn-out armchair in the corner. But something was different. The books glowed faintly, their words shifting and whispering as she passed. She pulled one from the shelf. The text rearranged itself before her eyes, alive.

'They are magical,' Alfie said. 'Stories from lost worlds. Forgotten knowledge. Some even contain doors to places beyond imagination.'

Her throat tightened.

'This is mine?'

Alfie nodded.

'It is yours. No Guardian, no pain. This is your life, and no one, no one will hurt you. You are in my land, Nina.'

'How... how? Did you rebuild my library?'

'I brought it here because I knew you would need it.'

'Why?'

'Because this is where you belong. You do not have a soul, Nina, just like me. You were never human. This is and always will be your place. Now you will have peace, just as you always wished for.'

For the first time in a long time, Nina felt calm. The constant fight, the endless running, and now... she had this. A home, a purpose, a place where she could simply exist.

Alfie leaned against the doorframe, arms crossed, smirking. 'You will be the Librarian of Death's world. The keeper of knowledge.'

Asim

TESSA SAT BACK IN THE cushioned chair, stretching her legs out and letting out a slow breath. The sky stretched wide and open above her, filled with floating lights that pulsed gently, like stars that had drifted too close. The air wasn't warm or cold. Just... still.

She had been here long enough to understand what this place was. Long enough to accept it. Unlike Nina and Asim, she hadn't clung to illusions or tried to piece together something that wasn't there. She had known the truth from the start. They were dead.

She swirled the whiskey in her glass, watching the way the amber liquid caught the glow from above. She had adjusted. Found a strange kind of peace in it. But Asim? Oh, he was about to get the shock of his life.

Footsteps approached, hurried, uneven. She didn't even turn. She already knew who it was.

'Tessa?' Asim called.

He reached her quickly, stopping just beside her chair. 'You're here.'

'Yep,' she said simply, taking another sip of her drink.

She could feel his stare, his relief, but underneath that—confusion.

'You're alive, but you said you are dead. Now, this party, my dad, and this strange place,' he said. 'Are we dead?'

'Dead? Yes, we are. All, everyone here, all this, this place.'

'How? But, I don't understand. And how are you here the whole time? What is...'

'Calm down, Asim. This place is good. You will love it. Forget what was, blah blah, I love it here, trust me.'

'How can you? I mean...'

'Asim, you lost the battle. Death gave you a new body, that's all. Now we have a new life. I feel like I'm repeating myself.'

'Oh, okay. Sorry, Tessa, I'm just confused, okay?'

'So was I... but trust me, we have eternity, Asim. We are immortal, and not living in Hell. Don't you get it?' said Tessa.

She set her glass down on the small table beside her and turned properly to face him.

'Calm down. You look like you're about to pass out.'

He didn't move.

'No. That's not... no... I... I remember the fight, the battle. We won. Alfie healed us. We got invited to that party. That happened. I remember it.'

Tessa rubbed her temples.

'Shhh, drink this.'

His stomach dropped. He ripped his shirt, saw his key—his key—even felt it.

'See? My key!'

'Yes, Asim. Because you will become the King of Dreams now. That's how you actually become one—you had to die first, you get it?'

His breathing turned sharp, uneven. His mind scrambled for an explanation, something logical, something that didn't make this real.

'No. No, no, no.'

Tessa stood up and grabbed his shoulders, shaking him just slightly.

'Asim, breathe. You have to listen to me. You're not in your body anymore. We all died. It's over.'

'But we were at the party. We danced. We drank. We laughed...'

'Yeah, because that's what this place does, Asim,' she said, her voice steady but firm. 'It's over. No more suffering, Asim, no more torture. I heard about it, and I don't want to even think or talk about it, okay? Let's just adjust. And trust me, you will love it, okay?'

He clenched his jaw, eyes fixed on the horizon. Something was off. It had been from the start, but he had been too busy getting caught up in the moment. The people, the faces, the strange relief of seeing them again. He hadn't noticed.

Now it was settling in. The quiet. The stillness. The way everything felt too carefully placed. Like a scene arranged to look perfect, yet the details didn't quite fit. The laughter sounded hollow. The air refused to move the way it should.

It hit him like a delayed reaction. None of this was real. It was like waking up from a dream and realising the details were wrong. The people were right. The setting was familiar. But the sequence, the way it played out, was not how it happened.

His pulse picked up. His chest tightened. A beat too late, his mind started piecing it together.

And then—a voice.

'Asim.'

His entire body stiffened. Slowly, he turned.

Near the entrance of the terrace stood his father, Samir. Tall, broad shoulders, dark beard speckled with grey.

Asim's breath hitched. 'Dad?'

Samir nodded, calm as ever. 'Son.'

Asim felt something inside him break.

'This party. Is this all a dream?'

Samir stepped forward, his voice as steady as ever.

'It's alright, Asim. You don't have to fight it.'

Everything in Asim's mind screamed that this was wrong. That this wasn't how things were supposed to be. But deep down, beneath the panic, beneath the fear—He knew.

He knew Tessa was right. He knew this was real. His legs gave out. He collapsed onto the terrace floor, head in his hands.

'What now?' he whispered.

Tessa knelt beside him, rubbing his back gently. 'I know, Asim. I know. Now, we're gonna have a lovely tea..

Part Two

Two months later...

NINA SANK INTO HER favourite armchair. It was a bit shabby, sure, but that didn't matter. It had that perfect way of wrapping around her. Tucked away in the back of her old library, it was her little sanctuary, far from people and noise. As if there were many people or much noise to begin with. But that spot? No doubt it was perfect for reading a good book. Even at thirty-one, she had the heart of an old soul. So peace, quiet, and comfort? That was her thing.

And now, she no longer had to get up to put out the bloody fire in the fireplace. No more struggling with the pain in her legs, no more worrying about debts, and not even about Tessa or Asim. She liked it here. Maybe too much. Everything was exactly the same, even her flat upstairs. Even the door in the basement.

But this time, that door did not lead to the Real World. It was something else. Something magical. A portal that allowed Nina to travel between worlds—Worlds of Hate, Lies, Love, Serpents, and many more. Each one had a purpose, but Nina did not care. She had already been to another, and it had left a hole in her heart so deep that she simply took the key, locked the door, and hid it away in a cupboard.

Asim lived in the Dream Realm now. He had taken the crown and stepped fully into his role as King of Dreams. Surprisingly, he didn't hate it. He could travel between worlds, appearing wherever he wanted, yet his place, his true home, remained there.

He had told Nina about the Dream Realm, about how it was shifting and changing, reshaping itself around him. She never asked questions or pried, and Asim understood. She had chosen this life of quiet, of stories. She had already walked through too many doors, seen too many worlds. So he let her be.

Two months had passed. No running, no fighting, no constant worry about what was coming next. She had found her place here, a librarian in Death's world, the keeper of stories, a quiet guardian of knowledge.

She took a slow sip of her coffee, letting the warmth settle deep.

Then someone knocked at the door. Nina frowned. Hardly anyone knocked. Especially not him. Asim didn't need doors. He could have walked in through a dream, stepped into her world like a passing thought. Yet today, he chose to knock.

'It's open,' she called.

Asim stepped inside.

He looked different. Lighter, more like someone who had finally put down a weight he'd been carrying for too long. The tension in his shoulders was gone, his usual frown had softened into something almost unrecognisable... a peace.

'Morning,' he said, holding up a small envelope.

Nina arched an eyebrow, setting her coffee down.

'What's this? A love letter?'

Asim rolled his eyes, but smirked as he handed it over.

'Not quite. Open it.'

She tore the envelope open, pulling out a neatly written invitation. Her eyes scanned over the words, her brain taking a moment to catch up.

"You are invited to the wedding of Asim and Hira."

Her mouth fell open.

'You're getting married?!'

Asim chuckled, rubbing the back of his neck.

'Yeah. Thought it was about time.'

Nina looked back down at the invitation, then back up at him.

'Bloody hell, Asim. You go from "we're dead" to "let's get married" in two months?'

'Life moves fast when you're not alive.'

'Look at you, huh?'

Nina leaned back in her chair, a small smile tugging at her lips. 'You deserve this, you know. After everything. I'm happy for you, Asim. Really.'

'Thanks, Nina. Means a lot.'

She tapped the invitation lightly.

'So, when's the big day?'

'Next week,' he said. 'It'll be small, just family and friends. And of course, you're coming.'

'Yes... I'll be there.'

Before Asim could say anything else, the door opened again.

'Hello? Am I interrupting something?' said Tessa.

Nina's chest warmed instantly. She turned to see Tessa standing there, grinning, looking as lively as ever. She hadn't changed one bit—still full of energy, still loud, still Tessa.

Asim smirked.

'Look what the wind dragged in.'

'Yeah, yeah, I know you both missed me,' Tessa said, waving them off as she strolled inside.

She plopped onto the couch, stretching out like she owned the place. Nina shook her head, amused as ever by how Tessa always made herself at home, anywhere she went.

'Alright, what's this about?' Nina asked, narrowing her eyes. 'You're smiling too much. I don't trust it.'

Tessa gasped dramatically.

'What? I can't just be happy to see my favourite people?'

'No,' Asim and Nina said at the same time.

Tessa grinned. 'Alright, alright. I actually came with an invitation of my own.'

She pulled out a small golden envelope and handed it to them. Nina flipped it open, eyes scanning the elegant script inside. Her stomach flipped.

'Tessa... is this...?' Nina said.

Tessa nodded.

'An invitation. To my land. The Snake Kingdom. My people. My son. It's time you two finally came to see it.'

Asim raised an eyebrow.

'Your land?'

'Well, technically, it belongs to my son,' Tessa said, crossing her legs. 'But since he's still a kid, I suppose I'm in charge for now.' She leaned forward, grinning. 'And I think it's about time you two visited. Think of it as a little holiday before Asim's big day.'

Nina smiled, her fingers brushing the edge of the golden envelope.

'Sounds nice.'

'It is,' Tessa said. 'And I know you both will love it.'

Asim smirked.

'So let me get this straight. We died, moved into Death's world, I'm getting married, and now we're taking a holiday to the Snake Kingdom?'

Tessa laughed.

'Life's weird. Even after death.'

Nina shook her head with a soft smile.

'You know what? I think I like it here.'

Tessa winked.

'Told ya.'

Asim let out a slow breath, leaning back in his chair.

'Yeah. Me too.'

For the first time in a long time, there was no running. No fighting. No surviving. They were living. A new world. A new life. Together. And maybe, just maybe, this was the happy ending they never thought they'd get.